PENGUIN  C

GISLI SURSSON'S
THE SAGA OF THE PE(

VÉSTEINN ÓLASON has been Head of the Árni Magnússon
Institute in Reykjavík since 1999. Previous positions in Icelandic
literature include teaching at the Universities of Copenhagen, Oslo
and Reykjavík and a visiting professorship to the University of
California, Berkeley. He has published a number of books of literary
history and criticism, and is the editor and co-author of *The Literary
History of Iceland I–II* (1992–3).

JUDY QUINN teaches Old Norse literature in the Department of
Anglo-Saxon, Norse and Celtic at the University of Cambridge.
When she translated *The Saga of the People of Eyri* she was
teaching in the English Department at the University of Sydney.
She has published on eddic poetry, on prophecy in Old Norse
poetry and prose, and on orality and literacy in medieval Iceland.
She is currently editing the verses of Eyrbyggja saga as part of the
international project to re-edit the corpus of skaldic poetry.

MARTIN S. REGAL teaches in the English Department at the University of Iceland. He has published mostly in the field of theatre and
drama and is currently engaged in writing a volume for the New
Critical Idiom series on tragedy. He also translated *The Saga of
the Sworn Brothers* for a Penguin anthology that appeared in
1999.

# Gisli Sursson's Saga
## *and*
# The Saga of the People of Eyri

*With an Introduction and Notes by*
VÉSTEINN ÓLASON

PENGUIN BOOKS

PENGUIN BOOKS

Published by the Penguin Group
Penguin Books Ltd, 80 Strand, London WC2R ORL, England
Penguin Putnam Inc., 375 Hudson Street, New York, New York 10014, USA
Penguin Books Australia Ltd, 250 Camberwell Road, Camberwell, Victoria 3124, Australia
Penguin Books Canada Ltd, 10 Alcorn Avenue, Toronto, Ontario, Canada M4V 3B2
Penguin Books India (P) Ltd, 11 Community Centre, Panchsheel Park, New Delhi – 110 017, India
Penguin Books (NZ) Ltd, Cnr Rosedale and Airborne Roads, Albany, Auckland, New Zealand
Penguin Books (South Africa) (Pty) Ltd, 24 Sturdee Avenue, Rosebank 2196, South Africa

Penguin Books Ltd, Registered Offices: 80 Strand, London WC2R ORL, England

www.penguin.com

Translations first published in *The Complete Sagas of Icelanders (Including 49 Tales)*, I and V,
edited by Viðar Hreinsson (General Editor), Robert Cook, Terry Gunnell, Keneva Kunz
and Bernard Scudder. Leifur Eiríksson Publishing Ltd, Iceland 1997
First published by Penguin Classics 2003

020

Translation copyright © Leifur Eiríksson, 1997
Editorial matter copyright © Vésteinn Ólason, 2003
All rights reserved

Leifur Eiríksson Publishing Ltd gratefully acknowledges the support of the
Nordic Cultural Fund, Ariane Programme of the European Union, UNESCO,
Icelandair and others.

Set in 10.25/12.25 pt PostScript Adobe Sabon
Typeset by Rowland Phototypesetting Ltd, Bury St Edmunds, Suffolk
Printed and bound in Great Britain by Clays Ltd, Elcograf S.p.A.

www.greenpenguin.co.uk

# Contents

# Acknowledgements

The translations of the two sagas printed here were originally published in *The Complete Sagas of Icelanders* by Leifur Eiríksson Publishing, Reykjavík, which contributed to the production of this volume. Gísli Sigurðsson read the Introduction and produced the genealogy and plot summary for *The Saga of the People of Eyri*, and notes to both sagas. Bernard Scudder read and coordinated the entire material, Jean-Pierre Biard drew the maps and Jón Torfason compiled the Index of Characters. Thanks are also due to Viðar Hreinsson and Örnólfur Thorsson, who were instrumental at early stages of the project and in compiling the Reference Section. Diana Whaley wrote the survey of Early Icelandic Literature.

Martin Regal would like to thank Eysteinn Björnsson for his assistance with the kennings and Ivor Regal for his many useful suggestions concerning the prose text.

Jóhann Sigurðsson, publisher of the Complete Sagas, and Alastair Rolfe, Hilary Laurie, Lindeth Vasey, Margaret Bartley, Laura Barber and others at Penguin are also kindly thanked for their advice, encouragement and patience.

Vésteinn Ólason

# Introduction

The two sagas in this volume recount feuds that are supposed to have taken place in Iceland in the last decades of the tenth century AD, although the narrative as a whole covers a much wider time-span. The sagas are to some extent based on oral traditions but in the form that they have come down to us they are literature. It is assumed that *Gisli Sursson's Saga* was originally composed just before or around the middle of the thirteenth century, while *The Saga of the People of Eyri* was originally composed around 1270. The oldest manuscripts, on the other hand, are from the fourteenth century or later.

On the surface the lives described in these sagas are radically different from anything experienced in modern society. Families totally dependent on themselves and their kin for safety and survival guard their honour jealously, and even peaceful men get involved in feuds where lives are at stake. Seemingly unimportant events release uncontrollable passions and violence, and a prosperous family can be destroyed in a short time in a chain of events driven forward by envy and hate, jealousy and pride. There is no clear line between the natural and the supernatural, between evil other-worldly forces and human passion. The need to maintain peace and keep the balance is also strong, however, and the tension between these forces keeps the reader in suspense.

The main characters in the respective sagas are uncle and nephew, although of almost opposite characters. The uncle Gisli is a Viking Age hero, clever and resourceful, a formidable fighter stubbornly sticking to the archaic ethics of revenge he has inherited. His story is tragic, and in the end he is killed after a glorious defence against all the odds, as befits a true hero. Gisli's sister and her two children survive the calamities that strike the family. Gisli's nephew Snorri, who is the most important character of *The Saga of the People of Eyri*, is shrewd and resourceful, but in addition he is a politician and survivor whose intelligence and single-mindedness enable him to acquire successively more authority. This concentration and consolidation of power in the hands of a strong chieftain can be seen as part of the civilization of society. While Gisli represents the individualistic heroic morality of the Viking Age, Snorri embodies secular order in the new medieval society. When read together the two sagas – through their connections and their differences – are an excellent introduction to the salient themes of saga literature, where the Viking Age and the unique type of society that developed in Iceland from the settlement beginning in the late ninth century to Christianization in AD 1000 are viewed through the eyes of an era that was more civilized, or at least believed and hoped itself to be.

# I. BACKGROUND TO THE SAGA TRADITION – THE GOLDEN AGE

The Sagas of Icelanders can be seen as an attempt by Icelandic writers of the thirteenth and fourteenth centuries to make sense of their past and their present by telling entertaining and engaging stories. Iceland was settled in the Viking Age, and the first Icelandic historians tell us that most of the inhabitable parts of the country were settled and the rule of law established in a few decades around AD 900. None the less, to talk about the 'rule' of law may be considered an exaggeration by modern standards. A certain code of law was commonly accepted, a legal assembly that discussed new laws for the country was held each year, and a system of local and centralized courts was established, but there was no public executive power.

The fundamental principle driving this society was a code of honour that demanded loyalty to kin and other allied parties (see Social, Political and Legal Structures, p. 219). This included the duty to take revenge by killing if honour demanded. The social system depended on the maintenance of a delicate balance of power between the farmer-chieftains, or 'godis'; if one became too powerful, others formed an alliance against him. In the thirteenth century internal contradictions and external political pressure caused the breakdown of this vulnerable social contract; the balance of power was disrupted, and the leaders of a handful of influential families waged brutal war with each other, until the Icelanders agreed in 1262 to pay tax to the Norwegian king in return for his promise to bring about peace. By around 1300 Iceland was gradually adapting to a new regime in which power emanated from the king and official punishment replaced personal revenge.

Iceland had been Christianized around AD 1000, and from around 1100 a literary culture began to develop. Initially, literature in the vernacular was a tool for both the missionary activities of the church and attempts to civilize society through the codification of law. The interest shown by the ruling class of chieftains in their own Viking Age past and roots soon found expression in historical and pseudo-historical narratives about the settlement of Iceland, the kings and legendary heroes of Scandinavia, and in sagas about Icelanders. At the time the sagas were written, from around AD 1200, the Icelanders seem to have been engaged in a process of creating a semi-legendary and heroic past from their collective memories of the first hundred and fifty years of their country's history. In creating the sagas, oral tradition was absorbed, refashioned and expanded using the resources of literary culture. Two significant events were seen as turning points: the settlement from roughly AD 870–930 and the conversion to Christianity. Most sagas are introduced by the story of how the most prominent family or families emigrated from Norway and settled in Iceland. The reasons for the settlement are usually presented as either conflict with or insurrection against the newly unified kingdom of Norway that had been established by Harald Fair-hair, or feuds between individuals or clans in the old country. This strong sense of individualism and defiance would live on in and pervade the new world that the pioneering settlers built for themselves at the westernmost limits of Europe. *The Saga of the People of Eyri* also describes the foundation and consolidation of social structures in Iceland, which are of crucial importance for the plot because all conflicts threaten stability and must be resolved within the social framework.[1] The conversion, often described or mentioned in the final section of a saga, marks the end, or the beginning of the end, of the old heroic age and heralds a fundamental if gradual change in world view and social structure.[2]

Around the middle of the thirteenth century the Icelanders still looked upon themselves as descendants of Vikings and heroes, whom they were supposed to emulate in guarding an honour that was considered to be the highest of values, superior to the life of an individual. The political realities of the time and the intellectual horizon of the most forward-looking sections of the chieftain class, however, were gradually changing. The new chieftains valued property and power higher than heroics – and according to their ideology power had to be centralized. They were well aware that Icelandic society was an anomaly among the countries under the spiritual hegemony of the Roman Catholic Church. All other countries in Europe had a king, and in the 1260s Iceland came under the rule of a monarch too, not someone from the ranks of the Icelandic chieftains who coveted such a position, but the king of Norway. This led to profound changes in society during the last decades of the thirteenth century. It was in this period that the sagas were created, depicting the old society from an increasing distance and acknowledging the limitations of its heroic ideals at the same time as they nostalgically portrayed the downfall of heroes.

During the thirteenth century the Sagas of Icelanders thus demonstrated an increasing awareness of the essential characteristics of the old society, its shortcomings as well as its glory. Grim Viking Age heroes such as Egil Skallagrimsson and Gisli Sursson, or more romantic ones such as Kjartan Olafsson of *The Saga of the People of Laxardal*, whom we meet in works from around or before 1250, still figured in the sagas from the last decades of that century, but by then a new kind of 'hero' had emerged, a man preoccupied not only with his own honour but also with more impersonal and social aims. Such a man is the wise Njal of *Njal's Saga*, and Snorri the Godi is cast in the same mould, although his personality is different – and the texture of their respective sagas even more so. The author of *Njal's Saga* has forged his new world view into a seamlessly integrated whole, while the author of *The Saga of the People of Eyri* either could not or did not want to achieve the same degree of artistic unity. Such diverse approaches to composition show the fertility and variety that are one of the hallmarks of Iceland's literary culture in the Middle Ages.

Just like mainstream classicism and romanticism in their respective periods, the sagas of the late thirteenth and fourteenth centuries created a golden age in the past. They express an underlying feeling that the old society was doomed, but they look back on it with a fond nostalgia. Their age of 'freedom' was not one of affluence but of heroic dignity and self-respect. It is this sense of the inherent nobility of man that gives the sagas much of their appeal, and the championing of this quality in a highly developed form of narrative art has earned them a status among the great masterpieces of world literature.

With its strong human perspective, this is clearly a far different conceptual world from that found in the bulk of other medieval European literature, which tends to build upon either timeless, escapist fantasy or a divinely decreed order. Important distinguishing features are also seen in the sagas' style and their devotion to historical and local detail – their world is tangible and earthy, not an ersatz transit lounge en route to blissful oblivion in the afterlife.

The generic saga style is renowned for its economy and clarity of expression. While much European narrative literature of the Middle Ages makes lavish use of exaggeration and often tries to achieve effects through the sheer weight of clustered synonyms, the sagas are characterized by a careful choice of words and subtle understatement. In direct speech, strong emotions are usually kept in check and utterances even have the appearance of bleak objectivity. Given the context of violent action in which it is set, dialogue of this kind can be used to exceptionally powerful effect, and the reader should stay alert to the spectrum of ironies that it can invite. The syntactical structure of the prose narrative is simple and mainly paratactic, but by contrast the verse adorning many of the sagas is intricate almost to the point of obscurity. Syntax and word order are subjugated to metrical rules bearing little relation to the prose, while the vocabulary draws on an almost completely separate poetic diction that is yoked together into complex and cryptic imagery. The action usually comes to a temporary halt when a verse is quoted, but this lyric element can provide insights into the state of mind of its composer – a subjective device not admitted by the prose conventions – thereby creating additional layers of narrative subtlety.

One of the features that give the sagas a strong historic and realistic flavour – borne out by the palpable facts of Icelandic geography to this day – is the precise location of events to particular places and regions. Both sagas in this volume are set in the western quarter of Iceland, in the West Fjords and the Breidafjord area (see maps, pp. 214–17). This would have resonated with the original audiences, and there is no doubt that these sagas are based on oral traditions that had developed in this part of the country. Many of the main characters belonged to well-known settlers' families, and their descendants by the time the sagas were written included people of importance in this area.[3]

Despite their clear local focus, however, both the sagas in this volume – like many others, in fact – begin with a prelude in Norway, and in *The Saga of the People of Eyri* also in the Hebrides. There is no conflict between close attention to local detail and history and the broader sweep of the entire Viking cultural area in northern Europe, where palpable facts tend to merge into generalization and received tradition. The Norwegian prelude of *Gisli Sursson's Saga* is more important for the narrative structure because it not only gives reasons for the emigration to Iceland but also introduces the central themes of the main part of the story: a love triangle, defence of family honour at all costs, and divided loyalties and conflicts among couples and siblings. Both sagas also reveal their historical provenance by the fact that cases are taken to local assemblies but no further. Society itself, in effect, is taking shape at the same time as the plot; we learn how a local assembly is established when people have settled in Iceland and see how it functions in the escalation of the feuds that form the backbone of the plot. In other works, such as *Njal's Saga*, important issues are decided at the national assembly, the Althing at Thingvellir, but the litigation that arises in our two is never taken that far. None the less, the respective feuds develop differently, driven by the interplay of character and circumstance in each. In *The Saga of the People of Eyri*, dramatic events involving a great number of individuals are viewed with a certain detachment, and the contours of the many individual destinies may seem to be of less importance than the mechanics of power-brokerage revealed by the story. *Gisli Sursson's Saga* focuses narrowly on the tragic fate of one individual and his family and through its scrutiny illuminates important contradictions in the ethics of the old society. Bearing in mind both their collective background and broad distinguishing features, we can now look at each in turn more closely.

## II. GISLI SURSSON'S SAGA

Forbidden love leading to violence and death is a central theme of this saga. From the very beginning we are given a foreboding of this theme with the story of how Gisli's two uncles are killed, one by a berserk and the other by a slave whose excellent sword Grey-blade he has borrowed and been reluctant to return.[4] The fighting starts with a stock motif when the berserk challenges the elder brother, Ari, to a duel for his wife and kills him. The widow advises the second brother, also named Gisli, to borrow the sword, adding meaningfully that she would rather have been married to him in the first place. It is tacitly implied that she has betrayed her husband by not giving him the same advice. Indeed, Gisli and Ingibjorg are wed after he has killed the berserk, although a slave puts a prompt end to that marriage by killing him in turn. Grey-blade remains in the possession of the family and, while enshrining the heroic values passed down from one generation to the next, also becomes a symbol of the bad luck that haunts it.

In the second generation a schism arises between Gisli Sursson and his older brother Thorkel. Encouraged by his father, Gisli kills a certain Bard whom they suspect of seducing his sister Thordis, while Thorkel, who has been friendly with the suitor, greatly resents his brother's violent reaction. He even goes to the lengths of urging Bard's kinsman to avenge the killing. When a second suitor has also been killed the family become embroiled in a feud and have no choice but to emigrate to Iceland.

## Honour and vengeance

Honour is central to any individual's self-respect in the Sagas of Icelanders, and it can be worth more than life itself. Inextricably linked to this concept is the obligation to take revenge when there is no other way of satisfying wounded honour; at the same time, people are expected to take such action only as a last resort. But this balance is difficult to strike, and external factors – the actions of others and an individual's own moral bent – can lead a man who is not normally aggressive to act in ways certain to result in misfortune. Gisli Sursson is such a man. His saga is a tragedy because conflicts flare up between individuals so closely linked that all options seem equally unappealing. Vengeance is bound to hurt the avenger himself.

A code of conduct with ancient roots, which demands that a man should guard the honour of himself and his family at all costs and always demand life in revenge for life, is obviously a categorical imperative for the main hero of our saga, Gisli, just as it was for his Norwegian father and forefathers; in his last stanza (verse 39) Gisli actually traces his courage and toughness to his father's influence. Other characters, including Gisli's brother Thorkel, do not adhere to this code with his degree of conviction. Should the saga then be interpreted as being critical of this severe code of conduct, or only as showing an awareness of the moral dilemmas it creates? When Gisli, as a young man in Norway, is forced by his father and by his own sense of honour to kill another young man, the reader may feel that he is impetuous about taking revenge. Once incited, he kills without warning. In another manuscript version, Gisli is strongly urged on by his father but nevertheless gives the offender two warnings and entreats him to mend his ways before finally killing him. Such behaviour would be more typical of the moderation that is the mark of a real hero. Whichever version is closer to the original at this point, the disagreement between the brothers about the killing shows that Gisli's reaction to his father's incitement is not the only possible recourse, yet at the same time conventional concepts of honour clearly demand that he should take action. His father is a spokesman for the honour and vengeance culture, and, viewing the saga as a whole, it is natural to conclude that Gisli behaves quite properly and does what family honour demands, although his reactions may be excessive or over-zealous. As subsequent events confirm, his brother Thorkel is definitely the lesser man.

Later in the saga Gisli is twice confronted by even more taxing demands imposed by the ideals of honour. These subsequent events highlight the essentially contradictory nature of the revenge ethic and the tragic consequences that can be triggered when ill fortune comes into play. On the first occasion, when his 'sworn brother' and brother-in-law Vestein has been murdered in secret, Gisli is certain that the deed was engineered by his own brother Thorkel, and that another brother-in-law, his sister's husband Thorgrim, must be the killer. Driven by the obligation to avenge his sworn brother, Gisli responds with another secret killing, stabbing Thorgrim while he is lying in the darkness of night in the arms of his wife Thordis. Later in the saga she exposes her brother, after he confesses to the killing in a verse which she overhears and interprets. Fateful events ensue: Gisli is condemned to outlawry, lives like a hunted animal for years, and is eventually killed in retribution. There is no indication in the text that he ever regrets having killed Thorgrim or that he is considered to have behaved improperly. His pursuers during his long years of outlawry are shown to be thoroughly disreputable people. In exposing Gisli, Thordis commands sympathy for being in no less a dilemma than he is: she naturally resents not only his killing of her husband, but also the implicit suggestion that his ties to Vestein were stronger than his ties to her husband. Moreover, she is carrying Thorgrim's baby, a son as it turns out – who will emerge as Snorri, the hero of *The Saga of the People of Eyri* – and does not want to leave their child with the terrible burden of being obliged to take revenge on his own uncle, a formidable champion to boot. When Thordis exposes her brother she is choosing the lesser of two evils. However, at the end of the saga she attempts to avenge Gisli's death and demonstrates her belief that by his outlawry her brother has atoned in full for killing her husband.

Though the saga never condemns Gisli for killing Thorgrim, there is a sense that the demands of vengeance can become so outrageous that it would be wrong to accede to them. To Vestein's sons, the killing of Thorgrim seems insufficient recompense and, while still boys, they kill Thorkel Sursson. They escape and seek out Aud, their paternal aunt, and her husband Gisli, who are both hiding at a remote location. Ch. 30 describes how Aud welcomes the boys warmly, but prevents them from meeting Gisli and sends them away. When she tells him about the killing, his immediate reaction is that he cannot live under the same roof as his brother's killers and must take vengeance, but he is easily convinced to let them get away. This episode shows that the saga's acceptance of the vengeance culture is not unconditional; there is no glorification of vendetta as such, but rather an awareness of its potentially terrible consequences. Accordingly the saga provides Gisli with the opportunity to take a further step along the road of vengeful extremism, and although good sense prevails and he is happy to let the matter rest, the listener or reader is left in no doubt that he would have thought nothing of pursuing and killing Vestein's sons had he really wanted to. By doing so, however, he would have killed the sons of the very man for whom he had sacrificed everything in his pursuit of vengeance. Such is the wretched fate stalking these families that, at the end of the saga, another of Gisli's brothers kills one of Vestein's two sons.

Some present-day readers have found Gisli's inflexible adher-
ence to the demands of vengeance unsympathetic, but they have
rarely given him credit for his own recognition that revenge has
its limits. The killing of Vestein is a shameful act, and Gisli
views it as completely without justification. Accordingly he
cannot tolerate the idea of allowing such a deed to stand un-
avenged, and in fact he does try to divert attention from his
brother Thorkel by killing Thorgrim. It seems unnecessary to
believe, as some scholars have suggested, that Gisli derived any
perverse pleasure from killing his brother-in-law in his marital
bed, yet the description of this killing is so powerful, its atmosphere so emotionally charged, that it is hardly surprising that
such thoughts have been entertained.

## Fate and other supernatural forces

'Thus Gisli's life came to an end, and although he was deemed
a man of great prowess, fortune was not always with him.' As
explicit a comment as this is rare in the sagas. With its typical
understatement, it refers to ideas about good or bad luck, which
in this saga are closely connected to the idea of fate. It is
emphasized time and again that the future course of events is
predetermined and nothing can change what lies ahead. This
can be seen from Gest's prophecy in Ch. 6, which earns symbolic
confirmation when the plan to avert it misfires, and from Gisli's
words towards the end of the same chapter: 'I suspect fate
will take its course now.' The event which sets in motion the
subsequent grim chain of events – the conversation between
Gisli's wife Aud and Thorkel's wife Asgerd about the latter's
love for Vestein – causes Gisli again to reflect on the forces ruling
his life: 'Fate must find someone to speak through. Whatever is
meant to happen will happen' (Ch. 9). The same idea is
expressed symbolically in Vestein's words in Ch. 12: 'now all
waters flow towards Dyrafjord and that is where I will ride.'
The plot is thus very much subject to fate and governed by
forces beyond the power of individuals.

Supernatural forces impact on the saga again when the sorcerer Thorgrim Nef (Nose) casts a spell to render ineffective any

help that may be given to Thorgrim's killer. All events conspire against Gisli: powerful opponents, fate and sorcery. The saga hinges on how individuals confront the burden of fate, living in accordance with their conscience and fighting for their lives until the bitter end, no matter how powerful the forces they have to face, nor how awful their lot must be. Compared to the laws inscribed in the consciousness of the individual, the laws and judgements of society count for little, and no attempts are ever made to pay material compensation for the various killings in this saga. Gisli is sentenced to outlawry in his absence, and the court case is only briefly described. As an outlaw his thoughts are with the judgements of fate rather than of society. In this sense *Gisli Sursson's Saga* is more individualistic and less socially aware than *The Saga of the People of Eyri*, and its preoccupations with fate and heroic ethics reflect a more archaic mindset.

If our only sources of information about Gisli's feelings were his own statements (in prose) and his actions, then the modern reader could be excused for regarding him as some kind of automaton, lacking all warmth of human feeling; but a careful reading of the saga hardly supports such an interpretation, and Gisli's poetry says more about his thoughts and feelings than the narrative reveals. Gisli is in fact deeply moved by the blood-stained life he has led, and anxious about the fate which awaits him. He never complains, but he expresses his feelings when he describes his dreams and makes verses about them, thus stepping into the area occupied by fate and other supernatural forces. As with the poetry of other saga heroes, it is disputed whether Gisli's verse was a part of oral traditions about him or composed for the written saga. Much of it has a Christian colouring and could not have been composed in the tenth century, but it could have been created later in either oral or written tradition. Be that as it may, it was included in the written text and stands there as an integral part of the saga we know.[5]

Gisli's dreams begin when he has been outlawed, and so does the poetry that accompanies them. Two dream-women visit him alternately while he sleeps: one is benevolent and brings him a Christian message, the other is malevolent and speaks the words of fate, the judgement from which no man may escape – she predicts evil fortune, washes him in blood and dresses him in bloodstained clothes. These women symbolize the conflicting forces of his fate and can be seen as projections of the roles his wife and his sister play in his life. Through the dreams and the verses the reader is offered a poignant insight into the hero's thoughts and feelings that cannot be presented in any other way. Gisli shows no remorse, but he seems conscious of his terrible fate in living a life dedicated to bloodshed – first the blood of others and, eventually, his own.

## Fate and sexuality

By no stretch of the imagination could *Gisli Sursson's Saga* be described as a love story, yet the relationship between men and women lies behind all the ill-fated events it narrates. Two women are all-important: Gisli's sister Thordis, the agent of fate, and his loyal wife Aud. When introduced, Thordis is described as 'good-looking and intelligent'. Yet the saga says so little about her that there is no way of knowing for certain whether she may be held responsible for her brother having to kill her suitors in defence of the family honour, nor do we know whether she was Thorgrim and Thorkel's accomplice in arranging the killing of Vestein. None the less, we can hardly avoid sympathizing with her when her husband is suddenly killed while she is carrying their first child. Twice more she contributes fatefully and memorably to the course of events. First, she interprets a verse spoken by Gisli as signalling his confession of guilt for Thorgrim's murder, and informs her husband Bork, Thorgrim's brother – albeit some time after she first realized the meaning of the verse, suggesting that her decision had not been an easy one. Second, it is clear that she endorses the archaic revenge ethic by which her brother lives when, after Gisli's death, she tries to kill Eyjolf the Grey and then divorces Bork. In one of his verses, Gisli contrasts his sister with the great heroine of eddic poetry, Gudrun Gjukadottir, feeling that she lacks Gudrun's steely strength.[6] These two figures certainly have much in common. In the ancient Germanic legends about the Volsungs and Nibelungs the great hero Sigurd is killed by his brother-in-law in the arms of his wife Gudrun. According to the eddic poem *Atlakviða*, which was recorded from oral tradition about the time *Gisli Sursson's Saga* was written, Gudrun later takes the most terrible revenge on her second husband Atli when he has deceived and killed her brothers; she kills Atli's and her two sons and serves their flesh and blood to him, and having told him what she has done she sets fire to his hall and burns him to death. Gisli expects his sister to behave like Gudrun and put the duties to her kin above those she owes her husband, but in fact her mind is torn. Thordis is the most purely tragic figure in the saga, and yet she brings forth the representative of more peaceful times to come in her son Snorri.

*Gisli Sursson's Saga* focuses more closely on Aud's words and actions than those of Thordis, even though she does not play the same key role in the plot. Aud is the ideal of the loyal and worthy wife, wholly supportive of her husband right up to his dying day. There are opportunities for her to demonstrate this loyalty, as when she refuses bribes from Eyjolf the Grey, strikes him on the nose with the money bag, and says, famously: 'remember, you wretch, for as long as you live, that a woman has struck you' (Ch. 32). Her support for Gisli during his last stand, however, is to no avail, and even does him harm as it turns out. Her actions are severely limited by the ideas of a male-dominated society; but within those constraints and by its standards she behaves blamelessly.

## Comic relief

For all its deeply tragic framework and core, *Gisli Sursson's Saga* has its comic episodes too. When Gisli has been outlawed, he repeatedly just manages to escape with his life, sometimes by valiant fighting and at other times by trickery, and indeed he takes on the shape of a trickster figure in several scenes. There is nothing heroic about the way he hoodwinks his slave Thord into exchanging cloaks with him with the result that he gets away while Thord is killed (Ch. 20). This is the first of the 'shape-shifting' ruses that Gisli employs to escape from his enemies; in Ch. 26 he dons another disguise and plays a fool or

'village idiot'. Another comic scene is acted out when he hides
in the hay in the bed of a poor but foul-mouthed woman
(Ch. 27). While we may see such interludes as 'playing to the
groundlings', they serve as in Shakespeare not only as relief but
also ultimately to heighten the tragic element still further.

A more discreet way of mixing comedy into the tragedy is the
description of characters who do not measure up to the standard
of heroism. Thordis's second husband Bork acts unheroically
when he initially hesitates to take action after learning the
identity of his brother's killer, and then relies exclusively on
hired men for the revenge. He is contrasted with his brother
Thorgrim, who is a man of immediate action, as he demonstrates
in Ch. 7. The opposition between the brothers Gisli and Thorkel
is striking, and it plays a part in the tragic fate of the family, but
the saga repeatedly portrays Thorkel as a comic character. The
fateful episode when Thorkel overhears his wife Asgerd and
Aud talking about the former's love for Vestein itself ends as
comedy, although it initiates a tragic course of events. The same
evening that Thorkel overhears the women's conversation there
is a confrontation between him and Asgerd (Ch. 9). Thorkel is
here portrayed as a wavering and cowardly man who, besides
being disloyal to his kinsmen, as he has already demonstrated,
makes empty threats. Asgerd is more like a traditional heroine,
determined and passionate. Obviously, she does not have the
fierce pride of an eddic Brynhild, who wants no one but the best
of men. But Asgerd is not prepared to accept any kind of
humiliation from her husband, and she has no scruples about
using her sexual power over him to ensure this. There are fine
psychological nuances here. Thorkel's lack of character is never
directly mentioned, let alone condemned, but is revealed
through the contrast between his brave words and his action.
Both spouses act according to practical, unheroic consider-
ations, but it is the woman who shows strength and determination, and the man who lets himself be dominated by his wife.
A description of a conversation between Gisli and Aud in the
same circumstances follows immediately, and the contrast is
striking: Aud confides in her husband and there is mutual trust
and affection between them.

## Narrative art

The plot of *Gisli Sursson's Saga* is not always very coherent or
logical, although the main events are well arranged and parallel
scenes are used with great effect (see, for example, Chs. 14 and
17). The dialogue is usually brief and to the point, effectively
enhancing the atmosphere and the urgent psychological and
even existential issues at stake in each situation. With his econ-
omical style the author clearly knows the art of arousing and
keeping the interest of the reader/listener by holding back information. The reader makes discoveries at the same time as characters in the narrative, and telling details that the characters see
or hear are effectively communicated. Descriptions of weather
conditions are cases in point. We read how Gisli painstakingly
covers his tracks in the snow when he sets off alone to kill
Thorgrim, but his boots, covered in ice and snow and noticed
only by Thorkel, almost give the game away (Chs. 16 and
17). Again, on Gisli's last day, tell-tale trails left by incidental
characters lead his enemies to him: 'It was the kind of weather
where the air is very still, but there was also a heavy frost . . .
The women were wearing tunics and they trailed along in the
frozen dew' (Ch. 34). Limiting the point of view is skilfully
applied in Chs. 13 and 16 where first Vestein and then Thorgrim
are killed. In Vestein's case the events are experienced exclusively from the point of view of the victims. The killer is present
only as experienced by what the witnesses hear and through the
result of his actions. The episode of the second murder is more
fully set in scene, and the narrative method is much more
nuanced; it is dominated by the point of view of the killer. This
manner of presentation has prompted twentieth-century readers
to ask whether it was in fact Thorgrim rather than Thorkel who
killed Vestein. Earlier readers do not seem to have been in any
doubt, since it is mentioned in both extant versions, either in
chapter headings or in the text itself, that Thorgrim was the
killer. This may not have been expressly stated in the original
written version, but it has been convincingly argued that,
although Thorkel certainly was the instigator, it was Thorgrim
who thrust the spear into Vestein's body. In any case it is

interesting that the storytelling is focused with such ingenuity that readers can still argue about this today.

The author of *Gisli Sursson's Saga* was a master at creating monumental scenes demonstrating the integrity of persons who face overwhelming odds. Examples include the scene in Ch. 26 where the poor tenant Ingjald of Hergilsey is threatened by his landlord Bork to make him reveal Gisli's whereabouts, and answers: 'My clothes are so poor that it would be no great grief if I stopped wearing them out. I'd rather die than not do all I can to keep Gisli from harm.' Aud's cutting retort to Eyjolf the Grey in Ch. 32 was quoted above. The personal integrity and fearless pride expressed in these scenes are in the spirit of Gisli's whole life, and the final episode of it, his defence and fall in Chs. 34 to 36, epitomizes this core quality. Thordis' attack on Eyjolf in Ch. 37 echoes the same sentiments.

## The outlawed hero

*Gisli Sursson's Saga* is the tale of an unfortunate man who acts according to his conviction when he is faced with a tragic choice, and as a result is outlawed, hunted and in the end killed. His heroic and glorious last defence clearly marks him out as a great hero, but so in fact does his whole story. In the words of Peter Foote: 'Gisli appears as the typical hero, a man of many parts, a fighter at once bold and resourceful and ruthless, good with his hands, a loyal friend, punctilious in matters of honour.'[7] His fate is the central concern of the saga, which does not involve itself with the broader issues of relevance to society as a whole that are of such great interest in *The Saga of the People of Eyri*, and certainly in others such as *Njal's Saga*. Nevertheless, *Gisli Sursson's Saga* can be read as something of a case study with a more general message than its author may have consciously intended. 'Law' was a complex concept in the Icelandic commonwealth: it designated a corpus of originally unwritten but memorized rules or 'articles', and also the community that accepted these rules and even the geographical area in which they were considered to be valid. The boundaries of the 'law' were not clearly demarcated, because although it was valid everywhere in Iceland, it could not be effectively implemented in the wilderness, and therefore it made sense to judge someone to be outside the law – one term for outlaw was *skóggangsmaðr* (literally 'forest-dweller'). The category of outlaw highlights the fundamental distinction between culture and nature, or the social and the 'wild'.

Ultimately the 'law' and the ethics of society are the same, but just as the law in Old Icelandic society was imperfect, and could only be implemented by someone who was able to back up his interpretation of it with physical force, it was also flawed because of an inherent contradiction in the ethical basis of society: the code of honour and revenge set against the rule of law. *Gisli Sursson's Saga* thematizes this contradiction. A man who acts according to his deepest ethical conviction may incur the ultimate penalty: to be outlawed and cast out of society so categorically that no one is allowed to grant him shelter or assistance and anyone may kill him. Characteristically, the only person who tries to take revenge for Gisli Sursson is his sister Thordis; by convention, women were considered irresponsible and not supposed to play an active part in such affairs. *Gisli Sursson's Saga* insists, if this reading is correct, that Gisli is an honourable man, but it does not claim that the verdict against him is unlawful or even unfair. Does the problem have any solution? It would be overinterpretation to say that *The Saga of the People of Eyri* is a kind of ethical sequel with a clear message suggesting how to resolve such conflicts. Nevertheless, it can be read as a chronicle pointing the way from the cruel and partly 'wild' community of feuding families to a better-functioning and safer society where strong chieftains secure the peace.

Although it is not obvious on first reading, *Gisli Sursson's Saga* is an important intertext for the reading of *The Saga of the People of Eyri*, whatever their differences. The family tragedy of the first looms as a dark and threatening background to the social comedy of the second. There is an undercurrent of passion flowing from the one into the other, which is most vividly present in passages describing magic and the supernatural where witches and ghosts create havoc and ultimately destroy the lives of innocent people. Other disasters arise when men are illicitly and fatally attracted to beautiful women. Female sexuality and secret knowledge of magic are seen as threats to the male-dominated social order. The menacing forces of female sexuality are personified in Gisli's sister Thordis, and they reappear in her daughter Thurid in *The Saga of the People of Eyri*. Both women are at the centre of events that lead to feuds and multiple killings. In spite of continuing vendettas, the fate of this family turns from disaster to success when the focus moves from the hapless but heroic outlaw Gisli to his circumspect and successful nephew, Snorri the Godi. In the latter's saga we see how bloody conflicts are solved and social order gradually established, and how the foundations are laid for a chieftaincy that can control and keep in check the powers that threaten social stability.

## III. THE SAGA OF THE PEOPLE OF EYRI

*The Saga of the People of Eyri* draws a memorable picture of a chaotic and half-wild society where either brutal force or sly deception seems to decide the issues. Underlying the apparent chaos, however, the reader will discover a certain order that is gradually strengthened as the story progresses. The main characters are involved in a passionate struggle for power – a struggle that is portrayed with an element of humour, inviting us to regard it as social comedy. This comedy has a dark and irrational aspect, frequently transgressing the borders of the supernatural and entering the world of the fantastic, where magic prevails and ghosts play important roles. While it contains some of the most vivid episodes in saga literature, with diverse and memorable characters, and the reader finds many instances of the laconic and witty dialogue that characterizes the best of the genre, anyone who looks in the first chapters to find heroic adventure or romance will be surprised, if not puzzled.[8] The approach is much more like that of a medieval chronicle or modern work of local history. The beginning of the saga presents armed conflicts, changing fortunes and the moving of whole clans from one country to another in such a summary fashion that the abundance of geographical and personal detail threatens to leave the reader confused and overwhelmed. Of course, these events are merely introductory material that readers should not try to commit to memory all at once, but it is often helpful to refer back to this section when trying to make sense of the relationships and importance of individuals of later generations, who dominate the scene in the main part of the saga. But even there it is often difficult to orientate oneself. Scenes, episodes and even whole sequences of events are recounted with marvellous clarity and poignancy, but it may take some effort to realize how they are connected to each other and to the whole. As the saga progresses it turns out to be composed of several narrative strands, which either follow upon each other or are woven together, and the pattern they produce is certainly an intricate and rewarding one.

In terms of its subject matter, the saga ranges from episodes that strike the modern mind as marvellous or fantastic to pieces of information apparently introduced purely for their historical interest. In between lies a wealth of immediately engaging excitement and action. On a closer look the human drama presented in the saga reveals a deep insight into the politics of power as well as keen observation of human wisdom and folly. In presenting his rich variety of material the narrator maintains a steady and apparently objective tone of voice, creating the impression that the entire work is history recorded on the basis of reliable sources. The reader should not be deceived by this apparent objectivity, however. Irony and warmth, sympathies and antipathies are discreetly conveyed. Thorleif Kimbi's homecoming with Snorri in Ch. 13 is described in concrete detail without evaluative comment, and it is only by contrasting his behaviour and his garb with that of his companions that the reader realizes he is a vain and somewhat ridiculous character. Likewise, the highly detailed account of the widow Thorgerd's wanderings from one of her kinsmen to another in order to organize revenge for her husband's death (Chs. 26 and 27) arouses sympathy and respect for the bereaved woman without any explicit comment to that effect. The episode with the slave Egil the Strong in Ch. 43 is a masterpiece of ironic narrative where sympathy is subtly mixed with contempt. The reader has to judge the characters and situation from several possibilities. One of the saga's most important qualities is precisely this avoidance of explicit moral or dogma, in which sense it is more akin to modern writing than to medieval traditions elsewhere in Europe.

The following outline of the composition of the saga is intended to help those reading the saga for the first time to find their way through the jungle of events, rather than to do justice to the lively and eventful narrative, the variety of characters or the world described.

## The plot – weaving the strands together

The saga opens with a matter-of-fact account of a number of people who settled the northern coast of the Snaefellsnes peninsula. Even though other settlers can claim a more noble lineage, it is the people of Thorsnes, the descendants of Thorolf Moster-beard, who receive most attention, signalling that they will occupy the centre stage in the story.[9] Thorolf settles at Hofstadir where he builds a temple (*hof*) and establishes an assembly on hallowed ground, literally and figuratively laying the foundations of a new society. The next generation moves the farm to Helgafell (later the site of a monastery), also on Thorsnes. Although the descriptions of these important events, the building of the temple and the establishment of the assembly, read like a trustworthy historical account, they are more likely to be the educated guesswork of a learned thirteenth-century writer than based on oral tradition.[10] Whether or not they have a historical basis, these descriptions serve as signals that the family of Helgafell will play an important social role in the saga. Much of the information given has the flavour of something gathered in a writer's study: oral traditions are so well integrated into the literary structure that it is impossible to distinguish the two.

After the introductory section, which describes the settlements and early rivalries between the chieftain families in the area, the pace of the saga is slowed down when Snorri Thorgrimsson (Snorri the Godi) enters the scene. From then on he is the central character who either is a direct party to conflicts or becomes involved in them, and almost without exception emerges each time with some gain in power and prestige. His position in the saga is emphasized by the detailed description in Ch. 15, by which time he has already demonstrated his most important qualities.

Snorri the Godi, of the Thorsnes family, was born after his father was killed by Snorri's maternal uncle, Gisli Sursson, as described in *Gisli Sursson's Saga*. While still an adolescent, Snorri demonstrates his qualifications by outwitting his paternal uncle Bork and taking over the farm at Helgafell and the position of godi. The plot that is subsequently developed consists of two main strands, each composed of several minor threads and episodes. One main strand describes a feud or series of feuds in which Snorri and Arnkel, another godi, are the principal actors. They live very close to each other and have thingmen in the same part of the district, so their rivalry is inevitable. The conflict that develops between Snorri's brother-in-law, Thorbjorn of Froda river (married to Thurid, Snorri's half-sister through his mother), and Arnkel's nephew Thorarin of Mavahlid (Chs. 15–16, 18–22) ends when Thorbjorn is killed and Thorarin is outlawed and leaves the country. The subtlety of the play for prestige and power among these chieftains is interesting: Arnkel gains honour from his success in supporting Thorarin, although the formal victory is Snorri's; the smaller figures are the losers. Snorri's sister Thurid takes no part in the action but is none the less indirectly implicated in an evil scheme with disastrous consequences for the very sympathetic couple Thorarin and Aud. Later on Thurid is repeatedly the cause of conflicts, as her mother was in *Gisli Sursson's Saga*. The feud between Snorri and Arnkel resumes when one of Snorri's men maims a relative of a worthy farmer, Vigfus, whose wife has a family connection with Arnkel. Snorri's strength is shown when it takes three important chieftains, including Arnkel, to form a sufficiently strong alliance against him, and this time he has to pay a heavy fine. Nevertheless, he has strengthened his position because of his firm handling of the case and through his marriage to the daughter of Styr, a strong and overbearing chieftain who up to that time had belonged to the alliance opposed to him. In typical style, Snorri wins Styr's favour by giving him clever advice about how he is to solve the threat posed by two berserks he has hired as workmen.

During the last feud in this strand Arnkel's weak position and slender power base are revealed when his aged father, Thorolf Lame-foot, becomes involved in conflicts with his neighbours and seeks Snorri's assistance when Arnkel does not want to support him in an unjust case. After Thorolf's death Snorri and Arnkel clash over a piece of land which Thorolf (unlawfully in Arnkel's opinion) has turned over to Snorri. The conflict escalates until Arnkel is attacked by Snorri and a group of his followers and killed after a heroic defence. This represents a total victory because there are no close relatives to take up Arnkel's case, and Snorri greatly strengthens his position by it, although without gaining any glory.

It is typical for this saga's composition that by the time Arnkel is killed another main strand has already been introduced (Ch. 29), in which Snorri's sister Thurid is directly involved. Married for the second time to a wealthy man and living at Froda river, she receives many visits from Bjorn the Champion of the Breidavik People, and they are thought to be having an affair. When her second husband's attempts at ending the affair misfire, Snorri, as head of the family, initiates legal proceedings which end with Bjorn being sentenced to lesser outlawry and having to leave Iceland for three years. In the process Bjorn is supported by the people of Eyri, who in this strand of the plot emerge as Snorri's most powerful opponents. This strand is elaborated upon in Chs. 39–48. Typically, the conflict is escalated by a series of seemingly trivial incidents. One of the men of Alftafjord, who are Snorri's most loyal supporters, fights with Bjorn's brother over a trifling issue, and to make matters worse, Bjorn returns to Iceland and begins courting the mistress of the house at Froda again. Finally, when one of the men of Alftafjord wants to marry a woman of the Eyri family he is turned down with contempt. After several incidents involving heavy fighting and some killings, Bjorn is forced to leave Iceland for good, while Snorri and Steinthor of Eyri, his most formidable opponent, are reconciled. The less important families of Breidavik and Alftafjord end up paying the price for all these conflicts, while Snorri emerges from them with such strength that his authority in the Snaefellsnes region is never challenged again.

Despite its chaotic surface appearance, this main part of the saga (Chs. 13–48) turns out to have a tightly woven underlying fabric, but the rest of the plot, where there is no interweaving of strands, is looser in composition. When Iceland is converted to Christianity, special mention is made of the fact that Snorri the Godi becomes a spokesman for the new faith. This is important because it makes him a representative of the new order. The ensuing chapters contain an independent tale, the wonders of Froda river, which are reported to have happened in the very first year of the conversion to Christianity. This is a mysterious account of strange, evil powers and revenants of a more traditional type, and again Thurid is at the centre of the events. An elderly foreign woman appears on the scene, and her death spawns mysterious and monstrous events: evil spirits are unleashed, and accidents and some sort of plague cause the death of many people, who all return as ghosts and haunt the place. A formal legal process is instigated against the ghosts to drive them away, and when they finally leave, consecrated water and sacred relics are carried around the house, and a mass is sung. Thus secular and spiritual powers are united in an ideal match and restore the natural order.

The final extended narrative is a lively and entertaining account of a dastardly leader of band of robbers who bullies some of Snorri's thingmen. Snorri takes action, killing the leaders and dissolving the band, by which he demonstrates not only his determination and skilful leadership, but also his sense of humour.

Concluding the plot are two folktale-like episodes that can be interpreted as aftermaths to the two main strands of the middle section of the saga: the first (Ch. 63) describes how the spirit of Thorolf Lame-foot reappears in the form of a bull and kills one of his and Arnkel's enemies, which can be taken as a belated revenge for Arnkel; in the second (Ch. 64) we are introduced to an elderly man in a distant mysterious country who turns out to be Bjorn, the Champion of the Breidavik People, Snorri's most prominent adversary in the second strand of the plot. Bjorn has therefore survived the feud, although he could not be accommodated in the space that Snorri occupied. With its summary of the last twenty years of Snorri the Godi's life and the enumeration of his children and some of their descendants, the final chapter reinforces the pseudo-historical mode of the narrative.

## Narrative art – humour and irony

Whichever manuscript version we read, the style of *The Saga of the People of Eyri* is concrete, broadly rational in thought and bristling with dry humour. Irony and understatement are characteristic devices, and the style is more polished than that of *Gisli Sursson's Saga*. For all the objective impression given by the style, the author is skilled at discreetly influencing the reader's sympathies. In Chs. 26 and 27, for example, we are told about the slaying of Vigfus at Drapuhlid and how his widow Thorgerd immediately rides from one chieftain to another to seek their assistance in bringing a case against the killers. In the end she is forced to dig up her husband from his grave and ride to another farm with his head. The saga apparently remains undisturbed by any qualms about the treatment dealt out to the poor woman. She is described as a true heroine, fiercely loyal to her dead husband's honour. However, when we read her own words carefully, they shed clear light on her sufferings and how cruelly she is treated by her own and her husband's kinsmen, who are loath to risk their honour on her behalf.

While the saga may take an intermittent interest in ordinary farmers, its point of view is that of the uppermost class in society, the chieftains. The class bias becomes very clear in its portrayal of working men and slaves, who are invariably ridiculed for their stupidity and lack of courage. When the Scot Nagli, scared out of his wits, flees from the fighting in Mavahlid he meets a couple of slaves who become smitten by his fear, and they all run off a promontory to their deaths (Ch. 18). Arnkel's slaves abandon him when he is under attack from a large band of men and forget (or pretend to forget) to tell his people about it when they return home (Ch. 37). If a slave has courage, like Egil the Strong in Alftafjord, he is presented as lacking in intelligence. Egil's desire for freedom is described with some sympathy, but it leads to his death. The tale of his attempt to kill Bjorn the Champion of the Breidavik People in Ch. 43 is an ironical masterpiece: 'Egil felt it would be only *a little while* before he earned for himself *everlasting* freedom.' Inevitably, the outcome is the complete opposite: he has only a few hours left to live. Egil's surprise attack on Bjorn, which he foresees as a great heroic act which will open his door to freedom, is a humiliating anticlimax: 'when he went to step across the threshold, he trod on the loose tassel. When he tried to step forward with his other foot, the tassel held fast, causing him to trip, and he fell forward on to the floor of the hall. There was a huge thud as if the skinned carcass of a cow had been thrown down on the floor.' This is one of many examples of the way this saga leaves the final interpretation of events to the reader. The humour of the concrete and detailed description of Egil's fatal journey can only be enjoyed in full by a reader who is attentive to the minutest of details, who in the end will have to decide whether this is black comedy or a mixture of contempt with compassion.

Snorri the Godi himself makes many ironical statements, sometimes even reported in indirect speech. A man named Alf the Short plays a role in Snorri's dealings with the robbers in Bitra. He is described as a coward who makes much fuss, and his main accomplishment, being an extremely swift runner, has a comic ring to it in the context. Another character in the same episode, Thrand Strider, is his exact opposite as far as courage and fighting skills are concerned. He walks great distances and is the most prominent of Snorri's men in the decisive fight. Ch. 61 tells how Alf the Short has run a long distance to report to Snorri about harassment by robbers: 'He strongly urged Snorri to go north at once to attack Ospak and his band. But first Snorri the Godi wanted to find out from the north whether they had done anything more than push Alf the Short out of the way . . .' Snorri's contempt for the man can be deduced from his words, but they are understated and entail no outright criticism or mockery.

Snorri the Godi is rather an unusual hero for a saga. He is neither particularly strong nor brave, nor is he much of a fighter, although he repeatedly leads groups of men to battle. But Snorri is more intelligent than any of his opponents, which can be judged not only by his actions and their results, but also by his comments on other people and their actions and by the characteristic irony and dry humour of his words. Moreover, some explicit comments about his wisdom are made by both the narrator and certain characters: for example, 'Snorri was a wise man and had foresight about many things, a long memory and a predisposition to vengeance. He gave his friends good counsel but his enemies felt the chill of his strategies' (Ch. 15). Snorri is also an atypical saga protagonist insofar as he is not always a prominent player in the events themselves. Frequently conflicts arise between other people, and at a later stage Snorri is drawn into them in his capacity of godi. His antagonists often seem to enjoy a more sympathetic portrayal than he does, and they may win temporary victories. Characters such as Arnkel or Bjorn certainly have more traditional heroic qualities and they gain honour in their dealings with him, but in the end Snorri carries the day when Arnkel is killed and Bjorn is forced to leave the country for good.

## Reality and myth

The events described in *The Saga of the People of Eyri*, from Ketil Flat-nose's sojourn in the Hebrides until the death of Snorri the Godi, are supposed to have taken place in the period from around 870 until 1030, although the main action would have been in the last two decades of the tenth century. The introduction, the account of the Christianization of Iceland and the genealogical information in the very end of the saga serve to give it the character of history or chronicle. Reinforcing this impression are several comments on the difference between the customs of former times and the time the story is told (see for instance Chs. 4 and 38). All this enhances what could be called the 'reality effect', to borrow Roland Barthes' term, rather than the 'realism' of the saga.[11] The same effect is achieved through the moderation of descriptions in general. Fighting is usually recounted without significant exaggeration or displays of heroics. Thus when Arnkel valiantly defends himself against fifteen attackers, his weapon is not the gleaming sword of a hero but the running-blade from a sled, and he does not kill or maim any of his assailants, as Gisli Sursson would surely have done. These trivial details in no way detract from the essentially heroic nature of his defence, but would have made it sound more real to the ears of the original audience. For modern readers such a narrative style is probably no less effective than the elevated style of heroic epos, and many parallels could be pointed out in realistic novels, crime fiction and westerns.

Strangely enough, the abundant descriptions of marvellous or supernatural events are also rendered in realistic style. On one level the stories of ghosts and monsters become even more effective or shocking when not distinguished from the reality of the everyday world than they would be in the consciously wrought setting of, say, a Gothic novel. The first appearance of other-worldly phenomena is as early as Ch. 11, when Thorstein Cod-biter has drowned and the shepherd has a vision of how the drowned men enter a mountain and are welcomed by Thorstein's father. This strongly atmospheric scene opens up a new dimension in the world of the saga. The immediate warning it provides of Thorstein's death is a well-known phenomenon from folklore. Here it is as if a curtain is suddenly drawn from the hidden world of the dead, then just as suddenly falls again. Apart from the shepherd's vision no contact is established between the two worlds, and the course of events taking place in the saga is in no way affected, but the narrative effortlessly glides into the sphere of the marvellous and uncanny both here and elsewhere.

Alerted by this description in the introductory section, we are not surprised to find further testimonies that people live on in some sense after death and can make themselves appear to the living or be revealed to them. Of course such events pose a threat when the dead seem to be malevolent and actively interfere in the world of the living, but they are described in such a matter-of-fact 'realistic' fashion that they obviously were considered, if not natural, then at least possible by the narrator and his audience. *The Saga of the People of Eyri* abounds in accounts of malevolent ghosts. Examples are Thorolf Lame-foot, who does not stay in his grave in spite of his son Arnkel's precautions at the burial, and the revenants at Froda river. Thorolf's story is forcefully told, the reader prepared for drama by the tension of anticipation. When Thorolf eventually dies, angry with his son and most other people around him ('growing more ill-natured, violent and unjust with the years'), the measures Arnkel takes to stop him leaving his grave to haunt his home are described in great detail: he takes care to approach the body from behind, wraps a cloak around its head so that no one comes to harm through looking in Thorolf's eyes; he breaks a hole in the wall behind Thorolf's seat through which he removes the body, as Egil Skallagrimsson does when disposing of his dead father in *Egil's Saga*; and then near the bottom of the valley where Thorolf lived he is buried in a 'strongly built cairn'. Inevitably, the precautions are to no avail and Thorolf does not 'lie still', as the saga says; in a vivid piece of scene painting (Ch. 34) his ghost wanders around, frightens and kills cattle, a shepherd, then more people, and eventually drives everyone from the valley. Finally, Arnkel succeeds in burying his father so far away that he is never bothered by his ghost again. Just as in the tale of the wonders at Froda river, where Kjartan alone has the strength of character to stand up against evil powers, the ghost's power is limited here. Ghosts seem to fear and respect individuals of great courage and integrity. Near the end of the saga, however (Ch. 63), Thorolf starts marauding again, and when his body is dug up it proves to be 'monstrous to look at. He was as black as Hell and as huge as an ox.' Fantastic and fear-inspiring as the episode may be, when it ends with the bull killing Thorodd Thorbrandsson and then disappearing, it is none the less related in the same straightforward terms as an event that could happen any day in the Icelandic countryside. Motifs related to the one of a cow licking the ashes of a burnt human body and becoming impregnated with a bull that embodies the man's anger and vengefulness are known from mythology and folklore. They probably enshrine the age-old wisdom that 'the evil that men do lives after them'.

The most mysterious happenings of the saga take place at Froda river (Chs. 50–55). Their uncanny atmosphere comes partly from how little background the reader is told. We never hear about Thorgunna's past, nor what strange kind of magic is attached to the precious things she leaves and wants to be burned. Her devout Christianity gives the narrative a religious flavour. The strange portent of the blood that rains on the hay is a powerful warning of things to come. The head of the seal that appears in the fireplace and the tail sticking out of the pile of dried fish could be incarnations of the devil. Revenants of a more traditional ghost-story type make appearances as well, such as the vivid and chilling image of the silent flock of ghosts who, in increasing numbers, invade the quarters of the living every night. The reader can only conclude that such fantastic events, unthinkable today, were an intrinsic feature of the world in which this saga's traditions lie, and even acceptable to its audience at the time it was written.

Magic and sorcery are another supernatural element that not only spices up the action but also affects the course of events. An example is the fate of the people of Mavahlid (Chs. 15–16, 18–22). The story takes place on two levels, as it were, mythical and social. At the mythical level the main antagonists are the sexually attractive witch Katla of Holt and the somewhat older Geirrid of Mavahlid, who is 'knowledgeable about magic'. It is Katla's black magic that initiates the feud between Thorarin of Mavahlid and Thorbjorn of Froda river, leaving the chieftains led by Arnkel, who skilfully handle the legal and violent aspects of the conflicts, helpless to deal with the evil witch until Geirrid comes to their assistance.

Sexuality is an undercurrent in the saga, releasing forces which threaten social stability and are hard for the mechanisms of power and authority to control. Katla's attempt to seduce the young Gunnlaug and her jealous revenge when she does not succeed lead to the killing of many men and the destruction of the Mavahlid family. The illicit love affair between Thurid and

Bjorn causes much disruption and costs many lives. Thurid's vanity is also the cause of the strange events at Froda, which begin when evil powers associated with Thorgunna and her treasures are released. It seems that Thorgunna's Christianity, practised with great devotion, holds in check these powers that are somehow connected with a past, possibly in the Hebrides where she is said to have her roots, about which the saga is confoundingly silent. It is tempting to read a Christian moral into this story, namely that Thurid is being punished for her infidelity and her wilfulness. But this is certainly not a simple cautionary tale, because she survives, and the only person at Froda who is endowed with the strength and integrity to oppose the evil powers and finally lead the process of driving them out is Kjartan, the offspring of her illicit love affair with Bjorn.

The female characters of *The Saga of the People of Eyri* are hardly described at all, with the exception of the Hebridean Thorgunna and the witch Katla, although a fairly clear picture is also given of her rival, Geirrid. There is no portrayal of the physical appearance of Thurid, who plays the most important female role, although it is obvious that she must have been an attractive woman with a strong will of her own. Married first to a much older man and after his death to a man who is rich but described in contemptuous terms, she does not hesitate to go her own ways. To a certain extent she plays the role of 'femme fatale' in *The Saga of the People of Eyri*, just as her mother Thordis does in *Gisli Sursson's Saga*. Thordis is involved in the action of *Gisli Sursson's Saga* from the outset, albeit mainly passively, and in the episode that unites the two sagas she tries to take action herself by attacking her brother's killer and subsequently renouncing her husband Bork. Thurid is more marginal in the action and seems to lack the strength to oppose the strong will of her brother Snorri. When she contravenes Thorgunna's explicit wishes about burning her belongings, Thurid's motive is pure desire for luxurious possessions, while her action also demonstrates the power she exerts over her weakling husband. Indeed, her dealings with Thorodd are more reminiscent of the comic quarrel and reconciliation of Asgerd and Thorkel in *Gisli Sursson's Saga*, Ch. 9, than of her mother's tragic life. Thus the fateful influence of female sexuality that is so destructive in *Gisli Sursson's Saga* is present but subdued and in the end brought under control in Snorri the Godi's saga.

## The chieftain and the heroes – decentralized narrative

The male sphere of action, centred around Snorri the Godi, is radically different from the female and mythical sphere. It is forward-looking and deals with social and practical problems, and its underlying concern is the mechanics and consolidation of secular power. Nevertheless, although Snorri the Godi is at the centre of the plot, figuratively speaking the sun of the solar system, other characters and episodes in orbit around him are given close attention for their own sake. Arnkel is a traditional kind of hero, a typical representative of early Icelandic society like Gisli, modest and unaggressive but a man who guards his honour zealously and defends himself bravely against insurmountable odds. His tale could be read separately as a tragedy about the downfall of a hero who succumbs to the schemes of less heroic figures. Bjorn the Champion of the Breidavik People is a romantic, almost chivalric, type. A born survivor, he realizes when the time has come to leave the scene and seek new pastures. Thus the saga tells an intertwined cycle of tales, with different protagonists who personify different values. This is the main reason for its apparent incoherence on first reading, an impression that gradually recedes. The different strands and episodes of *The Saga of the People of Eyri* ultimately advance the main story in contrast, for instance, to the cycles of King Arthur, where his court is the same when the knights return from their adventures. The saga as a whole is governed by an interest in the affairs of society, which are perceived as best handled by strong chieftains such as Snorri the Godi. However, long sections focus on and sympathize with individuals who do not fit into such a society. An aspect of this decentralization of the narrative is that the main characters of the various episodes differ significantly from each other – and it is the central figure, Snorri, who diverges most from the traditional saga hero mould. This difference is highlighted by the contrasts between Snorri and his maternal uncle Gisli. As a traditional hero, the latter is firmly anchored in a world which already belonged to the past by the time the saga was written. His character and his fate are one, and after a glorious last stand he is doomed to be destroyed, leaving no offspring; his weapon and the symbol of his dismal fate is the sword Grey-blade. In spite of all his good qualities his stubborn vengefulness is a threat to society. His nephew Snorri, on the other hand, is not a hero by any stretch of the imagination and his fate is unheroic: his weapon is his intelligence, he survives into a peaceful old age and brings forth a thriving family. He is the creator of his own fate and a stabilizing force in society.

Snorri's appearance and character are described in one passage (Ch. 15), but the real delineation of his personality progresses as the story unfolds, through his words and actions. His first move in the quest for power is deception. Returning from abroad after a brief but obviously very successful trading journey, he conceals his wealth and manages to trick the family farm out of the hands of his uncle and stepfather Bork without doing anything except waiting for him to make a false move. Bork underestimates Snorri and, blinded by greed into acting stupidly, easily falls prey to his scheme. In the main action of the saga Snorri always acts with caution and circumspection, but also with courage and resolution when that is called for. Slowly and methodically he takes advantage of every occasion to strengthen his position, without taking any unnecessary risks until his authority has been consolidated. One of Snorri's characteristics is that he always seems to be in full control of his emotions. In this respect he is a clear contrast to his sister Thurid and also to such male characters as Thorarin from Mavahlid and Bjorn the Champion of the Breidavik People. Thorarin is so quiet and peaceful that he is slandered for being unmanly, but when put to the test he demonstrates both courage and fighting skills, to the surprise of everyone, including himself. He is a poet, and in his verse he comments on the violent events he becomes involved in and his own reactions to them. It is his mother who eggs him on, while his wife Aud is even more peaceful than he is. When her hand is cut off as she and other women try to stop a fight, she even tries to hide the fact. These people are cast as totally innocent and sympathetic victims of an evil plot, and Thorarin reacts as an honourable man must do. However, his only way out of the difficulties is to seek the assistance of chieftains, and he is well connected. All the same, in the end he must leave the scene, and it is interesting to note the detachment with which the saga concludes: it simply states that Thorarin leaves for Norway, and the same year goes from there to the British Isles: 'Thorarin does not come into this story again.' Not a word is said about his wife or the other people in Mavahlid. What is of interest in the saga is the power play among chieftains; lesser people can enter the scene for a while, engage interest and be portrayed with great care, but when they have played out their role they are no longer of any concern.

Another character who plays an important role for a while, Bjorn the Champion of the Breidavik People, is also a poet. Stubbornly he persists in his visits to Thurid at Froda, expressing his love for her in beautiful stanzas (see in particular verse 24). He is contemptuous of danger and even death, yet is so brave that he always manages to defend himself even against overwhelming odds. In many respects he is favoured by fortune, but unlike Thorarin he does not mend his ways when he returns from his first outlawry. Repeated attempts to get rid of him prove unsuccessful, and the final encounter even leaves him with Snorri's life in his hands. However, at that point he realizes that the game is lost, that Snorri is too big for him to handle, and he consents to leave the country for good. He is none the less presented in such a favourable and sympathetic light – and perhaps viewed that way by generations of listeners to tales about him – that he cannot be dismissed entirely even when he has left the front stage. His strength and luck seem to live on in his son Kjartan of Froda river, while the folktale near the end of the saga, where we meet him again, portrays him living on as a leader of people in a mysterious 'other world'.

Numerous other minor characters are given a good deal of attention in their own right. Snorri's father-in-law Styr, for instance, merits a vivid description with an underlying reference to the great part he plays in *The Saga of the Slayings on the*

*Heath*, an earlier work. Episodes which feature in both sagas, such as his dealings with his brother Vermund and the Swedish berserks, are treated more rationally in *The Saga of the People of Eyri*, with a keener observation of his character and above all a touch of humour.

When Snorri moves from Helgafell for unspecified reasons, we are only given a hint in the final chapter as to how he overcame initial resistance and gained a superior position in his new district. However, he has clearly assumed the role of a major chieftain by Chs. 57–62, where he acts with determination in dealing with a band of robbers in Strandir, and solves the problem effectively, justly and above all memorably. The episode can be read as an exemplary tale about the importance and social role of chieftains, although the text itself draws no such general conclusions. In the course of the saga, therefore, there has been a development towards a well-ordered society in which the strong chieftain, wise and moderate but at the same time determined and unwavering, plays a crucial role as a stabilizing force. While *Gisli Sursson's Saga* ends in destruction, the saga about his nephew describes the development of a new order that can be read as a metaphor of the society of law and order about which the Icelanders must have dreamt during the tumultuous times of the thirteenth century (perhaps even earlier), and which they surely must have hoped to have achieved with the treaty they made with the King of Norway in 1262. Such an interpretation would be consistent with the assumption that *The Saga of the People of Eyri* was written around 1270. As in many other sagas, the conversion to Christianity around AD 1000, as depicted in literature, can be seen as symbolic of another watershed more than two and a half centuries later, when Icelandic chieftains began to accept and seek the protection of royal power. After the conversion, all disturbances of the peace that occur in this saga, whether mythical or social in nature, are settled by the authority of the clever and determined chieftain.

The author of *Gisli Sursson's Saga* moulds his material into a well-integrated whole with the apparent main purpose of giving voice to the system of values that inspired Gisli, and therefore concentrates single-mindedly on his tragic fate. The salient characteristic of *The Saga of the People of Eyri*, on the other hand, is its decentralization of focus. Although it turns out to be coherent when all the strands have been pulled together, its open form of narrative allows different voices expressing varying values to be heard. This structure must have been created by a skilled writer who worked with diverse oral tales and wanted to combine them and make them serve his own purpose without subduing their voices altogether. This saga therefore presents the reader with many voices orchestrated by a detached view of the traditional ideology and the old society. The saga might have been written a decade before *Njal's Saga*. It takes a similarly broad view of society, but just as Snorri the Godi is less sentimental and more governed by self-interest than Njal, Snorri's saga is more detached and even cynical in its attitude to politics and power. Ultimately, *Njal's Saga* demonstrates the futility of man's attempts to govern his affairs rationally, while *The Saga of the People of Eyri* firmly believes in reason and intelligence as crucial forces in a political game that serves the interests of the strong chieftain at the same time as ensuring peace and balance in society as a whole.

# IV. THE SECRET OF THE SAGAS

The sagas in this volume abound in qualities that appeal to the modern reader. The dignity and integrity of the main characters is a strong feature, but they draw a firm line between self-respect and comic self-importance, and are liberally laced with both humour and less transparent dramatic ironies. Ultimately, their success as narratives lies without doubt in the great restraint exerted by the narrators. While they are particular about the concrete details of major events they never tell us too much, always leaving gaps for us to fill and questions to answer. We see this in the descriptions of the most important killings in *Gisli Sursson's Saga*, when Vestein and then Thorgrim are secretly murdered. In both cases the accounts are concrete and detailed, yet the focus is so narrow that it blocks out as much as it brings into view. We are merely left to wonder about the nature of the relationship between Thordis and her Norwegian suitors: was it conversational, romantic or overtly sexual? How intimate was the 'affair' between Asgerd and Vestein? Was it really an affair or did she only 'have a crush' on him? People in the nineteenth and the late twentieth centuries differed widely in their judgements on these points, but that tells us more about the readers than about the saga. Turning to *The Saga of the People of Eyri* we see this narrative restraint applied from another angle, where things almost invariably go as Snorri has planned although we are not informed of those plans in advance. We are never told the details of the love affair between Bjorn and Thurid and only gradually and through hints is it confirmed that he is the real father of her son Kjartan. We learn to know the characters through what we hear and see, and only occasionally do they express their feelings openly. We never know what is deepest in their minds, and therefore have to judge them for ourselves, just like people we meet in our everyday lives. This withholding of information has a parallel in the style, in its concreteness, frequent understatement and the wry incisiveness of remarks made in the dialogue.

This introduction has argued that the difference in the age of these sagas – *Gisli Sursson's Saga* in all likelihood being a few decades older – is reflected in their respective portrayals of man and society. Such is the objectivity or inscrutability of the method of narration, however, that we can never be absolutely sure how much of the differences between the two sagas stems from differences in the traditional material and above all in the characters of the authors themselves. But on one point it is easy to agree: both these sagas are the work of writers with great imaginative and narrative powers.

## NOTES

1. The social is inextricably linked to the religious in this saga, and therefore the founding of the district assembly and the building of a temple in Ch. 4, despite the note of antiquarianism that they strike, have a deep significance for the story, as do the conversion

to Christianity and the building of a church at Helgafell, which is briefly described in Ch. 49.

2.  While there is no doubt about the importance of the conversion for the development of Icelandic society, the general image of the settlement and its causes as presented in the sagas is more likely to be a creation of the thirteenth century and its political conflicts than an accurate rendering of historical fact. The picture of the harsh rule of Harald Fair-hair in Norway, which was supposed to have driven the settlers of Iceland to seek freedom in a new country, could have been influenced or even have arisen while their descendants many generations on witnessed the consolidation of the Norwegian monarchy in the period during the reign of King Hakon Hakonarson (1217–63). Iceland's conversion to Christianity, on the other hand, has many affinities with the end of the Icelandic Commonwealth and the acceptance of Norwegian sovereignty in 1262–4; both events signify the coming of a new order, and the second completes what the first had begun. The country's adaptation to the common ideology of medieval Europe was not complete while it had no king.

3.  These significant families were headed by members of the Sturlung family, who amassed great wealth and power in the thirteenth century. From their ranks came great writers, scholars and men of authority and property, such as Snorri Sturluson (1179–1241) and his nephews Sturla Thordarson (1214–84) and Olaf Thordarson (d. 1259). Heroic traditions and saga writing seem to have flourished in the western quarter of Iceland. In these parts the monastery of Helgafell on the Snaefellsnes peninsula and Snorri Sturluson's farm at Reykholt in Borgarfjord were probably the most important centres of saga writing, although other places certainly played a role.

4.  Readers ought to be warned that the text is not very well preserved. The manuscript version translated for this edition dates from the fifteenth century. There are two other versions of medieval origin, one of them only a fragment, the other only preserved in eighteenth-century copies. None of those versions can be traced farther back than the fourteenth century. *Gisli Sursson's Saga* is commonly considered to have been composed on the basis of oral traditions around the mid thirteenth century or even a decade or two earlier, but we must accept the fact that the original written version is irretrievably lost. There are significant differences between the two main versions, especially in the introductory section, and scholars do not agree which is a better representative of the first, hypothetical

written version. It is most likely that both have been altered by scribes who left their individual imprint on the new versions, and these changes sometimes affect the interpretation of important events.

5. When *Gisli Sursson's Saga* was written the Icelanders had been Christian for more than two centuries, and there is no reason to believe that the author was not a good Christian. The events of the saga take place in pagan times, but in the final chapter we are told that Gisli's and Vestein's widows are baptized and go on a pilgrimage. However, the saga does not focus on religious issues, and no conflict can be detected between Christian and pagan ethics. Indeed, it is only in some of the stanzas that any influence from religious literature can be found.

6. The term 'eddic' is used of the poetry found in the *Elder Edda* or *Poetic Edda*, an Icelandic collection of narrative poems about pagan gods and legendary heroes written in the thirteenth century. Most of the poems derive from oral tradition.

7. Peter Foote, 'An Essay on the Saga of Gisli and its Icelandic Background', in *The Saga of Gisli*, trans. George Johnston (London: J. M. Dent & Sons, University of Toronto Press, 1963) pp. 93–134. Quotation on p. 108.

8. *The Saga of the People of Eyri* has been somewhat better preserved than *Gisli Sursson's Saga*, although the text also has to be based on versions that can be dated to the fourteenth and fifteenth centuries. These are preserved in incomplete vellum manuscripts or fragments, but what is lacking can be filled in with texts from much later paper copies. There do not seem to be any significant variations in content among these versions, although a chapter is lacking in the latest one. On the other hand, there is considerable variation in the wording, and we just do not have access to the text as it was originally phrased on vellum in the second half of the thirteenth century.

9. The traditionally accepted name of the saga is therefore a misnomer, and 'The Saga of the People of Thorsnes' would be more appropriate.

10. Modern scholarship has concluded that there were no buildings in Iceland in pagan times that functioned exclusively as temples; rather, big halls at the farms of godis were temporarily hallowed for sacrificial feasts. Their size could have been influenced by the intention to use them for this purpose, however. The description of the temple is probably based on literary sources, which in turn seem to be reconstructions modelled on church buildings. It is certain

that there was a local assembly at Thorsnes, but it is more doubtful whether it was established as early as in the lifetime of Thorolf Moster-beard.

11. Roland Barthes, 'L'effet de réel', *Communications*, 11 (1968), pp. 84–9.

# Further Reading

## GENERAL

Andersson, Theodore M., *The Problem of Icelandic Saga Origins: A Historical Survey* (New Haven: Yale University Press, 1964).

—, *The Icelandic Family Saga: An Analytic Reading* (Cambridge: Harvard University Press, 1967).

*The Book of Settlements* (*Landnámabók*), trans. Hermann Pálsson and Paul Edwards (Winnipeg: University of Manitoba Press, 1972).

Byock, Jesse L., *Feud in the Icelandic Saga* (Berkeley: University of California Press, 1982).

—, *Medieval Iceland: Society, Sagas, and Power* (Berkeley: University of California Press, 1988).

Clover, Carol J., *The Medieval Saga* (Ithaca: Cornell University Press, 1982).

—, and John Lindow (eds.), *Old Norse–Icelandic Literature: A Critical Guide, Islandica* xlv (Ithaca: Cornell University Press, 1985).

Hallberg, Peter, *The Icelandic Saga*, trans. Paul Schach (Lincoln: University of Nebraska Press, 1962).

Hastrup, Kirsten, *Culture and History in Medieval Iceland* (Oxford: Clarendon Press, 1985).

*Íslendingabók* (*The Book of the Icelanders*), trans. Halldór Hermannson (Ithaca: Cornell University Press, 1930).

Jesch, Judith, *Women in the Viking Age* (Woodbridge: Boydell Press, 1992).

Jochens, Jenny, *Women in Old Norse Society* (Ithaca: Cornell University Press, 1995).

—, *Old Norse Images of Women* (Philadelphia: University of Pennsylvania Press, 1996).

Ker, W. P., *Epic and Romance: Essays on Medieval Literature*, 2nd edn. (London, 1908; rpt. New York: Dover, 1957).

Kristjánsson, Jónas, *Eddas and Sagas: Iceland's Medieval Literature*, trans. Peter Foote, 3rd edn (Reykjavík: Hið íslenska bókmenntafélag, 1997).

Meulengracht Sørensen, Preben, *Saga and Society: An Introduction to Old Norse Literature*, trans. John Tucker (Odense: Odense University Press, 1993).

Miller, William Ian, *Bloodtaking and Peacemaking: Feud, Law, and Society in Saga Iceland* (Chicago: University of Chicago Press, 1990).

Nordal, Sigurður, *Icelandic Culture*, trans. Vilhjálmur T. Bjarnar (Ithaca: Cornell University Press, 1990).

Ólason, Vésteinn, *Dialogues with the Viking Age: Narration and Representation in the Sagas of Icelanders*, trans. Andrew Wawn (Reykjavík: Heimsringla, 1997).

Pulsiano, Phillip, and Kirsten Wolf, et al. (eds.), *Medieval Scandinavia: An Encyclopedia* (New York: Garland, 1993).

Sawyer, Birgit and Peter, *Medieval Scandinavia: From Conversion to Reformation, circa 800–1500* (Minneapolis: University of Minnesota Press, 1993).

Schach, Paul, *Icelandic Sagas* (Boston: Twayne, 1984).

Steblin-Kamenskij, M. I., *The Saga Mind*, trans. Kenneth H. Ober (Odense: Odense University Press, 1973).

Tucker, John (ed.), *Sagas of the Icelanders* (New York: Garland, 1989).

Turville-Petre, Gabriel, *Origins of Icelandic Literature* (Oxford: Clarendon Press, 1953).

# GISLI SURSSON'S SAGA

Foote, Peter, 'An Essay on the Saga of Gisli and its Icelandic Background', in *The Saga of Gisli* (London and Melbourne: Dent, 1963), pp. 93–134.

Ólason, Vésteinn, 'Gísli Súrsson – a Flawless or Flawed Hero?', in *Die Aktualität der Saga: Festschrift für Hans Schottmann* (Berlin, New York: Walter de Gruyter, 1999), pp. 163–75.

Schach, Paul, 'Some Observations on the Helgafell Episode in Eyrbyggja saga and Gísla saga', in *Saga och språk: Studies in Language and Literature*, ed. John M. Weinstock (Austin, Texas: Jenkins, 1972), pp. 113–45.

Turville-Petre, Gabriel, 'Gísli Súrsson and his Poetry: Traditions and Influences', *Modern Language Review*, 39 (1944), pp. 374–91. (Repr. with a postscript in his *Nine Norse Studies* (London: Viking Society for Northern Research, 1972), pp. 118–53.)

# THE SAGA OF THE PEOPLE OF EYRI

Hollander, Lee M., 'The Structure of Eyrbyggja Saga', *Journal of English and Germanic Philology*, 58 (1959), pp. 222–7.

McCreesh, Bernadine, 'Structural Patterns in *Eyrbyggja saga* and other Sagas of the Conversion', *Medieval Scandinavia*, 11 (1978–9), pp. 271–80.

McTurk, Rory, 'Approaches to the Structure of Eyrbyggja saga', in *Sagnaskemmtun: Studies in Honour of Hermann Pálsson*, ed. R. Simek et al. (Wien, Köln, Graz: Hermann Böhlaus Nachf., 1986), pp. 223–37.

Ólason, Vésteinn, ' "Máhlíðingamál": Authorship and Tradition in a Part of *Eyrbyggja saga*', in *Úr Dölum til Dala: Guðbrandur Vigfússon Centenary Essays*, eds. Rory McTurk and Andrew Wawn, Leeds Texts and Monographs, new series, 11 (Leeds: School of English, 1989), pp. 187–203.

Pálsson, Hermann and Paul Edwards, 'Introduction', in *Eyrbyggja Saga*, trans. Hermann Pálsson and Paul Edwards (London: Penguin Books, 1989).

# A Note on the Translations

The two translations in the present volume are reprinted, with only minor alterations, from *The Complete Sagas of Icelanders*, edited by Viðar Hreinsson and published in five volumes by Leifur Eiríksson Publishing, Reykjavík (1997):

*Gisli Sursson's Saga*, II, 1–48
*The Saga of the People of Eyri*, V, 131–218

The editions and manuscripts on which the translations are chiefly based are as follows:

## Gisli Sursson's Saga (*Gísla saga Súrssonar*)

Edition: In *Íslendinga sögur og þættir*, ed. Bragi Halldórsson et al., Reykjavík 1987, pp. 852–98 (shorter version – the main divergences from the longer version are discussed in the Introduction to this volume).

Manuscript: *AM 556 a 4to*, a fifteenth-century saga manuscript that also contains two other outlaw sagas.

## The Saga of the People of Eyri (*Eyrbyggja saga*)

Edition: In *Íslendinga sögur og þættir*, ed. Bragi Halldórson et al., Reykjavík, 1987, pp. 537–624.

Manuscripts: *AM 448 4to, AM 442 4to, AM 450 a 4to, AM 309 4to, AM 162 e fol., AM 446 4to, AM 445 b 4to, AM 445 a 4to, Lbs. 982 4to.*

The translators' aim in all cases has been to produce accurate and readable modern English versions of the original texts. This involves being as faithful as practicable to the spirit, style and detail of each saga, avoiding pedantic imitation of formal features, but also resisting the temptation to 'improve' the originals. The Complete Sagas project as a whole also sought to reflect the homogeneity of the world of the Sagas of Icelanders by aiming for consistency in the translation of certain essential vocabulary, for instance terms relating to legal practices, social and religious practices, farm layouts or types of ships.

As is common in translations from Old Icelandic, the spelling of proper nouns has been simplified, both by the elimination of non-English letters and by the reduction of inflections. Thus 'Þórólfr' becomes 'Thorolf', 'Börkur' becomes 'Bork' and 'Vésteinn' becomes 'Vestein'. The reader will soon grasp that '-dottir' means 'daughter of' and '-son' means 'son of'. Place names have been rendered in a similar way, often with an English identifier of the landscape feature in question (for example, 'Stafa river', in which '-a' means 'river'). A translation is given in parentheses at the first occurrence of place names when the context requires this, such as Dagverdardal (Breakfast dale). For place names outside Scandinavia, the common English equivalent is used if such exists; otherwise the Icelandic form has been transliterated. Nicknames are translated where their meanings are reasonably certain.

The translation of the poetry is particularly challenging, both because of obscurities and corruptions in the texts, and because its intricate metre, flexible word order and compressed and often riddling diction do not transpose well into English. Translators have attempted to render something of the meaning and style of the original, but the overriding aim has been to produce English verses that are comprehensible and poetically satisfying.

# GISLI SURSSON'S SAGA

1 | This story begins at the time when King Hakon, foster-son of King Athelstan of England,[1] ruled Norway and was near the end of his days.

There was a man named Thorkel, known as Skerauki, who lived in Surnadal and held the title of hersir. He had a wife named Isgerd and they had three sons. Ari was eldest, then came Gisli,[2] and finally Thorbjorn. All three were brought up at home. There was a man named Isi, who lived in the fjord of Fibule in North More with his wife, Ingigerd, and his daughter, Ingibjorg. Ari, son of Thorkel from Surnadal, asked for Ingibjorg's hand and she was given to him with a large dowry. A slave named Kol went with her.

There was a man named Bjorn the Black, a berserk. He went around the country challenging men to fight with him if they refused to yield or accede to his demands. One winter, he arrived at Surnadal while Thorkel's son Ari was taking care of the farm. Bjorn gave Ari a choice: either he fight him on the island of Stokkaholm in Surnadal or hand over his wife, Ingibjorg. Without hesitation, Ari decided that he would fight Bjorn rather than bring shame on himself or his wife. The duel was to take place three days later.

The time appointed for the duel arrived, and they fought – the result being that Ari fell and lost his life. Bjorn assumed he had won both the land and the woman, but Ari's brother Gisli said that he would rather die than allow this to happen. He was determined to fight Bjorn.

Then Ingibjorg spoke, 'I did not marry Ari because I preferred him to you. Kol, my slave, has a sword called Grasida

(Grey-blade).[3] You must ask him to lend it to you since whoever fights with it is assured of victory.'

Gisli asked the slave for the sword and Kol lent it to him, but with great reluctance.

Gisli prepared himself for the duel. They fought and Bjorn was slain. Gisli felt he had won a great victory, and it is said that he asked for Ingibjorg's hand because he did not want the family to lose a good woman. So he married her, took over her property and became a powerful figure. Thereafter Gisli's father died, and Gisli inherited all his wealth. Gisli saw to it that all the men who had come with Bjorn were put to death.

Kol demanded that his sword be returned. Gisli, unwilling to part with it, offered him money instead. Kol wanted nothing but the sword, but it was not returned. Greatly displeased with this, the slave attacked Gisli and wounded him badly. In response, Gisli dealt Kol such a blow to the head with Grasida that the blade broke as it smashed through his skull. Thus both men met their death.

2 | Thorbjorn then inherited all the wealth that previously belonged to his father and two brothers, and continued to live at Stokkar in Surnadal. He asked for the hand of a woman named Thora, the daughter of Raud from Fridarey, and his request was granted. The couple were well suited and soon began to have children. The eldest was a daughter named Thordis. The eldest of their sons was named Thorkel, then came Gisli and the youngest was named Ari. They were regarded in the district as the finest men of their generation. Ari was taken in as a foster-son by Styrkar, his mother's brother. Thorkel and Gisli were brought up at home.

There was a young man named Bard who lived in Surnadal, who had recently inherited his father's wealth. Another young man named Kolbjorn lived at Hella in Surnadal. He, too, had newly inherited his father's property.

There was a rumour abroad that Bard had seduced Thordis, Thorbjorn's daughter, a good-looking and intelligent girl. Thorbjorn took this badly and said that there would be trouble if his son Ari were living at home. Bard remarked that he took no heed of the words of idle men – 'I will continue as before,' he said.

Thorkel was a close friend of Bard's and party to this liaison. Gisli, however, was as deeply offended as his father by the way people were talking.

It is said that Gisli went along with Thorkel and Bard one time to Bard's farm at Granaskeid. When they were halfway there, with no warning whatsoever, Gisli dealt Bard his death blow. Thorkel was angry and told Gisli that he had done great wrong. Gisli told his brother to calm down and jested with him.

'We'll swap swords,' he said, 'then you'll have the one with the better bite.'

Thorkel composed himself and sat down beside Bard's body. Gisli rode off home to tell his father, who was greatly pleased by the news. There was never the same warmth between the two brothers after this. Thorkel refused the exchange of weapons and, having no desire to stay at home, he went to stay with a close relative of Bard's, called Skeggi the Dueller, who lived on the island of Saxo. He strongly urged Skeggi the Dueller to avenge his kinsman's death and take Thordis as his wife.

Twenty men set off for Stokkar and when they reached the farm, Skeggi the Dueller suggested to Thorbjorn that their families be united. 'I'll marry your daughter, Thordis,' he said.

But Thorbjorn did not want the man to marry his daughter. Thordis, it was said, had since become friendly with Kolbjorn. Suspecting this was the real reason his proposal had been rejected, Skeggi went to meet Kolbjorn and challenged him to a duel on the island of Saxo. Kolbjorn agreed to take up the challenge, saying that he would not be worthy of Thordis if he dared not fight Skeggi. Thorkel and Skeggi returned to Saxo and stayed there until the fight was due to be fought. Twenty other men went with them.

After three nights had passed, Gisli went to meet Kolbjorn and asked him if he was ready for the duel. Kolbjorn answered him by asking whether this was really the way to achieve what he wanted.

'What kind of talk is that?' said Gisli.

'I don't think I'll fight Skeggi to win Thordis,' said Kolbjorn.

Gisli told Kolbjorn he was the greatest scoundrel living – 'And though it shame you forever,' he said, 'I will go instead.'

Gisli went to the island of Saxo with eleven men. Skeggi had already arrived at the spot where the duel was to be fought. He announced the rules and marked out where Kolbjorn was to stand, but he could not see his opponent nor anyone to replace him.

There was a man named Ref, who worked for Skeggi as a carpenter. Skeggi asked him to make wooden effigies in the likenesses of Gisli and Kolbjorn.

'And one will stand behind the other,'[4] he said, 'and these figures of scorn will remain like that forever to mock them.'

Gisli, who was in the woods, heard this and answered, 'Find some better employment for your farmhands. Here is a man who dares to fight you.'

They took up their duelling positions and began to fight, each of them bearing a shield. Skeggi had a sword called Gunnlogi (War-flame) that rang loud in the air as it struck out at Gisli. Then Skeggi said,

1.
War-flame sang
Saxo is amused.

Gisli struck back with his halberd which sliced through the lower end of Skeggi's shield and cut off his leg. Then Gisli spoke:

2.
Spear swept
I struck at Skeggi.

Skeggi bought his way out of the duel, and from that time he walked with a wooden leg. Thorkel went home with his brother Gisli. The two of them were now on very good terms, and Gisli's reputation was thought to have increased considerably as a result of this affair.

3 | Two brothers are mentioned in the story: Einar and Arni, the sons of Skeggi from Saxo. They lived at Flyndrenes, north of Trondheim. The following spring, Einar and Arni gathered together a large party of men and went to see Kolbjorn in Surnadal. They offered him a choice – either he go with them and burn Thorbjorn and his sons to death in their house or they kill him on the spot. He chose to go with them.

Sixty of them left for Stokkar by night and set fire to the houses there. Thorbjorn, his sons and Thordis were all asleep in an outbuilding. In the same outbuilding were two barrels of whey. Gisli, his father and his brother took two goat hides, dipped them in the whey to fight the fire and managed to douse it three times. Then they broke down a wall, and ten of them succeeded in escaping to the mountainside, using the smoke as cover. They were now such a distance from the farm as to be out of range of the dogs' barking.[5] Twelve people were burned to death in the fire. The attackers believed they had killed everyone.

Those who went with Gisli journeyed until they reached Styrkar's farm on Fridarey. There they gathered a force of forty men, went to Kolbjorn's farm and, without warning, set fire to his house. Kolbjorn was burned to death with eleven other men. Then they sold up their lands, bought a ship and left with all their belongings. There were sixty of them on board.[6] They arrived at a group of islands called the Asen and laid over there before setting out to sea.

They left the Asen Islands in two boats, forty men in all, and sailed north to Flyndrenes. At the same time, Skeggi's two sons were on their way to collect land rent with a group of seven men. Gisli's party confronted them and killed them all. Gisli slew three men and Thorkel two. From there they went to the farm and took a great deal of goods and livestock. Skeggi the Dueller was there at his sons' farm. This time Gisli cut off his head.

4 | After this, they went back to their ship and set out to sea.
They sailed for more than sixty days and nights, finally
reaching the mouth of the Haukadalsa river on the south side
of Dyrafjord in the west of Iceland.

Two men are mentioned, both named Thorkel, who lived on
opposite sides of the fjord. One of them, Thorkel Eiriksson,
lived at Saurar in Keldudal on the south side, and the other,
known as Thorkel the Wealthy, lived on the north side at
Alvidra. Thorkel Eiriksson was the first man of standing to go
down to the ship to greet Thorbjorn Sur (Whey),[7] who was
called that since the time he used whey to escape being burned
to death. None of the lands on either side of the fjord were
settled at the time, so Thorbjorn Sur bought some land at Saebol
in Haukadal on the south side. Gisli built a farm there at which
they lived from that time on.

There was a man named Bjartmar who lived at the head of
Arnarfjord. His wife, Thurid, was the daughter of Hrafn from
Ketilseyri in Dyrafjord, and Hrafn was the son of Dyri who first
settled the fjord. Bjartmar and Thurid had several children. The
eldest was a girl named Hild, and their sons were named Helgi,
Sigurd and Vestgeir.

There was a Norwegian named Vestein, who arrived at the
time of the settlement. He lodged at Bjartmar's farm. Vestein
took Bjartmar's daughter, Hild, as his wife, and it was not long
before they had two children, a daughter named Aud and a son
named Vestein.

Vestein the Norwegian was the son of Vegeir, the brother of
Vebjorn the Champion of Sognefjord. Bjartmar was the son of
An Red-cloak, son of Grim Hairy-cheeks, brother of Arrow-
Odd, son of Ketil Haeng, son of Hallbjorn Half-troll. An Red-
cloak's mother was Helga, the daughter of An Bow-bender.

Vestein Vesteinsson eventually became a skilled seafarer,
though at this point in the story he lived on a farm in Onund-
arfjord below Hest mountain. He had a wife, Gunnhild, and
two sons, Berg and Helgi.

Soon after, Thorbjorn Sur passed away, followed by his wife,

Thora. Gisli and his brother Thorkel took over the farm.
Thorbjorn and Thora were laid to rest in a burial mound.


5 | There was a man named Thorbjorn, nicknamed Selagnup
    (Seals' Peak). He lived at Kvigandafell in Talknafjord. He
was married to a woman called Thordis and had a daughter
named Asgerd. Thorkel, the son of Thorbjorn Sur, asked for
Asgerd's hand and she became his wife. Gisli asked for the hand
of Aud, Vestein's sister, and married her. The two brothers lived
together in Haukadal.

One spring, Thorkel the Wealthy travelled to the Thorsnes
Assembly,[8] and Thorbjorn Sur's two sons accompanied him. At
that time, Thorstein Cod-biter,[9] the son of Thorolf Moster-beard,
was living at Thorsnes with his wife, Thora, the daughter of Olaf
Thorsteinsson, and their children, Thordis, Thorgrim and Bork
the Stout. Thorkel settled his business at the assembly, and when
it was over, Thorstein invited him, along with Gisli and Thorkel,
to his home. When they left, he gave them good gifts, and they
responded by inviting Thorstein's sons to their assembly in the
west the following spring.

Thorkel the Wealthy and the brothers Gisli and Thorkel
returned home. The following spring, Thorstein's sons went to
the Hvolseyri Assembly along with a party of ten men. On their
arrival they met up with Thorbjorn Sur's sons, who invited them
home when the assembly was over. They had already accepted
an invitation to the home of Thorkel the Wealthy, but after they
visited him they went off to Gisli and Thorkel's farm and enjoyed
an excellent feast there.

Thorgrim, the son of Thorstein, found Thordis, the sister of
Gisli and Thorkel, very attractive and asked for her hand in
marriage. She was betrothed to him and the wedding followed
soon in the wake of the betrothal. Thordis had the farm at
Saebol as her dowry, and Thorgrim moved west to live there
with her. Bork, however, remained at Thorsnes with his sister's
sons, Outlaw-Stein and Thorodd.

Thorgrim now lived at Saebol, and Gisli and Thorkel moved

to Hol where they built a good farmhouse. The two farms, Hol
and Saebol, lay side by side, divided by a hayfield wall, and both
parties lived on friendly terms. Thorgrim had a godord and
afforded both brothers considerable support.

One spring, they left for the Spring Assembly with forty
men, all of them wearing coloured clothes.[10] Vestein, Gisli's
brother-in-law, joined up with them and so did the men from
Surnadal.

6 | There was a man named Gest, son of Oddleif.[11] He arrived
    | at the assembly and shared a booth with Thorkel the
Wealthy. The men from Surnadal were sitting in the Haukadal
booth drinking, while the others were at court because there
were lawsuits to be heard.

A man came into the Haukadal booth, a noisy fellow named
Arnor, and spoke to them: 'You Haukadal people don't seem
to want to do anything other than drink while your thingmen are
dealing with important matters. That's what everyone thinks,
though I'm the only one to say so.'

Then Gisli said, 'Then we will go to court. It could well be
that the others are saying the same.'

So they all walked over to the court where Thorgrim asked if
any of them needed his support.

'Having pledged our support, we will do all in our power to
help you, as long as we are standing,' he told them.

Then Thorkel the Wealthy answered, 'The matters that men
are concerned with at present are of little importance, but we
will let you know if we need your support.'

People began to talk about how much finery the group pos-
sessed, how imposing they were and how well they spoke.

Then Thorkel said to Gest, 'How long do you expect the
ardour and arrogance of these people from Haukadal to last?'

Gest answered, 'Three summers from now, the men in that
party will no longer see eye to eye.'

Now Arnor was present while they were talking, and he
rushed into the Haukadal booth and told them what had been
said.

Gisli answered, 'I am sure this report is correct, but let us make certain that his prediction does not come true. And I see a good way to avert it. We four will make our bond of friendship even stronger than before by pledging our sworn brotherhood.'

This seemed good counsel to them, so they walked out to Eyrarhvolsoddi and scored out a long strip of turf, making sure that both ends were still attached to the ground. Then they propped up the arch of raised turf with a damascened spear so long-shafted that a man could stretch out his arm and touch the rivets. All four of them had to go under it, Thorgrim, Gisli, Thorkel and Vestein. Then they drew blood and let it drip down on to the soil beneath the turf strip and stirred it together – the soil and the blood. Then they all fell to their knees and swore an oath that each would avenge the other as if they were brothers, and they called on all the gods as their witnesses.

But as they all clasped hands, Thorgrim said, 'I will have enough trouble to deal with if I so bind myself to Thorkel and Gisli, my brothers-in-law, but I bear no obligation to Vestein' – and he quickly withdrew his hand.

'Then others may do the same,' said Gisli, and he withdrew his hand, too. 'I will not burden myself with ties to a man who refuses to bind himself to Vestein, my brother-in-law.'

They were all deeply affected by this. Then Gisli said to Thorkel, his brother, 'This is what I thought would happen. What has taken place here will come to nothing. I suspect fate will take its course now.'

After this, everyone went home from the assembly.

7 | That summer, a ship arrived in Dyrafjord owned by two brothers from Norway. One was named Thorir and the other Thorarin, and they were from Oslo Fjord. Thorgrim rode out to the ship and bought four hundreds of timber, paying part of the sum immediately and leaving the balance until later. Then the traders put up ship in the Sandar estuary and found a place to lodge.

There was a man named Odd, the son of Orlyg, who lived at Eyri in Skutilsfjord. Thorgrim lodged the skipper and the

helmsman at his house, then he sent his son, Thorodd, to stack
and count the timber because he wanted it brought to his house
soon. Thorodd went and took the timber and stacked it, and
found that it was far from being the bargain his father had
described. Then he spoke harshly to the Norwegians, which
they could not tolerate, and they set about him and killed him.

After this, the Norwegians left their ship and travelled about
Dyrafjord, where they obtained some horses, and then headed
off towards their lodgings. They travelled all day and night,
eventually arriving at a valley that leads up out of Skutilsfjord.
They ate breakfast there and then went to sleep.

When Thorgrim heard the news, he set out from home without delay, had someone ferry him across the fjord and then
pursued the Norwegians alone. He arrived at the spot where
they were sleeping and woke Thorarin by prodding at him with
the shaft of his spear. Thorarin jumped up and, recognizing his
assailant, was about to grab his sword, but Thorgrim thrust out
with his spear and killed him. Then Thorir awoke, ready to
avenge his brother, but Thorgrim speared him clean through.
The place is now called Dagverdardal (Breakfast dale) and
Austmannafall (Eastman's fall). This done, Thorgrim returned
home and became renowned as a result of this expedition.

Thorgrim remained at his farm for the winter, and when
spring arrived, he and his brother-in-law, Thorkel, fitted out the
ship that had belonged to the Norwegians. The two men from
Oslo Fjord had been great troublemakers in Norway and they
had not been safe there. With the ship fully ready, Thorgrim
and Thorkel set sail. That summer, Vestein and Gisli also set off
from Skeljavik in Steingrimsfjord. Thus both ships were at sea.
Onund from Medaldal was left in charge of Thorkel and Gisli's
farm, while Outlaw-Stein and Thordis took care of the farm at
Saebol.

All this took place when Harald Grey-cloak[12] ruled Norway.
Thorgrim and Thorkel came ashore in the north of that country
and soon afterwards arrived at the court, where they presented
themselves to the king and greeted him warmly. The king gave
them a friendly welcome, and they pledged themselves as his
followers. They became wealthy and well established.

Gisli and Vestein had been at sea for more than fifty days and nights when they eventually ran ashore at Hordaland. It was early winter, in the dead of night, and a great blizzard was blowing. Their ship was wrecked, but the crew escaped drowning and the goods were salvaged.

8 | There was a man named Beard-Bjalfi, who owned a trading ship and was about to set out south for Denmark. Gisli and Vestein asked him if they could buy a half share in the ship. He replied that he had heard that they were decent men and agreed to the deal. They responded at once by giving him gifts worth more than the price of their share.

They sailed south to Denmark and arrived at a place called Viborg, staying the winter there with a man named Sigurhadd. There were three of them, Vestein, Gisli and Bjalfi, and they were all good friends and gave each other gifts. Early in the spring, Bjalfi prepared his ship to sail for Iceland.

There was a man named Sigurd, a trading partner of Vestein's and a Norwegian by birth, who at that time was living out west in England. He sent word to Vestein, saying that he wanted to break up their partnership, claiming that he no longer needed Vestein's money. Vestein asked Gisli's leave to go and meet the man.

'Then you must promise me,' said Gisli, 'if you return safely, you will never leave Iceland again without my consent.'

Vestein agreed to these terms.

One morning Gisli arose early and went out to the smithy. He was a very skilled craftsman and a man of many talents. He made a coin, worth no less than an ounce of silver, and riveted it together with twenty studs, ten on each half, so that the coin appeared whole even though it could be separated into two halves.

It is said that he pulled the coin apart and gave one half to Vestein, asking him to keep it as a token.

'We will only have these sent to each other if our lives are in danger,' said Gisli. 'And something tells me that we will need to send them, even though we may never meet each other again.'

Vestein then went west to England. Gisli and Bjalfi made for Norway, and in the summer they sailed to Iceland. They became wealthy and well-respected men and eventually parted on good terms, Bjalfi buying Gisli's share of the ship.

Then Gisli went west to Dyrafjord on a cargo vessel with eleven men.

9 | Thorkel and Thorgrim made their ship ready in another place and they arrived at the Haukadal estuary in Dyrafjord later on the same day that Gisli had sailed in on board the cargo vessel. They met up soon afterwards and greeted each other warmly, then each of them went off to his own home. Thorgrim and Thorkel had also become wealthy.

Thorkel bore himself aloof and did not work on the farm. Gisli, on the contrary, worked day and night.

One day when the weather was fine, Gisli sent all his men out haymaking – except Thorkel. He was the only man left at the farmhouse, and he laid himself out in the fire room after having finished his breakfast. The fire room was a hundred feet long and sixty feet wide, and on its south side was the women's area, where Aud and Asgerd sat sewing. When Thorkel woke up he went over to the women's area because he heard voices coming from it, and he lay down close by.

Asgerd was speaking: 'Aud, could you please cut out a shirt[13] for my husband, Thorkel?'

'I'm no better than you at such things,' said Aud, 'and, besides, you would not have asked for my help if you had been cutting out a shirt for my brother, Vestein.'

'That's a separate issue,' said Asgerd, 'and, to my mind, will remain so for some time.'

'I've known what was going on for quite a while,' said Aud, 'and we will not say any more about it.'

'I cannot see anything wrong with my liking Vestein,' said Asgerd. 'What's more, I've heard tell that you and Thorgrim saw a lot of each other before you married Gisli.'

'There was no shame in that,' said Aud. 'I was never unfaithful to Gisli and have therefore brought no disgrace upon him. We will stop talking about this now.'

But Thorkel heard every word they spoke, and when they stopped, he said:

3.
Hear a great wonder,
hear of peace broken,
hear of a great matter,
hear of a death
– one man's or more.

And after this he went inside.

Then Aud spoke: 'Women's gossip often leads to trouble, and here it may turn out to be the worst kind of trouble. We must seek counsel.'

'I've thought of a plan,' said Asgerd, 'that I think will work for me. But I do not see what you can do.'

'What is it?' asked Aud.

'I'll put my arms around Thorkel's neck when we are in bed and say it's a lie. Then he'll forgive me.'

'That will not be enough to prevent harm coming from this,' said Aud.

'What will you do?' asked Asgerd.

'Tell my husband, Gisli, everything I have left unsaid as well as all that to which I cannot find a solution.'

That evening Gisli came home from the haymaking. Usually, Thorkel would have thanked his brother for doing this work, but now he was silent and did not utter a word. Gisli asked him if he was feeling unwell.

'I am not sick,' said Thorkel, 'but this is worse than sickness.'

'Have I done anything to upset you?' said Gisli.

'No, not a thing,' said Thorkel, 'but you will find out eventually what this is about.'

And then each of them went about his business, and there was no more talk of the matter at that time.

Thorkel ate very little that evening and was the first to retire to bed.

Once he was there, Asgerd came to him, lifted the blanket and was about to lie down when Thorkel said, 'I will not have you lying here tonight, nor for a very long time to come.'

Asgerd replied, 'Why this sudden change? What is the reason for this?'

'We both know what's behind this,' said Thorkel, 'though I have been kept in the dark about it for a long time. It will not help your reputation if I speak more plainly.'

'You think what you will,' answered Asgerd, 'but I am not going to argue with you about whether I may sleep in this bed or not. You have a choice – either you take me in and act as if nothing has happened or I will call witnesses this minute, divorce[14] you and have my father reclaim my bride-price and my dowry. Then you wouldn't have to worry about my taking up room in your bed ever again.'

Thorkel was quiet for a while, then he said, 'I advise you to do as you wish. I will not stop you from sleeping here all night.'

She soon made clear what she wanted to do, and they had not been lying together for too long before they made up as if nothing had happened.

Aud got into bed with Gisli and told him what she and Asgerd had been talking about. She asked him not to be angry with her, but to see if he could think of a reasonable plan.

'I see no plan that will work,' he said, 'but I will not be angry with you for this. Fate must find someone to speak through. Whatever is meant to happen will happen.'

10 | The year wore on and the Moving Days came round again. Thorkel asked his brother Gisli to have a talk.

'It's like this, brother,' he said. 'I have a few changes in mind that I'm disposed to carry out, and they are along these lines – I want to divide up our wealth and start farming with Thorgrim, my brother-in-law.'

Gisli answered him, 'What brothers own jointly is best seen together. I would appreciate having things remain as they are and that we make no division.'

'We cannot go on like this any longer,' said Thorkel, 'jointly owning the farm. It will lead to great loss. You have always dealt with the work and the responsibility of the farm alone, and nothing comes of anything I take a hand in.'

'Don't concern yourself with this,' said Gisli, 'while I make no complaint. We have been on both good and bad terms with each other.'

'That's not what's behind it,' said Thorkel. 'The wealth must be divided, and since I demand this division, you may have the farm and the land and I will take the movable goods.'

'If there is no other way than to separate, then do whatever you wish. I do not mind whether I do the dividing or the choosing.'

So it ended with Gisli dealing with the division. Thorkel chose the goods while Gisli had the land. They also divided the dependants – two children, a boy named Geirmund and a girl named Gudrid. The girl went with Gisli and the boy with Thorkel.

Thorkel went to his brother-in-law and lived with him, while Gisli was left with the farm which he felt was none the worse for the loss.

Summer drew to a close and the Winter Nights began. In those days it was the custom to celebrate the coming of winter by holding feasts and a Winter Nights' sacrifice. Gisli no longer sacrificed after he left Viborg, but he still held feasts and showed the same magnanimity as before. Then, as the aforementioned time approached, he made everything ready for a magnificent feast and invited both Thorkels – that is, Thorkel Eiriksson and Thorkel the Wealthy – as well as the sons of Bjartmar, who were Aud's uncles, and many other friends and acquaintances.

On the day the guests arrived, Aud said, 'If the truth be told, there is one person missing who I wish was here.'

'Who is that?' asked Gisli.

'Vestein, my brother. I wish he were here to enjoy this feast with us.'

'That's not how I feel,' said Gisli. 'I would gladly pay a great deal for him not to come here now.'

And that ended their conversation.

11 | There was a man named Thorgrim, who was known as
   | Thorgrim Nef (Nose). He lived at Nefsstadir on the east
side of the Haukadalsa river and was versed in all manner
of spells and magic – the worst kind of sorcerer imaginable.
Thorgrim and Thorkel invited him home because they were also
holding a feast. Thorgrim Nef was a very skilled blacksmith,
and it is told that both Thorgrim and Thorkel went to the smithy
and locked themselves in. Then they took the fragments of
Grasida, of which Thorkel had taken possession when he split
up with his brother Gisli, and Thorgrim Nef made a spearhead
out of them. By evening the spearhead was completely finished.
The blade was damascened, and the shaft measured about a
hand in length.

This matter must rest here for a while.

The story goes on to say that Onund from Medaldal came to
Gisli's feast and took him aside to tell him that Vestein had
returned to Iceland and 'is to be expected here'.

Gisli reacted quickly and summoned two of his farmhands,
Hallvard and Havard, whom he told to go north to Onund-
arfjord to meet Vestein.

'Give him my greetings,' said Gisli, 'and tell him to stay where
he is and wait until I come to visit him. He must not come to
the feast at Haukadal.'

He then handed them a small kerchief which contained the
half-coin token, in case Vestein did not believe their story.

They left and took the boat from Haukadal. Then they rowed
to Laekjaros and went ashore to see Bersi, a farmer who lived
at Bersastadir. They informed him that Gisli had requested that
he lend them two of his horses, which were known as Bandvettir
(Tied-together) – the fastest horses in the fjords. He lent them
the horses and they rode until they reached Mosvellir, and from
there towards Hest.

Now Vestein rode out from home, and it turned out that as
he rode below the sandbank at Mosvellir, the two brothers,
Hallvard and Havard, rode above it. Thus he and they missed
each other in passing.

12 | There was a man named Thorvard who lived at Holt. His farmhands had been arguing about some task and had struck each other with scythes, so that both were wounded. Vestein came by and had them settle their differences so that they were both satisfied. Then he rode on to Dyrafjord with his two Norwegian companions.

Hallvard and Havard reached Hest and learned where Vestein was actually heading. They rode after him as fast as they could and when they reached Mosvellir, they could see men riding down in the valley but there was a hill between them. They rode into Bjarnardal and when they reached Arnkelsbrekka both their horses gave out. They took to their feet and began to shout. Vestein and his companions had reached the Gemlufall heath before they heard the men shouting, but they waited there for Hallvard and Havard who conveyed Gisli's message and presented him with the coin which Gisli had sent him.

Vestein took a coin from the purse which hung from his belt and turned very red in the face.

'What you say is true,' he said. 'I would have turned back if you had met me sooner, but now all waters flow towards Dyrafjord and that is where I will ride. Indeed, I am eager to do so. The Norwegians will turn back, but you two will go by boat,' said Vestein, 'and tell Gisli and my sister that I am on my way to them.'

They went home and told Gisli what had happened, and he answered: 'Then this is the way it has to be.'

Vestein went to see his kinswoman, Luta, at Gemlufall and she had him ferried across the fjord.

'Vestein,' she said to him, 'be on your guard. You will have need to be.'

He was ferried across to Thingeyri. A man called Thorvald Gneisti (Spark) lived there. Vestein went to his house and Thorvald lent him his horse. Then he rode out with his own saddle gear and had bells on his bridle. Thorvald accompanied him as far as Sandar estuary and offered to go with him all the way to Gisli's. Vestein told him that was not necessary.

'Much has changed in Haukadal,' said Thorvald. 'Be on your guard.'

Then they parted.

Vestein rode onward until he reached Haukadal. There was not a cloud in the sky and the moon shone. At Thorgrim and Thorkel's farm, Geirmund and a woman named Rannveig were bringing in the cattle. Rannveig put them in stalls after Geirmund drove them inside to her. At that moment, Vestein rode by and met Geirmund.

Geirmund spoke, 'Don't stop here at Saebol. Go on to Gisli's. And be on your guard.'

Rannveig came out of the byre, looked at the man closely and thought she recognized him. And when all the cattle were inside, she and Geirmund began to argue about who the man was as they made their way to the farmhouse. Thorgrim was sitting by the fire with the others, and he asked what they were quarrelling about and whether they had seen or met anyone.

'I thought I saw Vestein stop by,' said Rannveig. 'He was wearing a black cloak, held a spear in his hand and had bells on his bridle.'

'And what do you say, Geirmund?' asked Thorgrim.

'I couldn't see very well, but I think he was one of Onund's farmhands from Medaldal, wearing Gisli's cloak. He had Onund's saddle gear and carried a fishing spear with something dangling from it.'

'Now one of you is lying,' said Thorgrim. 'Rannveig, you go over to Hol and find out what's going on.'

Rannveig went there, and arrived at the door just as the men had started drinking. Gisli was standing in the doorway. He greeted her and invited her inside. She told him that she had to get back home, but 'I would like to meet the young girl, Gudrid.'

Gisli called to the girl, but there was no response.

'Where is your wife, Aud?' asked Rannveig.

'She is here,' said Gisli.

Aud came out and asked what Rannveig wanted. Rannveig said that it was only a trivial matter, but got no further. Gisli told her either to come inside or go home. She left and looked even more foolish than before – if that were possible – and she had no news to tell.

The following morning Vestein had the two bags of goods

brought to him which the brothers, Hallvard and Havard, had brought back with them. He took out a tapestry[15] sixty ells long and a head-dress made from a piece of cloth some twenty ells long with three gold strands woven along its length, and three finger bowls worked with gold. He brought these out as gifts for his sister, for Gisli and for his sworn brother, Thorkel[16] – should he want to accept them. Gisli went with Thorkel the Wealthy and Thorkel Eiriksson to Saebol to tell his brother that Vestein had come and that he had brought gifts for both of them. Gisli showed him the gifts and asked his brother to choose what he wanted.

Thorkel answered, 'It would be better if you took them all. I don't want to accept these gifts – I cannot see how they will be repaid.'

And he was determined not to accept them. Gisli went home and felt that everything was pointing in one direction.

13 | Then something unusual happened at Hol. Gisli slept unsoundly for two successive nights and people asked him what he had dreamed. He did not want to tell them. On the third night, after everyone was fast asleep in bed, such a heavy gust of wind hit the house that it took off all the roofing on one side. At the same time, the heavens opened and rain fell like never before. Naturally, it poured into the house where the roof had split.

Gisli sprang to his feet and rallied his men to cover the hay. There was a slave at Gisli's house named Thord, known as the Coward. He stayed home while Gisli and almost all his men went out to attend to the haystacks. Vestein offered to go with them but Gisli did not want him to. And then, when the house began to leak badly, Vestein and Aud moved their beds lengthways down the room. Everyone else except these two had deserted the house.

Just before daybreak, someone entered the house without a sound and walked over to where Vestein was lying. He was already awake but before he knew what was happening, a spear was thrust at him and went right through his breast.

As Vestein took the blow, he spoke: 'Struck there,' he said.

Then the man left. Vestein tried to stand up, but as he did so he fell down beside the bedpost, dead. Aud awoke and called out to Thord the Coward and asked him to remove the weapon from the wound. At that time, whoever drew a weapon from a death wound was obliged to take revenge, and when a weapon was thus left in the fatal wound it was called secret manslaughter rather than murder.[17] Thord was so frightened of corpses that he dared not come near the body.

Then Gisli came in, saw what was happening and told Thord to calm down. He took the spear from the wound himself and threw it, still covered in blood, into a trunk so that no one might see it, then sat down on the edge of the bed. Then he had Vestein's body made ready for burial according to the custom in those days. Vestein's death was a great sorrow both to Gisli and the others.

Then Gisli said to his foster-daughter, Gudrid, 'Go to Saebol and find out what they are up to there. I'm sending you because I trust you best in this as in other matters. Make sure you tell me what they are doing.'

Gudrid left and arrived at Saebol. Both the Thorgrims and Thorkel had arisen and sat fully armed. When she came in no one hurried to greet her. Indeed, most of them said nothing at all. Thorgrim, though, asked her what news she brought and she told them of Vestein's death, or murder.

Thorkel answered, 'There was a time when we would have regarded that as news indeed.'

'A man has died,' said Thorgrim, 'to whom we must all pay our respects by honouring his funeral and by making a burial mound for him. There's no denying that this is a great loss. Tell Gisli we will come there today.'

She went home and told Gisli that Thorgrim sat fully armed with helmet and sword, that Thorgrim Nef had a wood-axe in his hand and that Thorkel had a sword which was drawn a hand's breadth – 'all the men there were risen from their beds, some of them were armed'.

'That was to be expected,' said Gisli.

14 | Gisli and all his men prepared to build a mound for Vestein
     | in the sandbank that stood on the far side of Seftjorn pond
below Saebol.

And while Gisli was on his way there, Thorgrim set out for
the burial place with a large group of men.

When they had decked out Vestein's body according to the
ways of the time, Thorgrim went to Gisli and said, 'It is a custom
to tie Hel-shoes[18] to the men that they may wear them on their
journey to Valhalla, and I will do that for Vestein.'

And when he had done this, he said, 'If these come loose then
I don't know how to bind Hel-shoes.'

After this they sat down beside the mound and talked
together. They thought it highly unlikely that anyone would
know who committed the crime.

Thorkel asked Gisli, 'How is Aud taking her brother's death?
Does she weep much?'

'It seems you know quite well,' said Gisli. 'She shows little
and suffers greatly.' Then he said, 'I dreamed a dream the night
before last and last night too, and though my dreams indicate
who did the slaying, I will not say. I dreamed the first night that
a viper wriggled out from a certain farm and stung Vestein to
death, and, on the second night, I dreamed that a wolf ran out
from the same farm and bit Vestein to death.[19] I have not told
either dream until now because I did not want them to come
true.'

And he spoke a verse:

4.
Better, I believed,
to remember Vestein
gladdened with mead
where we sat drinking
in Sigurhadd's hall,
and none came between us,
than to wake a third time
from so dark a dream.

Then Thorkel asked, 'How is Aud taking her brother's death? Does she weep much?'

'You keep asking this, brother,' said Gisli. 'You are very curious to know.'

Gisli spoke this verse:

5.
In secret, bowed beneath
the cover of her bonnet,
she, goddess of gold,                          *goddess of gold*: woman
lacks solace of sound sleep.
From both kindly eyes
and down her cheeks
flows the dew of distress                       *dew of distress*: tears
for a brother lost forever.

And again he spoke a verse:

6.
Like a stream fast flowing,
sorrow, the death of laughter,
through the brow's white woods,          *brow's white woods*: eyelashes
forces tears down into her lap.
The snake-lair's goddess,              *snake-lair*: bed of gold; its *goddess*:
her weeping eyes swollen                                              woman
with bitter fruit, looks to me,
Rögnir of praise, for consolation.     *Rögnir* (Odin's) *of praise*: poet

After that, the two brothers went home together.

Then Thorkel said, 'These are sad tidings and you will bear them with greater grief than we, but each man has to look out for himself, and I hope you don't let this affect you so much that people begin to suspect anything. I would like to have the games begin again and things to be as good as they have ever been between us.'

'That is well spoken, and I will gladly comply,' said Gisli, 'but on one condition – if anything takes place in your life that pains you as badly as this pains me, you must promise to behave in the same manner as you now ask of me.'

Thorkel agreed to this. Then they went home and Vestein's funeral feast was held. When it was over, everyone went back to his own home and all was quiet again.

15 | The games now started up as if nothing had happened. Gisli and his brother-in-law, Thorgrim, usually played against each other. There was some disagreement as to who was the stronger, but most people thought it was Gisli. They played a ball game[20] at Seftjorn pond and there was always a large crowd.

One day, when the gathering was even larger than usual, Gisli suggested that the game be evenly matched.

'That's exactly what we want,' said Thorkel. 'What's more, we don't want you to hold back against Thorgrim. Word is going around that you are not giving your all. I'd be pleased to see you honoured if you are the stronger.'

'We have not been fully proven against each other yet,' said Gisli, 'but perhaps it's leading up to that.'

They started the game and Thorgrim was outmatched. Gisli brought him down and the ball went out of play. Then Gisli went for the ball, but Thorgrim held him back and stopped him from getting it. Then Gisli tackled Thorgrim so hard that he could do nothing to stop falling. His knuckles were grazed, blood rushed from his nose and the flesh was scraped from his knees. Thorgrim rose very slowly, looked towards Vestein's burial mound, and said:

7.
Spear screeched in his wound
sorely – I cannot be sorry.

Running, Gisli took the ball and pitched it between Thorgrim's shoulder-blades. The blow pushed him flat on his face. Then Gisli said:

8.
Ball smashed his shoulders
broadly – I cannot be sorry.

Thorkel sprang to his feet and said, 'It's clear who is the strongest and the most highly accomplished. Now, let's put an end to this.'

And so they did. The games drew to a close, summer wore on, and there was a growing coldness between Thorgrim and Gisli.

Thorgrim decided to hold a feast at the end of autumn to celebrate the coming of the Winter Nights. There was to be a sacrifice to Frey,[21] and he invited his brother, Bork, Eyjolf Thordarson[22] and many other men of distinction. Gisli also prepared a feast and invited his relatives from Arnarfjord, as well as the two Thorkels, Thorkel the Wealthy and Thorkel Eiriksson. No fewer than sixty people were expected to arrive. There was to be drinking at both places, and the floor at Saebol was strewn with rushes from Seftjorn pond.

Thorgrim and Thorkel were getting their preparations under way and were about to hang up some tapestries in the house because the guests were expected that evening.

Thorgrim said to Thorkel, 'It would be a fine thing now to have those tapestries that Vestein wanted to give to you. It seems to me there's quite a difference between owning them outright and never having them at all. I wish you'd have them sent for.'

Thorkel answered, 'A wise man does all things in moderation. I will not have them sent for.'

'Then I will do it,' said Thorgrim, and he asked Geirmund to go.

Geirmund answered him, 'I don't mind working, but I have no desire to go over there.'

Then Thorgrim went up to him, slapped his face hard and said, 'Go now then, if that makes you feel any better about it.'

'I'll go,' said Geirmund, 'though it seems worse. But you may be certain that I will give a mare for this foal, and you will not be underpaid.'[23]

Then he left. When he reached Gisli's house, Gisli and Aud were about to hang up the tapestries. Geirmund told them why he was sent and all that had been said.

'Do you want to lend the tapestries, Aud?' asked Gisli.

'You know that I would have neither this nor any other good

befall them, nor indeed anything that would add to their honour. That is not why you asked me.'

'Was this my brother Thorkel's wish?' asked Gisli.

'He approved of my coming for them.'

'That is reason enough,' said Gisli, and he went with Geirmund part of the way and then handed over the tapestries.

Gisli walked as far as the hayfield wall with him and said, 'Now this is how things stand – I believe that I have made your journey worthwhile, and I want your help in a matter that concerns me. A gift always looks to be repaid. I want you to unbolt three of the doors tonight. Remember how you came to be sent on this errand.'

Geirmund answered, 'Will your brother Thorkel be in any danger?'

'None at all,' said Gisli.

'Then it will be done,' said Geirmund.

When he returned home he threw down the tapestries, and Thorkel said, 'There is no one like Gisli when it comes to forbearance. He has outdone us here.'

'This is what we needed,' said Thorgrim, and he put up the tapestries.

Later that evening the guests arrived and the sky began to thicken. In the still of the night the snow drifted down and covered all the paths.


16 | That evening Bork and Eyjolf arrived with sixty men, so that there were one hundred and twenty all told at Saebol and half as many at Gisli's. Later they began to drink and after that they all went to bed and slept.

Gisli said to his wife, 'I have not fed Thorkel the Wealthy's horse. Walk with me and bolt the door, but stay awake while I am gone. When I come back, unbolt the door again.'

He took the spear, Grasida, from the trunk and, wearing a black cloak,[24] a shirt and linen underbreeches, he walked down to the stream that ran between the two farms and that was the water source for both. He took the path to the stream, then waded through it until he reached the path that led to Saebol.

Gisli knew the layout of the farmstead at Saebol because he had built it. There was a door that led into the house from the byre, and that is where he entered. Thirty head of cattle stood on each side. He tied the bulls' tails together and closed the byre door, then made sure that the door could not be opened from the inside. After that he went to the farmhouse. Geirmund had done his work – the doors were unbolted. Gisli walked in and closed them again, just as they had been that evening. He took his time doing this, then stood still and listened to see whether anyone was awake. He discovered that they were all asleep.

Lights were burning in three places in the house. He picked up some rushes from the floor, twisted them together, then threw them at one of the lights. It went out. He waited to see whether this had wakened anyone and found that it had not. Then he picked up another bundle of rushes and threw it at the next light, putting that out too. Then he noticed that not everyone was asleep. He saw the hand of a young man reach for the third light, take down the lamp-holder and snuff the flame.

He walked farther into the house and up to the bed closet where his sister, Thordis, and Thorgrim slept. The door was pulled to, and they were both in bed. He went to the bed, felt about inside it and touched his sister's breast. She was sleeping on the near side.

Then Thordis said, 'Why is your hand so cold, Thorgrim?' – and thereby woke him up.

Thorgrim replied, 'Do you want me to turn towards you?'

She thought it had been his hand that touched her. Gisli waited a little longer, warming his hand inside his tunic, while the couple fell asleep again. Then he touched Thorgrim lightly, waking him. Thorgrim thought that Thordis had roused him and he turned towards her. Gisli then pulled the bedclothes off them with one hand, and with the other he plunged Grasida through Thorgrim so that it stuck fast in the bed.

Then Thordis cried out, 'Everyone wake up. Thorgrim, my husband, has been killed!'

Gisli turned quickly towards the byre, leaving the way he had planned, and then locked up securely after himself. He headed home the same way he had come, leaving no sign of his tracks.

Aud unbolted the door as he arrived, and Gisli went to his bed as if nothing were amiss and as though he had done nothing.

All the men at Saebol were exceedingly drunk and no one knew what to do. They had been caught off guard, and therefore did nothing that was either useful or appropriate in the situation.

17 | Eyjolf spoke, 'An evil and serious thing has happened here and no one has his wits about him. I think we had better light the lamps and man the doors quickly to prevent the killer from getting out.'

That was done, but when there was no trace of the killer, everyone thought it must have been one of their own number who did the deed.

It was not long until dawn came. Then Thorgrim's body was taken and the spear removed, and he was made ready for burial. Sixty men set out to Gisli's farm at Hol. Thord the Coward stood outside and when he saw the band of men he ran inside and said that an army was approaching the farm. He was jabbering wildly.

'This is good,' said Gisli, and he spoke a verse:

9.
Words could not fell me,
by the fullest of means.
I, battle-oak, have brought                          *battle-oak*: warrior
death's end to many a man,
making my sword's mouth speak.
Let us go our ways silently;
though the cove-stallion's rider          *cove-stallion's rider*: seafarer,
be fallen, trouble is astir.                                    i.e. warrior

Thorkel and Eyjolf came to the farmhouse and walked over to the bed closet where Gisli and his wife lay. Thorkel, Gisli's brother, went right up to the closet and saw that Gisli's shoes were lying there, covered in ice and snow. He pushed them under the footboard so that no one else would see them.

Gisli greeted them and asked what news they brought. Thorkel told him that there were ill tidings and of great magnitude, then asked Gisli what lay behind all this and what they should do.

'Great deeds and ill deeds often fall within each other's shadow,' said Gisli. 'We will take it upon ourselves to make a burial mound for Thorgrim. This we owe you, and it is our duty to carry it out with honour.'

They accepted his offer and all returned to Saebol together to build a mound. They laid Thorgrim out in a boat and raised the mound in accordance with the old ways.

When the mound had been sealed, Gisli walked to the mouth of the river and lifted a stone so heavy it was more like a boulder. He dropped it into the boat with such a resounding crash that almost every plank of wood gave way.

'If the weather shifts this,' he said, 'then I don't know how to fasten a boat.'

Some people remarked that this was not unlike what Thorgrim had done with Vestein when he spoke of the Hel-shoes.

Everyone then prepared to go home from the funeral.

Gisli said to his brother, Thorkel, 'I believe you owe it to me that we be as friendly as we have ever been in the past – and now let's begin the games.'

Thorkel agreed to this readily, and they both returned home. Gisli had a good many men at his house, and when the feast was over, he bestowed good gifts on all his guests.


18 | They drank at Thorgrim's wake and Bork gave good gifts of friendship to many of the company.

The next matter of account was that Bork paid Thorgrim Nef to perform a magic rite, and to this effect – that however willing people might be to help the man who slew Thorgrim, their assistance should be of no avail. A nine-year-old gelding ox was given to Thorgrim for the magic rite, which he then performed. He prepared what he needed to carry it out, building a scaffold on which he practised his obscene and black art in devilish perversity.

Another thing happened that was accounted strange – the snow never settled on the south-west of Thorgrim's burial mound, nor showed any sign of frost. People suggested that Frey had found the sacrifices Thorgrim made to him so endearing that the god had not wanted the ground between them to freeze.

Such was the situation throughout the winter while the brothers jointly held their games. Bork moved in with Thordis and married her. She was with child at the time, and soon gave birth to a boy. He was sprinkled with water and at first named Thorgrim after his father. However, when he grew up he was thought to be so bad-tempered and restless that his name was changed to Snorri[25] the Godi. Bork lived there for a while and took part in the games.

There was a woman named Audbjorg who lived farther up the valley at Annmarkastadir. She was Thorgrim Nef's sister and once had a husband whose name was Thorkel, but who was nicknamed Annmarki (Flaw). Her son, Thorstein, was one of the strongest at the games, aside from Gisli. Gisli and Thorstein were always on the same side in the games, pitched against Bork and Thorkel.

One day, a great crowd of people came to see the game because they wanted to find out who was the strongest and the best player. And it was the same here as anywhere else – the more people arrived to watch, the greater the eagerness to compete. It is reported that Bork made no headway against Thorstein all day, and finally he became so angry that he broke Thorstein's bat in two. In response to this, Thorstein tackled him and laid him out flat on the ice.

When Gisli saw this he told Thorstein that he must put his all into playing against Bork, and then he said, 'I'll exchange bats with you.'

This they did, then Gisli sat down and fixed the bat. He looked towards Thorgrim's burial mound; there was snow on the ground and the women sat on the slope. His sister Thordis was there and many others. Gisli then spoke a verse which should not have been spoken:

10.

| | |
|---|---|
| I saw the shoots reach up | |
| through the thawed earth | *Thor*: i.e. man; |
| on the grim giant-Thor's | *giant-Thor*: word-play on |
| mound; | Thorgrim's name |
| I slew that Gaut of | *Gaut* (Odin) *of battle-gleam* (sword): |
| battle-gleam. | warrior |
| Thrott's helmet | *Thrott's* (Odin's) *helmet*: warrior |
| has silenced the spear-rattler, | |
| given one, greedy for land, | |
| a plot of his own, forever. | |

Thordis remembered the verse, went home and interpreted what it meant. The game then came to a close and Thorstein went home.

There was a man named Thorgeir, and known as Orri (Grouse), who lived at Orrastadir. There was another man, named Berg, and known as Skammfot (Short-leg), who lived at Skammfotarmyri (Short-leg's marsh) on the east side of the river.

As the men made their way home from the game, Thorstein and Berg began to talk about how it was played, and eventually they began to argue. Berg supported Bork, while Thorstein spoke out against him. Berg hit Thorstein with the back of his axe, but Thorgeir came between them and prevented Thorstein from responding. Thorstein went home to his mother, Audbjorg, and she bound up his wound. She was displeased about what had befallen him.

Old Audbjorg was so uneasy that she had no sleep that night. It was cold outside, but the air was still and the sky cloudless. She walked several times withershins around the outside of the house, sniffing in all directions. As she did this, the weather broke and a heavy, blustering snowstorm started up. This was followed by a thaw in which a flood of water gushed down the hillside and sent an avalanche of snow crashing into Berg's farmhouse. It killed twelve men. The traces of the landslide can be seen to this day.

19 | Thorstein went to meet Gisli, who gave him shelter. From there, he went south to Borgarfjord and then abroad. When Bork received news of the disaster at Berg's house, he went to Annmarkastadir and had Audbjorg seized. From there she was taken out to Saltnes and stoned to death.

After this, Gisli left his home and went to Nefsstadir, seized Thorgrim Nef and took him to Saltnes where a sack was placed over his head[26] before he was stoned to death. He was covered over with mud and stones, beside his sister, on the ridge between Haukadal and Medaldal.

All was quiet now, and the spring wore on. Bork went south to Thorsnes and was going to settle down there. He felt that his journey west had brought him no honour – he had lost a man of Thorgrim's calibre and matters had not been put right. He now prepared to go, leaving plans and instructions for what he wanted done at the farm in his absence, since he intended to return to fetch his possessions and his wife. Thorkel Sursson also decided to settle at Thorsnes, and made preparations to accompany Bork, his brother-in-law.

The story has it that Thordis Sursdottir, who was Gisli's sister and Bork's wife, went part of the way with Bork.

Bork spoke: 'Now, tell me why you were so upset when we broke up the games in the autumn. You promised to tell me before I left here.'

They had arrived at Thorgrim's burial mound while they spoke. Suddenly, Thordis stopped and said she would venture no farther. Then she recited the verse that Gisli had composed when he looked at Thorgrim's burial place.

'And I suspect,' she said, 'that you need not look elsewhere concerning Thorgrim's slaying. He will rightly be brought to justice.'

Bork became enraged at this, and said, 'I want to turn back right now and kill Gisli. On the other hand, I can't be sure,' he said, 'how much truth there is in what Thordis says. It's just as likely that there's none. Women's counsel is often cold.'

Thorkel persuaded them to ride on until they reached Sandar estuary, where they stopped and rested their horses. Bork spoke very little. Thorkel said he wanted to meet his friend, Onund, and rode off so fast that he was soon out of sight.

Then, he changed direction and rode to Hol, where he told Gisli what had happened, how Thordis had discovered the truth and solved the meaning of the verse: 'You'll have to regard the matter as out in the open now.'

Gisli fell silent. Then he spoke a verse:

11.
My sister, too taken
with her fine clothes,
lacks the firm-rooted spirit          *Gudrun, Gjuki's daughter*: tragic
of Gudrun, Gjuki's daughter,          heroine of *The Saga of the Volsungs*
that sea-fire's goddess,                  *sea-fire*: gold; its *goddess*: woman
amber-Freyja, who killed                     *amber-Freyja*: woman
her husband with undaunted courage
to avenge her brave brothers.

'I don't think I deserved this from her,' said Gisli. 'I thought I made it clear several times that her honour meant no less to me than my own. There were even times when I put my life in danger for her sake, and she has pronounced my death sentence. But what I need to know now, brother, is what I can expect from you, considering what I have done.'

'I can give you warning if there is an attempt on your life,' said Thorkel, 'but I can afford you no help that might lead to my being accused. I feel I have been greatly wronged by the slaying of Thorgrim, my brother-in-law, my partner and my close friend.'

Gisli answered him, 'It was unthinkable that a man such as Vestein should not be avenged. I would not have answered you as you now answer me, nor would I do what you propose to do.'

Then they parted. Thorkel went to meet Bork and from there they went south to Thorsnes, where Bork put his house in order. Thorkel bought some land at Hvamm on Bardastrond.

Then the Summons Days came round, and Bork travelled west with forty men to summon Gisli to the Thorsnes Assembly. Thorkel Sursson was in his party, as were Thorodd and Outlaw-

Stein, Bork's nephews. There was also a Norwegian with them, named Thorgrim. They rode out to the Sandar estuary.

Then Thorkel said, 'I have a debt to collect at a small farm down here, a little farther on', and he named the farm. 'So I'll ride out there and pick up what's due to me. Follow me at your own pace.'

Thorkel then rode on ahead and when he reached the farmstead he had mentioned, he asked the farmer's wife if he might take one of the horses there and let his own stand by the front door.

'And throw some homespun cloth over the saddle of my horse,' he said, 'and when my companions arrive, tell them I'm sitting in the main room counting the silver.'

She lent him a horse and he rode with great haste to the woods at Haukadal, where he met Gisli and told him what was happening – that Bork had come from the west.

20 | Now, to return to Bork. He prepared a case against Gisli for the slaying of Thorgrim to be presented at the Thorsnes Assembly. At the same time, Gisli had sold his land to Thorkel Eiriksson and received payment in cash, which was especially convenient for him.

He asked his brother Thorkel for advice. In other words, he wanted to know what Thorkel was prepared to do for him and whether he would assist him. Thorkel's answer was the same as before – he would keep Gisli informed of any planned assault, but stay clear himself of any possible accusations.

Then Thorkel rode off and took a route that brought him up behind Bork and the others, thereby slowing down their pace a little.

Gisli took two cart-horses and headed for the woods with his valuables. His slave, Thord the Coward, went with him.

Gisli said, 'You have often shown obedience to me and done what I wanted, and I owe you some reward.'

As usual, Gisli was wearing his black cloak and was well dressed.

He removed his cape and said, 'I want to give you this cloak, my friend, and I want you to enjoy its use right away. Put it on and sit behind on the sled, and I'll lead the horses and wear your cloak.'

And that is what they did. Then Gisli said, 'Should some men call out to you, make sure you do not answer. If they intend to do you harm, make for the woods.'

Thord had as much wits as he had courage, for he had none of either. Gisli led the oxen and Thord, who was a big man, sat high up on the sled thinking he was very finely dressed and showing off. Now Bork and his men saw them as they made their way towards the woods, and they quickly pursued them. When Thord saw what was happening, he jumped down off the sled and made for the woods as fast as he could. They thought he was Gisli and chased him, calling out to him loudly as they ran. Thord made no reply. Instead, he ran as fast as his feet could carry him. The Norwegian, Thorgrim, threw his spear at Thord, catching him so hard between the shoulder-blades that he fell face forward to the ground. That was his death blow.

Then Bork said, 'That was a perfect throw.'

The brothers, Outlaw-Stein and Thorodd, agreed that they would pursue the slave and see whether he had any fight in him, and they turned off into the woods.

To return to Bork and the others – they came up to the man in the black cloak and pulled back his hood to discover that they had been rather less lucky than they imagined. They had killed Thord the Coward when they had meant to kill Gisli.

The story has it that the brothers, Outlaw-Stein and Thorodd, reached the woods and that Gisli was already there. He saw them and they saw him. Then one of them threw a spear at Gisli, which he caught in mid-flight and threw back at Thorodd. It struck the middle of his body and flew right through him. Outlaw-Stein returned to his companions and told them it was difficult to move around in the woods, but Bork wanted to go there anyway, so that is where they went. When they came to the woods, Thorgrim the Norwegian saw a branch move in one place and threw his spear directly at it, hitting Gisli in the calf of his leg. Gisli threw the spear back and it pierced right through Thorgrim and killed him.

The rest of them searched the woods, but they could not find Gisli so they returned to Gisli's farm and initiated a case against him for killing Thorgrim. They rode home, having taken no valuables from the house. Gisli went up the mountainside behind the farm and bound up his wound while Bork and the others were down at his farmstead. When they left, Gisli returned home. Gisli now prepared to leave. He got a boat and loaded it up with his valuables. His wife, Aud, and his foster-daughter, Gudrid, accompanied him to Husanes, where they all went ashore. Gisli went to the farm at Husanes and met a man there who asked him who he was. Gisli told the man as much as he thought he ought to know, but not the truth. Then he picked up a stone and threw it out to a small islet that lay offshore and asked the farmer to have his son do the same thing when he came home – then they would know who he was. But there was no man who could manage it, and thus it was proven once again that Gisli was more accomplished than most other men. After this, Gisli returned to the boat and rowed out around the headland and across to Arnarfjord, and from there across a smaller fjord that lies within it, known as Geirthjofsfjord. Here he prepared to settle down, and built himself a homestead where he stayed for the whole winter.

21 | The next thing that happened was that Gisli sent word to Vestein's uncles, Helgi, Sigurd and Vestgeir, the sons of Bjartmar, asking them to go to the assembly and offer a settlement for him so that he would not be outlawed.

They went to the assembly, but they made no headway with a settlement. Indeed, it was said that they handled matters so badly that they were close to tears before it was over. They related the outcome to Thorkel the Wealthy, saying that they dared not face Gisli to tell him he had been outlawed. Aside from Gisli's sentence nothing else of note took place at the assembly. Thorkel the Wealthy went to meet Gisli to tell him that he had been outlawed.

Then Gisli spoke these verses:

12.
The trial at Thorsnes
would not thus
have gone against me
if Vestein's heart
had beat
in the breasts
of the sons
of Bjartmar.

13.
My wife's uncles
were downcast
when they ought
to have been glad.
Those spenders of gold                          *spenders of gold*: men
behaved as if
they had been
pelted with rotten eggs.

14.
News comes from the north:
the assembly is over,
harsh sentence passed
on me – no honour there.
Giver of pure gold,                             *giver of pure gold*: generous man
this blue-armoured warrior
shall cruelly repay
both Bork and Stein.

Then Gisli asked the two Thorkels what he might expect of
them, and they both replied that they would give him shelter
provided it meant no material loss on their parts. Then Thorkel
the Wealthy rode home. It is said that Gisli spent three winters
at Geirthjofsfjord, staying some of the time with Thorkel Eiriksson. Then he spent another three winters journeying around
Iceland, meeting with various chieftains and trying to elicit their
support. As a result of Thorgrim Nef's evil arts, and the magic

rite and spells he had performed, Gisli had no success in persuading these chieftains to ally themselves with him; although their support sometimes seemed almost forthcoming, something always obstructed its course. Nevertheless, he spent lengthy periods with Thorkel Eiriksson. By this time he had been outlawed for six years.

At the end of this period, he dwelt partly in Geirthjofsfjord, at Aud's farm, and partly in a hut that he had built north of the river. He had another hideout by a ridge just south of the farm – and he also stayed there from time to time.

22 | Now when Bork heard of this, he left home and went to meet Eyjolf the Grey, who at that time was living at Otradal in Arnarfjord. Bork asked him to go and search for the outlaw Gisli and kill him, offering him three hundred pieces of silver[27] to do all in his power to find the man. Eyjolf took the money and promised to take care of the matter.

There was a man with Eyjolf named Helgi, who was known as Helgi the Spy. He was sharp-sighted, a fast runner, and he knew all the fjords. He was sent to Geirthjofsfjord to find out whether Gisli was there and discovered that there was indeed a man there, but he did not know whether it was Gisli or someone else. He went back and told Eyjolf the situation. Eyjolf said he was sure it was Gisli, and he reacted quickly by going to Geirthjofsfjord with six men. But he did not find Gisli, so he returned home.

Gisli was a wise man who dreamed a great deal and whose dreams were prophetic. All knowledgeable men agree that Gisli survived as an outlaw longer than any other man, except Grettir Asmundarson.[28]

It is said that one night, when Gisli was staying at Aud's farm, he slept badly and when he awoke she asked him what he had dreamed.

He answered her, 'There are two women I dream of. One is good to me. The other always tells me something that makes matters worse than ever, and she only prophesies ill for me. Just now I dreamed that I appeared to be walking towards a certain house or hall, and it seemed that I walked into the house and recognized there many of my kinsmen and friends. They sat by fires and drank. And there were seven fires, some of them almost burned out and some burning very bright. Then my good dream-woman came in and said that this signified how many years I had left to live, and she advised me to stop following the old faith for the rest of my life, and to refrain from studying any charms or ancient lore. And she told me to be kind to the deaf and the lame and the poor and the helpless, and that is where my dream ended.'

Then Gisli spoke some verses:

15.

| | |
|---|---|
| Bright land of wave's flame, | *wave's flame*: gold; its *land*: woman |
| goddess of gold, I came | *goddess of gold*: woman |
| to a hall where seven fires, | |
| to my anguish, were burning. | |
| On both sides, men on benches | |
| greeted me kindly, while I, | |
| wringer of verses, wished each | |
| and every man there good health. | |

16.

| | |
|---|---|
| 'Consider, tree of the sword,' | *tree of the sword*: warrior |
| said the Eir of ribbons, | *Eir of ribbons*: woman |
| 'how many fires burn | |
| brightly here in the hall – | |
| thus many winters are left | |
| unlived for him who bears | |
| the shield in battle's storm. | |
| Better things soon await you.' | |

17.

| | |
|---|---|
| 'Bringer of death in battle, | |
| from words spoken by poets, | |
| take and learn only what is good,' | |
| said Nauma of gold to me. | *Nauma of gold*: woman |
| 'Almost nothing is worse, | |

for the flame of shield,                    *flame of shield*: warrior
the spender of sea-fire,        *sea-fire*: gold; its *spender*: generous man
than to be versed in evil.'

18.
'Do not be the first to kill,
nor provoke into fight
the gods who delight in battle.       *gods* (Njord) *who delight in battle*:
Give me your word on this.                                        warriors
Help the blind and handless,
ring-giver, Balder of shield.              *Balder of shield*: warrior
Beware, evil resides in scorn
shown to the lame and needy.'


23 | To return to Bork, he began to put considerable pressure
     on Eyjolf. He felt that Eyjolf had not done what was
expected of him and that he had got less than he expected for
his money. Bork said he knew for certain that Gisli was in
Geirthjofsfjord, and he told Eyjolf's men, who were acting as
messengers between them, that either Eyjolf must go and search
for Gisli or he would go and do it himself. Eyjolf responded
quickly and sent Helgi the Spy back to Geirthjofsfjord. This
time he had enough food with him and was away for a week,
waiting for Gisli to appear. One day, he saw a man emerge from
a hiding place and recognized him as Gisli. Helgi made off
without delay and told Eyjolf what he had discovered.

Eyjolf got ready to leave with eight men, and went off to
Aud's farm in Geirthjofsfjord. They did not find Gisli there, so
they went and searched the woods, but they could not find him
there either. They returned to the farm and Eyjolf offered Aud
a large sum of money to disclose Gisli's whereabouts. But that
was the last thing she wanted to do. Then they threatened to
hurt her, but that produced no result, and they were forced to
return home. The whole expedition was considered humiliating,
and Eyjolf stayed at home that autumn.

Although he had eluded them this time, Gisli knew they would
catch him eventually because the distance between them was so

short.[29] So he left home and rode out to meet his brother, Thorkel, at Hvamm on Bardastrond. He knocked on the door of the chamber where his brother lay and Thorkel came out to greet him.

'I need to know,' said Gisli, 'whether you will help me. I expect it of you. I'm in a tight spot and I have long refrained from asking your assistance.'

Thorkel answered as before, and said that he would offer him no help that might lead to a case being brought against him. He was willing, however, to give him silver and some horses if Gisli needed them, or anything else he had mentioned earlier.

'I can see now,' said Gisli, 'that you don't want to give me any real help. Then let me have three hundreds of homespun cloth, and be comforted with the thought that from this time on I will ask very little of you.'

Thorkel did as he was asked. He gave Gisli the cloth and, in addition, some silver. Gisli said he would accept these but that he would not have acted so ignobly if he had been in his brother's position. Gisli was much affected when they parted. He headed out for Vadil, to Gest Oddleifsson's mother, Thorgerd. He arrived there before dawn and knocked on the door. Thorgerd came to answer. She often used to take in outlaws, and had an underground passage. One end of this passage was by the river, and the other led into the fire room of her farmhouse. Traces of this can still be seen.

Thorgerd welcomed Gisli warmly: 'I suggest you stay here for a while,' she said, 'but I don't know that I can give you much more than a woman's help.'

Gisli accepted her offer, and added that, considering the kind of help he had had from men, he did not expect to be done any worse by women. He stayed there for the winter and was nowhere treated as well during his days as an outlaw.

24 | When spring came round again, Gisli went to Geirthjofs-fjord because he could no longer be away from his wife, Aud – for they loved each other greatly. He stayed there in hiding until autumn and, as the nights lengthened, he dreamed

the same dreams over and over again. The bad dream-woman appeared to him and his dreams grew ever more troubled. One time, when Aud asked him what he had dreamed, he told her. Then he spoke a verse:

19.

If old age awaits this spear-breaker            *spear-breaker*: warrior
then my dreams lead me astray.
Sjofn of sewing, mead-goddess,          *Sjofn* (goddess) *of sewing*: woman;
comes to me in my sleep,                       *mead-goddess*: woman
and gives this maker of verses
no cause to believe otherwise.
Wearer of brooches,                           *wearer of brooches*: lady
this keeps me not from sleep.

Then Gisli told her that the evil dream-woman also came to him often, and always wanted to smear him with gore, bathe him in sacrificial blood and act in a foul manner.

20.

Not all my dreams bode well,
yet each of them must I tell.
That woman in my dreams
takes all my joy, it seems.
As I fall asleep, she appears,
and comes to me besmeared
hideously in human blood,
and washes me in gory flood.

And again he spoke:

21.

Once more have I told my dream
to the trees of arrow-torrents.         *trees of arrow-torrents*: warriors
And words did not fail me.
Eir of gold, battle-thirsty men              *Eir* (goddess) *of gold*: woman
had me made an outlaw.
They will surely
regret what they have done
if rage comes upon me now.

Things were quiet for a while. Gisli went back to Thorgerd
and stayed with her for another winter, returning to Geirthjofsfjord the following summer where he stayed until autumn. Then
he went once again to his brother, Thorkel, and knocked on his
door. Thorkel did not want to come out, so Gisli took a piece
of wood, scored runes on it and threw it into the house. Thorkel
saw the piece of wood, picked it up, looked at it and then stood
up and went outside. He greeted Gisli and asked him what news
he brought.

Gisli said he had none to tell: 'I've come to meet you, brother,
for the last time. Assist me worthily now and I will repay you
by never asking anything of you again.'

Thorkel gave him the same answer as before. He offered Gisli
horses or a boat, but refused any further help. Gisli accepted
the offer of a boat and asked Thorkel to help him get it afloat –
which he did. Then he gave Gisli six weights of food and
one hundred of homespun cloth. After Gisli had gone aboard,
Thorkel stood there on the shore.

Then Gisli said, 'You think you're safe and sound and living
in plenty, a friend of many chieftains, who has no need to be on
his guard – and I am an outlaw and have many enemies. But I
can tell you this, that even so you will be killed before me. We
take our leave of each other now on worse terms than we ought
and will never see each other again. But know this. I would
never have treated you as you have treated me.'

'Your prophecies don't frighten me,' said Thorkel, and after
that they parted.

Gisli went out to the island of Hergilsey in Breidafjord. There
he removed from his boat the decking, thwarts, oars and all else
that was not fastened down, turned the boat over and let it drift
ashore in Nesjar. When people saw the boat, wrecked and
washed ashore, they assumed that Gisli had taken it from his
brother Thorkel, then capsized and drowned.

Gisli walked to the farmhouse on the island of Hergilsey,
where a man named Ingjald[30] lived with his wife, Thorgerd.
Ingjald was Gisli's cousin, the son of his mother's sister, and
had come to Iceland with Gisli. When they met, he put himself
at Gisli's complete disposal, offering to do for him whatever

was in his power. Gisli accepted his offer and stayed there for a
while.

25 | There were both a male slave and a female slave at Ingjald's
   | house. The man was named Svart and the woman Bothild.
Ingjald had a son named Helgi, as great and simple-minded an
oaf as ever there was. He was tethered by the neck to a heavy
stone with a hole in it and left outside to graze like an animal.
He was known as Ingjald's Fool and was a very large man,
almost a troll.

Gisli stayed there for that winter and built a boat and many
other things for Ingjald, and everything he made was easily
recognizable because he was a superior craftsman. People
showed surprise at the number of well-crafted items that Ingjald
owned since it was known that he was no carpenter.

Gisli always spent the summers in Geirthjofsfjord, and by
now three years had passed since he had his dreams. Ingjald had
proven himself a faithful friend, but suspicions arose and people
began to believe that Gisli was alive and living with Ingjald, and
that he had not drowned as they had once thought. People
started to remark on the fact that Ingjald had three boats and
all were skilfully crafted. This gossip reached Eyjolf the Grey,
and he sent Helgi out again, this time to the island of Hergilsey.
Gisli always stayed in an underground passage when people
came to the island. Ingjald was a good host and he invited Helgi
to rest there, so he remained for the night.

Ingjald was a hard-working man and rowed out to fish whenever the weather permitted. The following morning, when he
was ready to go to sea, he asked Helgi whether he was not eager
to be on his way and why he was still in bed. Helgi said that he
was not feeling very well, let out a long sigh and rubbed his
head. Ingjald told him to lie still, and then went off to sea. Helgi
began to groan heavily.

It is said that Thorgerd then went to the underground hiding
place, intending to give Gisli some breakfast. There was a partition between the pantry and where Helgi lay in bed. Thorgerd
left the pantry and Helgi climbed up the partition and saw that

someone's food had been served up. At that very moment, Thorgerd returned and Helgi turned round quickly and fell off the partition. Thorgerd asked him what he was doing climbing up the rafters instead of lying still. He said he was so racked with pains in his joints that he could not lie still.

'Could you help me back to bed?' he said.

She did as he asked and went out with the food. Then Helgi got up and followed her and saw what was going on. After that he went back to bed, lay down and stayed there for the rest of the day.

Ingjald returned that evening, went to Helgi's bed and asked him if he felt any better. Helgi said he was improving and asked if he might be ferried from the island the following morning. He was rowed out to the island of Flatey, and from there he went south to Thorsnes, reporting that he had news that Gisli was staying at Ingjald's house. Bork set out with a party of fourteen men, boarded a ship and sailed south across Breidafjord. That day, Ingjald went fishing and took Gisli with him. The male and female slaves, Svart and Bothild, were in a separate boat, close to the islands known as Skutileyjar.

26 | Ingjald saw a ship sailing from the south, and said, 'There's a ship out there and I think it's Bork the Stout.'

'What do you suggest we do now?' asked Gisli. 'Let's see whether your wits match your integrity.'

'I'm not a clever man,' said Ingjald, 'but we have to decide something quickly. Let's row as fast as we can to Hergilsey, get up on top of Vadsteinaberg and fight them off as long as we can keep standing.'

'Just as I anticipated,' said Gisli. 'You hit on the very plan that best shows your integrity. But I would be paying you poorly indeed for all the help you have given me if you lose your life for my sake – and that will never happen. We'll use a different plan. You and your slave, Svart, row out to the island and make ready to defend yourselves there. They will think that it is I who am with you when they sail up past the ness. I'll exchange clothes with the slave, as I did once before, then I'll get into the boat with Bothild.'

Ingjald did as he was advised, but he was clearly very angry.

When they parted company, Bothild said, 'What can be done now?'

Gisli spoke a verse:

22.

| | |
|---|---|
| The shield-holder seeks | *shield-holder*: warrior |
| a plan to part with Ingjald. | |
| Let us pour Sudri's mead, | *Sudri's* (dwarf's) *mead*: poetry |
| slave-woman, though I | |
| accept my fate, whatever it be. | |
| Noble woman of low means, | |
| carrier of wave-fire: | *carrier of wave-fire* (gold): woman |
| I fear nothing for myself. | |

Then they rowed south towards Bork and his men, and behaved as if nothing were amiss.

Gisli told them how they should act. 'You will say,' he told her, 'that this is the fool on board, and I'll sit in the prow and mimic him. I'll wrap myself up in the tackle and hang overboard a few times and act as stupidly as I can. If they go past us a little, I'll scull as hard as I can and try to put some more distance between us.'

Bothild rowed towards them, but not close, and pretended to be moving from one fishing ground to another. Bork called out to her and asked her if Gisli was on the island.

'I don't know,' she answered. 'But I do know there's a man out there who surpasses all others in size and skill.'

'I see,' said Bork. 'Is Ingjald the farmer at home?'

'He rowed back to the island quite some time ago,' she said, 'and his slave was with him, as far as I know.'

'That is not what's happened,' said Bork. 'It must be Gisli who is with him. Let's row after them as fast as we can.'

The men answered, 'We're having fun with the idiot,' and looked towards him. 'Look at how madly he's behaving.'

Then they said what a terrible thing it was for her to have to look after this fool.

'I agree,' said Bothild, 'but I think it's just idle amusement for you. You don't feel sorry for me at all.'

'Let's indulge no further in this nonsense,' said Bork. 'We must be on our way.'

They left, and Bork and his crew rowed out to Hergilsey and went ashore. Then they saw the men up on Vadsteinaberg and headed that way, thinking they were really in luck. But it was Ingjald and his slave up on the crag.

Bork soon recognized the men and said to Ingjald, 'The best thing you can do is hand over Gisli – or else tell me where he is. You're an unspeakable wretch, hiding my brother's murderer like this when you're my tenant. Don't expect any mercy from me. You deserve to die for this.'

Ingjald replied, 'My clothes are so poor that it would be no great grief if I stopped wearing them out. I'd rather die than not do all I can to keep Gisli from harm.'

It is said that Ingjald served Gisli best, and that his help was the most useful to him. When Thorgrim Nef performed his magic rite, he ordained that no assistance Gisli might receive from men on the mainland would come to anything. However, it never occurred to him to say anything about the islands, and thus Ingjald helped him for longer than most. But this could not last indefinitely.

27 | Bork thought it was unwise to attack his tenant, Ingjald, so he and his men turned instead towards the farmhouse to search for Gisli. As was to be expected, they did not find him there, so they went about the island and came to a place where the fool lay eating in a small, grassy hollow, haltered by the neck to a stone.

Bork spoke: 'Not only is there a great deal of talk about this fool, but he seems to move around a lot more than I thought. There's nothing here. We have gone about this task so badly that it doesn't bear thinking about, and I have no idea when we'll be able to make matters right. That was Gisli in the boat alongside us, impersonating the fool. He's got a whole bag of tricks, as well as being a skilled mimic. But think how much it would shame us to let him slip through our fingers. Let's get after him quickly and make sure he doesn't escape our clutches.'

They jumped aboard their ship and rowed after Gisli and Bothild, pulling long strokes with their oars. They saw that the two of them had gone quite some distance into the sound, and now both vessels rowed at full pace. The one with the larger crew sped along faster, and finally it came so close that Bork was within spear-throwing range as Gisli pulled ashore.

Gisli said to the slave-woman, 'Here we part ways. Take these two gold rings – one you must take to Ingjald and the other to his wife. Tell them to give you your freedom and accept these as tokens. I also want Svart to be freed. You have truly saved my life and I want you to reap your reward.'

They parted and Gisli jumped ashore and ran to a ravine in Hjardarnes. The slave-woman rowed off and the sweat rose from her like steam.

Bork and his men rowed ashore and Outlaw-Stein was the first off the boat. He ran off to look for Gisli and when he reached the ravine, Gisli was standing there with his sword drawn. He drove it at once through Outlaw-Stein's head, split him down to the shoulders, and he fell to the ground, dead. Bork and the others then came on to the island and Gisli ran down to the water, intending to swim for the mainland. Bork threw a spear at him and it struck him in the calf of his leg, wounding him badly. Gisli removed the spear, but lost his sword, too weary to keep hold of it any longer. By then, the darkness of night had fallen.

When Gisli reached land he ran into the woods – at that time there was woodland in many places – and Bork and the others ran ashore to look for him, hoping to restrict him to the woodland. Gisli was so worn out and stiff that he could hardly walk, and he was also aware that he was surrounded on all sides by Bork's party of men.

Trying to think of a plan, he went down to the sea, and in the darkness he made his way along the shoreline under the shelter of the overhanging cliffs until he came to Haug. There he met a farmer named Ref,[31] a very sly man. Ref greeted him and asked him what was going on. Gisli told him all that had taken place between him and Bork and his men. Ref had a wife named Alfdis, a good-looking woman, but fierce tempered and thoroughly shrewish. She and Ref were more than a match for each other. When Gisli had given his account, he urged Ref to give him all the help he could.

'They will be here soon,' said Gisli. 'I'm in a very tight spot and there aren't too many people around to whom I can turn.'

'I will help you, but on one condition,' said Ref, 'that I alone decide how I go about matters, and you must not interfere.'

'I accept,' said Gisli. 'I will not venture any farther on my way.'

'Come inside then,' said Ref. And so they went in.

Then Ref said to Alfdis, 'Now, I'm going to give you a new bedfellow.'

And he took off all the bed covering and told Gisli to lie down on the straw. Then he put the covers back over him and now Alfdis lay on top of him.

'And now you stay put,' said Ref, 'whatever happens.'

Then he asked Alfdis to be as difficult to deal with as possible and to act as madly as she could.

'And don't hold yourself back,' said Ref. 'Say whatever comes into your mind. Swear and curse as much as you like. I'll go off to talk with them and say whatever occurs to me.'

When he went out again he saw some men coming – eight of Bork's companions. Bork himself had stayed behind at the Fossa river. These men had come to search for Gisli and to capture him if they found him. Ref was outside and asked them what they were doing.

'We can only tell you what you must already know. Have you any idea where Gisli has gone? Has he come by here by any chance?'

'First,' said Ref, 'he has not been here. If he had chanced it he would have met with a very swift end. And second, do you really think I am any less eager to kill him than you? I have sense enough to know that it would mean no small gain to be trusted by a man such as Bork and be counted his friend.'

They asked, 'Do you mind if we search you and the farm?'

'Of course not,' said Ref, 'please do. Once you're certain he's not here, you'll be able to concentrate on searching elsewhere. Come in and search the place thoroughly.'

They went in, and when Alfdis heard the noise they were making she asked what gang of thugs was out there and what kind of idiots barged in on people in the middle of the night. Ref told her to calm down, and she responded with a flurry of foul language that they were unlikely to forget. They continued to search the place even so, but not as carefully as they might have done if they had not had to suffer such a torrent of abuse from the farmer's wife. Having found nothing, they left and wished the farmer well. He, in return, wished them a good journey. Then they went back to meet Bork and were highly displeased with the whole trip. They felt they had lost a good man, been put to shame and achieved nothing.

News of this spread all over the country and people considered that the men had derived nothing from their futile search for Gisli. Bork went home and told Eyjolf how matters stood. Gisli stayed with Ref for two weeks and then left. They parted good friends and Gisli gave him a knife and a belt – both valuable possessions. Gisli had nothing else with him.

After that Gisli returned to his wife in Geirthjofsfjord. His reputation had increased considerably as a result of what had happened, and it is truly said that there has never been a more accomplished and courageous man than Gisli, and yet fortune did not follow him.

But now to other matters.

28 | To return to Bork. That spring, he went with a large group of men to the Thorskafjord Assembly, intending to meet with his friends. Gest travelled east from Bardastrond, as did Thorkel Sursson. They arrived in separate ships.

When Gest was ready to embark, two poorly dressed young men with staffs approached him, and it was noticed that Gest spoke to them in secret. They asked if they might go with him on his ship and he granted them that favour. They journeyed with him to Hallsteinsnes, then went ashore and walked on until they came to the Thorskafjord Assembly.

There was a man named Hallbjorn, a wanderer who travelled around the country, though always with a group of ten or twelve others. He raised a booth for himself at the assembly, and this is where the two young men went. They asked him for a place in the booth, saying that they, too, were wanderers, and he said he would give shelter to anyone who asked for it.

'I've come here many a springtime,' he said, 'and I know all the chieftains and godis.'

The lads said they would be pleased to be in his care and learn from him: 'We're very curious to see all the grand and mighty men we have heard so many stories about.'

Hallbjorn said he would go down to the shore and identify every ship as soon as it came in, and tell them which it was. They thanked him for his kindness, and then they all went down to the shore to watch the ships as they sailed in.

Then the elder lad spoke: 'Who owns the ship that is sailing in now?'

Hallbjorn told him it belonged to Bork the Stout.

'And who is that, sailing in next?'

'Gest the Wise,' he said.

'And that ship, coming in behind him, and putting up at the horn of the fjord?'

'That is Thorkel Sursson,' said Hallbjorn.

They watched as Thorkel came ashore and sat down somewhere while the crew carried their goods and provisions on to to dry ground, out of reach of the tides, and Bork set up their booth. Thorkel was wearing a Russian hat and a grey fur cloak that was pinned at the shoulder with a gold clasp. He carried a sword in his hand. Then Hallbjorn went over to where Thorkel was sitting, and the young men went with him.

One of the lads spoke – it was the elder. He said, 'Who is this noble-looking man sitting here? Never have I seen such a fine and handsome man.'

The man answered, 'Well spoken. My name is Thorkel.'

Then the lad said, 'That must be a very good sword you have there in your hand. Would you allow me to look at it?'

Thorkel answered him, 'Your behaviour is rather unusual,

but all right, I'll allow you to,' and he handed him the sword.

The young man took it, turned to one side, unfastened the peace straps and drew the sword.

When Thorkel saw that he said, 'I did not give you permission to draw the sword.'

'I did not ask your permission,' said the lad.

Then he raised the sword in the air and struck Thorkel on the neck with such a fearsome blow that it took off his head.

When this had happened, Hallbjorn leapt up and the lad threw down the blood-stained sword. He grabbed his staff and he ran off with Hallbjorn and the others in his band, who were almost out of their wits with fear, and they all ran past the booth that Bork had set up. People thronged around Thorkel, but no one seemed to know who had done this deed. Bork asked why there was so much noise and commotion around Thorkel just as Hallbjorn and about fifteen of his band ran past the booth. The younger lad was named Helgi, while his older companion, who had done the killing, was named Berg.

It was Helgi who answered: 'I'm not sure what they are discussing, but I think they're arguing about whether Vestein left only daughters behind him, or whether he had a son.'

Hallbjorn ran to his booth, and the lads hurried to some nearby woods and could not be found.

29 | People ran into Hallbjorn's booth and asked what had happened. The road-farers told them that two young men, about whom they knew nothing, had come into their group and that they had no idea this would happen. Then they gave descriptions of them and repeated what the young men had said. From what Helgi said Bork surmised that they were Vestein's sons.

Then Bork went to meet Gest and discuss with him what should be done.

Bork said, 'I bear a greater responsibility than anyone else to bring a suit in the wake of my brother-in-law Thorkel's slaying. We think it not unlikely that Vestein's sons did this deed. No one else could have had anything against Thorkel. And it looks as if they've escaped for the moment. Tell me how I should proceed with the case.'

Gest answered him, 'I know what I'd do if I had done the killing. I'd get out of it by changing my name, so that any case brought against me would come to nothing.'

And he discouraged Bork from pursuing the accusation. People were reasonably sure that Gest had conspired with the lads because he was a blood-relation of theirs.

They broke off their talk and the case was dropped. Thorkel was buried according to the old customs, and then everyone went home. Nothing else of note took place at the assembly. Bork was as displeased with this trip as he had often been with the others, and this matter brought much disgrace and dishonour to him.

The young men travelled until they reached Geirthjofsfjord, where they spent five days and five nights out in the open. By night they went to Aud's farm – where Gisli was staying – and knocked on the door. Aud went to the door to greet them and asked their business. Gisli lay in bed in the underground hideout, and she would have raised her voice if he had needed to be on his guard. They told her of Thorkel's slaying and what the situation was, and also how long they had gone without food.

'I'm going to send you,' said Aud, 'across the ridge to Mosdal, to Bjartmar's sons. I'll give you some food and some tokens so that they will give you shelter for a while, and I'm doing this because I'm in no mind to ask Gisli to help you.'

The young men went into the woods, where they could not be traced and, having gone without food for a long time, they ate. When they had satisfied their hunger, they lay down to sleep because by then they were very tired.

30 | At this point, the story turns to Aud. She went to Gisli and said, 'Now, it means a great deal to me how you will act and whether you choose to honour me more than I deserve.'

He answered her quickly, 'I know you are going to tell me of my brother Thorkel's death.'

'It is so,' said Aud, 'and the lads have come and want to join you. They feel they have no one else to rely on.'

Gisli answered, 'I could not bear to see my brother's killers or to be with them', and he jumped up and went to draw his sword as he spoke this verse:

23.
Who knows, but Gisli may
again draw cold sword
from sheath when warriors
from the assembly report
the slaying of Thorkel
to that sword-polisher.                    *that sword-polisher*: warrior
We will dare great deeds,
even to the very death.

Aud told him they had already left – 'for I had sense enough not to risk their tarrying here'.

Gisli said it was better that they did not meet. Then he soon calmed down and things were quiet for a while.

It is said that at this time, according to the prophecy of the dream-woman, Gisli had only two years of life remaining to him. As time passed, Gisli stayed in Geirthjofsfjord and all his dreams and restless nights began again. Now it was mainly the bad dream-woman who came to him, although the good one also appeared sometimes.

One night, Gisli dreamed again that the good dream-woman came to him. She was riding a grey horse, and she invited him to come home with her, to which he agreed. They arrived at a house, which was more like a great hall, and she led him inside. He saw cushions on the raised benches and the whole place was beautifully decorated.

She told him they would stay there and take their pleasure – 'and this is where you will come when you die,' she said, 'and enjoy wealth and great happiness'.

Then Gisli awoke and spoke several verses concerning what he had dreamed:

24.

The thread-goddess invited          *thread-goddess*: woman
the praise-maker to ride                *praise-maker*: poet
on a grey steed to her home.
And as we rode along
she was gentle to me,
that bearer of the ale-horn          *bearer of the ale-horn*: woman
swore she would heal me.
I remember her words.


25.

The good dream-woman
led me, the poet, to sleep
there, where soft beds lay.
From my mind this will not fade.
The thread-goddess led me
to her soft resting place,
so perfectly arranged,
and there I lay me down.


26.

'Here will you lie down
and breathe your last with me,'
said the Hild of the rings.    *Hild* (goddess) *of the rings*: the dream-woman
'And here, my warrior,
you will rule over all this wealth
and have dominion over me,
and we will have riches
beyond gold's measure.'


31 | It is said that on one occasion when Helgi was sent again
     to spy in Geirthjofsfjord – where everyone believed Gisli
to be staying – a man named Havard went with him. He had
come to Iceland earlier that summer and was a kinsman of Gest
Oddleifsson. They were sent into the woods to cut timber for
building, and although that was the apparent purpose of their

journey, it was really a ploy for them to look for Gisli and to see whether they could locate his hideout. One evening they saw a fire on the ridge, south of the river. This was at dusk, but it was very dark.

Then Havard asked Helgi what they should do – 'For you are more used to all this than I am,' he said.

'There is only one thing to do,' said Helgi, 'and that is to build a cairn here on this hillock, where we are now, so that it can be found tomorrow when it grows light enough to see.'

This is what they decided to do. When they had built the cairn, Havard said that he was so drowsy that he could do nothing else than go to sleep – which he then did. Helgi stayed awake and finished off building the cairn, and when he was done, Havard awoke and told him to sleep for a while, saying that he would keep watch. Then Helgi slept for a spell, and while he was sleeping, Havard began carrying away every single stone of the cairn under the cover of darkness. When he had done that, he took a great boulder and hurtled it down on the rock-face near Helgi's head so hard that the ground shook. Helgi sprang to his feet, shaking with fear, and asked what had happened.

Havard said, 'There's a man in the woods. Many such boulders have been cast down here tonight.'

'That must have been Gisli,' said Helgi, 'and he must know we're here. You must surely realize, my friend, that every bone in our bodies would have been smashed to pieces if that rock had hit us. There's nothing else to do but get out of here as quickly as possible.'

Then Helgi ran as fast as he could, and Havard went after him and asked him not to run so far ahead. But Helgi took no notice and ran as fast as his feet would carry him. Finally, they both reached the boat, jumped into it and rowed hard without pause until they came to Otradal. Helgi said that he now knew of Gisli's whereabouts.

Eyjolf acted quickly. He left immediately with eleven men – Helgi and Havard among them – and journeyed until they came to Geirthjofsfjord. They scanned the whole wood for the cairn and Gisli's hideout, but found neither. Then Eyjolf asked Havard where they had built the cairn.

He answered, 'I couldn't tell you. Not only was I so tired that I hardly knew what was going on around me, but it was Helgi who finished building the cairn while I slept. I think Gisli must have been aware of us being there, then taken the cairn apart when it was light and we were gone.'

Then Eyjolf said, 'Fortune is not with us in this matter, so we will turn back.'

And they did just that. But first Eyjolf wanted to go and see Aud. They reached the farmhouse and went in, where Eyjolf sat down to talk to Aud, and these were his words – 'I want to make a deal with you, Aud,' he said. 'You tell me where Gisli is and I will give you three hundred pieces of silver, which I have received as the price on his head, and you will not be present when we take his life. In addition, I will arrange a marriage for you that will be superior in every way to this one. And you must consider,' he said, 'how impractical it would be for you to linger in this deserted fjord and suffer from Gisli's ill fortune, never seeing your family and kinfolk again.'

This was her reply: 'I don't expect,' she said, 'that we'll reach agreement on your ability to find me as good a match as this one. Yet, it's true what they say, "death's best consolation is wealth", so let me see whether this silver is as plentiful or as fine as you say.'

So he poured the silver into her lap, and she held it there while he counted it and showed her its value.

Gudrid, her foster-daughter, began to cry.

32 | Then Gudrid went to meet Gisli and told him, 'My foster-mother has lost her senses and means to betray you.'

Gisli said, 'Think only good thoughts, for my death will never be the result of Aud's treachery.'

Then he spoke a verse:

27.

The sea-elk riders claim                    *sea-elk* (ship) *riders*: seafarers
the mead-goddess has sold                    *mead-goddess*: Gisli's wife
her man, with a mind
deep and treacherous as the sea.
But I know the land
of gold sits and weeps.                      *land of gold*: woman
I do not think this true
of the proud sea-flame's wearer.    *sea-flame*: gold; its *wearer*: woman

After that the girl went home, but did not say where she had been. By that time Eyjolf had counted all the silver.

Aud spoke: 'By no means is this silver any less or worse than you have said. And now you must agree that I may do with it whatever I choose.'

Eyjolf gladly agreed, and told her that, of course, she might do as she wished with it. Aud took the silver and put it in a large purse, then she stood up and struck Eyjolf on the nose, and blood spurted all over him.

'Take that for your gullibility,' she said, 'and all the harm that ensues from it. There was never any hope that I would render my husband into your hands, you evil man. Take this now for your cowardice and your shame, and remember, you wretch, for as long as you live, that a woman has struck you. And you will not get what you desire, either.'

Then Eyjolf said, 'Seize the cur and kill it, though it be a bitch.'

Then Havard spoke. 'Our expedition has gone badly enough without this disgraceful deed. Stand up to him, men. Don't let him do this.'

Eyjolf said, 'The old saying is true, "the treachery of a friend is worse than that of a foe".'

Havard was a popular man, and many of the party were ready to show him their support, as well as to prevent Eyjolf from carrying out this disgraceful act. So Eyjolf conceded to them and having done that he left.

But before Havard left, Aud spoke to him: 'It would be wrong to hold back the debt that Gisli owes you. Here is a gold ring I want you to have.'

'But it is not a debt I was looking to recover,' said Havard.

'Even so,' said Aud, 'I want to pay you back.'

Actually, she gave him the gold ring for his help.

Havard got himself a horse and rode south to Gest Oddleifs-son at Bardastrond, for he had no desire to remain any longer with Eyjolf. Eyjolf went back home to Otradal, and was thoroughly displeased with the outcome of his journey, especially since most people regarded it as disgraceful.

33 | As the summer wore on, Gisli stayed in his underground hideout and was very much on his guard. He had no intention of leaving and, besides, he felt that no other refuge was left him since the tally of years in his dreams had now passed away.

It happened that one summer night Gisli once again had a very fitful and restless sleep, and when he awoke Aud asked him what he had dreamed.

He told her that the bad dream-woman had come to him and said, 'Now I will destroy everything that the good dream-woman has said to you, and I will make certain that nothing comes of what she has promised.' Then Gisli spoke a verse:

28.
'Never shall the two of you
abide together. Your great love
will slowly turn to poison
and become sorrow,'
said the woman.
'He who rules all has sent you
alone from your house
to explore the other world.'

'Then in a second dream,' he said, 'this woman came to me and tied a blood-stained cap on my head, and before that she bathed my head in blood and poured it all over me, covering me in gore.'

And he spoke a verse:

29.
I dreamed a dream of her,
goddess of riches.                              *goddess of riches*: woman
She washed my hair in foam of          foam of *Odin's fires* (swords):
    Odin's fires                                                        blood
spilled from the well of swords.            *well of swords*: wound
And it seemed to me that
the bearer of hand-flame                   *bearer of hand-flame* (gold)
was blood-red from the wound-blizzard
of the fire-breaker of wrists.          *fire-breaker of wrists*: warrior

Then he spoke another verse:

30.
I thought I felt how
the valkyrie's hands,
dripping with sword-rain,                         *sword-rain*: blood
placed a bloody cap
upon my thickly grown,
straight-cut locks of hair.
That is how the thread-goddess          *thread-goddess*: woman
woke me from my dream.

Gisli began to have so many dreams that he became very
frightened of the dark and dared not be alone any longer.
Whenever he closed his eyes, he saw the same woman. On
yet another night, Gisli slept badly and Aud asked him what
happened to him in his dream.

'I dreamed,' said Gisli, 'that some men came upon us. Eyjolf
was among them and many others. We confronted each other,
and I know there was an exchange of blows between us. One of
them came first, really howling, and I think I must have cut him
in two at the waist. I thought he had the head of a wolf. Then
many others attacked me. I felt I had my shield in my hand and
that I fought them off for a long while.'

Then Gisli spoke a verse:

31.
My foes sought me out,
swinging their swords,
but I did not fall then.
I was outnumbered,
yet I fed the raven's maw.                    *fed the raven's maw*: killed men
But your white bosom
was reddened and steeped
in my crimson blood.

Then he spoke another:

32.
They could not mar my shield
with their resounding blows.
It protected the poet well.
I had courage enough,
but they were too many
and I was overcome,
swords singing loud
in the air around me.

And then another:

33.
I brought down one of them
before raven-feeders wounded me,        *raven-feeders*: warriors
I fed his corpse to the blood-hawk.          *blood-hawk*: raven
My sword's edge swung and cut
its way through his thighs
slicing his legs in twain.
His sudden fall beneath me
added to my greater glory.

Now autumn drew near, but Gisli's dreams did not ease;
indeed, they grew more frequent. One night, after he had slept
badly, Aud asked him again what had appeared to him. Gisli
spoke a verse:

34.
I felt my life's blood run
down both my sides.
I must bear this wound-flood bravely.
Goddess decked in gold,
these are the dreams
that trouble my sleep.
I am an outlaw to most men;
only arrow-storms await me.                    *arrow-storms*: battle

And then he spoke another:

35.
I felt my blood spilled
over my arched shoulders
by a corpse-net's wielder                      *corpse-net*: shield
with his sharp sword.
Wearer of golden rings,                        *wearer of golden rings*: woman,
my hopes of life were meagre                                   Gisli's wife
from that raven-feeder's fury;                 *raven-feeder*: warrior
herb-goddess, such was my solace.              *herb-goddess*: woman

And then another:

36.
I felt the shakers of shield-trolls            *shakers of shield-trolls*:
shear off both my hands                                      warriors
with their weapons.
I was mortally wounded.
Then I felt the edge slice
my helmet-stump and split it.                  *helmet-stump*: head
Thread-goddess, weapons hovered
above my head, threateningly.

And yet again:

37.
I felt, as I slept, that above me
stood silver-banded Sjöfn.                     *silver-banded Sjöfn*: woman
Her brow was wet, the eyes
of that bonnet-goddess were weeping.           *bonnet-goddess*: woman

And that fire-goddess of wave              *fire-goddess of wave*: woman
soon bound up my wounds.
What message, think you,
has this dream for me?

34 | Gisli stayed home that summer, and all was quiet. Then,
     | on the last night of summer, Gisli could not sleep and
neither could the other two, Aud and Gudrid.

It was the kind of weather where the air is very still, but there
was also a heavy frost. Then Gisli said he wanted to leave the
house and head south to his hideout under the ridge, to see if he
could get some sleep there. All three of them went. The women
were wearing tunics and they trailed along in the frozen dew.
Gisli had a piece of wood, on which he scored runes, and as he
did so the shavings fell to the ground.

They arrived at the hideout and Gisli lay down to see if he
could sleep, while the women stayed awake. A heavy drowsiness
came upon him and he dreamed that some loon birds, larger
than cock ptarmigans, came to the house. They screamed hor-
ribly and had been wallowing in blood and gore.

Then Aud asked what he dreamed.

'Yet again, my dreams were not good,' said Gisli, and he
spoke a verse:

38.

When we parted, flax-goddess,              *flax-goddess*: woman (Gisli's wife)
my ears rang with a sound
from my blood-hall's realm                 *blood-hall*: heart; its *realm*: the mind
– and I poured the dwarves'                *poured the dwarves' brew*:
     brew.                                  composed a verse (about this)
I, tree of the sword's din,                *tree of the sword's din*: warrior
heard two loon birds fighting
and I knew that soon the dew
of bows would be descending.   *dew of bows*: showers of arrows, battle

At the same moment, they heard men's voices – Eyjolf had
arrived with fourteen others. They had been to the farmhouse
and seen the trail in the frozen dew, as if it was pointing the

way. When Gisli and the two women became aware of the intruders, they climbed up on to the ridge where their vantage point was the best. Each of the women held a large club. Eyjolf and the others had come to the bottom of the ridge.

Then Eyjolf said to Gisli, 'I advise you to retreat no farther. Don't have yourself chased like a coward. You are said to have great courage. We have not met too often, but I'd prefer this encounter to be our last.'

Gisli answered him, 'Then attack like a man, and you may be sure I will retreat no farther. And you should lead the attack, since you bear a greater grudge than the men who come with you.'

'I won't have you decide,' said Eyjolf, 'how I deploy my men.'

'It comes as no surprise,' said Gisli, 'that a coward such as you would not dare to cross weapons with me.'

Then Eyjolf said to Helgi the Spy, 'You would win great acclaim if you were the first to climb the ridge and attack Gisli – a deed of heroism that would long be remembered.'

'I've often noticed,' said Helgi, 'that you usually want other people in front of you when there's any danger. Since you urge me so profoundly, I'll attempt it, but you must show enough courage to come with me and keep close behind – that is, if you're not a completely toothless bitch.'

Helgi found what seemed the best way up, and he carried a large axe in his hand. Gisli was also armed with an axe, and had a sword and shield at his side. He wore a grey cloak, which he had tied with a cord. Helgi made a sudden dash and ran up the slope at Gisli. Gisli turned and swung his sword, striking Helgi in the loins and cutting him asunder so that both halves of his body fell back off the edge of the ridge. Eyjolf made his way up in a different place, where he was confronted by Aud, and she struck him with her club so hard on the arm that it took away all his strength, and he staggered back down.

Then Gisli said, 'I knew long ago that I had married well, but never realized till now that the match was as good as this. Yet the help you gave me now was less than you wished or than you intended, even though the blow was good, for I might have dispatched them both in the same way.'

35 | Then two men went to grab hold of Aud and Gudrid, but
     | found the task was not so easy. Twelve men went for Gisli,
and made their way up on to the ridge. He fought them off with
rocks and weapons so well that his stand became famous.

Then one of Eyjolf's companions ran up to Gisli and said,
'Lay down your fine weapons and give them all to me – and give
me your wife, Aud, too.'

Gisli answered him, 'Then show your courage, because
neither befits you – neither my weapons nor my wife.'

The man thrust out at Gisli with a spear, and Gisli struck
back, shearing the head from the shaft. But the blow was so
fierce that his axe smashed against the rocky ground and the
blade broke off. He threw it down and took up his sword
instead, fighting on and guarding himself with his shield.

Then they launched a spirited attack, but Gisli defended
himself well and with great courage. It was a hard and closely
fought fight in which Gisli slew two more men, bringing the
tally now to four.

Eyjolf ordered them to attack as boldly as they could.

'We're having a hard time of it,' he said, 'but that will not
matter if we are rewarded for our efforts.'

Then, when it was least expected, Gisli turned around and
ran from the ridge up on to the crag known as Einhamar.
There, he faced them and defended himself. This caught them
completely off-guard, and they felt their position had worsened
considerably. Four of them were dead, and the rest were
wounded and weary, so they held off their attack for a while.
Then Eyjolf urged them on harder than ever, promising them
substantial reward if they defeated Gisli. Eyjolf had with him a
group of men of outstanding strength and hardiness.

36 | A man named Svein was the first to attack Gisli, but Gisli
     | struck at him, cleft him through the shoulder-blades and
threw him off the edge of the crag. The others began to wonder
where this man's capacity for slaughter was going to end.

Then Gisli said to Eyjolf, 'May the three hundred pieces of silver that you have received for my life be dearly earned, and may you wish that you had added another three hundred for us never to have met. On your head will fall the shame for this great slaughter.'

They looked for a plan – none among them would flee to save his own life. So they went at him in two flanks, and heading the attack with Eyjolf were two of his kinsmen, Thorir and Thord. Both were excellent fighters. The battle was fierce and they succeeded in wounding Gisli in several places with their spears, but he defended himself with great courage and strength, and they faced such an onslaught of rocks and powerful blows that none escaped being wounded. When Gisli struck out he never missed. Now Eyjolf and his kinsmen saw that their names and their honour were at stake, and they attacked harder than ever, thrusting at him with their spears until his guts spilled out. Gisli gathered them up together in his shirt and bound them underneath with the cord.

Then he told them to hold off a while. 'The end you wanted will come,' he said.

Then he spoke a verse:

39.
Goddess of golden rain,
who gives me great joy,
may boldly hear report
of her friend's brave stand.
I greet the sword's honed edge
that bites into my flesh,
knowing that this courage
was given me by my father.

This was Gisli's last verse. As soon as he had spoken it, he jumped off the crag and drove his sword into the head of Eyjolf's kinsman, Thord, and split him down to the waist. In doing so, Gisli fell down on top of him and breathed his last.

Everyone in Eyjolf's party was badly wounded, and Gisli had died with so many and such great wounds that it was an amazement to all. They say that he never once retreated, and as far as anyone could see his last blow was no weaker than his first.

Thus Gisli's life came to an end, and although he was deemed a man of great prowess, fortune was not always with him.

The men dragged his body down and took his sword from him. Then they covered him over with stones and went down to the sea. Then a sixth man died on the shore. Eyjolf invited Aud to accompany him, but she did not want to go. After that, Eyjolf and the remaining men returned to Otradal, and that same night a seventh man died. An eighth died after being bedridden with his wounds for a year, and although the other wounded men recovered they gained nothing but dishonour.

And it is said everywhere that no man in this land had ever been known to put up a greater stand than Gisli.

37 | Eyjolf set out from his home with eleven men and went south to meet Bork the Stout. He told him the news and gave a full account of what had happened. Bork was greatly pleased by this, and he asked Thordis to give Eyjolf a warm welcome.

'Remember,' he said, 'the great love you bore my brother Thorgrim and treat Eyjolf well.'

'I weep for my brother Gisli,' said Thordis. 'Would not a good bowl of gruel be warm enough a welcome for Eyjolf?'

And later in the evening, when she brought in the food, she dropped a tray of spoons. Eyjolf had laid Gisli's sword between the bench and his feet, and Thordis recognized it. When she bent down to pick up the spoons, she grabbed the sword by the hilt and thrust out at Eyjolf, meaning to strike him in the guts. But she had not noticed that the end of the hilt was turned upwards, and it caught against the table. She had struck him lower than she intended, hit him in the thigh and wounded him sorely.

Bork grabbed hold of Thordis and wrenched the sword away from her, and the others all jumped to their feet and overturned the tables and the food. Bork left it in Eyjolf's hands to decide the penalty for this deed, and he claimed full compensation –

the same as was imposed for slaying a man – and said he would have demanded more if Bork had handled this matter less fittingly.

Then Thordis named witnesses and declared herself divorced from Bork, saying that she would never again share his bed – and she stood by her word. She left and went to live at Thordisarstadir, out at Eyri. Bork, however, remained at Helgafell until Snorri the Godi drove him out.[32] After that he went to live at Glerarskogar. Eyjolf went home and was greatly displeased with his visit.

38 | Vestein's sons went to Gest Oddleifsson, their kinsman, and urged him to use his power to get them out of the country along with their mother Gunnhild, Gisli's wife Aud, Ingjald's daughter Gudrid and Geirmund her brother. They all went to the Hvita river and Gest paid for their passage abroad.

They were only at sea for a short time before they reached Norway. Berg and the other two men walked around town and tried to find a place to lodge. They met two men, one of whom was a young, well-built lad, dressed in fine red clothes. He asked Berg his name, and Berg told him his true identity and kin since he expected to gain more by using his father's name. The man in red pulled out his sword and dealt Berg a death-blow on the spot. He was Ari Sursson, brother to Gisli and Thorkel.

Berg's companions went back to the ship and told what had happened, and the skipper helped them escape, finding a place for Helgi[33] on board a ship bound for Greenland. Helgi arrived in that country, became prosperous and was held in great esteem there. Some men were sent out to kill him, but nothing came of it. He eventually died on a hunting expedition, and this was considered a great loss.

Aud and Gunnhild went to Hedeby[34] in Denmark, took the Christian faith and then went on a pilgrimage to Rome. They never returned.

Geirmund remained in Norway, married and prospered there. Gudrid, his sister, also married and was thought to be a woman of wisdom. Many can be counted as her descendants.

Ari Sursson went to Iceland and came ashore at Hvita river. He sold his ship and bought himself some land at Hamar, where he lived for several years. After that he lived in several other places in Myrar, and had many descendants.

And here ends the saga of Gisli Sursson.

*Translated by* MARTIN S. REGAL

# THE SAGA OF THE
# PEOPLE OF EYRI

1 | There was a man named Ketil Flat-nose[1] who was an excellent hersir in Norway. He was the son of Bjorn Buna, and the grandson of Grim, a hersir from Sogn. Ketil was married to Yngvild, the daughter of Ketil the Ram, a hersir from Raumarike. Their sons were named Bjorn and Helgi, and their daughters Aud the Deep-Minded, Thorunn Hyrna and Jorunn Manvitsbrekka. Ketil's son Bjorn was fostered in the east in Jamtland by Earl Kjallak who was a wise and excellent man. The earl also had a son named Bjorn as well as a daughter named Gjaflaug.

This was at the time when King Harald Fair-hair came to power in Norway. Because of hostilities, many distinguished men fled their ancestral lands in Norway, some east across the Kjolen mountains, and some west across the sea. Some of these men spent the winters in the Hebrides or the Orkney Islands and in summer returned to plunder Norway, causing great damage in Harald's realm. The farmers there complained to the king about this and appealed to him to protect them from hostilities.

The king responded by preparing an army to set out for the west and he summoned Ketil Flat-nose as the army's leader. Ketil tried to get out of it but the king insisted he go. When he realized how determined the king was, Ketil set out on the journey, taking his wife with him and those children who were at home. On his arrival in the west he fought several battles and always had victory. He took over the Hebrides and became the leader there, making settlements with the most powerful of the leaders in the Western Isles and forming strong alliances with them. He sent his army back east to Norway, and when they returned to King Harald they announced that Ketil Flat-nose was the leader of the Hebrides but that they were not certain whether he had extended Harald's realm into the Western Isles. When the king heard this, he confiscated Ketil's estates in Norway.

Ketil Flat-nose married his daughter Aud to Olaf the White, who was at that time the greatest warlord in the Western Isles. He was the son of Ingjald Helgason, whose mother, Thora, was the daughter of Sigurd Snake-in-the-eye, and the grandson of Ragnar Shaggy-breeches. Ketil married Thorunn Hyrna to Helgi the Lean, who was the son of Eyvind the Easterner and Rafarta, the daughter of King Kjarval of Ireland.

2 | Ketil Flat-nose's son Bjorn lived in Jamtland up until the time Earl Kjallak died. He married the earl's daughter, Gjaflaug, and then moved west over the Kjolen mountains, first to Trondheim and then south to reclaim his father's estates and drive away the agents King Harald had appointed there. King Harald was in Vik when he heard this news, and he travelled immediately to Trondheim by the highland route. On his arrival he called an assembly of eight provinces and there he declared Bjorn Ketilsson an outlaw in Norway, which meant he could be seized and killed wherever he was found. The king sent Hauk High-breeches and some other warriors to kill Bjorn if they could find him. When they arrived south in Stadir, Bjorn's friends found out about their mission and warned him about it.

Bjorn boarded a skiff he owned, taking his household and goods with him, and sailed south along the coast of Norway because it was then the depths of winter and he did not trust the open sea. He sailed until he came to the island of Moster, which lies off southern Hordaland, and there he was received by a man named Hrolf, the son of Ornolf Fish-driver. Bjorn stayed there in hiding with him for the rest of the winter. The king's men turned back once they had taken over Bjorn's estates and placed men in charge of them.

3 | Hrolf was a prominent chieftain and a man of great lar-
  | gesse. He maintained a temple to Thor on the island and
was a great friend of Thor's. It was because of this that he was
known as Thorolf. He was a big man, handsome and strong
and he sported a huge beard, which led to him being nicknamed
Moster-beard. He was the most eminent man on the island.

In the spring Thorolf gave Bjorn a good longship and provided
him with a good crew, including his own son, Hallstein, to
accompany him on his westward journey to visit his kinsmen.
But when King Harald heard the news that Thorolf Moster-
beard had sheltered the outlaw Bjorn Ketilsson, he sent men to
order him off his lands and he threatened to make him an
outlaw like his friend Bjorn unless he came before the king and
submitted himself entirely to him.

This happened ten years after Ingolf Arnarson[2] had left to
settle in Iceland and his journey had become very famous,
because men who returned from Iceland spoke of the good
quality of the land.


4 | Thorolf Moster-beard held a great sacrificial feast during
  | which he consulted his dear friend Thor about whether he
should reconcile himself with the king or leave the country and
seek another fate. The oracle directed Thorolf to Iceland. He
got himself an ocean-going ship and prepared it for the journey
to Iceland, taking with him his household and all his goods.
Many of his friends decided to go on the journey with him. He
dismantled the temple and transported most of its timbers,
together with the earth from underneath the pedestal on which
Thor had been placed.

Thorolf then sailed out to sea with a fair wind and came
within sight of land, sailing then west along the southern coast
and around cape Reykjanes. The wind dropped and they could
see on the shore where broad fjords cut into the land. Thorolf
cast overboard the high-seat pillars which had been in his
temple, one of which had Thor carved on it. Thorolf declared
that he would settle in Iceland in whatever place Thor directed

the pillars to land. As soon as the pillars were thrown overboard, they were swept towards the more westerly of the fjords and seemed to travel faster than might be expected.

A sea breeze then sprang up and they sailed west around the headland of Snaefellsnes and into the fjord. They saw that the fjord was extremely broad and long and that it was bordered on both sides by high mountains. Thorolf named the fjord Breidafjord (Broad Fjord). He put in to land halfway along the southern shore of the fjord and anchored his ship in a cove there, which has since been named Hofsvog. After that they explored the area and found that Thor and the pillars were already ashore at the tip of the headland north of the cove. The headland has been named Thorsnes ever since.

Then Thorolf carried fire around his land-claim,[3] from the Stafa river as far as the river he named Thorsa (Thor's river). He established settlements for his crew and set up a large farm by the cove, Hofsvog, which he named Hofstadir. There he had a temple built,[4] and it was a sizeable building, with a door on the side-wall near the gable. The high-seat pillars were placed inside the door, and nails, that were called holy nails, were driven into them. Beyond that point, the temple was a sanctuary. At the inner end there was a structure similar to the choir in churches nowadays and there was a raised platform in the middle of the floor like an altar, where a ring weighing twenty ounces and fashioned without a join was placed, and all oaths had to be sworn on this ring. It also had to be worn by the temple priest at all public gatherings. A sacrificial bowl was placed on the platform and in it a sacrificial twig – like a priest's aspergillum – which was used to sprinkle blood from the bowl. This blood, which was called sacrificial blood, was the blood of live animals offered to the gods. The gods were placed around the platform in the choir-like structure within the temple. All farmers had to pay a toll to the temple and they were obliged to support the temple godi in all his campaigns, just as thingmen are now obliged to do for their chieftain. The temple godi was responsible for the upkeep of the temple and ensuring it was maintained properly, as well as for holding sacrificial feasts in it.

Thorolf named the headland between Vigrafjord and Hofsvog Thorsnes. The headland is in the form of a mountain, and Thorolf invested so much reverence in it that no one was allowed to look towards it without having washed and nothing was allowed to be killed on the mountain, neither man nor animal, unless it died of natural causes. He named this mountain Helgafell and believed that he and all his family on the headland would go there when they died. At the place where Thor had come ashore, on the point of the headland, Thorolf held all court sessions and he established a district assembly there. He considered the ground there so sacred that he would not allow it to be defiled in any way, either by blood spilt in rage, or by anybody doing their elf-frighteners[5] there – there was a skerry named Dritsker (Shit-Skerry) for that purpose.

Thorolf became a splendid farmer and kept a large household, since at the time there was plenty of food to be had from the islands and from the sea.

5 | The story now turns to Bjorn, the son of Ketil Flat-nose, who sailed west across the sea to the Hebrides after parting with Thorolf Moster-beard, as was told earlier. By the time he arrived there his father Ketil had died, but he was met by his brother Helgi and his sisters who invited him to share their prosperity. Bjorn became aware that they now practised a different religion, and he found it degrading that they had rejected the traditional faith their ancestors had revered. He therefore could not find much pleasure in the place and did not want to settle there. Still, he did spend the winter with his sister Aud and her son Thorstein.[6] But when they discovered that he was not receptive to his family's ideas, they named him Bjorn the Easterner and took a dim view of his reluctance to settle there.

6 | Bjorn stayed in the Hebrides for two winters before he made his journey to Iceland, accompanied by Hallstein Thorolfs-son. They arrived in Breidafjord and following Thorolf's advice, Bjorn settled the land between Stafa river and Hraunsfjord,

establishing his home at Borgarholt in Bjarnarhofn.[7] He was an eminent man in the district.

Hallstein Thorolfsson thought it was beneath him to accept land from his father and travelled west across Breidafjord and took land there, making his home at Hallsteinsnes.

A few years later Aud the Deep-Minded came out to Iceland and spent her first winter with her brother Bjorn. She then took all the land in the valley in Breidafjord, between the Skraumuhlaupsa and Dagverdara rivers, and lived at Hvamm. All of Breidafjord was settled at this time but settlers who take no part in this saga do not need to be mentioned here.

7 | A man named Geirrod settled the land from the Thorsa river to Langidal and lived at Eyri. He travelled to Iceland with Ulfar the Champion, to whom he gave land round Ulfarsfell, and Finngeir, the son of Thorstein Ondur. Finngeir lived at Alftafjord, and his son was Thorfinn, the father of Thorbrand of Alftafjord. Another man, Vestar, who was the son of Thorolf Blister-pate, came to Iceland with his elderly father and settled the land west of Urthvalafjord and lived at Ondurdareyri. His son, Asgeir, lived there after him.

Bjorn the Easterner was the first of these settlers to die, and he was buried in a mound at Borgarlaek. He was survived by two sons. One of them was Kjallak the Old who lived at Bjarnarhofn after his father. He married Astrid, who was the daughter of Hrolf the hersir and the sister of Steinolf the Short, and they had three children. Their son was Thorgrim the Godi and their daughter Gerd was married to Thormod the Godi, the son of Odd the Bold. Their third child, Helga, was married to Asgeir of Eyri. From the children of Kjallak a large family is descended, and they are known as the Kjalleklings. Bjorn's other son was named Ottar, and he married Groa, the daughter of Geirleif and the sister of Oddleif of Bardastrond. Their sons were Helgi, the father of Osvif the Wise, and Bjorn, the father of Vigfus of Drapuhlid. Vilgeir was the third son of Ottar Bjarnarson.

In his old age, Thorolf Moster-beard married a woman named

Unn. Some people say she was the daughter of Thorstein the Red, but Ari Thorgilsson the Learned does not count her among his children.[8] Thorolf and Unn had a son named Stein, whom Thorolf dedicated to his friend Thor, calling him Thorstein. The boy matured very quickly. Hallstein Thorolfsson married Osk, the daughter of Thorstein the Red. Their son was also named Thorstein and he was fostered by Thorolf. Thorolf called him Thorstein Surt (Black), and his own son Thorstein Cod-biter.

8 | At this time Geirrid, the sister of Geirrod of Eyri, came out to Iceland and Geirrod gave her a farm in Borgardal, an inland valley of Alftafjord. She had her hall built across the public path and insisted that all travellers pass through there. She always kept a table laden with food, which was freely offered to anyone who wanted it. Because of this, she was thought of as the most generous of women.

Geirrid had been married to Bjorn, the son of Bolverk Blind-pout, and their son was named Thorolf. He was a zealous Viking. He arrived in Iceland sometime after his mother and stayed with her for the first winter. Thorolf considered his mother's land inadequate and challenged Ulfar the Champion for his land, inviting him to a duel because Ulfar was old and childless. Ulfar would rather have died than be cowed by Thorolf. They fought a duel in Alftafjord and Ulfar was killed, but Thorolf was wounded in the leg and always walked with a limp after that. He became known as Lame-foot because of it.

Thorolf established a farm at Hvamm in Thorsardal. He took over Ulfar's lands and was a great troublemaker. He sold land to slaves freed by Thorbrand of Alftafjord: Ulfarsfell to Ulfar and Orlygsstadir to Orlyg and they lived there for a long time. Thorolf Lame-foot had three children. Arnkel was the name of his son and Gunnfrid his daughter, who was married to Thorbeinir of Thorbeinisstadir at Vatnshals, east of Drapuhlid. Their sons were Sigmund and Thorgils, and his daughter, Thorgerd, was married to Vigfus of Drapuhlid. Thorolf Lame-foot's other daughter was named Geirrid, and she was married to Thorolf, the son of Herjolf Holkinrassi. They lived at

Mavahlid and their children were Thorarin the Black and
Gudny.

9 | Thorolf Moster-beard died at Hofstadir. His son,
Thorstein Cod-biter, inherited the farm and married
Thora, the daughter of Olaf Feilan and the sister of Thord
Bellower[9] who then lived at Hvamm. Thorolf Moster-beard was
buried in a mound at Haugsnes west of Hofstadir.

At that time the Kjalleklings were so fiercely arrogant that
they believed themselves to be better than other men in the
district. What's more, Bjorn's relatives outnumbered any other
family in Breidafjord. One of the relatives, Barna-Kjallak, lived
at that time on Medalfellsstrond, which is now called Kjal-
laksstadir. He had many sons and they were all accomplished,
and they offered support to their relatives south of the fjord at
assemblies and meetings.

One spring at the Thorsnes Assembly Thorgrim Kjallaksson
and his brother-in-law, Asgeir of Eyri, declared that they would
not put up with the arrogance of the people of Thorsnes any
longer and that they would relieve themselves on the grass, as
they usually did at meetings, even though the people of Thorsnes
were so proud that they claimed their land was more sacred
than any other land in Breidafjord. They announced that they
did not intend to wear out their shoes by walking out on to a
skerry to do their elf-frighteners.

When Thorstein Cod-biter got word of this he was in no mind
to allow them to defile the ground that his father Thorolf had
worshipped above all other parts of his estate. He summoned
his friends and intended to defend the ground by force if they
proposed to defile it. He was supported in his plan by Thorgeir
Keng, the son of Geirrod of Eyri, and the people of Alftafjord,
Thorfinn and his son Thorbrand, Thorolf Lame-foot and many
others of Thorstein's thingmen and friends.

In the evening when the Kjalleklings had finished eating they
took their weapons and walked out on to the headland. But
when Thorstein and his men saw them turning off the trail
which led to the skerry, they leapt up with their weapons and

ran after them with shouts and challenges. When the Kjalleklings saw this they grouped together to defend themselves, but the attack by the people of Thorsnes was so fierce that the Kjalleklings lost ground and were driven down on to the beach. Then they retaliated and a very hard battle was fought between them. The Kjalleklings were fewer but they were a select band.

When the people from Skogarstrond, Thorgest the Old and Aslak of Langidal, became aware of the fight, they ran to intervene between the sides, but each side was as furious as the other and Thorgest and Aslak were unable to separate them until they threatened to support whichever side would listen to their arguments. With this the two sides separated, but in such a way that the Kjalleklings were not able to go back to the assembly ground and so boarded their ship and sailed away from the assembly. Men had been killed on both sides, but more on the Kjalleklings' side, and many had been wounded. A truce was impossible because neither party would make any concessions and both threatened retaliation at the first opportunity. Where they had fought the ground was covered in blood – there where the people of Thorsnes had stood in battle.


10 | After the assembly both sides kept forces at the ready, and the hostility between them was intense. Their friends made the decision to send for Thord Bellower who was at that time the most prominent chieftain in Breidafjord. He was a blood relation of the Kjalleklings but also related by marriage to Thorstein. He was thought to be the most likely one to be able to reconcile them. As soon as Thord received this request he set out with a large number of men to try to bring about a settlement. He found their differences to be great but nevertheless he managed to arrange a truce and a peace meeting between them. The eventual resolution of the case was that Thord was to arbitrate between them, taking into account the Kjalleklings' stipulation that they would never go out and use Dritsker and Thorstein's insistence that the Kjalleklings not be allowed to defile the ground now any more than before. The Kjalleklings declared all of Thorstein's men who had died in the battle to be

beyond the protection of the law because of their premeditated intention to fight. But the people of Thorsnes claimed all the Kjalleklings beyond the protection of the law on account of the breach of law they had committed at a sacred assembly. In spite of the difficulties in the case, Thord agreed to arbitrate rather than have them part on feuding terms.

Thord began the settlement by stating that the gains of each side should be preserved: he declared that no compensation should be paid for the killings or bloody wounds which had been caused at Thorsnes and he argued that since the ground had been defiled by blood spilt in rage, the earth could no longer be considered more sacred there than anywhere else. Furthermore, he identified those at fault as those who first caused bloody wounds to others, declaring it to have been a disturbance of the peace, and he announced that no more assemblies would be held there any more. In order that they might be reconciled and become friends from then on he con- cluded that Thorgrim Kjallaksson should bear half the cost of maintaining the temple and likewise get half the temple-toll and half the thingmen. Thorgrim also had to back Thorstein in all his lawsuits from then on and support him in keeping the assembly site sacred wherever it was next established. This done, Thord Bellower married his niece, Thorhild, daughter of his neighbour Thorkel Meinak, to Thorgrim Kjallaksson. From then on Thorgrim was called Thorgrim the Godi.

They moved the assembly farther up the headland to where it is now held. When Thord Bellower established the Quarter Assemblies he made it the site for the West Fjords Quarter Assembly, at which men from all over the West Fjords would meet. It is still possible to see the judgement circle in which men were sentenced to be sacrificed. Within the ring stands Thor's stone, across which men's backs were broken when they were sacrificed, and the stain of blood can still be seen on the stone. The site of the assembly was the holiest of places, but it was not forbidden to relieve oneself there.

11 | Thorstein Cod-biter became a very prosperous man and always kept sixty freed slaves with him. He was a responsible provider and often went out fishing. The first farm he had built was at Helgafell, where he moved his household and established a temple that was the greatest temple of its day. He also had a farm built on the headland, near the site of the first assembly. This farm was built with the greatest attention to detail and when it was ready he gave it to his cousin, Thorstein Surt (Black), who lived there after that and he became a particularly wise man.

Thorstein Cod-biter had a son who was called Bork the Stout.[10] In the summer of Thorstein's twenty-fifth year his wife Thora gave birth to a boy who was named Grim and sprinkled with water. Thorstein dedicated this child to Thor and declared that he would be a temple godi and named him Thorgrim. The following autumn Thorstein went out to Hoskuldsey island for provisions.

One evening that autumn Thorstein's shepherd was rounding up his sheep north of Helgafell when he saw the northern side of the mountain open up. He saw great fires burning inside and heard the sound of feasting and good cheer. When he listened closely in order to hear what was being said, he heard that Thorstein Cod-biter and his men were being welcomed there and that Thorstein was being told to sit in the high seat opposite his father. The shepherd reported this apparition to Thorstein's wife, Thora, that same evening. She appeared indifferent to the account and said it may well be a foreboding of much graver tidings. The following morning men came ashore from Hoskuldsey with the news that Thorstein Cod-biter had drowned while fishing. Everyone considered this a great loss. Thora kept the farm and hired a man named Hallvard to help her. They had a son named Mar.

12 | The sons of Thorstein Cod-biter grew up with their mother
     and were promising young men, though Thorgrim was
ahead of his brother in all things and became a temple godi as
soon as he was old enough. Thorgrim married Thordis Sursdottir in Dyrafjord,[11] and moved west to live with his brothers-
in-law Gisli and Thorkel. Thorgrim killed Vestein Vesteinsson
during an autumn feast in Haukadal. The following autumn
when Thorgrim was twenty-five, the same age his father had
been when he died, his brother-in-law Gisli killed him during
an autumn feast at Saebol. A few nights later his wife Thordis
gave birth to a child. It was a boy and was named Thorgrim
after his father.

A little later Thordis married Thorgrim's brother, Bork the
Stout, and moved in with him at Helgafell. Her son Thorgrim
was fostered by Thorbrand at Alftafjord. He was an unruly
child and was therefore called Snerrir (Twist) and later Snorri.

Thorbrand of Alftafjord married Thurid, the daughter of
Thorfinn Seal-Thorisson from Raudamel. Their children were
Thorleif Kimbi, who was the eldest, then Snorri, Thorodd was
the third, the fourth was Thorfinn, the fifth Thormod and their
daughter was named Thorgerd. They were all blood-brothers
of Snorri Thorgrimsson.

At that time Arnkel, Thorolf Lame-foot's son, lived at Bolstad
near Vadilshofdi. He was the biggest and strongest of men, a
knowledgeable lawman and very clever. He was a man of sound
character and surpassed other men in that part of the country
in both popularity and valour. He was also a temple godi and
had many thingmen.

Thorgrim Kjallaksson lived at Bjarnarhofn, as was told
earlier, and he and Thorhild had three sons. Brand, the eldest,
lived in Krossnes near Brimlarhofdi. The second was Arngrim.
He was a tall, strong man with a large-boned face and a prominent nose. He had light red hair with a prematurely receding
hairline, shaggy eyebrows and large, well-shaped eyes. He had
a wild temper and was very unjust and because of this he
was called Styr. Vermund was the youngest of Thorgrim

Kjallaksson's sons. He was a tall man, lean and handsome. He was called Vermund the Slender.

Asgeir of Eyri's son was named Thorlak and he married Thurid, the daughter of Audun Stoti from Hraunsfjord. Their children were Steinthor, Bergthor, Thormod, Thord Blig and Helga. Steinthor was the foremost of Thorlak's children. He was a big, strong man, the most skilled in weaponry of all men and highly accomplished. He was usually a quiet man. Steinthor was regarded as one of the best three warriors in Iceland, along with Helgi Droplaugarson and Vemund Fringe.[12] Thormod was a wise and self-controlled man while Thord Blig was an excitable man with a quick tongue. Bergthor was the youngest but the most promising.

13 | Snorri Thorgrimsson was fourteen years old when he sailed abroad with his foster-brothers Thorleif Kimbi and Thorodd. His uncle, Bork the Stout, gave him fifty ounces of silver for his journey. They had a good passage and arrived in Norway in the autumn and spent the winter in Rogaland. Snorri stayed with Erling Skjalgsson at Sola who was kindly disposed to Snorri because of the friendship between their forebears Horda-Kari and Thorolf Moster-beard.

The following summer they returned to Iceland but they were late getting ready to sail and had a difficult passage, reaching Hornafjord just before winter. When the men of Breidafjord came ashore there was a striking difference between Thorleif Kimbi's and Snorri's outfits. Thorleif bought the best horse he could get there and he had a splendid coloured saddle. He carried an ornamented sword, a gold-inlaid spear, an elaborately gilded dark blue shield and all his clothing was exquisite. He had spent almost all his travel money on his apparel. Snorri, on the other hand, wore a black cloak and rode a good black mare. He had an old trough-shaped saddle and carried unornamented weapons. Thorodd's attire was somewhere between the two.

They rode from the east through Sida and followed the usual route to Borgarfjord and from there they went west across Fletir,

breaking their journey at Alftafjord. Then Snorri rode on to
Helgafell, intending to stay there for the winter. Bork received
him coolly and Snorri became a laughing stock because of his
outfit. Bork concluded that he must have been unlucky with his
travel money to have squandered it all.

One day in early winter, twelve fully armed men entered the
house at Helgafell. One of them was Bork's cousin, Eyjolf the
Grey, son of Thord Bellower. He lived in the west at Otradal in
Arnarfjord. When they were asked their news they announced
the death of Gisli Sursson and of those men he had killed before
he fell.[13] Bork was in high spirits at this news and asked Thordis
and Snorri to welcome Eyjolf as warmly as possible, as the man
who had rid their kin of such great shame.

Snorri appeared indifferent but Thordis said that it would be
a good enough welcome 'if gruel is given to Gisli's killer'.

'It's not for me to decide on the food,' replied Bork.

Bork placed Eyjolf in the high seat with his companions beside
him towards the door. They threw their weapons on to the floor.
Bork sat next to Eyjolf on the inner side with Snorri next to
him. Thordis brought in gruel troughs with wooden spoons in
them, but when she placed Eyjolf's serving before him the spoon
fell down in front of her. She stooped down to pick it up but
took Eyjolf's sword instead and swiftly thrust it up under the
table. It stabbed Eyjolf in the thigh and even though the hilt had
rammed into the table, the wound was quite severe. Bork shoved
the table away from them and struck at Thordis. Snorri pushed
Bork so that he fell down, and he pulled his mother into the seat
beside him, saying that she had enough distress without being
beaten. Eyjolf and his men leapt up from their seats and it was
man restraining man after that.

The situation was resolved by Bork giving Eyjolf the right to
decide the amount of compensation owed him and he claimed
a very high price for his bloody wound. He then went away
with his payment. Ill-feeling developed between Bork and Snorri
as a result of this incident.

14 | At the District Assembly the following spring Snorri demanded his inheritance from Bork. Bork agreed to pay him his share, 'but I have no intention of dividing up Helgafell. I can see that we cannot run the farm together so I want to buy out your share.'

'I think it is fairest for you to assess the value of the land as you see fit,' Snorri replied, 'but I will decide which one of us should buy the other one out.'

Bork thought this over and guessed that Snorri would not have ready cash to pay for the land if he had to pay immediately. He therefore valued half the land at sixty ounces of silver, excluding the islands belonging to Helgafell, because he expected they would be sold cheaply once Snorri had bought another farm. It was a condition of the price that it had to be paid immediately, without a loan from anyone else as part payment.

'Now you can choose, Snorri, which option you want,' said Bork.

'This shows that you think I am short of money, kinsman Bork,' Snorri replied, 'since you place such a low value on Helgafell's land. But I have decided to take the option of buying my father's estate at this price, so give me your hand and let's shake on the deal.'

'Not until every penny has been paid for it,' said Bork.

Snorri turned to his foster-father Thorbrand and said, 'Didn't I give you my money pouch last autumn?'

'Yes,' said Thorbrand and pulled out the pouch from underneath his cloak.

The silver was then counted and even after every penny had been paid for the land there were still sixty ounces of silver left in the pouch. Bork took the money and handed over the estate to Snorri.

Then he said, 'You have proven yourself richer in silver than I expected, kinsman. I would now like us to forget the ill-feeling between us and I propose that we both live here at Helgafell together for the next season since you have so little livestock.'

'You can enjoy your livestock away from Helgafell,' replied Snorri. It had to be as Snorri wanted it.

When Bork was ready to leave Helgafell, Thordis came up and named witnesses to her declaration of divorce from her husband Bork, giving as her reason the fact that he had hit her and she did not want to put up with his violence any more. Their property was then divided and Snorri acted for his mother since he was her heir. Bork then had to accept the terms that he had intended for others, of getting a low price for the islands. After that Bork left Helgafell and went west to Medalfellsstrond, living first at Barkarstadir between Orrahvol and Tunga. He later moved to Glerarskogar and lived there till his old age.

15 | Snorri Thorgrimsson settled at Helgafell and his mother ran the household for him. Snorri's uncle, Mar Hallvardsson, came to live with them and brought with him a lot of livestock and took over the management of Snorri's farm. He then had a prosperous estate and a large household.

Snorri was a man of medium height but rather thin, and he was handsome, with regular features and fair skin. His hair was red-gold and his beard red. He was usually an even-tempered man, and did not readily show his likes and dislikes. Snorri was a wise man and had foresight about many things, a long memory and a predisposition to vengeance. He gave his friends good counsel, but his enemies felt the chill of his strategies. He maintained a temple and was therefore known as Snorri the Godi. He became a prominent chieftain but his power also occasioned envy since there were many who believed that their lineage gave them no lesser claim to leadership than his, and rather more in terms of the strength of their following and their proven valour.

Bork the Stout and Thordis Sursdottir had a daughter named Thurid who was then married to Thorbjorn the Stout of Froda river. He was the son of Orm the Slender who had been the first settler in Frodaland. He had previously been married to Thurid, the daughter of Asbrand from Kamb in Breidavik. She was the sister of Bjorn the Champion of the Breidavik People, who will come into this saga later, and Arnbjorn the Strong. Her sons with Thorbjorn were Ketil the Champion, Gunnlaug and Hallstein. Thorbjorn was an unbalanced man who bullied weaker men.

At this time Geirrid, the daughter of Thorolf Lame-foot, lived at Mavahlid with her son Thorarin the Black. He was a big, strong man, ugly and taciturn, but usually self-composed, and he had a reputation as a peacemaker. He was not a rich man, although he had a profitable farm. Thorarin was so impartial that his enemies said his disposition was as much a woman's as a man's. He was married and his wife was named Aud. Gudny was the name of his sister and she was married to Vermund the Slender.

There was a widow named Katla living west of Mavahlid at Holt. She was good-looking but there was something peculiar about her. Her son was named Odd, and he was a big, energetic man, boisterous and very talkative, a troublemaker and a slanderer.

Gunnlaug, the son of Thorbjorn the Stout, was eager for knowledge and spent a lot of time at Mavahlid learning from Geirrid Thorolfsdottir because she was very knowledgeable about magic.

One day Gunnlaug called in at Holt on his way over to Mavahlid and had a long talk with Katla. She asked him whether he was going to Mavahlid again 'to stroke the old woman's groin'.

Gunnlaug said that was not his purpose, adding 'you are hardly so young, Katla, that you can afford to blame Geirrid for ageing'.

'I wasn't thinking of comparisons, but it makes no difference,' Katla replied. 'No woman except Geirrid will be able to please you now, but there are other women who know a thing or two apart from her.'

Katla's son Odd often accompanied Gunnlaug to Mavahlid. When they were late coming back Katla often invited Gunnlaug to stay the night but he always went home.

16 | Early in the first winter after Snorri had set up his farm at Helgafell, Gunnlaug Thorbjarnarson went to Mavahlid with Odd Kotluson. Gunnlaug and Geirrid spent the whole day talking together.

Late in the evening, Geirrid said to Gunnlaug, 'I don't want you to go home tonight, because it's a night of much spirit-movement and many a witch wears a fair face. You don't strike me as a lucky-looking man right now.'

'Nothing can happen to me while the two of us are together,' Gunnlaug replied.

'You won't get much help from Odd,' said Geirrid. 'Indeed, you alone will pay for your wilfulness.'

With that Gunnlaug and Odd left and walked until they reached Holt. Katla had already gone to bed by that time. She asked Odd to invite Gunnlaug to stay the night. He said he had already offered, 'but he wants to go home'.

'Let him go, just as he's determined it, then,' she said.

Gunnlaug did not arrive home that evening and there was some discussion about mounting a search for him but nothing came of it. During the night Thorbjorn looked outside and saw his son Gunnlaug lying unconscious in front of the door. He was carried indoors and when his clothes were pulled off, his shoulders were all bruised and bloody and the flesh was torn from the bone. His injuries kept him in bed for the whole winter and were the subject of much discussion. Odd Kotluson suggested that Geirrid must have ridden him, adding that they had parted abruptly that evening. Most people were inclined to agree with him.

The next spring on the Summons Days, Thorbjorn rode to Mavahlid and summonsed Geirrid, accusing her of being a night-rider and having caused injury to Gunnlaug. The case went before the Thorsnes Assembly with Snorri the Godi supporting his brother-in-law, Thorbjorn, and Arnkel the Godi defending the charge on behalf of his sister Geirrid. A panel of twelve was appointed to judge the case but neither Snorri nor Arnkel could give a decision in the case because of their kinship with the plaintiff and the defendant. Helgi, the godi of Hofgard, was called on to deliver the verdict. He was the father of Bjorn, grandfather of Gest, and great-grandfather of Ref the Poet.

Arnkel the Godi went up to the court and swore an oath on the altar-ring that Geirrid had not caused Gunnlaug's injuries. Thorarin and ten other men swore the same oath. After that

Helgi announced the verdict, and Snorri and Thorbjorn's case was quashed, which brought them dishonour.

17 | At the same assembly, Thorgrim Kjallaksson and his sons quarrelled with Illugi the Black over the dowry and bride-price of Illugi's wife, Ingibjorg Asbjarnardottir, which had been entrusted to Tin-Forni. There were wild storms at the time of the assembly so that no one from Medalfellsstrond could reach the site, and Thorgrim's strength in numbers was very much weakened by his kinsmen's absence. Illugi had a hundred well-chosen men and he pressed on with his case, but the Kjalleklings went into the court with the intention of breaking it up. The result was a great throng and even more men became involved in separating them. In the end, Tin-Forni paid out the money as Illugi demanded.

The poet Odd said this in his drapa on Illugi:

1.
There was a throng in the west
at the Thorsnes Thing
when the luck-studded fighter
firmly demanded the hoard.
Then the load of Forni's purse
landed in the hands of the resolute
feeder of battle-swallows.                    *battle-swallows*: ravens; their
Settlement was made in danger.                    *feeder*: warrior

After that the storm let up and the Kjalleklings arrived from the west of Medalfellsstrond. Thorgrim Kjallaksson no longer wanted to hold to the agreement and attacked Illugi and his men. A fight broke out and Snorri the Godi appealed for mediators who managed to arrange a truce between them. Three of the Kjalleklings' men were killed and four of Illugi's men. Styr Thorgrimsson killed two men there.

Odd said this about it in his drapa on Illugi:

2.

| They openly breached the settlement, | |
|---|---|
| and three stirrers of wakeful shields | *stirrers of wakeful shields*: |
| fell there before the bearer | warriors |
| of the ice-sharp blade; | *bearer of the ice-sharp* |
| until Snorri – the warrior who feeds | blade: warrior |
| the giant-wife's wolf-kin – | *giant-wife's wolf-kin*: |
| fixed a settlement between them. | carrion beasts |
| His leadership grew famous. | |

Illugi thanked Snorri the Godi for his support and offered to pay him, but Snorri said he did not want payment for his first offer of support. Illugi then invited him home and Snorri accepted, and he received valuable gifts while he was there. Snorri and Illugi were then friends for the time being.

18 | That summer, Thorgrim Kjallaksson died and his son Vermund the Slender took over the farm at Bjarnarhofn. He was a clever man and always reliable in his advice. At that time, Styr had been living for a while at Hraun inland from Bjarnarhofn. He was a clever and courageous man. He was married to Thorbjorg, the daughter of Thorstein Sleet-nose. Their sons were Thorstein and Hall, and their daughter was named Asdis, an honourable woman but rather strong-willed. Styr had a lot of influence in the area and many followers.[14] He was also involved in a lot of disputes because he had committed many killings without ever paying any compensation. The same summer a ship that was half-owned by Norwegians arrived in Salteyraros estuary. Their skipper was named Bjorn and he went to stay with Steinthor at Eyri. The other half-share of the ship belonged to some Hebrideans and Alfgeir was the name of their skipper. He went to stay with Thorarin the Black at Mavahlid and was accompanied by his friend Nagli, who was a large man and fleet of foot. He was of Scottish origin.

Thorarin had a good fighting stallion which he grazed up on the mountain. Thorbjorn the Stout also grazed many stud horses up on the mountain pastures and each autumn he used to choose a few of them for slaughter. That autumn it happened that Thorbjorn's horses could not be found. A thorough search was made for them, but the weather was particularly severe that autumn.

Early in the winter Thorbjorn sent Odd Kotluson south across the heath to Hraun to where a man called Seer-Gils lived. He had foresight and a sixth sense for solving thefts or other things he wanted to get to the bottom of. Odd asked whether Thorbjorn's horses had been stolen by men from abroad, or men from another district, or by his own neighbours.

'Tell Thorbjorn exactly what I am telling you,' Seer-Gils answered, 'that I believe his horses have not strayed far from their usual pasture. But it is difficult to name the men and it is better to carry one's loss than to end up in serious trouble.'

But once Odd returned to Froda, Thorbjorn and his men believed that Seer-Gils had implicated the people of Mavahlid in this matter. Odd added that Seer-Gils had said that those most likely to be the horse thieves were those who were short of money themselves, but who had a larger household than usual to provide for. It seemed to Thorbjorn that this wording implied the people of Mavahlid.

After that, Thorbjorn rode from home with eleven men. His son Hallstein was in the party, but his other son, Ketil the Champion, was abroad at the time. Thorbjorn's neighbour, Thorir Arnarson of Arnarhvol, was with them and he was the bravest of men. Odd Kotluson was also on the expedition. When they arrived at Katla's place at Holt, she gave her son a dark-brown tunic which she had just made. Then they rode to Mavahlid where Thorarin and his men were outside, and they watched the party approaching. They greeted Thorbjorn and asked his news.

'Our purpose in coming here, Thorarin,' said Thorbjorn, 'is to look for the horses that were stolen from me last autumn. We would like to make a search of your property.'

'Is this search being done according to the law, and have you appointed appropriate witnesses to investigate this case?' asked Thorarin. 'Can you assure us of our safety during the search? And how far afield are you conducting this search of yours?'

'We don't expect we'll need to search farther afield,' replied Thorbjorn.

'Then we flatly refuse your request to search, if you wish to go about it unlawfully,' Thorarin said.

'Then we'll assume you're guilty of the crime if you will not co-operate with the search,' Thorbjorn answered.

'Do as you like, then,' said Thorarin.

After that Thorbjorn established a door court[15] and named six men to judge the case. Thorbjorn brought a charge of horse-theft against Thorarin. Just at that moment, Geirrid came out the door and saw what was happening.

'That judgement is all too true,' she said, 'that you, Thorarin, have as much a woman's disposition as a man's, when you tolerate every disgrace from Thorbjorn the Stout. I don't understand why I have such a son.'

Then Alfgeir, the ship's skipper, said to Thorarin, 'We will support you in any way we can, whatever action you decide to take.'

'I don't feel like standing around here any longer,' replied Thorarin. At that, Thorarin and his men ran out intending to break up the court. There were seven of them in all, and a fight began immediately. Thorarin killed a farmhand of Thorbjorn's and Alfgeir another. A farmhand of Thorarin's was also killed there. But no weapon could touch Odd Kotluson. Aud, the mistress of the house, called on the women to separate them and they threw clothes over their weapons. Thorarin and his men went indoors after that and Thorbjorn and his men rode away intending to take the matter up at the Thorsnes Assembly. They rode up along the estuary and bandaged their wounds under a haystack wall at a place named Korngard.

In the hayfield at Mavahlid a hand was found where the fight had taken place. It was shown to Thorarin, and he saw that it was the hand of a woman. He asked where Aud was, and was told that she was lying in her bed. He went in to see her and asked her whether she was wounded. Aud told him not to worry about it, but he realized none the less that it was her hand that had been cut off. He called his mother in and asked her to bandage the wound.

Then Thorarin went out with his companions and ran after Thorbjorn and his men. When they were a short distance from the haystack they overheard Thorbjorn and his men talking. Hallstein was speaking.

'Thorarin fought off any suggestion of cowardice today,' he said.

'He fought boldly,' said Thorbjorn, 'but many a man becomes brave in dire straits, though they're not at all brave the rest of the time.'

'Thorarin may be the best of fighters,' replied Odd, 'but it will be considered a mishap that he chopped off his wife's hand.'

'Is that true?' said Thorbjorn.

'True as daylight,' said Odd.

With that they all fell about laughing and ridiculing Thorarin. At that moment, Thorarin and his men came upon them, with Nagli at the forefront. But when Nagli saw them brandishing their weapons he lost his nerve and ran away up on to the mountain, scared out of his wits. Thorarin went for Thorbjorn and struck him on the head with his sword, splitting it in two down to the jaw. Then Thorir Arnarson and two other men attacked him and Hallstein and a second man fought Alfgeir. Odd Kotluson and another man set upon Alfgeir's companion. Three of Thorbjorn's men fought two of Thorarin's men and the fighting between them was very fierce.

The result was that Thorarin cut off Thorir's leg at the thickest part of the calf, and killed both his companions. Hallstein was mortally wounded by Alfgeir, and once Thorarin was free, Odd Kotluson ran off with two other men. He was not wounded because no weapon could get through his tunic. All their other companions were left lying there, and both of Thorarin's farm-hands were dead.

Thorarin and his men took Thorbjorn's horses and rode them home. On the way, they saw Nagli running along the hillside. By the time they reached the hayfield, they saw that Nagli had passed the farm and was headed towards the promontory named Bulandshofdi. There he ran into two of Thorarin's slaves who were driving sheep back from the brink of the promontory. He told them about the clash and what the odds were. He said he was certain that Thorarin and his men were all dead. Just at that moment they saw men riding towards them from the farmstead across the field. Thorarin and his men began to gallop because they wanted to help Nagli and stop him from jumping into the sea or over the cliffs.

When Nagli and the slaves saw that the men were riding furiously towards them they assumed it must be Thorbjorn and his men. They all raced off again towards the promontory and ran until they came to the place now called Thraelaskrida. Thorarin and his men finally caught up with Nagli there because his lungs had almost exploded from panting, but the slaves ran ahead and jumped off the promontory and were killed, which was to be expected because the cliff is so high that everything perishes that goes over it.

Then Thorarin and his company went home. Geirrid was waiting in the doorway and asked them how it had gone. Thorarin then spoke this verse:

3.
I – murderous wielder of the death-edge –          *death-edge*: sword
defended myself against women's
taunts when I dared to fight;
the eagle got to eat fresh corpses.
I didn't spare the sword there
in the stir of slay-adders.          *slay-adders*: swords; their *stir*: battle
I seldom boast of this
in front of the war-god's worshippers.

'Are you announcing the killing of Thorbjorn?' asked Geirrid. Thorarin replied:

4.
My razor-sharp sword
sought its mark under his hood
and the bloody flood streamed
from the fight-seeker.          *fight-seeker*: warrior
Blood poured from his ears
and filled his fame-room          *fame-room*: mouth
but his sword still
strayed too close to me.

'The whetting paid off, then,' Geirrid replied. 'Come in and let's see to your wounds.' And so it was.

Now to return to Odd Kotluson. He went on until he came to Froda and announced the news. Thurid, the mistress of the house, assembled men to go and fetch the bodies and bring home the wounded. Thorbjorn was laid in a burial mound but his son Hallstein recovered from his injuries. Thorir of Arnarhvol also recovered but walked with a wooden leg after that, so he was called Thorir Wood-leg. He married Thorgrima Magic-cheek, and their sons were Orn and Val, who were both honourable men.

19 | Thorarin spent one night at home at Mavahlid. The next
   | morning, Aud asked him what his plans were.

'We don't want to kick you out,' she said, 'but I fear that there will be more door courts this winter because I know that Snorri the Godi will mount a case following the killing of his brother-in-law, Thorbjorn.'

Then Thorarin said:

5.
The wily law-wrecker
won't outlaw me this winter
if I can get hold of Vermund,
the hastener of battle-din.          *hastener of battle-din*: warrior
I have to praise my protector,
if my hopes are to have a chance.
I made the raven's young
rejoice on the field of the dead.

'It would be most prudent, now,' said Geirrid, 'to seek help from kinsmen such as Vermund or my brother Arnkel.'

'It is more likely that both of them will be needed before the end of this case, though I will begin by placing my trust in Vermund,' Thorarin replied.

That same day all those who had been involved in the killings rode east along the fjords and arrived at Bjarnarhofn in the evening, going inside after everyone had already taken their

seats. Vermund greeted them and at once made room on the
high seat for Thorarin and his men. When they had sat down
Vermund asked their news.

Thorarin spoke:

6.

| | |
|---|---|
| I shall tell the clash-trees | *clash-trees*: warriors |
| the whole story – | |
| how the trees of battle, shield-bearers, | *trees of battle*: warriors |
| bullied me with the law. | |
| Listen to me meanwhile: | |
| men of iron should expect | *men of iron*: warriors; |
| arrow-sport. | *arrow-sport*: battle |
| I saw the valkyrie's hand-reed | *valkyrie's hand-reed*: sword |
| reddened by blood. | |

'What more is there to be told, kinsman?' asked Vermund.
Thorarin spoke again:

7.

| | |
|---|---|
| They attacked me at home, | |
| sword-gods who imperil lives: | *sword-gods*: warriors |
| in the fight, the flash of battle | *flash of battle*: sword |
| cut the keeper of the spears' path. | *keeper of the spears' path*: |
| So, attacking, we offered | warrior |
| the sword-god few options. | |
| I did not break the sport | *sport of comfort*: peace |
| of comfort willingly. | |

His sister, Gudny, took her place on the floor and asked, 'Did
you clear yourself of their taunts out there?'

Thorarin replied:

8.

| | |
|---|---|
| I had to defend myself | |
| against the valkyrie's derision: | |
| the dart-of-wounds was driven, | *dart-of-wounds*: spear |
| and the raven delighted in gore. | |
| When the sword of my father's son | |
| rang against helmets in the field, | |

gashes spurted blood
and wound-streams ran.

'It seems to me you dealt with them swiftly,' Vermund said.
Thorarin replied:

9.

| | |
|---|---|
| Sinister darts of prophecy | *darts of prophecy*: arrows |
| sang against my shield | |
| from the valkyrie's dire battle-plain, | |
| when the bent beam of Frodi's arm | *Frodi*: a sea king; the *bent beam* |
| was splattered with gore. | of his arm: shield |
| There, before the ghost | *land of the shield-rings*: shield; |
| of the land of the shield-rings, | its *ghost*: dead warrior |
| weapons' lake lapped on the field. | *weapons' lake*: blood |

'Have they found out yet whether you are a man or a woman?'
asked Vermund.
Thorarin replied:

10.

| | |
|---|---|
| I consider myself cleared | |
| of the cutting warrior's calumny, | |
| the steerer of the famous | |
| horse of planks sank there. | *horse of planks*: ship |
| The raven tore into flesh | |
| no matter what the warrior | |
| – gladdened by the fish of armour – | *fish of armour*: sword |
| tells his girlfriend. | |

After that, Thorarin told all the news.
Then Vermund asked, 'Why did you go after them? Didn't
you think you'd done enough the first time?'
Thorarin replied:

11.

| | |
|---|---|
| It will be said, wielder | *Odin's fire*: sword; its *wielder*: warrior |
| of Odin's fire, that I waged | |
| she-wolf's joy out of spite | *she-wolf's joy*: battle |
| – I used to master the ship off Enni. | |
| When the traitors, entanglers | |

of truth, pretended
I had hurt Hlin of the fine raiments,                    *Hlin* (goddess) *of the fine*
I made fit retaliation.                                          *raiments*: woman

'It's understandable that you didn't put up with that,' said
Vermund. 'But how well did the foreigners serve you?'
Thorarin replied:

12.
Most of the corpse-geese                                *corpse-geese*: ravens
got a poor feed from Nagli;
faint-hearted, the one                        *the one familiar with the sea's sun*
    familiar                                              (gold): man
with the sea's sun fled into the hills;
With rather more spirit, Alfgeir
advanced into the song of weapons,             *song of weapons*: battle
hidden by his helmet. Fire                         *fire of the battle*: spears
of battle whistled overhead.

'Didn't Nagli acquit himself well?' asked Vermund.
Thorarin replied:

13.
Crying, the keeper of the swords' path            *swords' path*: shield; its
ran away from combat.                                      *keeper*: warrior
There didn't seem much chance of peace
to the guardian of the helmet,               *guardian of the helmet*: warrior
so the mare-driver                                      *mare-driver*: man
preferred to dive into the sea;
cowardice was on the mind
of the cup-bearer, wreck of a man.                    *cup-bearer*: man

After Thorarin had spent the night at Bjarnarhofn, Vermund
said, 'You won't find my offer of support very generous, kinsman. I'm reluctant to help you out of your difficulties without
the support of other men, so let's ride over to Bolstad today to
talk to your kinsman, Arnkel, and find out what help he'll give
us. I expect Snorri the Godi will be severe in this action.'
'It's up to you to judge,' replied Thorarin.
Once they were on their way, Thorarin spoke:

14.

Vermund and I will remember
how once we were cheerful together,
before I, fir-tree of riches,                    *fir-tree of riches*: man
caused a man to fall.
Now I fear, linen-goddess,                        *linen-goddess*: woman
we will have to flee
the proud thane. The rain                         *rain of red shields*: battle
of red shields is repugnant to me.

This was directed towards Snorri the Godi. Vermund and
Thorarin rode into Bolstad where Arnkel welcomed them and
asked their news.

Thorarin replied:

15.

It was frightening to think
of the storm of ravens' wine          *ravens' wine*: blood; its *storm*: battle
at my farm – fire of Munin's meal      *Munin*: one of Odin's ravens; the
swept through men –                     *fire* of its meal (corpses): weapons
when the shimmering linden                    *shimmering linden*: spear
sheared the vikings' moon;                       *vikings' moon*: shield
at the meeting of warriors
swords passed through shields.

Arnkel enquired further about the events in the report Thorarin had given.

And when he had retold the events as they happened, Arnkel
said, 'You really must have been angry, kinsman, since you are
usually such a moderate man.'

Thorarin replied:

16.

Those who enjoy the snow-drift   *hawks' spur*: hand; *snow-drift*: silver;
of the hawks' spur                      *those who enjoy* its silver: men
accused me of easy living
– until now I have frustrated feuds.
A cloudburst, furious torrent,
often comes in still weather.

Now the land of the wrist's lightning          *wrist's lightning*: gold; its
will learn of my words.                                        *land*: woman

'That may be,' said Arnkel, 'but I want to propose that you stay with me, kinsman Thorarin, until the case is settled, one way or another. And although I am assuming leadership in this matter, I'd still like you, Vermund, not to abandon the case, even though I'm taking responsibility for Thorarin.'

'I am obliged to help Thorarin in any way I can,' said Vermund, 'no less so now that you have taken charge of the action.'

'It's my view that we all should spend the winter together here, close to Snorri the Godi,' said Arnkel. And so they did, so that Arnkel had a full house that winter. Vermund divided his time between Bjarnarhofn and Arnkel's farm. Thorarin remained in his usual mood and was quiet for long periods of time. Arnkel was a very houseproud and cheerful host, taking it badly if others were not as happy as he was. He often mentioned to Thorarin that he should cheer up and not be concerned about the future, saying he had heard that the widow at Froda was bearing her sorrows well, 'and she would think it ridiculous if you didn't cope well.'

Thorarin answered:

17.
The fine-dancing widow,
ale-drunk, won't deride me
– I know the raven feasted on
pieces of corpse flesh –
because I shudder at the thought                          *sword-dew*:
of sword-dew; the hawk of corpses           blood; *hawk of corpses*: raven
enjoys the hard play of grief;                      *hard play of grief*: battle
hatred has come among men.

Then one of Arnkel's men replied, 'You won't know until spring, when the Thorsnes Assembly is over, whether you can do without support in this affair.'

Thorarin replied:

18.

| Men say that the shield-holders | *shield-holders*: warriors |
| might face shouting brawls | |
| at court; we will seek | |
| the support of a powerful man, | |
| unless tactful Arnkel conducts | |
| our case to great acclaim. | |
| I put my trust in the keeper | |
| of helmet-song completely. | *helmet-song*: battle; its *keeper*: warrior |

20 | The mistress of the house at Mavahlid, Geirrid, sent word to Bolstad that she had found out that it was Odd Kotluson who had chopped off Aud's hand. She claimed to have Aud's own word on this, and she also said that Odd had boasted about it to his friends. When Thorarin and Arnkel heard this news they rode from home out to Mavahlid with ten men, and stayed the night there. The following morning they rode towards Holt where their approach could be seen from the farmstead. There was not a man on the farm except Odd.

Katla sat on the cross-bench spinning yarn. She told Odd to sit beside her, 'and be quiet and still.'

She told the women to stay in their places, 'and be quiet. I will speak for us all.'

When Arnkel and the others arrived, they went straight inside. As they came into the main room Katla greeted Arnkel and asked him the news. Arnkel said he did not have any, and asked where Odd was.

Katla said he had gone south to Breidavik bay, 'but he wouldn't have avoided seeing you if he were at home, because we believe you to be honourable men.'

'That may well be,' said Arnkel, 'but we want to search your house.'

'Do as you please,' said Katla, and asked the cook to carry a light for them, and to unlock the storeroom, 'that is the only locked room on the farm.'

They noticed that Katla was spinning yarn on her distaff.

They searched the buildings but could not find Odd and after
that they left.

When they had ridden a little distance from the farm buildings, Arnkel stopped and said: 'Is it possible that Katla could
have pulled the wool over our eyes? Could that have been her
son Odd who appeared to us to be her distaff?'

'She'd be quite capable of that,' said Thorarin, 'so let's go
back.'

And they did. When the people at Holt saw that men were
returning, Katla said to the women, 'You should still stay in
your places, but Odd and I are going outside.'

When they reached the front door, Katla went into the hall-
way directly opposite the door and started combing her son's
hair and cutting it. Arnkel and the others ran through the door
and saw Katla playing with a goat there, trimming its forelock
and beard and grooming its coat. Arnkel and his men went into
the main room but could not see Odd. Katla's distaff was lying
there on the bench. They were now convinced that Odd had not
been there, and so they went out and rode away.

But when they reached the spot where they had turned back
before, Arnkel said, 'Don't you suspect that Odd could have
been disguised as a goat?'

'Who knows,' said Thorarin, 'but if we go back now we
should take hold of Katla.'

'Let's try once more,' said Arnkel, 'and see what happens.'

Once again, they turned back.

When Katla saw them returning, she asked Odd to come with
her for a walk.

Once they were outside, she went to the rubbish-pile and
told Odd to lie down under the pile 'and stay there whatever
happens.'

When Arnkel and his men arrived, they ran into the main
room where Katla was sitting spinning. She greeted them and
said they were becoming regular visitors. Arnkel said that was
quite true. His companions took Katla's distaff and broke it
in two.

'Tonight at home,' said Katla, 'you won't be able to say you had no purpose here at Holt since you have broken my distaff.'

Then Arnkel and his men searched for Odd inside and out but saw no living creature except a domestic boar that Katla owned, which was lying under the rubbish-pile. They went away after that, but when they were half-way to Mavahlid, Geirrid came to meet them with one of her farmhands and asked them how it had gone. Thorarin told her.

She said they had not made a proper search for Odd, 'and so I want you to go back again, but I will come with you this time. Where Katla is concerned, you won't make any headway using frail sail-cloth.'

And so they turned back again. Geirrid had a black cloak on. When the party was seen returning to Holt, Katla was told that there were now fourteen men and one of them was wearing coloured clothing.

'That will be the troll, Geirrid, coming with them,' said Katla, 'and simple illusions will not be enough now.'

She got up from her cross-bench and took away the cushions from under her. Underneath them was a trap-door with a storage space beneath it. She made Odd get in there and rearranged the cross-bench as before. She sat down again and said that she felt rather strange. When they came into the main room there were no greetings between them. Geirrid threw off her cloak and walked toward Katla with a sealskin bag she had brought with her which she pulled over Katla's head. Her companions tied it tightly around her neck. Then Geirrid told them to open up the cross-bench. Odd was discovered underneath it and then he was tied up.

After that they were taken to Bulandshofdi and Odd was hanged there.

While he was kicking on the gallows, Arnkel said to him, 'You got an evil end because of your mother. It might also be said that you have an evil mother.'

'Maybe he doesn't have a good mother,' said Katla, 'but I never wished him to get such an evil end because of me. It's my will that you all get an evil end because of me, and I expect that will be the case. I'll no longer hide the fact that I was responsible for Gunnlaug Thorbjarnarson's injuries which were the cause of all this trouble. And you Arnkel,' she said, 'cannot get an evil end from your own mother because she's no longer alive, but I want my curse to work on you so that you come off worse because of your father than Odd has because of me, because you stand to lose more than he has. I expect it will be said before long that you have an evil father.'

After that they stoned Katla to death under the promontory. Then they went to Mavahlid and spent the night there, and rode back home the following day. The news quickly travelled everywhere, but no one thought it was sad. And so the winter passed by.

21 | One day in spring, Arnkel called over his kinsman, Thorarin, as well as Vermund and Alfgeir, for a talk and asked them what kind of support they would like the most, whether they should go to the assembly, 'and try out all our friends on this matter. There seem to be two possible outcomes if we do that,' said Arnkel. 'A settlement could be reached, in which case you would have to pay a high price for all the men who were killed or wounded. But riding to the assembly might also be a dangerous option if, by pressing our case too forcefully, our situation becomes more difficult. The other option is to put all our energy into helping you get away with your money, and then to deal with whatever land we cannot sell as luck allows us.'

Alfgeir was most enthusiastic about this course of action. Thorarin said he would not be able to afford to pay compensation to all those involved in the case, and Vermund declared he would not desert Thorarin, whether he wanted him to travel abroad with him or to help him fight here in Iceland. But Thorarin chose Arnkel's offer to help them travel abroad. Afterwards a man was sent out to Eyri to tell Bjorn, the ship's skipper, that he should make every effort to prepare their ship to sail as soon as possible.

22 | Now to turn back to Snorri the Godi, who took charge of
the action over the killing of his kinsman, Thorbjorn. He
had his sister, Thurid, move back to Helgafell because it was
being said that Bjorn, the son of Asbrand of Kamb, was making
frequent visits to her home to seduce her. Snorri thought he
could see through Arnkel's plans when he heard about the ship
being made ready, realizing that they were not planning to pay
compensation for the killings since no offer of settlement had
been made by them. None the less, all was quiet right up until
the Summons Days.

When that time came, Snorri assembled men and rode to
Alftafjord with a force of eighty men, because it was then the
law that the summons for a killing had to made where the
killers could hear it, or at their home, but neighbours were not
summoned until the assembly itself. When Snorri and his party
were seen approaching Bolstad, the men there discussed whether
they should attack them since they had the numbers.

Arnkel said that was not the way, adding that 'we shall allow
Snorri to use legal means.' He said that the only thing to do now
was whatever was necessary.

When Snorri arrived at Bolstad there was no violence between
the men. Snorri summonsed Thorarin to the Thorsnes Assembly
along with all those who had taken part in the killings. Arnkel
listened carefully to the summons. After that Snorri and his men
rode away in the direction of Ulfarsfell.

When they had gone, Thorarin spoke this verse:

19.

It is not because of my crime
that I, caster of the bright hail's fire,          *bright hail's* (i.e. battle's) *fire*:
have been robbed of my rights                                          weapons
if experts in the gleaming roof          *gleaming roof of Valhalla*: shields;
of Valhalla make me an outlaw.                    their *experts*: warriors
I see they outnumber us.
May the gods enforce our victory,          *hand's beautiful fire*: gold or ring;
field of the hand's beautiful fire.                    its *field*: woman

Snorri the Godi rode across the ridge to Hrisar and then on to Drapuhlid that morning, riding from there out to Svinavatn lake and on to Hraunsfjord, and from there he followed the path out to Trollahals, never breaking his journey until he reached the Salteyraros estuary. When they arrived, some of his men captured the Norwegians while others burned the ship. With all this done, Snorri the Godi and his men rode back home.

Arnkel heard the news that Snorri had burnt the ship. He, Vermund, Thorarin and a few other men then boarded a ship and rowed north through the fjords to Dagverdarnes, where a ship belonging to some Norwegians was beached. Arnkel and Vermund bought the ship and Arnkel gave his half to Thorarin while Vermund kept his own half. They sailed the ship out to Dimun and fitted it out there. Arnkel stayed with them until they were ready and then accompanied them out to Ellidaey island where they parted the best of friends. Thorarin and his companions sailed out to sea and Arnkel went home to his farm. It was generally acknowledged that the support he had given had been splendid.

Snorri the Godi went to the Thorsnes Assembly and prosecuted the case. Thorarin and all those who had participated in the killings were sentenced to lesser outlawry, and after the assembly, Snorri collected whatever property he could as compensation, and that was the end of the case.

23 | Vigfus, the son of Bjorn Ottarsson, lived at Drapuhlid, as was told earlier. He married Thorgerd Thorbeinisdottir. Vigfus was a respected farmer but very difficult to get on with. His sister's son, Bjorn, was staying with him, and he was a quick-tongued and useless sort of boy.

In the autumn after the Mavahlid incident, Thorbjorn the Stout's horses were found in the mountains. His stallion had been unable to hold the pasture against Thorarin's stallion and the whole herd had been snowed under. When they were discovered, they were all dead.

That same autumn a large number of people gathered at Tunga between the Laxa rivers inland from Helgafell to sort the sheep. Men from Snorri the Godi's farm were there for the sorting, and they were led by Snorri's uncle, Mar Hallvardsson. Helgi was the name of his shepherd. Bjorn, Vigfus's nephew, was lying on top of the wall of the sheep-pen, holding a shepherd's staff, and Helgi was sorting the sheep. Bjorn asked which sheep he had just separated out. When it was checked, it was found to have Vigfus's brand on it.

'You're sorting the sheep rather casually today, Helgi,' said Bjorn.

'It's more dangerous for someone like you,' replied Helgi, 'sitting on common pasture.'

'What would a thief like you know about that,' said Bjorn, who then leapt up and struck Helgi with his staff so that he fell down unconscious.

When Mar saw this he drew his sword and lunged at Bjorn, striking his arm below the shoulder and causing a serious wound. At that, men rushed to join the two sides, but others went between them and separated them so that nothing of note happened.

The following morning, Vigfus rode down to Helgafell and demanded compensation for the injury, but Snorri said he would not make anything out of the incidents that had occurred there. Vigfus did not like this answer and they parted with great coolness.

In the spring, Vigfus brought a charge of inflicting a bloody wound at the Thorsnes Assembly but Snorri argued that Bjorn had provoked the incident. The outcome of the case was that Bjorn was unprotected by the law for his assault against Helgi, and got no compensation for his bloody wound, although he carried his arm in a sling after that.

24 | At the same assembly, Thorgest the Old and the sons of Thord Bellower brought an action against Eirik the Red for the killing of Thorgest's sons who had died the autumn before when Eirik had fetched his bench-boards at Breidabolstad. The assembly was very well-attended, and large forces had already been gathered together. During the assembly, Eirik made

his ship seaworthy at Eiriksvog on Oxnaey island, assisted by Thorbjorn Vifilsson, Killer-Styr, the sons of Thorbrand of Alftafjord, and Eyjolf Æsuson from Svinaey island. But Styr was the only one of Eirik's supporters at the assembly, and he tried to dissuade whomever he could from supporting Thorgest. Styr also asked Snorri the Godi not to join Thorgest's attack on Eirik after the assembly, and promised him in return that he would support him in the future if he was in any difficulty. Because of Styr's pledge, Snorri took no part in the action.

After the assembly, Thorgest and his men travelled in a large fleet towards the islands, but Eyjolf Æsuson kept Eirik's ship hidden in the bay at Dimunarvog where Styr and Thorbjorn came to join Eirik. Eyjolf and Styr then followed Arnkel's example and each of them accompanied Eirik in their own ferry out to Ellidaey island.

It was on this journey that Eirik the Red discovered Greenland and he stayed there for three winters before returning to Iceland for one winter.[16] He then went back to settle Greenland, and this happened fourteen years before Christianity was adopted by law in Iceland.

25 | Now to turn to Vermund and Thorarin the Black, who reached land in Norway north of the mouth of Trondheim, from where they sailed into Trondheim. At that time Earl Hakon Sigurdsson ruled Norway[17] and Vermund went to see the earl and became one of his men. Thorarin sailed west to the British Isles with Alfgeir that same autumn, and Vermund gave his share of the ship to them. Thorarin does not come into this story again.

Earl Hakon spent the winter at Lade, and Vermund was one of his favourite men there. The earl treated him well because he knew that Vermund was from a distinguished family in Iceland. There were two Swedish brothers also staying with the earl, one named Halli and the other Leiknir. They were men of much greater size and strength than any other men in Norway or farther afield at the time. They both went into berserk fits and once they had worked themselves up into a frenzy they were not like human beings. They went mad like dogs and had no fear of either fire or iron. But on a daily basis they were not difficult to get along with, as long as they were not crossed; once roused, they turned into the most erratic men. The Swedish King Eirik the Victorious[18] had sent the berserks to the earl with the warning that he should treat them well, adding that they would be of great assistance if their moods could be kept under control.

The following spring after he had been with the earl for the winter, Vermund wanted to return home to Iceland and asked the earl for permission to make his journey.

The earl said he could travel wherever he wished, but asked him to consider before he left 'whether there is any particular thing in my possession that you would accept from me to contribute to your success, which would increase the honour and esteem of both of us.'

When Vermund considered what he should ask for from the earl, the idea occurred to him that his success in Iceland would be greatly strengthened if he had supporters such as the berserks. So he became determined to ask if the earl would give him the berserks as supporters. The reason behind his request was that Vermund thought his brother Styr was assuming more than his fair share of power and treating him unfairly, just as he treated many other people whenever he could get away with it. Vermund thought Styr would find it more difficult to bully him if he had followers like the brothers with him. Vermund then told the earl that he would accept the honour of being given the protection and backing of the berserks.

'It seems to me,' replied the earl, 'that you have asked for the one thing that will be of no use to you, even if I granted it. I think they will prove obstinate and arrogant whenever you have to deal with them. I also think it would be too much for any farmer's son to control them and keep them subservient, even though they have been obedient in their service to me.'

Vermund said he would risk taking them if the earl would hand them over to him. The earl told him to find out first from the berserks if they would go with him. Vermund did so, asking if they would travel with him to Iceland and give him support and backing in return for his assurance that he would treat them well and give them anything they needed when they asked for it. The berserks replied that they had never thought of going to Iceland, and that they had not thought there were suitable chieftains there for them to serve.

'But if you are so keen for us to go to Iceland with you, Vermund, you should also realize that we will behave very badly if you do not grant us whatever we ask for if you have the means to give it to us,' they said.

Vermund said that would never happen. After that he got their consent to accompany him to Iceland if that was the earl's wish and he gave them his approval.

Vermund then told the earl what had happened, and he made the decision that the berserks should go with him to Iceland, 'if you believe that will do most for your honour.'

But he also warned him that he would regard it as an insult if he mistreated them once they had come under his control. Vermund replied that he need not be concerned about that. After that Vermund sailed to Iceland with the berserks and had a good journey, arriving at his farm at Bjarnarhofn the same summer that Eirik the Red sailed to Greenland, as was told earlier.

Soon after Vermund got home, the berserk Halli advised him that he wanted Vermund to find him a suitable wife. Vermund did not think he knew a likely woman of good family who would want to tie herself to a berserk for the rest of her life, so he kept putting it off. But when Halli realized this, his wolf mind took over and he became ill-tempered and everything between them went awry. The berserks became arrogant and disobedient towards Vermund, and he began to regret having taken them on.

In the autumn Vermund hosted a great feast and invited his brother Styr, Arnkel the Godi, and the people of Eyri. When the feast was over, Vermund offered the berserks as a gift to Arnkel calling it a most suitable tribute, but Arnkel would not accept it. Then Vermund sought Arnkel's advice about how to rid himself of this problem, and Arnkel suggested he hand them on to Styr, saying he would be best suited to having such men because of his arrogance and injustice.

When Styr was ready to leave, Vermund went up to him and said, 'Now, brother, I would like us to end the coolness that has been between us since before I went away. We should renew our loyal kinship and good friendship, and to that end I will give you the men that I brought to Iceland to serve and support you, for I know no man confident enough to fight you if you have supporters like them.'

'I welcome a better relationship between us, kinsman,' Styr replied, 'but the only news I've heard of these men that you brought back suggests they would bring trouble rather than prestige or fortune. I'll never take them into my household, having enough enemies of my own without them adding to my troubles.'

'What advice can you give me then, kinsman,' Vermund asked, 'to rid myself of this problem?'

'That's another matter entirely,' said Styr. 'Helping you solve your problem is one thing, but receiving these men from you as a gift is another, and I do not want it. But solving your problem is no man's responsibility as much as mine, if we are now on friendly terms again.'

Even though Styr spoke in this way, Vermund still wanted him to take the berserks, and so the brothers parted with great affection. Styr went home with the berserks, although they were not at all keen on this to begin with, saying Vermund had no right to sell them or give them away like slaves, but nevertheless, they admitted that it was more to their liking to serve Styr rather than Vermund. And at first their relationship looked quite promising.

The berserks were with Styr when he went west across the fjord to kill Thorbjorn Kjalki who lived in Kjalkafjord. He had a very sturdy bed closet made of timber beams, which the berserks broke open by forcing the joints apart in no time at all, though it was Styr who killed Thorbjorn Kjalki.

26 | During the autumn when the berserks had come to stay with Styr, Vigfus of Drapuhlid set out one day with his three slaves to make charcoal at a place named Seljabrekkur. One of the slaves was called Svart the Strong.

Once they were in the woods, Vigfus said, 'It's a great shame, and one that you must feel quite strongly, Svart, that you should be an enslaved man when you are as strong and manly as you appear to be.'

'Certainly I find it hard to bear,' he said. 'But it's not within my power to do anything about it.'

'What would you do in return for me granting your freedom?' asked Vigfus.

'I can't pay for it with money, since I have none, but I won't spare any effort in whatever other ways there may be.'

'Go over to Helgafell and kill Snorri the Godi,' said Vigfus, 'and after that you will certainly have your freedom as well as valuable goods which I will give you.'

'I'd never be able to bring that off,' said Svart.

'I'll give you directions,' replied Vigfus, 'so that it can be done without endangering your life.'

'I'd like to hear about it then,' said Svart.

'You go over to Helgafell and get into the loft which is above the front door and remove enough floor boards so that you can fit your halberd through the gap. And when Snorri goes out to the toilet, thrust the halberd through the loft's floor into Snorri's back so hard that it goes through the belly. Then run out on to the roof and down the wall and you'll be able to get away under cover of darkness.'

With this plan in mind Svart went over to Helgafell and tore open the roof above the front door and got into the loft. This was at the time of evening when Snorri and his men were sitting by the fire eating their meal. At that time all farms had outdoor toilets. When Snorri and his men got up to go outside, Snorri led the way and was already out the door by the time Svart struck. But Mar Hallvardsson was walking behind Snorri and Svart's halberd got him, striking him on the shoulder-blade and cutting through beneath the arm, but it was not a serious wound.

Svart ran out on to the roof and down on to the wall, but he slipped on the paving stones and had quite a bad fall. Snorri got hold of him before he could get up. They got the whole story out of him, including the deal Vigfus had made with him, as well as the fact that Vigfus was then at Seljabrekkur burning charcoal. Then Mar's wound was dressed.

Snorri went with a party of six men to Drapuhlid. As they came over a rise they saw the fire where Vigfus and his farmhands were burning charcoal. They took them by surprise and killed Vigfus but spared the lives of his farmhands. Snorri returned home and Vigfus's slaves told the news back at Drapuhlid. Vigfus was placed in a burial mound later that day.

The same day, Vigfus's widow, Thorgerd, went to Bolstad to tell her kinsman Arnkel the news, and ask him to take up the case of Vigfus's killing. But Arnkel declined, saying it was the duty of his kinsmen, the Kjalleklings. He directed the case instead to Styr, as the kinsman most appropriate to bring a suit following the killing, since he was always keen to get involved in everything.

Thormod Trefilsson made this verse about the killing of Vigfus:

20.
The leader of the people first
felled the one who toppled                    *the one who toppled gold-bristled*
gold-bristled boar-helmets.                         *boar-helmets*: warrior
He was known by the name Vigfus.
After that the young wound-mews                     *wound-mews*: ravens
tore at the wound-flesh
of the warrior there,
of Bjorn's heir.

27 | After that Thorgerd travelled out to Hraun and asked Styr
    | to bring a suit following the killing of his kinsman, Vigfus.

'I promised Snorri the Godi last spring, when he distanced himself from the dispute between us and Thorgest's sons, that I would not turn against him in any case in which others more involved than myself could act,' Styr said. 'You should approach my brother Vermund to take up this case, or some of our other relatives.'

So Thorgerd went out to Bjarnarhofn and asked Vermund

for support, saying he was the most obliged to help 'since Vigfus trusted you most of all his kinsmen'.

'I'm bound by duty to contribute something towards the action,' Vermund replied, 'but I'm not willing to take on the problem on behalf of our other relatives. None the less, I will offer both my support and advice to the best of my ability. First I want you to go out to Eyri and see Vigfus's kinsman, Steinthor. He's always spoiling for a fight, and it's time he tried himself out in some kind of legal action.'

'You're putting me to a lot of trouble for this lawsuit, but I don't mind how much effort I put in if it's a success,' Thorgerd said.

Then she went out to Eyri and visited Steinthor and asked him to take charge of the action over the killing.

'Why do you ask me to do this?' asked Steinthor. 'I am a young man and have never taken any part in a lawsuit, whereas Vigfus's kinsmen who are more closely related than I am are much pushier than me. There is no chance of my taking the case off their hands, although I will stick by any of my kinsmen who take on the case.'

That was the only answer Thorgerd got there. She then went across the fjord to see Vermund and told him how things stood, saying that her whole case was lost unless he took the lead in the action.

'There's still a good chance that a prosecution will result from this case,' Vermund replied, 'which should be some consolation. I'll give you some further instructions if you will carry them out.'

'I'm still willing to do more in order to achieve this,' she replied.

'Go home now,' said Vermund, 'and have your husband Vigfus's body dug up. Then remove his head and take it to Arnkel and tell him that this head would not have left it to others to bring a suit on his behalf if it had been necessary.'

Thorgerd said she did not know where that kind of talk would lead and she could see they were not going to spare her any hardship or misery.

'But I am willing to do this,' she said, 'if it will make things worse for my enemies than before.'

After that she went home and made all the preparations she had been instructed to. When she arrived at Bolstad she told Arnkel that Vigfus's kinsmen wanted him to take charge of the action over Vigfus's killing and that they all promised their support. Arnkel said he had already said how he felt about the matter.

Then Thorgerd brought out the head from underneath her cloak and said, 'Now here is the head that would not have refused to bring a suit on your behalf if it had been necessary.'

Arnkel was very shocked by this and pushed her away from him, saying, 'Go away and tell Vigfus's kinsmen that they may no longer fail me in their support against Snorri the Godi, any more than I may flag in pursuing this prosecution. But my instincts tell me that however things turn out, they will give in before I do. And I can see that it is Vermund's strategy you are following here, but he won't need to egg me on whenever we are standing together as kinsmen.'

Thorgerd returned home and the winter passed. In the spring Arnkel started a case against all those involved in the killing of Vigfus except for Snorri the Godi. Snorri brought his own case against those who plotted against his life and another for the bloody wound dealt to Mar, arguing that these served to put Vigfus beyond the protection of the law. Both parties turned out in great numbers at the Thorsnes Assembly, but all the Kjalleklings supported Arnkel and so their side had the numbers. Arnkel pressed his charges with great determination.

When the time came for judgement, men intervened and the case was submitted to arbitration and all the matters dealt with by negotiation, with the result that Snorri agreed to their verdict on the killing of Vigfus, and had to pay a heavy fine and Mar had to spend three years abroad. Snorri paid his fine on the spot and the assembly closed with all these cases settled.

28 | Now to pick up the story, as was written before, at the point where the berserks went to live with Styr. They had only been there a short while when Halli took to chatting with Asdis, Styr's daughter. She was a young woman of firm

character, very proud and rather strong-willed. When Styr found out about their conversations, he told Halli not to bring disgrace on him or try to provoke him by seducing his daughter.

'It is not a disgrace for you if I talk to your daughter,' replied Halli, 'and I'm not doing this to dishonour you. To come to the point, I've fallen so in love with her that I can't get her out of my mind. I now wish to strengthen the friendship between us by asking you to allow me to marry your daughter, Asdis. In return I will pledge my friendship and loyal support and such backing and might from my brother Leiknir and me that no two other men in Iceland could possibly bring you such renown through their support. Our prowess will do more to strengthen your leadership than marrying your daughter to the greatest farmer in Breidafjord. That should make up for the fact that we are not wealthy men. But if you turn me down that will be the end of our friendship, and we will both do whatever we like with our affairs. It wouldn't be much use criticizing me then for talking to Asdis.'

When Halli had said his piece Styr was silent and found it difficult to come up with an answer.

Finally he said, 'Is this an honest proposal or are you just throwing words around and trying to sound me out?'

'You must give me a proper answer,' replied Halli, 'as mine are not empty words. Our whole friendship depends on how you answer this question.'

'In that case,' said Styr, 'I want to discuss this matter with my friends and get their advice about how I should answer.'

'You can discuss this with anyone you like within the next three days,' said Halli. 'I won't wait any longer than that for an answer because I don't want to be a suitor left in the lurch.'

After that they parted. The next morning Styr rode over to Helgafell. When he arrived Snorri invited him to stay but Styr said he just wanted to have a talk and then ride home. Snorri asked whether it was a difficult problem he wanted to discuss.

'It seems like one to me,' Styr replied.

'Then let's walk up on to Helgafell,' said Snorri. 'Plans made there have less chance of coming to nothing.'

'Whatever you think,' said Styr.

They walked up on to the mountain and sat there talking right up until evening. No one knew what they were talking about. Then Styr rode back home.

The following morning he and Halli talked. Halli asked Styr what the situation was with his proposal.

'It's generally thought that you are rather too poor,' replied Styr. 'How will you make up for the fact that you have no money to offer?'

'I am willing to do whatever I can, but I can't produce money when there is none,' Halli replied.

'I see that you wouldn't like it if I refused to marry my daughter to you,' said Styr. 'So I will do as men of the past used to do, and set you certain tasks to perform in order to win her hand.'

'What are they?' Halli asked.

'You shall clear a road across the lava field out to Bjarnarhofn, build a field-wall over the lava between our pastures and make an enclosure on this side of the wall. When you have completed these tasks, I will give my daughter Asdis to you in marriage,' said Styr.

'I'm not used to hard work,' said Halli, 'but I'll agree to it if it enables me to get married.'

Styr then announced that they had struck a deal. Following this the berserks began to clear the road, which was quite a physical feat. They also built the wall, traces of which can still be seen, and after that they built the enclosure. But while they were doing this work, Styr had a bathhouse built on his farm at Hraun. It was dug deep into the ground and had a window above the stone oven so that water could be poured through it from the outside, which made the bathhouse incredibly hot. When all the work was nearly finished and the berserks were spending their last day on the enclosure, Styr's daughter, Asdis, walked past them near the farm. She was dressed in her finest clothes, but when they addressed her, she did not answer.

Then Halli spoke this verse:

21.

Where are you going,
Gerd of the forearm's fire,                    *Gerd* (goddess) *of the forearm's*
walking past so elegantly                              *fire* (gold): woman
– never lie to me, linen-decked one –
for I have never seen you
dressed in such splendour,
walking from the house this winter,
wise goddess of table-games.                   *goddess of table-games*: woman

Then Leiknir spoke another verse:

22.

Seldom has the field of the sea's sun    *sea's sun*: gold; its *field*: woman
been seen with a head-dress so high.
The tree of the hand's fire                    *hand's fire*: gold; its *tree*: woman
is finely attired today.
Woman, what more is there
than we see beneath your conceit,
goddess of the drinking-horn,                   *goddess of the drinking-horn*:
smiling-voiced one.                                               woman

After that she walked away from them. The berserks went
home that evening and were extremely exhausted, as is the way
with those men who are not always in human shape; they
become completely drained whenever the berserk fit leaves them.
Styr went to see them and thanked them for the work they had
done. He suggested they take a bath and then have a rest, which
is what they did. When they were in the bath, Styr had the
bathhouse closed off and piled rocks on top of the trap-door
over the entrance, and had a wet ox-hide spread out in front of
the landing. Then he had water poured through the window
above the stone oven, which made the bathhouse so hot that
the berserks could not bear to stay in the bath and rushed at the
door. Halli managed to break open the trap-door and get out
but he fell on the ox-hide. Styr then gave him his death-wound.
But when Leiknir tried to rush up through the door, Styr thrust
a spear through him and he fell back into the bathhouse and
died there. Then Styr arranged a burial for the bodies. They

were carried out across the lava field and buried in a pit in the lava which was so deep that nothing could be seen from the bottom except the sky above. The pit was close to the path. Styr spoke this verse at the burial of the berserks:

23.

| | |
|---|---|
| It seemed the strengtheners | *strengtheners of the spears' meeting*: |
| of the spears' meeting | berserks |
| might never be easy for | |
| the battle-hardeners to deal with. | *battle-hardeners*: warriors |
| I do not fear the fierce | |
| foes' tyranny against me. | |
| The bold man's blade has shown | |
| the berserks their resting place. | |

When Snorri the Godi heard about this he rode over to Hraun where he and Styr spent the whole day talking together again. The upshot of their conversation was that Styr betrothed his daughter, Asdis, to Snorri the Godi, and the wedding took place the next autumn. Everyone thought that both men's prestige was increased through this liaison. Snorri the Godi was a better strategist and smarter, but Styr was more aggressive. Both of them had a great many kinsmen and many followers in the district.

29 | There was a man named Thorodd whose family came from Medalfellsstrond. He was a trustworthy man and a great merchant who owned his own ship. Thorodd had sailed to Ireland to do some trading in Dublin. At that time Earl Sigurd Hlodvesson of the Orkney Islands[19] had been raiding in the Hebrides and all the way west to the Isle of Man. He imposed taxes on the inhabitants of Man, and when they had accepted his terms he appointed men to collect the tax, which was paid mainly in refined silver. The earl himself sailed back north to the Orkneys.

When those who had collected the tax were ready to sail, they set out into a south-westerly wind. After they had been at sea a while the wind swung round to the south-east, and then to the east, and a storm blew up and drove them north of Ireland where their ship broke up on the shore of an uninhabited island. It was there that Thorodd found them on his voyage back from Dublin. The earl's men called out to the traders for help, and Thorodd had a boat launched and went in it himself. When they met, the earl's men begged Thorodd to help them and offered him money to take them back to the Orkneys to Earl Sigurd, but Thorodd did not think he could do that since he was already on course to Iceland. They kept pleading with him because they believed their property and lives were at stake if they were taken captive in Ireland or the Hebrides where they had just been raiding. Finally Thorodd sold them the boat from the ship for a large portion of the tax they had collected. They then set off for the Orkneys in their boat, and Thorodd travelled to Iceland without a lifeboat. He arrived in Iceland on the southern coast and sailed west along the coast and into Breidafjord. He arrived safely at Dagverdarnes and went to stay with Snorri the Godi at Helgafell during the autumn. From that time on he was known as Thorodd the Tax-trader.

This was just after the killing of Thorbjorn the Stout. That winter, Snorri's sister, Thurid, who had been married to Thorbjorn, was staying at Helgafell. It was not long after Thorodd had been back from abroad that he raised with Snorri the Godi the prospect of marrying his sister, Thurid. Since he was a wealthy man and Snorri knew his background well, and since Thurid needed to be well looked after, Snorri thought it was altogether appropriate that he should marry her, and he hosted their wedding there at Helgafell the same winter. The next spring Thorodd took over the farm at Froda and became a good and honest farmer.

But once Thurid was back at Froda, Bjorn Asbrandsson started making regular visits there and the talk was on everybody's lips that he and Thurid were lovers. Thorodd started to find fault with Bjorn's visits but this had no effect.

At that time, Thorir Wood-leg lived at Arnarhvol. His sons Orn and Val were now fully grown and were very promising young men. They scorned Thorodd for putting up with the shameful treatment he was getting from Bjorn and offered to support Thorodd if he wanted to retaliate.

Once when Bjorn came to Froda and sat talking to Thurid, Thorodd was nowhere to be seen, although he usually stayed in the same room with them while Bjorn was there.

'Take care when you leave, Bjorn,' warned Thurid, 'because I think Thorodd has decided to put an end to your visits here and I suspect that they are lying in wait for you. He won't be intending to give you an even chance.'

Then Bjorn spoke this verse:

24.
We would wish this day the longest
between wood's early glow and darkness
– sometimes the pillar of strings          *pillar of strings*: woman
brings sorrow to me –
since I prepare this evening,
pine-tree of the arm's serpent,          *pine-tree of the arm's serpent*:
to drink a funeral toast                                    woman
to the disappearance of my joy.

After that Bjorn took his weapons and went out heading for home. When he came up around the hill at Digrimuli, five men ambushed him. They were Thorodd, two of his farmhands and the sons of Thorir Wood-leg. They attacked Bjorn but he defended himself well and valiantly. The sons of Thorir were his most spirited attackers. They dealt him some bloody wounds but he killed them both. At this Thorodd retreated with his men. He had minor injuries but they had none.

Bjorn walked on his way until he came home and went into the main room. The mistress of the house asked a servant woman to look after him, but when she came into the room carrying a light she saw that Bjorn was covered in blood. She went straight to his father Asbrand and told him that Bjorn had come home all bloodied.

Asbrand went into the room and asked Bjorn why he was bloodied, 'or did you meet Thorodd?'

Bjorn answered that that was the case. Asbrand asked how things had gone between them.

Bjorn replied:

25.

It won't be as easy for the brave
breaker of battle-storm's fire                    *battle-storm's fire*: sword;
to harm me as for the shield-wielder                    its *breaker*: warrior
to tumble with the woman,
or to trade Draupnir's treasure                    *Draupnir's treasure*: gold
with the cowardly bowman
– since I have put to death
two of Wood-leg's sons.

Then Asbrand dressed his wounds and he recovered completely. Thorodd sought Snorri the Godi's support in the prosecution over the killing of Thorir's sons, and Snorri started a case for the Thorsnes Assembly. The sons of Thorlak of Eyri, however, lent their support to the people of Breidavik in these matters. The outcome of the case was that Asbrand gave surety for his son, Bjorn, and paid the fines for the killings, but Bjorn was outlawed for three years, and went abroad the same summer. The same summer Thurid gave birth to a boy at Froda who was given the name Kjartan. He was raised at Froda and was soon a big and promising boy.

When Bjorn had crossed the ocean he went south to Denmark and from there south to Jomsborg. At that time Palna-Toki was the leader of the Jomsvikings.[20] Bjorn joined them and he was called a champion among them. He was in Jomsborg when Styrbjorn the Strong conquered it, and he travelled to Sweden when the Jomsvikings supported Styrbjorn. He was also at the battle of Fyrisvellir when Styrbjorn fell, and he escaped into the woods with other Jomsvikings. As long as Palna-Toki lived, Bjorn stayed with him and was considered a man of strong character and the bravest one in dangerous situations.

30 | Now we turn back to Thorolf Lame-foot. He began to age quickly, growing more ill-natured, violent and unjust with the years. His relationship with his son Arnkel grew very hostile. One day Thorolf rode over to Ulfarsfell to see the farmer Ulfar. He was a very hard worker and known for harvesting hay faster

than other farmers. He was also so lucky with his livestock that none of his animals ever died from starvation or in blizzards. When Thorolf and Ulfar met, Thorolf asked what advice he would give him about conducting his farm work and what sense he had about how good a summer it would be for drying hay.

'I can't give you any advice other than what I do myself,' replied Ulfar. 'I am going to have the scythes brought out today and have as much grass as possible cut all through this week because I think it might become rainy, but after that my guess is that we will have good drying weather for the next fortnight.'

It turned out just as he had said, for it was often the case that he could predict the weather better than others. Then Thorolf went home and ordered his many farm-workers to get to work at once on the meadows. The weather turned out exactly as Ulfar had said. Thorolf and Ulfar owned a common meadow up on the ridge where they both cut a lot of hay, which was then dried and gathered into haystacks. Early one morning when Thorolf got up and looked outside, the weather was cloudy and he thought that it would be no good for drying. He told his slaves to get up and gather the hay together, telling them to work as hard as they could all day, 'because the weather doesn't look reliable to me.'

The slaves got dressed and went to work on the hay while Thorolf stacked it up and urged them on to get as much work done as they could. That same morning Ulfar went out early to look around and when he came back inside his workmen asked what the weather was like. He told them to sleep on undisturbed.

'The weather is good,' Ulfar said, 'and it will clear up during the day. Today you will cut hay in the homefield, and we'll look after the hay we have up on the ridge tomorrow.'

The weather turned out just as he had said. In the evening Ulfar sent men up to the ridge to check on their haystacks there. Thorolf had three oxen carting hay all day, and they had gathered in all the hay he owned by mid afternoon. Then he told his men to cart Ulfar's hay back to their farm, and they did as they were told. When Ulfar's man saw this he ran back and told Ulfar. Ulfar went up to the ridge very angry, and asked Thorolf why he was robbing him. Thorolf declared he did not care what he said, and started using violent language and became very difficult to deal with. They came close to blows, but Ulfar saw that there was nothing else to do except turn away.

Ulfar then went to see Arnkel, and told him of his loss and asked for his help, saying that without it he would not be able to do anything. Arnkel said he would ask his father to pay compensation for the hay, although he doubted very much that it would make any difference. When Arnkel and his father next met, Arnkel asked him to pay Ulfar for the hay he had taken, but Thorolf replied that the slave was much too wealthy already. Arnkel asked him to pay for the hay for his sake. Thorolf said he would not do anything for Ulfar except make things worse for him, and with that they parted.

Arnkel told Ulfar how Thorolf had answered when he next saw him. It seemed to Ulfar that Arnkel had not pushed the matter very hard, and he said that he could handle his father in such matters if he wanted to. Arnkel paid Ulfar for the hay at the price he wanted. When Arnkel and his father next met, Arnkel again tried to collect the cost of the hay from him but Thorolf's answers did not improve matters and they parted in anger. The next autumn Arnkel had seven of his father's oxen driven down from the mountain pasture and had them all slaughtered for his own household. This displeased Thorolf intensely and he demanded payment for them from Arnkel, who replied that they covered the cost of Ulfar's hay. Thorolf was even more displeased than before and blamed everything on Ulfar, and said he would take care of him.

31 | That winter around Yule Thorolf held a great feast and was very generous in providing his slaves with drinks. Once they were drunk, he egged them on to go over to Ulfarsfell and burn Ulfar to death inside his house. In exchange, he promised them their freedom. The slaves said they would do that for their freedom as long as he kept his word. Then six of them went together over to Ulfarsfell. They took a load of wood and piled it up against the house and set fire to it.

Arnkel and his men were sitting drinking at Bolstad at the

time. When they were on their way to bed, they saw the fire at Ulfarsfell, and rushed over there at once and took hold of the slaves and put out the fire. The house was only slightly burnt. The next morning Arnkel had all the slaves taken over to Vadilshofdi where they were hanged. After that Ulfar handed over all his property to Arnkel, who became Ulfar's legal guardian.

This exchange of property did not please the Thorbrandssons at all. They considered themselves the owners of all Ulfar's property since he was their freed slave. Relations between them and Arnkel soured to the point where they did not even play games together any more, whereas before they had often held matches. Arnkel was the strongest competitor in the games, followed closely by a man named Freystein Bofi, who was Thorbrand's foster-son, and allegedly, according to most people's opinion, his own son, but his mother was a slave. Freystein Bofi was an honourable man and a very strong one.

Thorolf Lame-foot was not at all happy with Arnkel for killing his slaves and sought compensation for them, but Arnkel flatly refused to pay a penny for them. And Thorolf liked that even less. One day Thorolf rode out to Helgafell to visit Snorri the Godi who invited him to stay, but Thorolf said he did not need to eat his food.

'I have come here because I want you to right the wrongs done against me,' said Thorolf, 'since I consider you the leading man in this district, who is therefore obliged to right wrongs on behalf of those who have been unfairly dealt with.'

'Who has been dealing unfairly with you, farmer?' asked Snorri.

'My son Arnkel,' Thorolf replied.

'You shouldn't complain about that,' Snorri said, 'for you'd do well to stay on the same side as him since he's a better man than you are.'

'That's not how it is,' replied Thorolf, 'because he's attacking me directly now. I would like to become a very good friend of yours, Snorri, if you will take up the prosecution of Arnkel for killing my slaves. I wouldn't claim all the compensation for myself.'

'I don't want to get involved in a quarrel between father and son,' Snorri replied.

'You're no friend of Arnkel's,' Thorolf said. 'It may well be that you consider me stingy with money, but that's not how it is now. I know that you would like to own Krakunes and its woods, which are the most precious in this district. I will hand all that over to you if you take up the case of my slaves and pursue it so vigorously that your reputation is enhanced by it and those who dishonoured me consider themselves harshly dealt with. I don't want mercy shown to any member of my family, whether he is a close or distant relative.'

Snorri considered himself very much in need of the woods. And so the story goes that he took over ownership of the land and took on the case of the slaves' killing. Thorolf rode home after that, feeling very pleased with himself, but no one else had much to say in favour of the arrangement.

In the spring Snorri brought a case at the Thorsnes Assembly against Arnkel over the killing of the slaves. There were large numbers on both sides at the assembly and Snorri was the prosecutor. But when the case came before the court, Arnkel called for an acquittal verdict, bringing forward evidence in his defence that the slaves were caught with fires lit for the burning of the farm.

Snorri advanced the argument that the slaves were beyond the protection of the law at the place of the action, 'but the fact is you took them over to Vadilshofdi and killed them there, and, in my opinion, they were not without legal rights there.'

Snorri held the case together and Arnkel's call for an acquittal was dismissed. After that men were appointed to mediate between them and a settlement was reached. The brothers Styr and Vermund had to arbitrate the case. They determined that twelve ounces of silver should be paid for each of the slaves, and it should be paid on the spot at the assembly. Once the fine was paid, Snorri gave the purse to Thorolf. He took it, saying, 'I never expected when I gave you my land that you would follow this up so half-heartedly. I know that Arnkel would not have slighted me by paying me this kind of compensation for my slaves, if I had referred the matter to him.'

'I don't consider you to have been disgraced by this,' replied Snorri, 'but I don't want to stake my reputation on your malice and injustice.'

'It's very likely that I won't often come to you with my problems,' Thorolf said, 'but there'll be other disasters to stop people in the neighbourhood from sleeping.'

After that men left the assembly, with Arnkel and Snorri feeling unhappy about the outcome of the case, but Thorolf was feeling worse.

32 | The story goes that Orlyg of Orlygsstadir became ill. His brother Ulfar sat by him as his life began to slip away. He died from this illness, and as soon as he was dead, Ulfar sent for Arnkel. Arnkel went at once to Orlygsstadir and he and Ulfar laid claim to all the property and possessions there. When the Thorbrandssons heard about Orlyg's death, they went to Orlygsstadir and claimed all the property and possessions that their freed slave had owned, but Ulfar declared himself to be his brother's legal heir. They asked Arnkel which side he would back. Arnkel said that if he had anything to do with it, Ulfar was not going to be robbed by anyone as long as their fellowship continued.

The Thorbrandssons went away then and rode over to Helgafell to tell Snorri the Godi what had happened and to ask for his help. But Snorri said he did not want to get embroiled in a dispute with Arnkel since they had been so slack in taking action to begin with, by letting Arnkel and Ulfar get their hands on the property first. The Thorbrandssons told him that he would not be able to manage bigger issues if he did not take care of matters such as this one.

The next autumn Arnkel held a grand autumn feast at his farm. It was his habit to invite his friend Ulfar to all his feasts, and he always left with fine gifts. On the day when men were to leave the feast at Bolstad, Thorolf Lame-foot rode out from home. He went to visit his friend Seer-Gils, who lived at Seer-Gilsstadir in Thorsardal, and asked him to ride with him up to the ridge at Ulfarsfellshals. Thorolf's slave went with them.

Once they were up on the ridge, Thorolf said, 'That's where Ulfar will be riding back from the feast, and more than likely, he will have valuable gifts that he's taking home. Now I would like you, Seer-Gils, to ride towards him and ambush him beneath the farm-wall at Ulfarsfell, and then I want you to kill him. In return I will give you three marks of silver and I will undertake to pay the compensation for the killing. Once you have killed Ulfar, you can take from him the treasures which he was given by Arnkel. Then run west along Ulfarsfell to Krakunes. If anyone follows you, you'll be able to hide in the woods. Then come back to see me, and I'll make sure that you are not harmed.'

Because Seer-Gils had many dependants and was in much need of money, he accepted this lure and went out to the wall across the hayfield at Ulfarsfell. Then he saw Ulfar going down from Bolstad with a fine shield that Arnkel had given him and a decorated sword. When they met, Seer-Gils asked to see the sword. He praised Ulfar highly, saying he was a noble man to be so worthy of receiving such honourable gifts from chieftains. Ulfar began twirling his finger in his beard and gave him the sword and the shield. At once Gils drew the sword and ran it through Ulfar. After that he ran away from Ulfarsfell to Krakunes.

Arnkel was standing outside when he saw a man running along with a shield, and he thought he recognized the shield. It occurred to him that Ulfar would not have given up the shield willingly.

Arnkel then ordered his men to chase the man, saying, 'because it looks like my father is behind this, and if this man has already killed Ulfar, you should kill him as soon as you get him, whoever he is, and don't let him come into my sight.'

Then Arnkel went up to Ulfarsfell and found Ulfar dead. Thorolf Lame-foot was watching when Seer-Gils ran along Ulfarsfell with the shield, so he assumed he knew what had happened to Ulfar.

He said to the slave who was with him, 'Go east to Karsstadir and tell the Thorbrandssons to go to Ulfarsfell and make sure they're not robbed of their freed slave's estate as they were before, now that Ulfar is dead.'

After that Thorolf rode home, considering himself to have done rather well. Those chasing Seer-Gils got hold of him out at a cliff which rises up from the foreshore. They got the whole story out of him there, and when he had finished telling them all that had happened, they killed him and buried him below the cliff. They took the treasures back to Arnkel.

Thorolf's slave arrived at Karsstadir and told the Thorbrandssons Thorolf's message. They went straight out to Ulfarsfell but when they arrived Arnkel was already there with a lot of men. The Thorbrandssons claimed the property that Ulfar had owned, but Arnkel brought forward the testimony of witnesses who had been present when Ulfar gave him possession of the property. Arnkel said he intended to retain it because it had not been contested at law, and he told them not to make any claims on the property since he was determined to keep it as if it were his own inheritance.

The Thorbrandssons realized that they had no choice but to go away. They went on to Helgafell and told Snorri the Godi what had happened and asked for his support.

Snorri said once again that they had been one move behind Arnkel, 'and you won't be able to wrest the property from his hands now that he has already taken everything into his possession. You have just as good a claim on the property, but it will go to the one who is physically stronger. And it's very likely that Arnkel has more of a chance in this, just as he has had in all your other dealings with him. But it's true to say that what happens to most others will happen to you, since Arnkel gets the better of everyone here in the district, and he will continue to do so while he lives – whether that's for a long or a short time.'

'It's true what you say, Snorri,' Thorleif Kimbi replied. 'You might be said to be excused from defending our rights against Arnkel since you never get the better of him, no matter what the matter is that you are contending with him.'

After that the Thorbrandssons went home in a very sombre mood.

33 | Snorri the Godi started exploiting Krakunes woods with a great deal of tree-felling. Thorolf Lame-foot thought the woods were being destroyed, so he rode over to Helgafell and asked Snorri to give him back the woods, claiming he had only lent them and not given them to him. Snorri said that could be cleared up by asking the opinion of those who had witnessed the deal, adding that he would not give up the woods unless they testified against him. Thorolf then rode away and was in an extremely bad mood. He rode over to Bolstad to see his son Arnkel, who welcomed his father warmly and asked what his business was.

'My purpose in coming here,' said Thorolf, 'is that I'm unhappy that we are getting along so badly. I'd like us to put that behind us and to renew our kinship because it's unnatural for us to be on bad terms. It seems to me we could become the most powerful men in the district with your courage and my plans.'

'I'd certainly like it better if we were closer,' Arnkel replied.

'I propose, then, that we begin our reconciliation and friendship by getting back Krakunes woods from Snorri the Godi, because I think it's the worst thing in the world that he oppresses us and won't give me back the woods. He even says that I have given them to him, but that's a lie,' Thorolf said.

'It wasn't out of friendship for me that you gave the woods to Snorri,' Arnkel said, 'and I'm not going to get involved in a dispute with Snorri about the woods on account of your slander. I know that he doesn't have any legal rights to the woods, but I don't want to see you, through your maliciousness, gloating over a quarrel between Snorri and me.'

'In my opinion,' said Thorolf, 'it is more your meanness, than your denying me the pleasure of a quarrel between the two of you.'

'Believe whatever you like about it,' Arnkel replied, 'but as matters stand, I'm not going to quarrel with Snorri over the woods.'

With that, father and son parted. Thorolf went home, very unhappy with his lot, thinking that he would not be able to get his own way easily. Thorolf Lame-foot arrived home in the evening and did not speak to anyone. He sat down in his high seat and did not eat anything all evening. He sat there after everyone else had gone to bed. In the morning when they got up, Thorolf was still sitting there and he was dead.

The mistress of the house sent a messenger to Arnkel to advise him of Thorolf's death. Arnkel rode over to Hvamm with some of his men. When they arrived at Hvamm, Arnkel made sure that his father was dead, sitting there in the high seat, but everyone else was terrified because his death seemed to them so unpleasant. Then Arnkel went into the fire room, and walked up along the benches behind Thorolf. He told everyone to beware of walking in front of him until his eyes had been closed. Then Arnkel took hold of Thorolf's shoulders and he had to exert more force than he expected in order to move him. He wrapped some clothes around Thorolf's head and prepared his body according to the customs of the time. After that he had the wall behind him broken down to drag the body outside. Oxen were harnessed to a sled on which Thorolf's corpse was laid, which was then driven up into Thorsardal, but not without a lot of effort, until he was brought to the place where he was to be buried. They buried Thorolf in a strongly built cairn.

After that Arnkel rode home to Hvamm and claimed as his own all the property and possessions his father had owned. Arnkel stayed there for three nights and this was an uneventful time. Then he went back home.

34 | After the death of Thorolf Lame-foot, it seemed to many people worse to be out of doors once the sun went down. As the summer passed, they became aware that Thorolf was not resting in peace. People could never go outside in peace once the sun had set. As well as that, the oxen that had hauled Thorolf to his grave had been ridden by trolls, and all livestock which came anywhere near Thorolf's cairn ran wild and bellowed themselves to death. The shepherd at Hvamm often came running home because Thorolf had chased him.

Then there was an incident at Hvamm during the autumn when neither the shepherd nor the livestock came home, and in the morning when a search was made for them, the shepherd was found dead a short distance from Thorolf's cairn. His body was coal-black all over and every bone was broken. He was buried beside Thorolf. All the livestock which had been in the valleys were either found dead or they had strayed into the mountains, never to be found again. And if any birds landed on Thorolf's cairn, they fell down dead at once.

Things got to the stage where no one dared to graze their animals up in the valley. People often heard loud noises outside during the night at Hvamm, and they often became aware that there were people outside riding on their roofs. Once winter came Thorolf often appeared on the farm, pursuing the mistress of the house most of all. Many people were harmed by this, but it drove her out of her wits, and she ended up dying because of it. She was carried up into Thorsardal and buried beside Thorolf.

After that everyone fled from the farm. Thorolf now began walking around the valley so widely that he devastated all the farms. It got so bad that his ghost killed some men and some fled. And all those people who died were then seen in Thorolf's company. People were now complaining a lot about this menace. Arnkel seemed to them to be the one responsible for setting things right. He invited anyone to stay with him who thought they were better off there than anywhere else. Wherever Arnkel was, there was never any trouble from Thorolf and his company. People grew so afraid of Thorolf's ghost during the winter that no one dared to go about their usual business, even if it was urgent.

But winter passed and fine spring days began to thaw the earth. Once it was completely thawed, Arnkel sent a messenger over to Karsstadir to the Thorbrandssons and asked them to go with him to move Thorolf out of Thorsardal and to find another burial site. According to the laws of the time, everyone was bound to help move dead people into graves if they were asked, just as they are obliged to do now. But when the Thorbrandssons heard this they said they saw no need to do anything to get Arnkel or any of his men out of their difficulties.

Then the old man Thorbrand said, 'It is necessary to do whatever the law requires people to do, and you have been asked to do something you cannot refuse to do.'

Thorodd then said to the messenger, 'Go back and tell Arnkel that I will help him with this on behalf of us brothers. I'll go to Ulfarsfell and meet him there.'

The messenger went back and told Arnkel this. He got ready for his journey straightaway and left with eleven men, a sled and digging tools. First they went up to Ulfarsfell, where they met up with Thorodd Thorbrandsson and two of his men. They rode up along the ridge and came into Thorsardal, where they broke open Thorolf's cairn. Thorolf's body had not decayed but he was very hideous to look at. They took him out of the grave and laid him on the sled which was drawn by two strong oxen. They hauled him up to Ulfarsfellshals but the oxen were so exhausted by it that they had to be replaced by two others to drag him farther along the ridge. Arnkel was planning to take him over to Vadilshofdi and bury him there, but when they came to the edge of the ridge, the oxen went crazy and broke loose. They ran down the ridge and headed out along the hillside above the farm at Ulfarsfell, and from there out to the foreshore where they both collapsed and died. Thorolf was by now so heavy that they could hardly manage to lift him at all. They dragged him across to a small headland which was nearby and buried him there. It has been known as Lame-foot Headland ever since. Then Arnkel had a wall built across the headland above the cairn, so high that no one could see over it except a bird in flight, and remains of the wall can still be seen. Thorolf lay there quietly as long as Arnkel lived.

35 | Snorri the Godi continued to exploit Krakunes woods despite the fact that Thorolf Lame-foot had raised objections to it, but Arnkel the Godi soon made it known that he did not think the title to the woods had been legally transferred. In his opinion, Thorolf had defrauded his rightful heirs by handing over the woods to Snorri the Godi.

One summer Snorri sent his slaves to work in the woods. They chopped down a great deal of timber, stacked it up and then went back to the farm. When the timber was drying, Arnkel pretended as if he were going to have the timber brought to his

farm, but that is not what he did. Instead he told his shepherd
to keep watch and tell him when Snorri had the timber fetched.
When the timber was dry, Snorri sent three of his slaves to fetch
it. He got his follower, Hauk, to accompany the slaves and
support them. They set off and loaded the timber on to twelve
horses and then turned on their way back to the farm.

Arnkel's shepherd watched their movements carefully and
told Arnkel. He took his weapons and rode after them, catching
up with them between the Svelgsa river and Holar. When he
approached them, Hauk jumped off his horse and thrust at
Arnkel with his spear, but the blow landed on the shield and
did not cause any injury. Then Arnkel jumped off his horse and
thrust at him with his spear, and that blow went through his
belly and he fell there at the place now known as Hauksa river.

When the slaves saw Hauk was dead, they took off and ran
home along the path with Arnkel chasing them all the way
past Oxnabrekkur. He turned back there and drove the horses
carrying the timber back to his farm. He unloaded the timber
and let the horses loose after tying the ropes up on their backs.
They were then shown the way out along the hillside, which
they followed until they came to Helgafell. News of this soon
got around, but everything stayed quiet for the rest of the year.

The next spring Snorri the Godi brought a case over the killing
of Hauk at the Thorsnes Assembly, and Arnkel brought a charge
of assault against Hauk to invalidate Snorri's case. There were
many supporters on both sides at the assembly, and the case
was contested with vehemence. The result of the case was that
Hauk was found to have been beyond the protection of the law
on account of his assault, so Snorri's charge was quashed.
Everyone rode away from the assembly after that. But there was
much resentment among people for the rest of the summer.

36 | Thorleif was the name of a man from the East Fjords
     | who had been sentenced to lesser outlawry for seducing a
woman. He came to Helgafell in the autumn and asked Snorri
the Godi to take him in. Snorri turned him away, but they talked
for a very long time before he went away. After that, Thorleif

went over to Bolstad, arriving in the evening and staying there for two nights. Arnkel got up early in the morning and was repairing his outside door. When Thorleif got up, he went to Arnkel and asked him to take him in. Arnkel answered rather hesitantly, and asked him if he had been to see Snorri the Godi.

'I saw him,' said Thorleif, 'and he would not have me on any account. Still I don't think much of supporting a man who always lets someone else get the better of him.'

'I don't think Snorri would make much of a bargain by offering to feed you in return for your support,' Arnkel replied.

'I'd rather be taken in by someone such as yourself, Arnkel,' Thorleif said.

'I'm not in the habit of receiving people from outside the district,' Arnkel replied.

They kept on arguing about this for quite a while. Thorleif kept on about the matter, but Arnkel turned him down. Arnkel was then drilling into the cross-plank of the door, and had laid aside his adze while he did it. Thorleif picked it up and lifted it quickly up above his head, intending to bring it down on Arnkel's head. But when Arnkel heard the whistling sound of the adze through the air, he jumped out of the way of the blow. He lifted Thorleif up to his chest, and the difference in their strength was soon apparent, for Arnkel was a very powerful man. He dashed Thorleif down on to the ground with such force that he almost lost consciousness and the adze was flung out of his hand. Arnkel took hold of it and struck into Thorleif's head with it, giving him a fatal wound.

There was talk that Snorri the Godi had sent this man after Arnkel's head. Snorri did not get involved in the discussion, and let people say whatever they wanted to, and so the year passed without incident.

37 | The next autumn at the Winter Nights, Snorri the Godi hosted a great autumn feast and invited his friends to it. Ale was served and the drinking was heavy. People grew merry with the ale, and there was a lot of talk about who the most eminent man or the greatest chieftain in the district was. People

were by no means of one opinion on this, as is often the way when there is talk of comparing men. Most of them thought Snorri the Godi was the most eminent man, but some went for Arnkel. A few even named Styr.

While they were discussing this, Thorleif Kimbi had his say: 'Why are you all arguing about this when everyone can see who the greatest man is.'

'What's your opinion then, Thorleif,' they asked, 'if you are going to be so frank about the matter?'

'Arnkel seems by far the best to me,' he said.

'What makes you think that?' they asked.

'It's the truth, that's all,' he said. 'In my opinion, Snorri the Godi and Styr count as one man because of their kinship, but none of Arnkel's household lies dead and unatoned beside his farm, killed by Snorri, whereas Snorri's supporter, Hauk, lies here beside Snorri's farm, killed by Arnkel.'

People thought that was going too far, considering where they were, even though it was true, and the conversation died down.

When everyone was leaving the feast, Snorri chose gifts for his friends. He accompanied the Thorbrandssons to their ship at Raudavikurhofdi headland.

When they were ready to part, Snorri went up to Thorleif Kimbi and said, 'Here is an axe, Thorleif, which I want to give you. It has the longest handle of any I own, but it is not long enough to reach Arnkel's head while he is haymaking at Orlygs-stadir, if you should take it with you from home in Alftafjord.'

Thorleif accepted the axe and said, 'Bear in mind that I will not hesitate to raise my axe against Arnkel once you are ready to avenge your supporter, Hauk.'

'I think you Thorbrandssons owe it to me to keep a look out for when I might have a chance with Arnkel. If I don't join you, when you've warned me that something could be done, then you can blame me.'

They parted at that, both sides saying they were prepared to kill Arnkel, but the Thorbrandssons were to keep a watch on his movements. Early in the winter there was a severe freeze, and all the fjords iced over. Freystein Bofi was looking after sheep in Alftafjord, and was also meant to be looking out for an opportunity to get Arnkel. Arnkel was a hard worker and made his slaves work from sun-up to sun-down. He had responsibility for both the farm at Ulfarsfell and the one at Orlygsstadir, since no one else was prepared to farm that land in the face of the Thorbrandssons' hostility.

During the winter it was Arnkel's habit to move hay from Orlygsstadir during the night by the light of the moon, since the slaves worked all through the day. He did not care at all that the Thorbrandssons were well aware whenever hay was being moved. One winter's night before Yule, Arnkel got up during the night and woke up three of his slaves, including one named Ofeig. Arnkel the farmer went with them over to Orlygsstadir, and they had four oxen and two sleds with them. The Thorbrandssons became aware of their journey and Freystein Bofi went over the ice to Helgafell at once, arriving at night when everyone had been in bed for a while. He woke up Snorri the Godi.

Snorri asked him what he wanted, and he answered, 'The old eagle has flown after its prey at Orlygsstadir.'

Snorri stood up and told everyone to get dressed. When they were dressed, they took their weapons and nine of them went out together across the ice to Alftafjord. When they reached the head of the fjord, the Thorbrandssons met up with them, and there were six of them. They all went up to Orlygsstadir together. When they arrived, one of the slaves had already taken back a cartload of hay, and Arnkel and the others were at work on the next load. Then they saw that armed men were coming up from the foreshore.

Ofeig was afraid that there might be trouble, saying, 'the only thing to do is for us to go back home.'

'I think the best policy here is for each of us to do whatever he thinks best,' said Arnkel. 'You should run home and wake up my supporters, who will get here quickly. The haystack is a good place to fight from, and I will defend myself from here if these men are hostile, because that seems better to me than running away. I will not weaken quickly. My men will arrive quickly to support me if you carry out your mission honourably.'

By the time Arnkel had said this, the slaves were on the run. Ofeig was the faster of the two. He was so scared that he nearly went out of his wits. He raced up into the mountain and fell into a waterfall and died. The waterfall is called Ofeigsfoss. The other slave ran back to the farm and as he went past the barn, his companion was there carting in the hay. He called out to the slave running past to help him bring in the hay, and it so happened that he had no objection to this work and joined him.

To return to Arnkel, he had recognized the party of men as Snorri the Godi's. He ripped the running-blade from the sled and took it up into the haystack with him. The haystack wall was tall on the outside and the hay was piled up even higher inside, except for at the end inside the wall, which was a good place to fight from. When Snorri and his men arrived at the haystack, it is not mentioned that they exchanged any words. They launched their attack at once, mostly with spears, and Arnkel defended himself with the running-blade. Many of their spear-shafts were broken but Arnkel was not wounded. When they had run out of missiles, Thorleif Kimbi ran towards the haystack and climbed up it with a drawn sword, but Arnkel swung the running-blade at him and Thorleif had to fall down backwards from the haystack to avoid the blow. The blade hit the haystack wall and went over on to the frozen turfs, where it broke at the strap holes, with one half flying out of the haystack. Arnkel had brought his sword and shield up into the haystack, and he took up his weapons now to defend himself, although he was in great danger of being wounded. They came up into the haystack and attacked him, but Arnkel climbed higher up on to the hay and held his position for a while. But in the end Arnkel was killed, and they hid his body under the hay in the haystack. After that Snorri and his men went back to Helgafell.

Thormod Trefilsson composed this verse in his long praise poem about Arnkel:

26.
With his sword the stout-hearted
warrior provided enough food
for the bird of wounds – young Snorri          *bird of wounds*: raven

won fame for himself in victory;
when he felled Arnkel,
the gladdener of Leifi's gull                *Leifi*: sea-king; his *gull*: raven; its
struck at the chest of life                                     *gladdener*: warrior
with the wound-sea's fire.                *wound-sea*: blood; its *fire*: sword

To return now to Arnkel's slaves, they went inside after they had finished unloading the hay, and took off their leather cloaks. Arnkel's followers woke up and asked them where he was. It was as if the slave awoke from a dream, and he replied:

'The truth is, he must be fighting Snorri the Godi at Orlygsstadir now.'

The men leapt up, got dressed and went as quickly as they could over to Orlygsstadir, where they found their master Arnkel dead. His death was mourned by everyone because he had been the most accomplished of all men in ancient times. He was the wisest of them all, even-tempered, stout-hearted, braver than anyone else, determined and very moderate. He always came out best in lawsuits, no matter who his adversary was. He was envied because of this, as the final events of his life show. They took Arnkel's body and prepared it for burial. Arnkel was placed in a burial mound by the sea out on Vadilshofdi headland, and the mound is as big as a large haystack.

38 | Arnkel's only heirs were women, and because of this the prosecution for his killing was not taken up with as much energy as might have been expected for such a great man. Nevertheless, the case was settled at the assembly, but only one man was outlawed for it: Thorleif Kimbi had to go abroad for three years after being charged with giving Arnkel his death-wound.

Since the outcome of this case was not as honourable as was thought fitting for a great chieftain such as Arnkel, the leading men of the land made a law that a woman or a young man under the age of sixteen could never prosecute a manslaughter case, and this has been the law ever since.

39 | Thorleif Kimbi made his journey that summer with some
     | traders who were preparing their ship at Straumfjord, and
he kept company with the leading men. It was the custom of
traders not to have a cook, but for the messmates themselves to
cast lots to decide which of them would prepare the food each
day. All the sailors had to get their drinking water from a cask
with a lid over it which stood by the mast. Extra water was kept
in barrels which was used to replenish the cask when it was
emptied.

When they were very nearly ready to set off, a man arrived at
Budarhamar. He was a very big man, and he carried a load on
his back. He struck people as rather strange. He asked to see
the skipper and was shown to his booth. He took off his bundle
by the door of the booth, and then went inside. He asked the
skipper if he would grant him passage on his ship. They asked
him his name and he said it was Arnbjorn, son of Asbrand of
Kamb. He said he wanted to travel abroad to look for his
brother, Bjorn, who had gone abroad several winters before,
but had not been heard of since he was in Denmark. The
Norwegians said that the cargo was already fastened down and
they did not think it could be undone at this stage. He said he
had so little baggage for the journey that it could lie on top of
the cargo. Because he seemed to them to need to make this
journey, they took him on board, but he prepared his meals by
himself and slept on the forward deck. In his baggage were three
hundred ells of homespun cloth, twelve homespun cloaks and
the provisions for his journey. Arnbjorn was handy around the
ship and ready to help, and the traders held him in high regard.

They had a good outward passage, arriving in Hordaland at
one of the outer islands, where they went ashore to prepare their
meal. It was Thorleif Kimbi's turn to cook, and he was supposed
to make gruel. Arnbjorn was already on shore making gruel for
himself, using the pot that Thorleif also wanted to use. Thorleif
went ashore and asked Arnbjorn to give him the pot, but he had
not yet thickened his gruel, and kept stirring the pot. Thorleif
was left standing there. Then the Norwegians called out from
the ship to Thorleif, telling him to get their meal ready, adding

that it was typical of an Icelander to be so casual about his task. Thorleif lost his temper and grabbed the pot and took it away, spilling Arnbjorn's gruel. Arnbjorn was left sitting there holding the ladle, but then he struck at Thorleif with it and hit him on the neck. It was a light blow, but because the gruel was hot, Thorleif's neck was burnt.

'Since we are both Icelanders, the Norwegians aren't going to get a chance to laugh at us by having to drag us apart like dogs,' said Thorleif. 'But I'll remind you of this when we're both back in Iceland.' Arnbjorn did not respond.

They remained at anchor there for a few nights before they got a favourable wind to sail ashore and unload the ship. Thorleif found lodgings there, but Arnbjorn got a passage east with some merchant-seamen to Vik, and from there to Denmark to look for his brother Bjorn.

40 | Thorleif Kimbi spent two years in Norway and returned to Iceland with the same traders as he had travelled with before. They arrived in Breidafjord and came ashore at Dagverdarnes. Thorleif went home to Alftafjord in autumn, and was very pleased with himself as usual.

The same summer the brothers Bjorn and Arnbjorn arrived back in Iceland at Hraunhofn estuary. Bjorn was now known as the Champion of the Breidavik People. Arnbjorn had made quite a lot of money abroad, and bought land at Bakki in Hraunhofn as soon as he got back that summer. He established a farm there the following spring, after spending the winter with his kinsman, Thord Blig.

Arnbjorn was not a showy sort of person, and had little to say on most matters, but he was nevertheless a great man in all respects. His brother, Bjorn, was a very showy man when he returned to Iceland, dressing very well according to the fashion of continental leaders. He was a much more handsome man than Arnbjorn, but he was by no means worthless, having proven himself in battle and distinguished himself while abroad.

During the summer when they had just come back, there was a large gathering of people north of the heath beneath

Haugabrekkur, east of the Froda river estuary. All the traders rode over to it, dressed in brightly coloured clothes. When they arrived, there were already many people there. Thurid, the mistress of the house at Froda, was there and Bjorn went to talk to her, though no one thought much of it since it was to be expected they would have a lot to talk about, having not seen each other for so long.

A skirmish between some of the men broke out during the day, and one of the northerners was fatally wounded. His body was carried underneath a bush which grew on the gravel-bank by the river. So much blood flowed out of the wound that a pool of blood formed next to the bush. Kjartan, the son of Thurid of Froda, had a small axe in his hand, and he ran over to the bush and dipped the axe in the blood. When the people who lived south of the heath rode back south from the meeting, Thord Blig asked how Bjorn's talk with Thurid of Froda had turned out. Bjorn said it had gone well. Then Thord asked whether he had noticed during the day the young boy Kjartan, the son of Thorodd's household.

'Yes, I saw him,' Bjorn replied.

'What did you think of him?' asked Thord.

Then Bjorn spoke this verse:

27.

I saw where the boy ran
to the wolf's well by the bush;　　　　　*wolf's well*: pool of blood
ferocity in his eyes –
in my exact likeness;
spenders of the river's fire　　　　　*river's fire*: gold; its *spenders*: men
say the child hardly recognized
his father, the helmsman
of the rolling current's horse.　　　　　*the rolling current's horse*: ship

'What will Thorodd have to say about which of you is the boy's father?' asked Thord.

Bjorn spoke this verse:

28.

| | |
|---|---|
| Then will the slender fir-tree of the tapestry | *fir-tree of the tapestry*: |
| affirm Thorodd's guess – | woman |
| that the snow-white land | *land of the head-dress*: woman |
| of the head-dress loved me – | |
| if the well-bred woman | |
| had a son so like me; | |
| I yearn for the goddess | *wave's fire*: gold; its *goddess*: woman |
| of the wave's fire yet. | |

'It may be in your best interest not to have anything to do with Thurid, and to stop thinking about her,' said Thord.

'That may be so,' said Bjorn, 'but that's far from how I feel, even though it will mean taking on a powerful man like Snorri the Godi, her brother.'

'Then you'd better work out your own plan of action,' said Thord, and that was the end of their conversation.

Bjorn went back to Kamb where he took over the management of the farm, since his father was by now dead. That winter he set out on a journey north over the heath to visit Thurid. Even though Thorodd felt uneasy about it, he could not see a way of putting a stop to it, since it kept going round in his head how difficult it had been for him when he had interfered in their affair before, and he saw that Bjorn was much stronger now.

That winter Thorodd paid Thorgrima Magic-cheek to bring about a wild storm while Bjorn was crossing the heath. One day Bjorn went over to Froda, but when he left to go home that evening, the sky was overcast and it had started to rain, and he was rather late getting going. By the time he came up to the heath, the weather had turned very cold and there were snow-drifts. It was so dark that he could not see the path in front of him. After that a blizzard blew up with so much force that he could hardly stand up. His clothes, which were soaked through, began to freeze, and he had completely lost his bearings and did not know which way he was going. He came upon a cave jutting out of the land, and went into it to shelter for the night, but it was a cold campsite.

Then Bjorn spoke this verse:

29.

The goddess of the sea's flame          *sea's flame*: gold; its *goddess*: woman
– she who spreads the cloth
over the wide bed – would hardly
think well of my lot,
if the goddess of wave-fire          *wave-fire*: gold; its *goddess*: woman
knew that I, courtly fir-tree
of the sea's steed, lay frozen,          *sea's steed*: ship; its *fir-tree*: man
alone, in a cave of stones.

And then he spoke another verse:

30.

From the east, my laden ship of planks
has plied the ice-cold earth of swans,          *earth of swans*: sea
ever since the flirting bride
brought us straight to love;
many a hardship I've endured,
but now the hardy battle-tree          *battle-tree*: warrior
lives here in a cave for a while,
instead of on a woman's pillow.

Bjorn was in the cave for three days and nights before the storm let up, and walked back across the heath on the fourth day and got back to Kamb. He was completely exhausted. Men on the farm asked him where he had been during the storm.

Bjorn replied:

31.

Our deeds became famous
under Styrbjorn's gilded standards;
iron-clad Eirik piled up
men in the din of spears;          *din of spears*: battle
I have trodden the heath-land
lost as a bewildered hound,
stumbling across the wide ways
in the woman's wet magic snow-drift.

Bjorn spent the rest of the winter at home. In the spring his brother Arnbjorn established a farm at Bakki in Hraunhofn, but Bjorn continued to farm at Kamb, and his farm became a great estate.

41 | The same spring at the Thorsnes Assembly Thorleif Kimbi asked to marry Helga, the daughter of Thorlak of Eyri and the sister of Steinthor of Eyri. Her brother Thormod, who was married to Thorleif Kimbi's sister, Thorgerd Thorbrandsdottir, was very much in favour of this. But when the matter was raised with Steinthor, he responded hesitantly, and passed the decision over to his brothers.

Then they went to see Thord Blig, who responded by saying, 'I'm not going to leave this matter up to other people; I'm going to take it on myself. What I have to say to you, Thorleif, is that those scars on your neck, that you got from the burning porridge three winters ago in Norway, will have to heal before I will marry my sister to you.'

'I don't know what can be done about that,' replied Thorleif. 'But whether this is avenged or not, I hope someone gets the better of you before another three winters pass.'

'Your threats don't unsettle me,' Thord replied.

The next morning there was a turf-game[21] going on outside the Thorbrandssons' booth when the Thorlakssons were walking by. Just as they were going past, a big sandy sod flew up and hit Thord Blig on the neck with such force that his legs were thrown up over his head. When he stood up, he saw that the Thorbrandssons were all laughing at him. The Thorlakssons turned back at once and drew their weapons. The two sides attacked each other and started fighting. Some men were wounded, but nobody died. Steinthor had not been with them when this happened; he had been talking to Snorri the Godi.

When the sides were separated, a settlement was sought and it was decided that Snorri and Steinthor should arbitrate. The wounds on each side were roughly equal, as was the aggression on each side, but any disparities had to be compensated for. Everyone had been nominally reconciled by the time they rode home from the assembly.

42 | That summer a ship arrived at the mouth of Hraunhofn, and another at Dagverdarnes. Snorri the Godi had business to do with the ship at Hraunhofn, and rode there with fifteen men. As they rode south over the heath into Dufgusdal, six fully armed men galloped after them. They were the Thorbrandssons. Snorri asked them where they were intending to go. They answered that they were going to the ship at Hraunhofn mouth. Snorri said he would do their business on their behalf and asked them to ride back home without taunting anyone, saying that it often took very little to provoke people who had previously been on cool terms, if they should happen to meet.

Thorleif Kimbi replied, 'It will never be said of us that we didn't dare ride through the Breidavik people's territory, but you may well ride home yourself if you don't dare ride on your way, even though you have business to do.'

Snorri did not reply. Then they rode out across the ridges and on to Hofgard, and from there out over the sand banks along the coast. When they were right out towards the mouth of the inlet, the Thorbrandssons rode apart and went up to Bakki. When they came to the farmstead, they leapt down from their horses and intended to go inside, but they could not break open the door. They then jumped up on to the roof of the building and started to tear it off. Arnbjorn took up his weapons and defended himself from inside the farmstead, thrusting his spear through the roof, which caused them a few injuries. It was then early in the morning and the weather was clear.

The men of Breidavik had risen early that morning, intending to ride down to the ship. As they came past Oxl they saw a man in fine clothes on the roof of the farm at Bakki. And they knew that was not Arnbjorn's attire. Bjorn and his men then changed direction and rode up there. When Snorri the Godi realized that the Thorbrandssons had ridden apart from his company, he rode back after them. When they reached Bakki, they were still madly trying to tear off the roof of the farmstead. Snorri asked them to leave and not to cause trouble while in his company. Since they had not managed to get inside the farmstead, they gave up their attack as Snorri directed, and then rode down to the ship with Snorri.

The men of Breidavik arrived at the ship during the day, and each side kept to itself. There were a lot of hard feelings and wariness between them, but neither side attacked the other. The men of Breidavik had greater numbers at the marketplace. In the evening Snorri the Godi rode south to Hofgard, where Bjorn lived with his son Gest, the father of Hofgarda-Ref. Bjorn the Champion of the Breidavik People and his men offered to ride after Snorri and his supporters but Arnbjorn did not want that, saying that each side should be content for now with what they had achieved. Snorri and his men rode home the next day and the Thorbrandssons now considered themselves worse off than before. And so the autumn passed.

43 | Thorbrand of Alftafjord had a slave called Egil the Strong. He was the biggest and strongest of men, and was unhappy with his life as a slave, and often asked Thorbrand and his sons to give him his freedom, offering to do whatever he could to earn it. One evening Egil went to herd the sheep along Alftafjord out to Borgardal. As evening drew on he saw an eagle flying from the west across the fjord. Egil had with him a large foxhound, which the eagle swooped on and lifted up in its talons, flying back to the west across the fjord to the cairn of Thorolf Lame-foot, and then it disappeared into the mountain. Thorbrand believed this sighting to be an omen.

Around the Winter Nights it was the custom of the people of Breidavik to hold ball games under Oxl mountain, south of Knorr. The spot is still called Leikskalavellir (Game-shed plains), and people from the whole district would come there. Large sheds were built for them to stay in, and some of them stayed for a fortnight or longer. At that time there was a good supply of fit men, as the district was well populated and most of the young men, except Thord Blig, were in the games. He would not join in on account of his aggressive temperament – not because he was so strong that he was not able to take part.

He sat on a stool and watched the games. Because of their strength, it was not considered fair for the brothers Bjorn and Arnbjorn to play except against one another.

That same autumn the Thorbrandssons told their slave Egil to go to the ball games and kill one of the Breidavik men, either Bjorn, Thord or Arnbjorn, and in return he would receive his freedom. According to some this was done on the advice of Snorri the Godi, who had given instructions to Egil to find out if he could hide inside the shed and make his attack from there. He was to go down the mountain pass which rises up from Leikskalar, but he was only to go down after the fires for the evening meal had been made, because he said there was usually an evening breeze from the sea which would blow the smoke up into the mountain pass then. He told him to wait until the mountain pass was filled with smoke before going down.

Egil went on this journey, going first out along the fjord asking after the Alftafjord sheep and pretending that he was looking for them. But while he was on this journey, Freystein Bofi was looking after the sheep back at Alftafjord. On the evening that Egil left, Freystein went west across the river to check on the sheep, and when he came to the avalanche, named Geirvor, on the other side of the river, he saw a severed human head lying out in the open.

The head spoke this stanza:

32.
Geirvor is bloodied
by the gore of men,
she will hide
the skulls of men.

He told Thorbrand about this apparition, and he thought it was portentous. Meanwhile Egil made his way out along the fjord and up on to the mountain east of Bulandshofdi, and then south over the mountains, heading for the mountain pass down to Leikskalar. He hid there during the day and watched the games. Thord Blig was sitting on the sidelines.

'I'm not sure what it is I see up there in the mountain pass,' said Thord, 'whether it's a bird or a man hiding, but it comes into view from time to time. It's certainly alive,' he said. 'I think it would be a good idea to investigate it,' but that was not done.

That day it was the turn of Bjorn the Champion of the Breidavik People and Thord Blig to do the cooking, and Bjorn was to make the fire and Thord to fetch the water. When the fire was made, the smoke drifted up into the mountain pass just as Snorri had said. Then Egil made his way down under the cover of the smoke towards the shed.

The games were not yet finished, but it was very late, and the fires were now blazing away so that the shed was full of smoke. And Egil made his way there. He had got quite stiff crouching up on the mountain. He had tasselled shoe-laces, as was the custom then, and one of the laces had become untied so that the tassel trailed along the ground. The slave went into the entrance hall of the shed. When he went into the main hall, he wanted to move silently because he could see Bjorn and Thord sitting by the fire, and Egil felt it would only be a little while before he earned for himself everlasting freedom. But when he went to step across the threshold, he trod on the loose tassel. When he tried to step forward with his other foot, the tassel held fast, causing him to trip, and he fell forward on to the floor of the hall. There was a huge thud as if the skinned carcass of a cow had been thrown down on the floor.

Thord leapt up and asked what enemy was there. Bjorn leapt up too and grabbed hold of Egil before he could get to his feet, and asked him who he was.

'It's Egil here, Bjorn, my friend,' he said.

'Who is this Egil?' Bjorn asked.

'Egil from Alftafjord,' he replied.

Thord drew his sword and wanted to kill him.

Bjorn took hold of Thord and told him not to kill the man so quickly, saying, 'we want to get the whole story out of him first.'

Then they put fetters on Egil's feet. In the evening when people had come back to the shed, Egil recounted how his journey was meant to have turned out, in full hearing of everyone. He stayed there that night, but the next morning they led him up the mountain pass, which is now known as Egilsskard, and there they killed him.

It was the law in those days that if a man killed another man's slave, he had to take the compensation payment of twelve ounces of silver to his home, beginning his journey there no later than the third sunrise after the killing of the slave. If the payment for the slave was legally made, there was no case to be answered for the killing of the slave.

After the killing of Egil the men of Breidavik decided to discharge the slave payment according to the law, and chose thirty men from those at the Leikskalar games, and that was a select band. They rode north across the heath and spent the night at Eyri with Steinthor. He joined them on their journey, bringing the total number in their band to sixty. They rode east along the fjord and spent the second night at Bakki with Thormod, Steinthor's brother. They asked their kinsmen, Styr and Vermund, to join them, making their number eighty altogether.

Then Steinthor sent a man over to Helgafell to find out what Snorri the Godi would do when he found out about the band of men they had gathered together. When the messenger arrived at Helgafell, Snorri the Godi was sitting in his high seat, and there was nothing unusual about the household. Steinthor's messenger was none the wiser about Snorri's intentions. When he returned to Bakki, he described the situation at Helgafell to Steinthor.

'It was to be expected that Snorri would abide by the law,' said Steinthor. 'And if he's not going to Alftafjord, I don't see why we need a large force, because I want us to behave prudently, even though we are conducting our case legally. It would seem a good idea to me, kinsman Thord,' Steinthor went on, 'for you and the rest of the Breidavik men to stay here, because it will only take the smallest incident to start a fight between you and the Thorbrandssons.'

'Well I'm certainly going,' replied Thord, 'because Thorleif Kimbi is not going to have cause to mock me for not daring to deliver the slave payment.'

Then Steinthor said to Bjorn and his brother Arnbjorn, 'I would like you two to stay behind with twenty men.'

'I'm not going to fight to come along with you, if you don't

think it's appropriate,' said Bjorn, 'but this will be the first time
I've ever been rejected from a band of men. It's my opinion
that Snorri the Godi will outsmart you in his actions. I'm not
clairvoyant, but I've got a hunch how this journey will turn out,
and before we next meet you will have found yourself with too
few men to support you.'

'I will make the decisions here while I am in charge,' said
Steinthor, 'even though I'm not as clever as Snorri the Godi.'

'You can do whatever you like, kinsman, as far as I'm concerned,' Bjorn replied.

After that Steinthor and his men rode away from Bakki, and
there were almost sixty of them altogether, riding east along
Skeid to Drapuhlid, then over Vatnshals and across Svelgsardal,
from where they headed east to Ulfarsfellshals.

44 | Snorri the Godi had sent word to his neighbours asking
   | them to move their ships under the headland at Rauda-
vikurhofdi. As soon as Steinthor's messenger had left the farm,
Snorri and his men went to the ships. He did not leave earlier
because he felt certain a man would be sent to spy on his
activities. Snorri sailed in along Alftafjord on the three ships,
which had almost fifty men on them, arriving at Karsstadir
before Steinthor and his men.

When people saw Steinthor's party from Karsstadir, the Thorbrandssons said they should advance to meet them, and stop
them reaching the hayfield, 'because we have a large force of
fine men.'

There were eighty of them altogether.

Then Snorri the Godi replied, 'They must not be denied access
to the farm, and Steinthor must get his legal rights, because he
will conduct his case sensibly and quietly. I would like everyone
to stay inside and not to exchange words with them, because
that will only add to the troubles between us.'

After that everyone went into the main room and sat down
on the benches, but the Thorbrandssons paced the floor.
Steinthor and his men rode up to the door, and it is said that
Steinthor was wearing a red tunic and had tucked the front of

the skirt up under his belt. He had a beautiful shield and helmet, and on his belt a sword, which was elaborately decorated. The boss shone white with silver, and the hilt was bound in beautifully gilded silver. Steinthor and his men dismounted and Steinthor went up to the door and fastened to the door-hinge a purse containing twelve ounces of silver. He named witnesses to testify that the slave payment had been legally made. The door was open and one of the women of the farm was standing in the doorway listening to the naming of witnesses.

She went into the main room and said, 'That Steinthor of Eyri is brave, and indeed he spoke very well when he delivered the slave payment.'

When Thorleif Kimbi heard that, he rushed forward and was followed by the other Thorbrandssons, and everyone else who had been in the main room went out after them. Thorleif was first to the door, and saw that Thord Blig was standing in front of the door with his shield, but Steinthor was by that time walking back across the hayfield. Thorleif grabbed a spear that was standing by the doorway and hurled it towards Thord Blig, hitting his shield, glancing off on to his shoulder, and causing a serious wound. After that the other men ran out, and a battle began in the hayfield. Steinthor was the most aggressive and struck out on both sides. When Snorri the Godi came out, he told men to stop the brawling and asked Steinthor to ride away from the hayfield, saying that he would not come after him. Steinthor and his men left the field and the fight broke up.

When Snorri the Godi turned back to the door, his son Thorodd was standing in front of him and he had a serious wound to his shoulder. He was then twelve years old. Snorri asked who had wounded him.

'Steinthor of Eyri,' he said.

Thorleif Kimbi responded, 'He has now repaid you fairly for not wanting to go after him. In my opinion we should not settle for this.'

'That's how it will have to be for now,' said Snorri the Godi, 'but it won't be the end of the matter.' He asked Thorleif to tell the men that they would be going after them.

Steinthor and his men had left the field by the time they saw men riding after them. They went across the river and then turned up into an avalanche named Geirvor, and prepared themselves for the encounter there, since it was a good place for a fight because of all the rocks. When Snorri's troop came up the avalanche, Steinthor shot a spear over them for good luck, according to ancient custom,[22] and the spear found its mark, hitting Snorri's kinsman, Mar Hallvardsson, rendering him unfit to fight.

When Snorri the Godi was told this, he said, 'It's been proved true then, that it's not always best to walk last.'

After that a serious battle began. Steinthor was at the forefront of his troop, striking on both sides, but the ornamented sword was not much good whenever it hit a shield, and he had to keep straightening it out under his foot. He kept attacking wherever Snorri the Godi was, and his kinsman, Styr Thorgrimsson, was fighting fiercely beside him. He was the first to kill a man from his son-in-law Snorri's side.

When Snorri the Godi saw that, he said to Styr, 'That's how you avenge Thorodd, your daughter's son, whom Steinthor has mortally wounded. You're no average villain.'

'I can quickly compensate you for that,' replied Styr.

And he shifted the direction of his shield and joined Snorri the Godi's troop and killed a second man, this time from Steinthor's troop.

At that moment Aslak and his son Illugi the Mighty arrived from Langidal, and tried to intervene in the fight. They had thirty men with them. Vermund the Slender joined their side, and they pleaded with Snorri the Godi to stop the killing. Snorri asked the people of Eyri to accept a truce, and the peacemakers asked Steinthor to make a truce on behalf of his men. Steinthor then asked Snorri to stretch out his hand, and he did. Steinthor raised up his sword and struck at Snorri the Godi's hand, causing a loud crash. The blow landed on his temple ring and almost broke it in two, but Snorri was not hurt.

Then Thorodd Thorbrandsson called out, 'They won't keep any truce, and we won't stop now until all the Thorlakssons are killed.'

Snorri the Godi replied, 'There will be turmoil in the district if all the Thorlakssons are killed, so we should keep the truce if Steinthor will abide by what we agreed to before.'

Then everyone urged Steinthor to accept the truce. In the end a truce was arranged so that everyone could travel safely back to their homes.

To turn to the men of Breidavik, they found out that Snorri the Godi had gone with a large following to Alftafjord. They took their horses and rode after Steinthor as hard as they could, reaching the ridge at Ulfarsfell when the battle was being fought on the avalanche. Some people say that Snorri the Godi could see Bjorn and his men up on the ridge when he turned in that direction, which was why the truce-making with Steinthor was so easy.

Steinthor and Bjorn met at Orlygsstadir, and Bjorn said that things had gone according to his prediction.

'In my opinion,' he said, 'you should turn back and pursue them now.'

'I want to hold my truce with Snorri the Godi however our dealings with him turn out in the future,' Steinthor replied.

After that everyone rode back to his own home, except Thord Blig, who had to stay at Eyri to recover from his wounds. In the battle of Alftafjord five men on Steinthor's side were killed, and two from Snorri the Godi's side, and many were wounded on both sides, since it was such a fierce battle.

Thormod Trefilsson described it in his poem 'Words of the Raven':

33.

| The feeder of the swan | *battle-din's swell*: blood; its *swan*: raven; |
| of battle-din's swell | *feeder* of the raven: warrior |
| filled the eagle with a wolf's | |
| feast in Alftafjord. | |
| There at the storm of swords | *storm of swords*: battle |
| Snorri robbed the lives | |
| from five seized men; | |
| so he punishes his enemies. | |

Thorbrand had been at the battle as a peacemaker along with Aslak and Illugi, and he had asked them to look for a settlement.

He thanked them warmly for their support, and Snorri for his assistance. Snorri the Godi went back home to Helgafell after the battle.

The arrangement then was that the Thorbrandssons should divide their time between Helgafell and home at Alftafjord until the case was resolved, since there were still hard feelings, as might be expected when there was no truce at all between men once they were back home after the fight.


45 | That summer, before the battle at Alftafjord, a ship had docked at Dagverdarnes, as was told earlier. Steinthor of Eyri had bought a good ten-oared boat from the men on the ship, but when he was taking the boat back home he was caught in a strong westerly gale that swept them east around Thorsnes and landed them at Thingskalanes, where they brought their boat ashore at Gruflunaust. They then walked across the ridges to Bakki, and from there home by ship. But the ten-oared boat was not fetched that autumn, and remained at Gruflunaust.

One morning, just before Yule, Steinthor got up early and said he wanted to fetch his boat from Thingskalanes. His brothers, Bergthor and Thord Blig, joined him on the journey. Thord's wounds were now very well healed so that he could bear weapons again. Also in the party were two Norwegians staying with Steinthor. Altogether there were eight of them and they sailed across the fjord to Seljahofdi, from where they walked over to Bakki, where their brother Thormod joined them, making them nine altogether.

Hofstadir bay was completely frozen over right out to Bakki the Greater, so they walked across the ice and on over the isthmus to Vigrafjord, which was also entirely iced over. In that fjord the water ebbed all the way out until it was dry, so that the ice rested on mud at low-tide, and the rocks in the fjord jutted up out of the ice, which was broken up around them. There were a lot of uneven ice floes past the rocks, and powdery snow had fallen over the ice, making it very slippery.

Steinthor and his men went over to Thingskalanes and dragged the boat out of the boat shed. They took both the oars and the benches out of the boat, leaving them on the ice along with their heaviest weapons and clothes. Then they hauled the boat along the fjord and across the isthmus to Hofstadir bay and all the way out to the rim of the ice. Then they went back for their clothes and other things. On their way back to Vigrafjord, they saw six men going north from Thingskalanes and they were travelling fast across the ice, headed for Helgafell.

Steinthor and his men suspected that it might be the Thorbrandssons, on their way to Helgafell for Yule. They started going very fast back across the fjord to where their clothes and weapons were. And it was the Thorbrandssons in fact, just as Steinthor suspected. When they saw that there were men running out along the fjord, they believed they knew who they must be and thought that the men of Eyri were intending to attack them. They too started moving very fast, heading towards the rock where they intended to take them on. The race was on, both sides moving as fast as they could, but the Thorbrandssons arrived at the rock first.

When Steinthor's men raced towards the rock, Thorleif Kimbi hurled a spear into their midst and it hit Bergthor Thorlaksson in his stomach, putting him out of the fight. He walked across the ice and lay down there, but Steinthor and some of his men launched an attack on the rock, while others went to get their weapons. The Thorbrandssons defended themselves courageously. They had a good position for fighting because there were ice-sheets jutting up all around the rock and they were extremely slippery. They had therefore hardly sustained any wounds by the time the others who were getting the weapons came back.

Steinthor and five of his men attacked the rock but the easterners ran out of range across the ice from the rock. They had bows and shot at those on the rock, making it very dangerous for them.

When he saw that Steinthor was drawing his sword, Thorleif Kimbi said, 'You're still using the white-hilted sword, Steinthor, but I don't know whether you're still using the blunt edge you had last autumn at Alftafjord.'

'I'd like you to find out for yourself before we part whether or not I have a blunt edge,' Steinthor replied.

Their attack on the rock was slow, and when they had fought for quite some time, Thord Blig made a run at the rock, trying to lunge his spear into Thorleif Kimbi since he was always at the forefront of his men. The spear hit his shield, but in fending it off so powerfully, his feet slipped from beneath him on the broken ice that was on a slope, and he fell down and slipped backwards off the rock. Thorleif Kimbi ran after him, wanting to kill him before he could get to his feet. Freystein Bofi ran after Thorleif, and he had ice-spurs on his shoes.

Steinthor ran up too and brought his shield down over Thord when Thorleif tried to strike him, and with his other hand he struck at Thorleif Kimbi and cut away his leg below the knee. At that Freystein Bofi lunged at Steinthor, aiming at his stomach, but seeing this Steinthor leapt up into the air and the spear passed between his legs. Steinthor performed these three things at once, just as described.

After that Steinthor struck at Freystein with his sword, and the blow landed on his neck and made a loud noise.

'Was that one bad for you, Bofi?' asked Steinthor.

'A bad one indeed,' Freystein replied, 'but not as bad as you thought, because I'm not hurt.'

He was wearing a felt hood with a piece of horn sewn into the collar, which is where the blow landed. Freystein then turned back up towards the rock. Steinthor told him not to run if he was not hurt. Freystein turned to meet the attack and they fought hard, but Steinthor was in danger of slipping since the blocks of ice were both steep and slippery, while Freystein stood firmly on his ice-spurs and struck both hard and often. Their contest ended when Steinthor struck Freystein above the hips with his sword so that the man was cut in two.

After that they went up on to the rock and did not stop fighting until all the Thorbrandssons had fallen. Then Thord Blig said that they should sever the heads from the bodies of all the Thorbrandssons, but Steinthor said he did not want to slay men who were lying down. Then they went down from the rock to where Bergthor lay, and he was still able to speak. They carried him with them back over the ice and across the isthmus to their boat. Then they rowed their boat over to Bakki in the evening.

Snorri the Godi's shepherd had been at Oxnabrekkur during the day and had seen the clash at Vigrafjord from there. He went home at once and told Snorri the Godi that there had been an encounter that day at Vigrafjord and it was hardly a friendly one. Snorri and eight of his men took their weapons and went over to the fjord. But by the time they got there, Steinthor and his men had made their way across the iced-over fjord.

Snorri and his men examined the men's wounds, and while only Freystein Bofi was dead, they all had serious wounds. Thorleif Kimbi called out to Snorri the Godi and told him to go after Steinthor and his men, and not to let any of them get away. Then Snorri the Godi went over to where Bergthor had lain and saw a large bloodstain there. He lifted up the blood and snow together in his hand, squeezed it and put it in his mouth, and asked who had bled there. Thorleif Kimbi said that Bergthor had been bleeding. Snorri said that it was blood from an internal wound.

'That may be,' said Thorleif, 'because it was caused by a spear.'

'I think that this is the blood of a doomed man,' said Snorri, 'and we won't go after him.'

Then the Thorbrandssons were carried back to Helgafell and their wounds bandaged. Thorodd Thorbrandsson had such a serious wound at the back of his neck that he could not hold up his head. He was wearing trousers with feet in them and they were completely soaked in blood. Snorri the Godi's servant had to pull them off him, but when he tried to remove the trousers, he could not get them off.

'They're not lying about you Thorbrandssons when they call you stylish dressers,' he said, 'since you have such tight-fitting clothes that they can't be taken off you.'

'You can't be pulling hard enough,' said Thorodd.

He then pressed one of his feet against the bench and tugged with all his might, but the trousers would not come off. Then Snorri the Godi went up and felt around the leg and discovered that a spear was lodged in it between the Achilles tendon and the shin, and it had pinned the trouser to the leg. Snorri then said that he was no average fool not to have considered such a possibility.

Snorri Thorbrandsson was the fittest of the brothers and in the evening he sat at the table next to his namesake, and they had curds and cheese. Snorri the Godi noticed that his namesake was not making much headway with the cheese, and asked him why he was eating so slowly. Snorri Thorbrandsson answered, saying that lambs that had been recently gagged were the most reluctant to eat. Then Snorri the Godi felt around his throat, and discovered an arrow sticking through the throat and into the base of the tongue. Snorri the Godi then took a pair of pincers and pulled out the arrow, and after that he could eat.

Snorri the Godi healed all the Thorbrandssons. And when Thorodd's neck began to heal, his head drooped to one side slightly. Thorodd said that Snorri wanted to heal him by leaving him maimed, but Snorri the Godi said he expected his head would stand up once the sinews knitted. Thorodd wanted nothing less than that the wound be opened up and the head set straighter. But it turned out as Snorri thought, that when the sinews knitted his head straightened up, although afterwards he was only able to bend his head slightly. Thorleif Kimbi always walked with a wooden leg after he was wounded.

46 | When Steinthor of Eyri and his men arrived at the boat shed at Bakki, they brought their boat up on to the shore, and the brothers went back up to the farm. Down at the shore a tent was put up over Bergthor for the night. It is said that Thorgerd, the mistress of the house, would not go to bed with her husband Thormod that evening. But just then, a man came up from the boat shed and told them that Bergthor was dead. When she heard that, the mistress of the house got into bed and there is no mention of any further quarrelling by the couple over this. Steinthor went home to Eyri in the morning and the rest of the winter passed without any violent incidents between men.

But in the spring as it was getting on to the Summons Days,

people of goodwill considered it a perplexing matter that the leading men of the district should be at odds with each another and having fights. The best men, who were friends with both sides, came forward to try to find a settlement between them. Their leader was Vermund the Slender, and they included many people of goodwill who were related to both sides. In time a truce was arranged and they were reconciled, and it is the opinion of most people that Vermund delivered the verdict in the case. He arbitrated the settlement at the Thorsnes Assembly and he had behind him all the wisest men who were present.

The details of the settlement were that all the killings and assaults on each side were weighed up. Thord Blig's wound from Alftafjord was equated with the wounding of Snorri the Godi's son, Thorodd. Mar Hallvardsson's wound and the blow Steinthor delivered to Snorri the Godi were set against the killing of the three men who died at Alftafjord. The killings by Styr of one man from each side were said to be equal. The death of Bergthor at Vigrafjord was considered the same as the wounding of the three Thorbrandssons, and the killing of Freystein Bofi was set against the man from Steinthor's side, who was previously not in the tally, but who died at Alftafjord. Thorleif Kimbi was compensated for the severing of his leg. And the man from Snorri the Godi's side who was killed at Alftafjord made up for Thorleif Kimbi's assault when he started the fight. Then everyone else's wounds were weighed up and compensation awarded for any disparity that seemed to exist, and so everyone left the assembly reconciled, and this settlement lasted as long as both Steinthor and Snorri the Godi were alive.

47 | The same summer after the settlement Thorodd the Tax-trader invited his brother-in-law Snorri the Godi to a feast at his farm at Froda, and Snorri went with eight men. While Snorri was at the feast, Thorodd complained to him that he considered himself to have been provoked and humiliated by the visits Bjorn Asbrandsson made to his wife Thurid, who was Snorri the Godi's sister. Thorodd told him that he thought Snorri ought to do something about this awkward situation.

Snorri stayed at the feast for several nights and then Thorodd saw him off with fine gifts. Snorri the Godi rode south across the heath, declaring that he planned to go to the ship at the mouth of Hraunhofn. This was during the hay harvest in summer.

When they came south to Kamb heath, Snorri said, 'We can ride down here from the heath to Kamb. I want you to know that I am planning an attack on Bjorn, to kill him if possible. But I don't want to attack him inside his farmhouse, because it's strongly built and Bjorn is strong and brave, and we only have a small force. Those men who have attacked such an outstanding man inside his house have not had much success, even with a greater force, such as the time when Geir the Godi and Gizur the White attacked Gunnar inside his house at Hlidarendi[23] with a force of eighty men. He was fighting alone from inside, but still some men were wounded and some killed and they were giving up the assault until Geir the Godi worked out with his own wits that Gunnar was running out of arrows. Now in the light of this, if Bjorn is outside, as might be expected since it is a good day for drying hay, then I want you, Mar, to deal him some wounds. But be careful, because he isn't a chicken-hearted man and a hard fight is likely from the vicious wolf that he is, if the first blow he gets doesn't cause his immediate death.'

When they rode down from the heath to the farm, they saw that Bjorn was outside in the home meadow working on a barrow, and there was no one with him and no weapons were around except a small axe and a large carving-knife that he was using to bore holes in the barrow. The knife's blade was a hand wide at the handle. Bjorn saw that Snorri and his men were riding down from the heath and on to the field. He recognized the men at once. Snorri the Godi was wearing a black cloak and rode in front of the party. Then Bjorn made a clever move, taking the knife and walking quickly over towards them. With one hand he grabbed Snorri's cloak-sleeve when he came up to them, and with the other hand he grasped the knife and held it as if he were ready to plunge it into Snorri's chest if he felt like it.

Bjorn greeted them as soon as they met and Snorri returned his greeting, but Mar's hand failed him because he thought Bjorn could harm Snorri very quickly if any attack was made on him. Then Bjorn walked along with them and asked the news, maintaining his original grip on Snorri.

Then Bjorn said, 'There's no denying, farmer Snorri, that I have done things to you which you may well hold against me, and I've been told that you bear hard feelings towards me. To my mind, it would be best if you made clear if you have some purpose in coming here other than visiting me on your way past. If you don't have one, then I would like you to agree to a truce between us, and I will go back home, because I am not going to be made a fool of.'

'You've been so lucky in the way our meeting has turned out,' Snorri replied, 'that you will get your truce this time, whatever else I might have intended before. But I want to ask this of you, that from now on you stop toying with my sister Thurid, because things won't get any better between us if you keep carrying on like that.'

'I will only promise you what I can deliver,' Bjorn replied, 'and I don't know how I will manage that while Thurid and I are living in the same district.'

'There's not so much for you here,' Snorri said, 'that you mightn't just as well leave the district.'

'What you say is true,' Bjorn replied. 'And it will be so, since you have come over yourself to see me and our meeting has turned out like this, that I will promise you that you and Thorodd won't be irritated by my visits to Thurid next winter.'

'You do well, then,' said Snorri.

After that they parted. Snorri the Godi rode to his ship and then went home to Helgafell.

The next day Bjorn rode south to the ship at Hraunhofn and took a passage abroad that summer, but they were rather late setting sail. They were caught in a north-easterly wind which blew for most of that summer, and nothing was heard of the ship for a long time.

48 | After the reconciliation between the people of Eyri and
     | the people of Alftafjord, the Thorbrandssons, Snorri and
Thorleif Kimbi went to Greenland. Kimbavog bay, which lies
between the glaciers in Greenland, is named after him, and
Thorleif lived in Greenland until his old age. Snorri went to
Vinland the Good with Karlsefni, and while fighting against the
Skraelings,[24] Snorri, the bravest of men, was killed. Thorodd
Thorbrandsson went back to farming at Alftafjord. He married
Ragnhild Thordardottir, the granddaughter of Thorgils Eagle
and the great-granddaughter of Hallstein the Godi of Hall-
steinsnes, who owned the slaves.[25]

49 | The next story to be told is about Gizur the White and his
     | son-in-law Hjalti, who came out to Iceland to preach the
Christian faith, and everyone in Iceland was baptized[26] and
Christianity was legally adopted at the Althing. Snorri the Godi
was most influential in persuading the people of the West Fjords
to adopt Christianity. When the Thing was over, Snorri the
Godi had a church built at Helgafell and his father-in-law,
Styr, had a second church built at Hraun. Men were greatly
encouraged to build churches by the priests' promise that they
would have the right to places in heaven for as many people as
could stand in the church they had built. Thorodd the Tax-trader
had a church built on his farm at Froda, but there was no priest
to perform mass at the church once it was built, because there
were so few of them in Iceland at that time.

50 | In the summer when Christianity was adopted by law in
     | Iceland, a ship landed at Snaefellsnes. It had come from
Dublin and had Irish and Hebridean men aboard, as well as a
few Norwegians. They stayed at Rif long into the summer,
waiting for a good wind to sail east along the fjord to Dagverdarnes, where many people from around Nes travelled to trade
with them.

There was a Hebridean woman named Thorgunna on the

ship. The crew of the ship said that she had brought finery with her that was very hard to get in Iceland. When Thurid, the mistress of the house at Froda, heard this she was very curious to see the finery, since she was fond of fine things and given to showy display. She went to the ship and found Thorgunna and asked her if she had any women's clothing that was particularly fine. Thorgunna said she had no finery for sale, but added that she herself had such finery as to be unashamed at feasts or other public gatherings. Thurid asked if she could see her things, and she agreed, and they seemed to her very nice and well tailored, but not costly.

Thurid made an offer to buy the finery but Thorgunna would not sell it. Then Thurid invited her to come and stay with her, because she knew Thorgunna was very well dressed and she thought she might get the clothes from her at her leisure.

'I like the idea of coming to stay with you,' Thorgunna replied, 'but you should know that I'm not keen to pay for my keep while I am still able to work. Hard work isn't disagreeable to me, as long as I don't have to work in the wet. But I will decide myself what I will pay you for my keep, from the money I have.'

Thorgunna spoke rather bluntly, but Thurid still wanted her to come to stay. Thorgunna's belongings were then carried off the ship. She owned a very heavy chest as well as a portable chest, which were both taken over to Froda. When Thorgunna arrived at her lodgings, she asked for her bed. She was given a place in the inner part of the hall. She then opened up her chest and took out of it some beautifully worked bedclothes. She spread fine English sheets and a silken quilt over the bed. She also took out of the chest bed-curtains and a canopy to go all around the bed. These were all so well made that people thought nothing like them had been seen before.

Then Thurid, the mistress of the house, said, 'What price do you put on the bedclothes?'

'I'm not going to lie in straw for your sake,' Thorgunna replied, 'even though you are well bred and carry yourself proudly.'

This displeased Thurid, and she did not make another offer for the finery. Thorgunna worked at weaving every day when there was no haymaking to be done. But when the weather was fine, she worked outside drying hay in the cultivated home field, and had a special rake made for herself, which only she was allowed to use.

Thorgunna was a well-built woman, both big and tall and very stout, with dark eyebrows and narrow eyes, and a full head of chestnut hair. She was generally well mannered and she went to church every day before starting work, but she was neither cheerful nor normally very talkative. It was general opinion that Thorgunna must have reached her sixth decade, but she was still a very vigorous woman.

At that time Thorir Wood-leg and his wife Thorgrima Magic-cheek had come to live in the Froda household, and they were not getting on well with Thorgunna. The farmer's son, Kjartan, was the only person with whom Thorgunna was on good terms. She liked him very much but he was rather reserved towards her, which often irritated her. Kjartan was then thirteen or fourteen, and was both well built and of imposing appearance.

51 | That summer was not very dry but the weather was fine in the autumn. By then the haymaking at Froda had got to the stage where the cultivated hayfield had been mown and nearly half its hay was completely dried. This was followed by a good drying day when the weather was still and clear so that no cloud could be seen in the sky. Thorodd the farmer got up early that morning and organized the day's work. Some men were put to carting hay, and some to stacking it, and the farmer directed the women to dry the hay, with the work divided between them. Thorgunna was given enough hay to dry for a cow to have lived off over the winter.

A lot of work was done during the day, but towards mid afternoon a black cloud appeared in the sky to the north over Skor, and quickly swept across the sky straight towards the farm. People thought it looked as if the cloud would bring rain. Thorodd told everyone to rake up the hay but Thorgunna kept turning her hay as energetically as she could. She did not rake it up even though she had been told to. The cloud quickly scudded

across the sky and when it was over the farm at Froda it grew
so dark that people could not see beyond the home meadow,
and they could scarcely distinguish their own hands. So much
rain fell from the cloud that all the hay lying on the ground
became soaked. The cloud suddenly drew past and the weather
cleared up. People could then see that blood had rained down
in the shower.

In the evening there were good drying conditions and the
blood quickly dried out of all the hay except that which Thorgunna was drying. It would not dry and the rake she had been
using did not dry out either. Thorodd asked what Thorgunna
thought this marvel might mean.

She said she did not know, 'but it seems most likely to me,'
she said, 'that it is a foreboding of doom for someone who is
here.'

Thorgunna went home that evening and took to her bed,
taking off her blood-soaked clothes. She then lay down in her
bed and heaved a great sigh. People realized that she had taken
ill. This shower had not fallen anywhere except at Froda. Thorgunna would not eat any food that evening. In the morning the
farmer Thorodd went to see her and asked how long she thought
her illness might last. She said she thought she would not have
any further illnesses.

Then she said, 'I consider you to be the wisest man here on
the farm. So I want to tell you what arrangements I want made
for everything I leave behind, and for myself, because things
will turn out just as I say. Even though you may think there is
not much remarkable about me, I think little good will come of
disregarding what I say. Things have started out in such a way
that I don't suppose the damage can be contained unless strong
measures are taken at once.'

'It's not unlikely that you're close to the truth about this,'
Thorodd replied. 'So I will promise not to disregard your
instructions.'

'What I want is to have my body carried to Skalholt[27] if I die
from this illness,' Thorgunna said, 'because something tells me
that place will one day be the most venerated in Iceland. And I
also know that there are priests there now who can sing mass

for me. That's why I want to ask you to have me taken there. In return you can have whatever property of mine you want to recompense you. But before my property is divided up, Thurid is to be given the scarlet cloak I own. I'm doing this as some relief for her because I will dispose of the rest of my possessions as it suits me. But I would like you to take whatever you or she likes of what I leave as compensation for any costs you have born on my behalf. The gold ring that I own must go to the church with me, and I want my bed and bedclothes to be burnt in a fire since they will be of no use to anybody. I'm not saying this because I would begrudge anyone enjoying this finery if I knew it might be useful to them. I'm saying this so insistently because I wouldn't like it if, because of me, people became as badly afflicted as I know they will be if what I say is disregarded.'

Thorodd promised to do just as she instructed. After that, the illness took hold of Thorgunna, and she did not lie there many days before she died. Her body was taken to the church and Thorodd had a coffin made for it. The next day Thorodd carried her bedclothes outside, and collected wood and built a big bonfire. Then Thurid, the mistress of the house, went outside and asked him what he was intending to do with the bedclothes. He said he was going to burn them in the fire as Thorgunna had asked.

'I won't have that,' said Thurid, 'such fine things being burnt.'

'She insisted,' Thorodd replied, 'that no good would come of disregarding her instructions.'

'That's nothing but malicious talk,' said Thurid. 'She didn't want anyone else to enjoy them, that's why she told you to do this. But no harm will come of it, whatever instructions of hers we disregard.'

'I'm not sure,' he said, 'if this is going against her instructions.'

Then she put her arms around his neck and asked him not to burn the bedclothes. She pleaded with him so much that she changed his mind with the result that Thorodd burnt the feather-bed and pillows but she kept the quilt and the sheets and the whole canopy, but neither of them was very pleased.

After that they prepared for the funeral journey, and got trustworthy men to travel with the body on good horses that

Thorodd owned. The body was wrapped in a linen cloth without seams, and then it was laid in the coffin. They travelled south across the heath, following the established tracks. Nothing is told of their journey until they came south of Valbjarnarvellir. There they came to very wet boggy ground and the body often fell off the horse, but they kept going south to Nordura river, which they crossed at Eyjarvad ford through deep water. The weather was stormy and there was very heavy rain.

They came at last to a farm in Stafholtstungur named Lower Nes, where they asked for lodgings but the farmer would not put them up. Since it was nearly night, they did not think they would be able to travel any farther because it did not seem sensible to them to tackle the Hvita river by night. They unloaded their horses and carried the body into a store-room outside the main door, and then went into the main room and took off their clothes, intending to spend the night there without food. The people of the farm went to bed while it was still daylight.

Once they were in their beds, they heard a great racket in the pantry, and wondered whether thieves had got inside. When they came to the pantry, they could see a tall woman standing there. She was completely naked, without a stitch on, and she was preparing a meal. The people who saw her were so frightened that they did not dare go near her. When the coffin-bearers heard this, they went to see what was going on. It was Thorgunna, and they all thought it wise not to interfere with her. And when she had done what she wanted, she carried the food into the main room, set the table and served her meal.

Then the coffin-bearers said to the farmer, 'It may well be that before we leave, you'll consider yourself to have paid a high price for not putting us up.'

The farmer and the mistress of the house replied, 'We will gladly give you food and whatever other hospitality you need.'

As soon as the farmer had offered them hospitality, Thorgunna walked out of the main room and she was not seen again. After that a fire was lit in the main room, and the wet clothes taken off the guests and replaced with dry ones. Then they sat at the table and made the sign of the cross over their food, and the farmer had the whole building sprinkled with holy water. The guests ate their food, and no one found fault with it even though Thorgunna had prepared it. They slept through the night and found the place very comfortable.

The next morning they prepared to go on with their journey and things went very smoothly for them, because wherever this news was heard, most people thought it advisable to show them whatever hospitality they required. From then on, their journey went without incident. When they arrived at Skalholt, the gifts that Thorgunna had left the Church were presented. The priests accepted them gladly. Thorgunna was then buried and the coffin-bearers went home. Their journey back went smoothly and they arrived home safely.

52 | At the Froda farm there was a large fire room that had a bed closet behind it, as was customary in those days. In front of the fire room were two store-rooms, one on each side, with dried fish stored in one and flour in the other. Every evening fires were lit in the fire room, as was the custom then. People would sit in front of the fires for a long time before they had their meal.

On the evening when the coffin-bearers came back, everyone was sitting in front of the fire at Froda, when they saw on the room's wainscoting that a half-moon had appeared. Everyone in the room could see it. It went backwards around the house, against the motion of the sun. It did not disappear as long as people were sitting in front of the fire. Thorodd asked Thorir Wood-leg what it might mean.

Thorir said it was a weird-moon, 'and it will be followed by someone's death here,' he said.

This kept happening there all week, the weird-moon appearing every evening just like the night before.

53 | The next thing that happened was that a shepherd came inside, and he was very downcast. He had little to say, and what he did say was irritable. People thought he must have been bewitched because he was beside himself, and kept talking to himself. This went on for some time. After two weeks of winter had passed, the shepherd came home one evening, went to his bed and lay down. In the morning he was found dead by people who went looking for him, and he was buried there at the church.

Soon after that serious hauntings began. One night Thorir Wood-leg went outside when nature called and was on his way back to the door, but when he tried to go back inside, he saw that the shepherd was standing in front of the doorway. Thorir wanted to go in, but the shepherd certainly did not want him to. Then Thorir tried to get away, but the shepherd went after him and took hold of him and threw him back against the door. He was hurt, but managed to get back to his bed, black and blue all over. He became ill because of this, and died. He was buried there at the church. The shepherd and Thorir Wood-leg were always seen in each other's company after that. As might be expected, this terrified everyone.

After Thorir's death one of Thorodd's farmhands became ill, and he lay in bed for three nights before dying. Then one after another died until six people had died altogether. It was coming up to Advent, although at that time it was not observed in Iceland. The store-room was so well stocked with dried fish that the door could not be closed. The pile went right up to the cross-beam and a ladder had to be used to get to the pile from above. Then things started to happen in the evenings. Just as people sat by the fire, they could hear the dried fish being torn at in the store-room, but whenever they went to look, they could find nothing alive in there.

During the winter just before Yule, Thorodd the farmer went out to Nes to fetch his dried fish. There were six men altogether in the ten-oared boat, and they spent the night out there. The same night that Thorodd had left, when the people at Froda came up to the fireside in the evening, they saw a seal's head coming up out of the fireplace. One of the servants saw it first when she came in. She took a club that was inside the doorway and struck the seal on the head. But the seal rose up with the blow and reared up towards Thorgunna's bed-curtains. Then one of Thorodd's men went up and started beating the seal, but with every blow it rose up further until its flippers appeared, and then the man fell down unconscious. Everyone else who was present became very frightened.

Then the boy Kjartan rushed forward and lifted up an iron sledgehammer and brought it down on the seal's head. It was a tremendous blow but the seal just shook its head and looked around. Kjartan kept going, with blow after blow, and the seal went back down as if he were driving in a nail. He kept beating until the seal went so far down that he hammered the floor over its head. And so it went on throughout the winter, with all the revenants fearing Kjartan the most.

54 | The next morning when Thorodd and his men were coming back from Nes with the dried fish, they were all drowned out near Enni. The boat and the fish were washed ashore beneath Enni, but the bodies were never found. When this news reached Froda, Kjartan and Thurid invited their neighbours to a funeral feast. They took the Yule ale and used it at the funeral.

On the first night of the funeral feast, once everyone was in their seats, Thorodd the farmer and his companions came into the fire room, completely drenched. People welcomed Thorodd warmly, thinking it was a good omen, because at that time they believed that the drowned had been well received by the sea-goddess Ran if they attended their own funeral feast. There was still a small degree of belief in heathen ways, even though people had been baptized and called themselves Christians.

Thorodd and his companions walked all the way across the sleeping hall, which had two doors, and into the fire room without responding to anyone's greeting. When they sat down by the fire, the people of the farm rushed out of the fire room, but Thorodd and his companions stayed there until the fire had turned to ashes. Then they went away. It went on like this every evening during the funeral feast, with the drowned men coming in and sitting by the fire. So there was much to talk about at the feast, but some people thought that it would end once the feast was over. The guests went home after the feast, and the homestead seemed rather dull afterwards.

On the evening after all the guests had left, the evening fire was lit as usual. As soon as the fire was burning, Thorodd and his companions came in and they were all soaking wet. They sat down by the fire and started to wring out their wet clothes. After they had sat down, Thorir Wood-leg and his six companions came in too. They were all covered in earth, and they began shaking out their clothes and splattering mud on to Thorodd and his men. The people of the farm rushed out of the fire room, as might be expected, and had neither evening light nor heating-stones nor anything else that they usually got from the fire.

The next evening the fire was made in another room, in the hope that they were less likely to come there. But it did not turn out that way, and everything went just as it had the previous evening, with both parties coming to the fireside.

The third evening Kjartan came up with a plan to make a very long fire in the fire room, and a fire for cooking in another room. And this was done. And it worked, with Thorodd and his companions sitting by the long fire and the people of the farm sitting by the little fire, and this went on all through Yule.

But more and more noise was coming from the pile of dried fish, so that night and day dried fish could be heard being torn up. Then they reached the point when the dried fish needed to be used for meals, so they went to look at the pile. The man who climbed up on to the pile saw that there was a tail coming up through it, which was like a singed oxtail, but it was short and covered in seal hair. The man at the top of the pile took hold of the tail and tugged at it, and then asked other men to come up and help him. Both women and men climbed up on to the pile, and tugged at the tail but they could not budge it. It did not occur to anyone that the tail was anything but dead. But when they tugged their hardest, the tail stripped the skin off the palms of the hands of those tugging hardest. Nothing was ever seen of the tail again. The dried fish was then unpiled, and each fish in it had been ripped from its skin so that there was no fish left right down through the pile, but there was also nothing alive in the pile.

The next thing that happened is that Thorir Wood-leg's wife, Thorgrima Magic-cheek, became ill. She lay in bed for a little while before she died, and the same evening that she was buried she was seen among her husband Thorir's company. Then there was a second wave of the sickness that had come when the tail first appeared, and more women than men died. Six people died this time, and some people fled because of the hauntings and ghosts. In the autumn there had been thirty servants there, but eighteen had died and five had run away, so there were only seven left.

55 | One day after these strange things had happened, Kjartan went over to Helgafell to see his uncle, Snorri the Godi, and get his advice about what to do about the strange happenings. There was a priest at Helgafell at the time who had been sent to Snorri the Godi by Gizur the White. Snorri sent the priest over to Froda with his son Thord Cat and Kjartan, as well as six other men. He advised them that Thorgunna's bed-canopy should be burnt, and all the revenants prosecuted at a door court. Then the priest should say mass, consecrate water and hear everybody's confession. They rode back to Froda, and on the way they asked the people from the neighbouring farm to come with him. They arrived on the evening before Candlemas, at the time when the evening fires were being lit. The mistress of the house, Thurid, had taken ill with the same sickness that the others had died of.

Kjartan went inside at once, and saw that Thorodd and his companions were sitting by the fire as usual. Kjartan took down Thorgunna's bed-canopy, and then went into the fire room and took some embers from the fire and went outside with them. Then all the bedclothes that Thorgunna had owned were burnt. After that Kjartan summonsed Thorir Wood-leg, and Thord

Cat summonsed the farmer Thorodd for walking around the homestead without permission, and depriving people of both their life and health. Everyone sitting by the fire was summonsed. A door court was held and charges were pronounced, with the whole procedure following that of a court at an assembly. Decisions were made, and cases summed up and judged.

When the sentence was being passed on Thorir Wood-leg, he stood up and said, 'I sat here as long as I could.'

After that, he went out through the door at which the court was not being held. Then sentence was passed on the shepherd.

When he heard it, he stood up and said, 'I will leave now, but I think it would have been better if I'd left earlier.'

When Thorgrima Magic-cheek heard that sentence had been passed on her, she stood up and said, 'I stayed here as long as it was peaceful.'

Then each and every one of them was charged, and as sentence was passed they stood up in turn and all responded in the same way. Then they went outside, and it was obvious from each of their statements that they left reluctantly. Eventually Thorodd the farmer was sentenced.

And when he heard it, he stood up and said, 'I think there's little peace to be had here, so we will all get going.'

And with that he left.

Then Kjartan and his companions went inside. The priest carried consecrated water and sacred relics around the whole house. The next day the priest sang all the prayers and celebrated mass solemnly, and after that all the revenants and ghosts left Froda, and Thurid began to recover from her sickness and finally she recuperated completely. In the spring after these marvels, Kjartan took on new servants and lived at Froda for a long time after that, and he turned into the greatest of champions.

56 | Snorri the Godi lived at Helgafell for eight years after Christianity was adopted by law in Iceland. During his last winter there his father-in-law, Styr, was killed at Jorvi in Flisa district. Snorri the Godi travelled south to collect the body and when he went into the women's room at Hrossholt, Styr

was sitting up and holding the farmer's daughter around the waist. The next spring Snorri the Godi exchanged land with Gudrun Osvifsdottir and moved his household to Tunga in Saelingsdal. That was two years after the death of Bolli Thorleiksson, Gudrun Osvifsdottir's husband.[28]

The same spring Snorri the Godi travelled south to Borgarfjord with four hundred men to bring an action over Styr's killing. Styr's brother, Vermund the Slender, who was then living in Vatnsfjord, was with him. Also there were Steinthor of Eyri, Thorodd Thorbrandsson from Alftafjord, Styr's nephew Thorleik Brandsson from Krossnes, as well as many other men of distinction. The furthest they got on their journey south was the Hvita river, at Haugsvad across the river from Baer. To the south of the river were Illugi the Black, Kleppjarn the Old, Thorstein Gislason, Gunnlaug Serpent-tongue, and Thorstein Thorgilsson from the island of Hafsfjardarey, who was married to Vigdis, Illugi the Black's daughter. There were many other men of distinction there, and their company was five-hundred strong.

Snorri the Godi and his men were not able to continue south across the river, so they began proceedings when they had come as close to them as they safely might. Snorri summonsed Gest for the killing of Styr, but the same charge by Snorri was quashed at the Althing that summer. The same autumn Snorri the Godi rode south to Borgarfjord, and killed Thorstein Gislason and his son Gunnar. Steinthor of Eyri was with him then, as was Thorodd Thorbrandsson, Bard Hoskuldsson, Thorleik Brandsson and ten other men.

The next spring Snorri the Godi and Thorstein of Hafsfjardarey, Illugi the Black's son-in-law, met at the Thorsnes Assembly. Thorstein was the son of Thorgils and the grandson of Thorfinn Seal-Thorisson from Raudamel. His mother was Aud, the daughter of Alf from Dalir, so Thorstein was the cousin of Thorgils Arason of Reykjaholar, Thorgeir Havarsson, Thorgils Holluson, Bitra-Oddi and the people of Alftafjord, Thorleif Kimbi and the Thorbrandssons. Thorstein had presented many cases at the Thorsnes Assembly.

One day on the assembly slopes Snorri the Godi asked

Thorstein whether he had many cases to bring at the assembly. Thorstein said he had prepared several cases.

'You would probably like us to support your cases as you and the men of Borgarfjord supported our cases last spring,' said Snorri.

'I'm not keen on that at all,' Thorstein replied.

After Snorri the Godi had said this, his sons and many of Styr's other kinsmen spoke aggressively to Thorstein, saying that it would be best if every case he brought was dismissed there, and that it would serve him right if he had to pay with his own life for the humiliating treatment that he and his father-in-law, Illugi the Black, had dealt them the previous summer. Thorstein had little to say in response, and everyone left the assembly slopes. Thorstein and his kinsmen from Raudamel had gathered together a large force. When it was time to go to court, Thorstein was planning to proceed with all the cases he had brought. When Styr's blood-relatives and kinsmen by marriage found this out, they took their weapons and positioned themselves between the court and the path the men of Raudamel would take to the court. A battle began between the two sides.

Thorstein of Hafsfjardarey only cared about attacking Snorri the Godi. Thorstein was a tall, strong man, and a brave fighter. As Thorstein was making a fierce attack on Snorri, Snorri's nephew, Kjartan from Froda, ran up in front of him. Thorstein and Kjartan fought for a long time, and the exchange of blows was fierce. Then friends of both of them came between them and arranged a truce.

After the battle Snorri the Godi said to his nephew Kjartan, 'You fought hard today, Breidavik-man.'

Kjartan replied rather angrily, 'You don't need to reproach me for my pedigree.'

In this battle, seven of Thorstein's men were killed and many from both sides were wounded. The case was brought to a settlement there at the assembly, and Snorri the Godi was not ungenerous in the terms of the agreement, because he did not want the case to be taken up again at the Althing since no compensation had yet been paid for the killing of Thorstein

Gislason. He thought he had enough to answer for at the Althing, without having to debate this case.

Thormod Trefilsson described all these events, the killing of Thorstein Gislason and his son Gunnar and the battle at the Thorsnes Assembly that followed, in this verse from his poem 'Words of the Raven':

34.
And still the stoic
destroyer of the spear-strip                    *spear-strip*: shield
slew two men south of the river
at the quarrel of swords;                    *quarrel of swords*: battle
seven warriors lay
robbed of life after that
at the ness of troll's harm;         *troll's harm*: the god Thor; his *ness*:
such is the evidence.                                          Thorsnes

It was a condition of their settlement that Thorstein should be able to present all the cases he had prepared at the Thorsnes Assembly. And in the summer at the Althing a settlement was made over the killing of Thorstein Gislason and his son Gunnar. Those men who had participated in the killings with Snorri the Godi went abroad. That summer Thorstein of Hafsfjardarey withdrew the godi's right of authority over the people of Rauda-mel from the Thorsnes Assembly, because he considered he had been overpowered there by Snorri and his supporters. Thorstein and his kinsmen then set up an assembly at Straumfjord and it remained there for a long time afterwards.

57 | At the time when Snorri the Godi had been living for a few years at Saelingsdalstunga, there was a man named Ospak living further north at Eyri in Bitra. He was the son of Kjallak from Kjallaksa river near Skridinsenni, and he was a married man, with a young son named Glum. Ospak was a big, strong man, very unpopular and troublesome. He had seven or eight men with him who were involved in many quarrels with the men up in the north. They usually travelled by ship close to the coast,

robbing people of their belongings or anything that had drifted on to their land as they saw fit.

There was a man called Alf the Short who lived at Thambardal in Bitra. He was a wealthy man and a notable farmer. He was a thingman of Snorri the Godi's, and took care of his driftage rights under the headland at Gudlaugshofdi. Alf believed he was treated coldly by Ospak and his companions and complained repeatedly about this treatment to Snorri the Godi whenever they met.

Thorir Gold-Hardarson was then living at Tunga in Bitra. He was a friend of Sturla Thjodreksson, nicknamed Killer-Sturla, who lived at Stadarhol in Saurbaer. Thorir was a successful farmer and was the leading man in the Bitra district. He was in charge of looking after Sturla's driftage rights in the north. Ospak and Thorir were often on bad terms and it varied who had the upper hand. Ospak was the leading man to the west in the Krossardal and Enni districts.

One winter there was an early cold snap that meant there was no grazing pasture around Bitra. People then faced serious losses, and some drove their livestock on to the heath. The previous summer Ospak had built a fortification around his farm at Eyri. It was a secure fortification if properly defended. In the depths of winter a fierce storm blew down from the north and raged for a week. When the storm let up, people could see that drift ice had come all the way up into the outer reaches of the fjord, but not as far in as Bitra. People then went to search the foreshores of their land. Word got around that a large fin whale had been beached between Stika and Gudlaugshofdi. Snorri the Godi and Sturla Thjodreksson had the largest legal stakes in the whale, but Alf the Short and several other farmers also had a share in it. Some men from Bitra travelled to where the whale was and cut it up according to Thorir's and Alf's instructions.

When the men were in the middle of flensing the whale, they saw a boat coming towards them across the fjord from Eyri, and they recognized it as the twelve-oared boat that Ospak owned. The boat landed near the whale and fifteen fully armed men came ashore. When Ospak got ashore, he went straight to the whale and asked who was in charge of it.

Thorir said that he was responsible for his and Sturla's share, and that Alf was looking after his share and Snorri the Godi's share, 'and each of the other farmers is taking care of his own share.'

Ospak asked how much of the whale they would give him.

'I won't give you any of the portion I am responsible for,' Thorir replied, 'but I don't know if the other farmers want to sell you what they have. How much are you offering?'

'You should know, Thorir, that I'm not in the habit of paying for whale-meat from you men of Bitra,' said Ospak.

'Well, I don't expect you'll get much for free,' Thorir replied.

The whale-meat that had been cut up already was lying in a pile, but it had not yet been divided up. Ospak told his men to get the meat and load it on to their boat. The men who had been cutting up the whale had few weapons except axes which they had been using to cut it. When Thorir saw that Ospak and his men were approaching the whale-meat, he called on his men not to let themselves be robbed. They all rushed to the other side, away from the whale carcass, and Thorir led the charge. Ospak turned at once towards him and dealt him a blow with the back of his axe. The blow landed on his ear, and he fell down unconscious. Those near him grabbed him and pulled him over to them, crowding around him as he lay there unconscious. As a result the whale was left unguarded. Then Alf the Short came forward and asked them not to take the whale-meat.

'Don't come any farther, Alf,' said Ospak. 'You've got a thin skull and I have a heavy axe. You'll end up worse off than Thorir if you come a step closer.'

Alf took this good advice, just as he was directed. Ospak and his men carried the whale to the boat, and had finished before Thorir came to. When he realized what had happened, he reproached his men for being worthless, standing by while some were being robbed and others beaten. Then Thorir leapt up, but by then Ospak had launched his boat and was well out from land. They rowed west across the fjord to Eyri and started work on their catch. Ospak would not let anyone who had been with him on the journey leave, and they all settled in and readied themselves inside the fortification. Thorir and his companions divided up what was left of the whale, with each person bearing a share of the loss according to how much of the whale they owned. After that they all travelled back home, but there was great enmity between Thorir and Ospak. Because Ospak had so many men with him, they quickly went through their provisions.

58 | One night Ospak and fourteen of his men went over to Thambardal. They walked into Alf's home and drove everyone in his household into the main room, while they stole from the farm and carried away their loot on four horses. When the people of Fjardarhorn became aware of their journey, a man was sent over to Tunga to tell Thorir. Thorir gathered a force of eighteen men together at once, and they rode down to the head of the fjord. Then Thorir saw Ospak and his men riding past and heading north from Fjardarhorn.

When Ospak saw the men riding after them, he said, 'Men are approaching and it's probably Thorir. He must be intending to avenge the blow I dealt him last winter. There are eighteen of them, and fifteen of us, but we are better equipped. It's difficult to say who is the more enthusiastic for a fight. The horses that we got from Thambardal might be eager to go back home, but I will not give up what we now have in our possession. Two of our men, who are least ready to fight, should drive the pack-horses back over to Eyri, and have the men who are there come over to join us, while the thirteen of us who are here will face them however it turns out.'

They did as Ospak told them. When Thorir and his men came up, Ospak greeted them and asked the news. His conversation was very smooth, as he tried to buy time from Thorir and his men. Thorir asked where they had got all their loot. Ospak said they had got it from Thambardal.

'How exactly did you come by it?' asked Thorir.

'It was neither given nor sold,' Ospak replied, 'and nothing was paid for it.'

'Will you give it up into our hands, then?' Thorir asked.

Ospak said he did not feel inclined to do so.

Then they made at one another and the fighting began. Thorir and his men fought very fiercely, but Ospak's men defended themselves valiantly. None the less they were short of men, and some on their side were soon wounded and others killed. Thorir had a bear-hunting knife in his hand and rushed at Ospak, lunging at him, but Ospak averted the blow. Since Thorir had thrown himself into a lunge which did not find its mark, he fell forward on to his knees with his head bent over. Ospak then struck down on Thorir's back with his axe and there was a loud crack.

'That will dampen your enthusiasm for long journeys, Thorir,' said Ospak.

'It might,' Thorir said, 'but I think I'll still make full-day journeys despite you and your blow.'

Thorir had had a knife hanging on a strap around his neck, as was the practice in those days, and the knife was around the back when the blow fell there, so he only got a slight scratch on either side of the knife. Then one of Thorir's companions rushed up and struck at Ospak, but he parried with his axe, the blow striking the shaft so that it broke in two, the axe then falling down. Ospak called out to his men and told them to try and get away. He took off running himself. As soon as Thorir stood up, he threw his short sword after Ospak, and it hit him in the thigh and ran through to the other side. Ospak pulled the sword out of his wound, turned around, and sent the sword back. It hit the belly of a man who had struck him previously, so that he fell down dead on the ground.

After that Ospak and his followers ran away, and Thorir and his men chased them out along the shore right up to Eyri. Men and women then came running down from the farm, so Thorir and his men turned back. The rest of the winter passed without incident, but in that fight, three of Ospak's men had died, and one of Thorir's, and many had been wounded on both sides.

59 | Snorri the Godi took up the case of Alf the Short against Ospak and his men, who were all sentenced to lesser outlawry at the Thorsnes Assembly. After the assembly Snorri the Godi went back to Tunga, and stayed at home until the

confiscation court. Then he went north to Bitra with a large body of supporters, but by the time he arrived there, Ospak had got away with all his belongings. He and fourteen men had sailed north to Strandir in two boats, where they stayed for the summer and caused a great deal of trouble. They settled in the north at Tharalatursfjord, and collected more men around them. A man named Hrafn, known as the Viking, joined them. He was a particularly evil man, who had been living as an outlaw in North Strandir. They did a great deal of damage there in robberies and murders, and the band stayed together right up until the Winter Nights. Then the men of Strandir gathered a force together, with Olaf Eyvindarson from Drangar and other farmers joining him. Ospak's band had built a fortification around their farm at Tharalatursfjord, and there were now thirty of them altogether. Olaf and his men laid siege to the fortification, which seemed impenetrable. They then held talks with the men inside, and the troublemakers offered to travel away from Strandir and cause no further disturbances in the district if they could leave the fortification. Since they did not think it would be to their advantage to continue dealing with them, they accepted the offer and swore an oath to this effect. The farmers then went back home.

60 | To turn back now to Snorri the Godi, he went north to the court of confiscation at Bitra, as was written earlier. By the time he came to Eyri Ospak had already left, but Snorri the Godi conducted the confiscation proceedings according to the law, and claimed all the property of the outlaws, dividing it up among the men who had suffered the most damage, Alf the Short and the other men who had been robbed. Then Snorri the Godi rode home to Tunga and so the summer passed.

Ospak and his men left Strandir at the Winter Nights with two large boats. They sailed along the coast of Strandir and then north across Floi bay to Vatnsnes. They went ashore and looted there, and loaded both boats as high as the sides would allow them, then sailed north across Floi into Bitra, landed at Eyri, and carried their loot up into the fortification. Ospak's wife and their son Glum had spent the summer there, along with two cows. The same night that they had come home, they rowed their boats up to the head of the fjord and walked up to the farmstead at Tunga and broke into the house. They dragged the farmer Thorir out of his bed, led him outside and killed him. Then they stole all the property that was in the house and took it down to the boats.

They then rowed to Thambardal, leapt ashore and broke down the doors just as they had done at Tunga. Alf the Short was lying in bed with all his clothes on, and when he heard the doors being broken down he jumped up and ran through a secret doorway at the back of the house. He got away and ran up into the valley. Ospak and his men stole everything they could get their hands on and took it to their boats, travelling back to Eyri with both boats fully laden. They carried their loot into the fortification and then hauled their boats in too. They filled them both with water and then closed up the fortification so that they were in the best position for a battle, and there they sat out the winter.

61 | Alf the Short ran south across the heath and did not stop until he came to Snorri the Godi's at Tunga, and told him about his troubles. He strongly urged Snorri to go north at once to attack Ospak and his band. But first Snorri the Godi wanted to find out from the north whether they had done anything more than push Alf the Short out of the way and whether they had taken up residence somewhere in Bitra. Some time later they heard from Bitra in the north about the killing of Thorir and the preparations which Ospak had made there. People found out that it would not be easy to overpower them. Then Snorri the Godi had Alf's family and what was left of his livestock fetched, and they all came to Tunga and stayed there for the winter. Snorri the Godi's enemies condemned him for being slow in righting Alf's lot. Snorri the Godi let anyone say whatever he wanted, but none the less, nothing was done.

Sturla Thjodreksson sent word from the west that he was ready to move against Ospak's band as soon as Snorri wished, claiming he was no less bound to make the journey than Snorri. During the winter right up until Yule reports kept coming from the north of destruction by Ospak and his men. The winter was very severe and all the fjords had iced over. Just before Lent Snorri the Godi sent a message over to Ingjaldshvol in Nes, to a man named Thrand Strider. Thrand was the son of the Ingjald after whom the farm at Ingjaldshvol was named, and he was the biggest and strongest of men, as well as a very fast runner. He had once been in Snorri the Godi's household. When he was a heathen he was known as a shape-shifter, but most people gave up magic when they were baptized. Snorri sent word to Thrand, asking him to come over to Tunga to see him, and to prepare himself for a journey that might involve certain dangers.

When Snorri the Godi's message reached Thrand, he said to the messenger, 'You should rest here for however long you like, but I will set off on Snorri the Godi's mission. We won't end up travelling together anyway.'

The messenger said that would only be known after it had been tried. But in the morning when the messenger woke up, Thrand was already well on his way. He had taken his weapons and walked east below Enni, and from there he followed the path over to Bulandshofdi, and then around the head of the fjord to the farmstead named Eid. Then he travelled across the ice, onwards across Kolgrafarfjord and Seljafjord, and from there east into Vigrafjord, and farther east across the ice all the way to the head of the fjord. He arrived at Tunga in the evening when Snorri was sitting at the table. Snorri greeted him warmly. Thrand responded in kind, and asked him what he wanted him to do, adding that he was prepared to travel anywhere he wanted to send him. Snorri asked him to stay there and rest the night, and Thrand's clothes were then taken off him.

62 | The same night Snorri the Godi sent a man west to Stadar-
   | hol to ask Sturla Thjodreksson to come and join him the
following day at Tunga north in Bitra. Snorri also sent men to the next farm to gather more men. The next day they left for the north across the Gaflfell heath, and there were fifty of them

altogether. They arrived at Tunga in Bitra in the evening, where Sturla was ready with thirty men, and they all left for Eyri that night. When they arrived, Ospak and his men came out on to the fortification wall and asked who the leaders of the band were. They told them, and ordered them to give up the fortification, but Ospak said he would not give up.

'But we will give you the same choice as we gave to the men of Strandir,' he said. 'We'll leave this district if you go away from the fortification.'

Snorri replied that they were not in a position to lay down hard terms. The next morning as soon as it was light, they divided themselves up to storm the fortification. Snorri the Godi got the side of the fortification to attack which Hrafn the Viking was defending, and Sturla was assigned the side which Ospak was defending. Sam and Thormod, the sons of Bork the Stout, attacked another side and Snorri's sons Thorodd and Thorstein Cod-biter were to attack the remaining side. Ospak and his men mainly used rocks to defend themselves as best they could. They fought on determinedly, for they were valiant fighters. Snorri and Sturla's side had mainly missiles for weapons, both for shooting from bows and hurling by hand. They had brought a lot of them, since they had spent some time preparing themselves to storm the fortification. The assault was a fierce one, and many were wounded on both sides, but no one was killed.

Snorri and his supporters kept up such a barrage of missiles that Hrafn and his men retreated behind the wall of the fortification. Then Thrand Strider made a running leap at the wall, jumping high enough to be able to hook his axe over the top of the wall and then pull himself up by the axe-handle until he got on to the fortification. When Hrafn saw that a man had got into the fortification, he rushed at Thrand with his spear, but Thrand warded off the lunge and swung at Hrafn's shoulder, cutting off his arm. Many men then rushed at him, but he jumped off the wall of the fortification and got back to his men.

Ospak urged his men to keep up the defence, and fought on bravely himself. He kept going out on to the fortification wall and throwing stones. At one point when he was making a bold defence by hurling a stone into Sturla's troop, Sturla threw a thonged spear at him, which hit him in the stomach, knocking him down outside the fortification. Sturla ran up to him straightaway and took hold of him, not wanting anyone else to wound him, because he wanted there to be no dispute that he was Ospak's killer. A third man was killed on the side of the wall that Bork's sons were attacking.

After that, the Vikings offered to surrender the fortification, if they could have a truce to protect their lives and limbs, and they said they would accept whatever conditions Snorri the Godi and Sturla demanded. Since Snorri the Godi's side was fast running out of missiles, they agreed to this. Then the fortification was given up, and the men in it surrendered to Snorri the Godi, who let them all get away without injury to life or limb as they had asked. Both Ospak and Hrafn died there, as well as a third man from their side, and there were many wounded on both sides.

This is how Thormod described the event in 'Words of the Raven':

35.
There was a battle at Bitra
and I believe the trouble-stirrer
provided bountiful flesh there                        *victory-women*:
for the birds of the victory-women;          valkyries; their *birds*: ravens
three steerers of sea-riders                 *sea-riders* (i.e. chariots): ships;
lay there, scant of life,                              their *steerers*: warriors
before the courage-sweller;                    *courage-sweller*: warrior
the raven got carrion there.

Snorri the Godi let Ospak's wife and his son Glum keep their farm there. Glum later married Thordis, the daughter of Asmund Grey-locks and the sister of Grettir the Strong,[29] and their son was Ospak, who quarrelled with Odd Ofeigsson of Midfjord.[30] Snorri the Godi and Sturla dispersed the Viking band, sending each of them on his way, and then they went back home. Thrand Strider stayed for a short while with Snorri the Godi before he returned to Ingjaldshvol. Snorri thanked him generously for his excellent support. Thrand Strider lived for a long time at Ingjaldshvol, and then later on at Thrandarstadir; he was a commanding figure.

63 | Thorodd Thorbrandsson was living at Alftafjord at this
   | time, and he had estates at both Ulfarsfell and Orlygsstadir.
Thorolf Lame-foot's ghost had been so active that people did
not think they could live on either of the estates. Bolstad was
now deserted, because Thorolf had begun to haunt it as soon as
Arnkel died, and both people and livestock had been killed
there. No one had dared to farm there after that happened.
When it was derelict, Lame-foot moved up to Ulfarsfell and
caused a lot of trouble there. Everyone was terrified whenever
they caught sight of Lame-foot.

The farmer at Ulfarsfell, Thorodd's tenant, went over to
Karsstadir to complain about the problem to him, saying everyone felt that Lame-foot would not let up until he had cleared
the whole district of both people and livestock, unless a solution
was found.

'And I won't be able to hold out much longer if nothing is
done,' he said.

When Thorodd heard this, he could not think of any good
way out of it. The next morning Thorodd had his horse brought,
and he summoned his farmhands to join him. He also got men
from neighbouring farms to come along. They travelled over to
Baegifotshofdi (Lame-foot's headland), to Thorolf's cairn. They
broke into it and found Thorolf's body, still unrotted and
monstrous to look at. He was as black as Hell and as huge as
an ox. When they tried to move him, they could not budge him.
Then Thorodd had a lever pushed underneath him, and by this
means they were able to lift him out of the cairn. Then they
rolled him down to the foreshore, and cut wood for a great
funeral fire, set fire to it, rolled Thorolf into it and burnt him to
cold coals. None the less, it took a long time before the fire had
any effect on Thorolf. The wind was strong and blew the ashes
far and wide once the burning took off, but whatever ashes they
could collect they scattered on the sea. When they had finished,
they went home.

It was about time for the night meal when Thorodd got
back to Karsstadir, and the women were doing the milking. As
Thorodd rode up to the milking-pen, one of the cows started

away from him, and fell over and broke one of her legs. They examined the cow, but she was too lean to be worth slaughtering, so Thorodd had her leg bound. The cow stopped producing any milk and when her leg was healed, she was taken for fattening at Ulfarsfell because the pasture there is as good as on an island. The cow often went down to the foreshore where the funeral fire had been, and licked the stones on to which the ashes had drifted.

According to some people, when the men from the islands sailed along the fjord with their cargo of dried fish, they could see the cow up on the mountain side with a dapple-grey bull, but no one thought this likely. In autumn Thorodd intended to kill the cow, but when men went to look for her, she was nowhere to be found. Thorodd often had searches made for her that autumn, but she was never found. People therefore assumed that the cow must either be dead or have been stolen.

Early one morning just before Yule the cowherd at Karsstadir went to the cowshed as usual, where he saw a cow standing in front of the door, and at once he recognized her as the missing cow with the broken leg. He led the cow into a stall and tied her up, and then he told Thorodd. Thorodd went out to the cowshed and looked over the cow. They realized that she was in calf, and therefore could not be killed. Thorodd had already slaughtered enough cattle for his household's needs. In the spring as summer was approaching the cow bore a calf, and it was a heifer. A little later she bore another calf, and this one was a young bull. The delivery was very difficult because the calf was so big, and a little while later the cow died. The big calf was taken into the main room. He was dapple-grey and a very fine-looking beast. Both calves were then kept in the main room, including the first-born one.

There was an old woman sitting in the main room. She was Thorodd's foster-mother, and she was now blind. In years gone by she was thought to have been foresighted, but when she grew old, whatever she said was treated as the fancies of old age. None the less a lot of what she said came true. When the big calf had been tethered to the floor, he bellowed loudly.

On hearing that, the old woman feared the worst and said, 'That's the sound of a troll, not the sound of a natural beast, and you'd do well to kill this ill-boding creature.'

Thorodd replied that the calf could not be killed, since he was such a fine one, which he said would turn into an excellent beast when full-grown. Then the calf bellowed a second time.

The old woman spoke, shuddering all over, 'Foster-son, have the calf killed because we will have nothing but ill fortune from him if he is reared.'

'The calf will be killed, if you so wish, foster-mother,' Thorodd replied.

Then both the calves were taken outside. Thorodd had the heifer-calf killed and the other one taken out into the barn. He warned everyone not to tell the old woman that the calf was still alive. The calf grew bigger day by day so that by the spring, when the calves were let out, he was no smaller than the calves born at the beginning of winter. He ran around a lot in the home meadow as soon as he got out and bellowed loudly like a roaring bull, so that it could be clearly heard inside the house.

Then the old woman said, 'So the troll was not killed. We will suffer more from him than we might find words to describe.'

The calf grew quickly and grazed out on the home meadow during the summer. By autumn he was so large that few of the yearlings were any bigger. He had fine horns and was the best looking of all the cattle. The bull was named Glaesir. By the time he was two years old, he was as large as a five-year-old ox. Glaesir always stayed with the cows near the farm, and whenever Thorodd went to the milking-pen, Glaesir went up to him and sniffed around him, licking his clothing while Thorodd patted him. He was as gentle as a lamb with both people and cattle, but whenever he bellowed he caused great alarm. When the old woman heard him, she was always greatly startled. When Glaesir was four years old, he would not walk ahead of women, children or young men, and if men went up to him, he would thrash his head around and behave suspiciously, but in the end he would walk away.

One day when Glaesir came back to the milking-pen, he

roared very loudly so that he was heard as clearly inside the
house as if he were inside. Thorodd was in the main room and
so was the old woman.

She sighed deeply and said, 'You don't put much store by my
advice to have that bull killed, foster-son.'

'You may rest easy, foster-mother,' Thorodd replied. 'Glaesir
will only live until autumn, and then once he's got his summer
fat on him, he'll be killed.'

'That will be too late,' she said.

'It's hard to see how,' Thorodd replied.

While they were talking, the bull responded, sounding even
worse than before.

Then the old woman spoke this verse:

36.
The king of the herd strains
his skull with blood-knowing bellow;
he will take the life of a man;
– the shaker of grey tresses totters –            *shaker of grey tresses*: old
he will show you the way                                                    woman
to the sword-slashed earth-wound;               *sword-slashed earth-wound*:
it will be: the beast will steal                                                 grave
your life – I see that clearly.

Thorodd replied, 'Now you're talking like an old fool, foster-
mother. You can see no such thing.'

She spoke again:

37.
Often you say she is mad when
the treasure-seat stirs her tongue,                      *treasure-seat*: woman
but I see wound-tears                                         *wound-tears*: blood
on your bloodied trunk.
This bull will be your killer
because it has begun to turn
in fury against men. Gerd       *Gerd* (goddess) *of the ringing gold*: woman
of the ringing gold sees that.

'That's not going to happen, foster-mother,' said Thorodd.
'What's worse is that it certainly will,' she replied.

In the summer when Thorodd had the hay from the home meadow raked into large haystacks, a heavy shower began to fall. The next morning when people came outside, they saw that Glaesir had come into the hayfield, and the wooden stocks that were put on his horns when he became vicious were off. He was not behaving in his usual manner, for he never normally destroyed haystacks when he was in the hayfield. But now he charged at the stacks and stuck his horns into them, tossing them up and flinging them all over the meadow. As soon as he had broken up one, he would go on to the next haystack, and so he went, bellowing around the meadow, sounding terrifying. People were so afraid of him that no one dared to approach him and drive him away from the hay.

When Thorodd was told how Glaesir was behaving, he rushed outside at once. There was a pile of wood stacked beside the outer door, and Thorodd took a large birch log and swung it over his shoulder, holding it by its branches. Then he ran down into the meadow to face the bull. When Glaesir saw him coming, he held his position and turned towards him. Thorodd shouted at him, but the bull was no more submissive for that. Then Thorodd hoisted the log and brought it down between the bull's horns with such force that the log split apart at the branches. Glaesir bridled at the blow and charged Thorodd, who grabbed him by the horns and swung him to the side. This went on for a while, with Glaesir charging and Thorodd jumping out of the way and forcing him to one side or the other, until Thorodd began to tire. Then he leapt up on to the bull's neck and clasped his arms below his throat, lying there on the bull's head between his horns, in the hope of tiring him out. But the bull raced back and forward across the field with him on top.

Thorodd's servants saw that the situation was looking very dangerous, but they did not dare to intervene without weapons. They went inside to get their weapons, and when they came back out, they ran down to the field with spears and other weapons. When the bull saw that, he drove his head down between his legs and twisted his head about so that he got one of his horns under Thorodd. Then he suddenly tossed his head, sending Thorodd's torso into the air so that he seemed to be performing a headstand on the bull's neck. As Thorodd fell back, Glaesir swung his head under him so that one of his horns plunged into Thorodd's belly, making him sink down at once. Thorodd's hands went loose, and the bull charged across the field and down to the river with a terrifying roar.

Thorodd's servants raced after Glaesir, chasing him all the way across Geirvor and on until they came to a bog beneath the farm at Hellar. There the bull charged out into the bog and sank down, never to come up again. The place has been called Glaesiskelda ever since. When the servants came back up to the home meadow, Thorodd was gone. He had gone back into the farmhouse, and when they came inside, they found him lying dead in his bed. They had his body taken to the church. Thorodd's son Kar took over the farm at Alftafjord after his father, and lived there for a long time. The farm at Karsstadir is named after him.

64 | There was a man named Gudleif who was the son of Gudlaug the Wealthy of Straumfjord, and the brother of Thorfinn from whom the Sturlung clan is descended.[31] Gudleif was an experienced merchant, and owned a large knorr. Thorolf, the son of Loft from Eyri, owned another knorr, and the two of them had fought against Gyrd, the son of Earl Sigvaldi, in the battle at which Gyrd had lost an eye. In the last days of St Olaf,[32] Gudleif went west on a trading journey to Dublin, intending to go on from there to Iceland. As he was sailing to the west of Ireland, he came up against an easterly gale and then a north-easterly one, which drove him far out across the sea to the west, and then south-west, so that they could not get their bearings from land. It was late in the summer and they swore many oaths in the hope they might be driven ashore.

Eventually they caught sight of land. It was a large land-mass, and none of them knew what land it was. Gudleif and his crew decided to go ashore since none of them felt like spending any longer on the high seas. They found a good place to anchor, and when they had been ashore for a little while, some men came down to meet them. They did not recognize any of them, but thought they were speaking Irish. Suddenly a large number of supporters joined them, making them several hundred strong. The inhabitants then attacked the travellers, taking them prisoner and binding them, after which they herded them farther up the shore. Then they were taken to an assembly and judgement was passed on them. They realized that some people wanted them put to death, and some wanted them divided up among various households as slaves.

While this was being debated, they saw a band of men carrying a banner riding towards them. They thought a chieftain of some kind might be in the band. When the band drew nearer, they saw that beneath the banner rode a tall, brave-looking man, very advanced in years, with a head of white hair. Everyone present bowed before this man and greeted him as their lord. The travellers quickly realized that all matters of importance and decisions were left up to him. After a while this man sent for Gudleif and his men, and when they came before him, he spoke to them in Icelandic, and asked them what lands they came from. They told him that they were mainly Icelanders, and the man asked which of them were the Icelanders. Gudleif stepped forward and greeted the man, who responded warmly and asked him what part of Iceland he came from. Gudleif told him he was from Borgarfjord. Then the man asked him whereabouts in Borgarfjord he lived, and Gudleif told him. After that the man asked for details about all the leading men of Borgarfjord and Breidafjord. When they had told him, he asked about Snorri the Godi and his sister, Thurid of Froda, making precise enquiries about every detail concerning Froda, in particular about the boy Kjartan, who was now the farmer there.

The inhabitants called out that something had to be done about the ship's crew. The tall man walked away from them and named twelve of his own men to come with him. They sat together for a long time talking, and then they rejoined the meeting.

The tall man said to Gudleif and his crew, 'The people of this land have discussed your case, and have left the judgement up to me. I wish to give you leave to travel wherever you want to go. Even though you might think it very late in the summer, I would advise you to get away from here, because the people here are untrustworthy, and very difficult to deal with. And they think that their laws have been broken.'

'What will we say about who has given us our freedom, if we get back to our homeland?' Gudleif asked.

'I can't tell you that,' the man replied, 'because I love my kinsmen and foster-brothers too much to want them to come here and be treated as you might have been, if you had not had the benefit of my intervention. I am now so old that I expect old age will overcome me at any moment. Even if I live a little while longer, there are more powerful men than me here in this land who won't grant much freedom to foreigners. It just so happens they weren't nearby when you arrived.'

Then the man had their ship made ready and stayed with them until a fresh wind arose, enabling them to sail out to sea. Before they parted the man took a gold ring from his finger and gave it to Gudleif, along with a fine sword.

Then he said to Gudleif, 'If you manage to get back to your foster-land, give this sword to Kjartan, the farmer at Froda, and the ring to his mother Thurid.'

'What will I tell them about the man who sent them these valuable things?' asked Gudleif.

'Say that the sender was a better friend to the mistress of the house at Froda than to her brother, the godi at Helgafell,' he replied. 'If anyone thinks they know from this who has sent these valuable things, tell them I forbid anyone coming to look for me, because this is a most dangerous place to get to, unless you have the kind of luck you had in landing here. This is a big country, without good harbours, and foreigners will be greeted with hostility everywhere, unless things turn out as they have for you.'

After that they parted. Gudleif and his men set out to sea and arrived in Ireland late in autumn, spending the winter in Dublin. The next summer they sailed to Iceland and Gudleif handed over the valuables. People came to the conclusion that the man must have been Bjorn the Champion of the Breidavik People, but there is no other evidence for this except what has just been narrated.

65 | Snorri the Godi lived at Tunga for twenty years and held
   | a rather precarious position while powerful men such as
Thorstein Kuggason, Thorgils Holluson and the other important men who were his enemies were still alive. He plays a part
in many other sagas other than this one, including *The Saga of
the People of Laxardal*, as many people know. He was a great
friend of Gudrun Osvifsdottir and her sons. He also comes into
*The Saga of the Slayings on the Heath*, where, apart from
Gudmund the Powerful, he was the strongest supporter of Bardi
after the slayings on the heath.

When Snorri started growing old, his honour and popularity
began to grow, partly because his enemies grew fewer. His
popularity was boosted by the marriage alliances he arranged
between his family and the men of distinction in Breidafjord
and farther afield. He married his daughter Sigrid to Brand
Vermundarson the Generous, and she later married Kolli, the
son of Thormod Thorlaksson of Eyri, and they lived at Bjarnarhofn. Snorri married his daughter, Unn, to Killer-Bardi, and she
later married Sigurd, the son of Thorir Dog from Bjarkoy island
in Halogaland. Their daughter, Rannveig, married Jon, the son
of Arni Arnason and the great-grandson of Arnmod, and their
son was Vidkunn of Bjarkoy, who was one of the noblest of the
landholders in Norway. Snorri the Godi married his daughter,
Thordis, to Bolli Bollason, and the Gilsbakki family are descended from them. And Snorri married his daughter, Hallbera,
to Thord, the son of Sturla Thjodreksson. Their daughter was
named Thurid and she married Haflidi Masson, and from them
comes a great family line. Snorri's daughter, Thora, was married
by him to Cart-Bersi, the son of Halldor Olafsson from Hjardarholt. She later married Thorgrim Svidi, and from them comes a
great and noble family line.

Snorri's other daughters were all married after his death. His
daughter Thurid the Wise was married to Gunnlaug, the son of
Steinthor of Eyri. Gudrun Snorradottir was married to Kolfinn
from Solheimar, Halldora Snorradottir to Thorgeir from As-
gardsholar, and Alof Snorradottir to Jorund Thorfinnsson, the
brother of Gunnlaug from Straumfjord.

Halldor was the most eminent of Snorri the Godi's sons. He lived at Hjardarholt in Laxardal, and the Sturlung and Vatnsfjord families are descended from him. Thorodd was the second most eminent of Snorri the Godi's sons, and he lived at Spakonufell in Skagastrond. Snorri's son, Mani, lived at Saudafell, and his son Ljot, who was nicknamed Mani-Ljot, was known as the greatest of Snorri the Godi's grandsons. Thorstein, another of Snorri the Godi's sons, lived at Laugarbrekka and the Asbjorn clan of Skagafjord are descended from him, as are many other people. Snorri the Godi's son Thord Cat lived at Dufgusdal, while Snorri the Godi's son Eyjolf lived at Lambastadir in Myrar. Snorri the Godi's son Thorleif lived at Medalfellsstrond, and the Ballara clan are descended from him. Snorri the Godi's son Snorri lived at Saelingsdalstunga after his father died. Snorri the Godi had another son, named Klepp, but no one knows where he lived, nor whether he had any descendants known from the sagas.

Snorri the Godi died at Saelingsdalstunga a year after the killing of St Olaf. He was buried there at the church he himself had established. When the graveyard there was dug up, his bones were taken up and moved to where the church now is on their estate. When this happened Gudny Bodvarsdottir was present, and she is the mother of Sturla's sons Snorri, Thord and Sighvat, and she reported that they were the bones of a medium-sized man, and not a tall one. She also said that the bones of Bork the Stout, Snorri the Godi's uncle, were moved at the same time, and they were extremely large. The bones of the old woman, Thordis, the daughter of Thorbjorn Sur and the mother of Snorri the Godi, were also moved, and Gudny said they were small female bones, and as black as if they had been singed. All of these bones were reburied in the graveyard where the church now stands.

This is the end of the saga of the people of Thorsnes, Eyri and Alftafjord.

*Translated by* JUDY QUINN

Translator's note: The translation of this saga began as a collaboration between myself and Kristín Hafsteinsdóttir, who unfortunately was unable to continue because of other commitments. Nevertheless, her insights and wit gave the translation its impetus, as well as making the task of collaborating by e-mail a delight.

# Notes

## GISLI SURSSON'S SAGA

1. *King Hakon, foster-son of King Athelstan of England*: Ruler of Norway *c.*934–60. He was the son of King Harald Fair-hair, and was born around 920 and died in 960 or 961. King Athelstan reigned 924–39.

2. *Gisli*: Gisli, son of Thorkel, is the uncle of the eponymous hero of the saga. Gisli Sursson himself is not introduced until Ch. 2.

3. *Grasida (Grey-blade)*: A feminine word in Icelandic (all other sword names are masculine) which may refer simply to the metal colour of the weapon. However, grey has symbolic associations with trickery and deception. The noun used for blade (*síða*) has a verbal homograph meaning 'to perform magic'. The sword is later forged into a spear (Ch. 11) which plays a vital role in the saga.

4. *And one will stand behind the other*: A direct charge of homosexuality, considered among the worst insults in the world of the sagas.

5. *out of range of the dogs' barking*: That is, because they could not hear the dogs, they were safe.

6. *There were sixty of them on board*: These are the somewhat confusing figures given in the original.

7. *Thorbjorn Sur (Whey)*: Later, Gisli is referred to, not as Thorbjornsson (son of Thorbjorn), but Sursson after his father's nickname.

8. *Thorsnes Assembly*: Thorsnes was originally a sacred site dedicated to the god Thor by its first settler, Thorolf Moster-beard, who also established a district assembly there (see *The Saga of the People of Eyri*, Chs. 4 and 9).

9. *Thorstein Cod-biter*: The chronologies of *Gisli Sursson's Saga* and *The Saga of the People of Eyri* are not in harmony here as Thorstein Cod-biter should be long dead according to the latter. It has been suggested that the chronologies would match if the writer of *Gisli*

*Sursson's Saga* is confusing Thorstein Cod-biter with his cousin and foster-brother Thorstein Surt, who lived on Thorsnes and, according to *The Saga of the People of Laxardal*, died around the time that Thorgrim, son of Thorstein Cod-biter, took Thordis as his wife (AD 955–9).

10. *coloured clothes*: An indication of social status and prosperity, often associated with people who have travelled abroad and bought their clothes there – rather than wearing Icelandic homespun cloth.

11. *Gest, son of Oddleif*: Known from several sagas (*The Saga of the People of Laxardal*, *Njal's Saga*, *The Saga of Ref the Sly* and *The Saga of Havard of Isafjord*) as a wise man, just and well-intentioned, even gifted with prophetic vision.

12. *Harald Grey-cloak*: Ruler of Norway 961–74, after the death of King Hakon, foster-son of King Athelstan.

13. *cut out a shirt*: In the sagas it is considered a sign of a woman's attraction to a man if she cuts out a shirt for him. Aud's words should therefore be taken as an accusation of Asgerd's love for Vestein.

14. *divorce*: Divorce was a relatively easy process for women in the sagas. Complaints about the husband's unmanly behaviour or, as here, his refusal to share the marital bed with his wife were legal and acceptable grounds for a divorce. In such an event the woman could reclaim her bride-price and dowry which was formerly administered by the husband (see Glossary).

15. *tapestry*: The sagas mention the use of tapestries for decorative purposes in festive halls. It is believed that these may often have had pictures on them, telling stories of well-known legendary characters and events.

16. *his sworn brother, Thorkel*: This shows that the oaths between Gisli, Thorkel and Vestein held, whereas Thorgrim had not fulfilled the ceremony of sworn brotherhood with Vestein (in Ch. 6). Gisli did not become Thorgrim's sworn brother either.

17. *secret manslaughter rather than murder*: This distinction is only found here and not in any other sagas or law codes. The more common distinction is between a publicly announced manslaughter and a secret murder.

18. *Hel-shoes*: This is the only extant reference to special shoes tied to the feet of a dead man, but reflects the general belief that the dead had to make a long journey to their destination in the afterlife. The northern 'Hel' appears to have resembled the Greek Hades without the punitive aspects of the Christian Hell.

19. *viper ... wolf ... to death*: The two beasts in Gisli's dream are

reminiscent of the Midgard serpent and the wolf Fenrir which fight Thor and Odin in the doom of the gods (Ragnarok). One of Odin's most frequent pseudonyms is Grim, thus implanting the idea of Thorgrim as Vestein's killer.

20.  *ball game*: A game played with a hard ball and a bat, possibly similar to the Gaelic game known as hurling which is still played in Scotland and Ireland. The exact rules are uncertain; the game appears to have involved two players at any one time, although sides are arranged in Ch. 18. Clashes at ball games often herald full-scale feuds, although in *The Saga of the People of Eyri*, Ch. 43, the setting is more gratuitous.

21.  *sacrifice to Frey*: Frey is a fertility god in the old Nordic mythology. Thorgrim enjoys a special relationship with him, as shown by the belief stated in Ch. 18 that Frey prevented Thorgrim's mound from freezing. Thorgrim thus has the divine forces on his side, bearing the names of both Thor and Odin (whose pseudonym was Grim) and making sacrifices to the third main divinity, Frey.

22.  *Eyjolf Thordarson*: A cousin of Bork and Thorgrim on their mother's side, the son of Thord Bellower. His nickname 'Grey' may reflect his guileful character.

23.  *give a mare for this foal . . . not be underpaid*: The word for a slap to the face is *buffeit* or *kinnhestur*, the latter literally meaning 'cheek-horse'. Thus Geirmund's pun suggests that he intends to pay back Thorgrim in kind for the blow.

24.  *black cloak*: Saga characters commonly don clothes of black (or a dark blue) when intending to kill.

25.  *Snorri*: A twin form of the name Snerrir which means 'unruly', 'argumentative'. Snorri is the main character in *The Saga of the People of Eyri* (see Introduction, pp. xxvii–xxxi).

26.  *a sack was placed over his head*: In order to avoid the Evil Eye, similar to the precautions taken by Arnkel in *The Saga of the People of Eyri* (Ch. 33) when he approaches his father's corpse from behind.

27.  *three hundred pieces of silver*: The price offered for Gisli is three times the normal amount for an outlaw.

28.  *Grettir Asmundarson*: Hero of *The Saga of Grettir the Strong*. Together with Gisli Sursson, Grettir was the best-known – and most admired – outlaw, with a whole saga to his name. Grettir is said to have survived for nineteen years as an outlaw. Gisli is six years short of Grettir's achievement.

29.  *the distance between them was so short*: The distance between Gisli's hideout (Geirthjofsfjord) and Otradal where Eyjolf lived.

30.  *Ingjald*: This son of an unnamed aunt of Gisli is a well-respected person in other sagas. His son was married to the sister of Thord Glumsson, the second husband of Gudrun Osvifsdottir in *The Saga of the People of Laxardal*.

31.  *Ref*: Literally 'fox', which might suggest links with Reynard in European beast fables and a possible allegorical interpretation of this episode. One of the wiliest characters in the saga literature is the eponymous hero of *The Saga of Ref the Sly*.

32.  *until Snorri the Godi drove him out*: This episode is recounted in full in *The Saga of the People of Eyri* (Ch. 14).

33.  *Helgi*: Vestein's son.

34.  *Hedeby*: The largest town in Scandinavia during the Viking Age with 1000–1500 inhabitants, an international trading centre with its own mint. Harald the Stern, King of Norway, sacked the town in 1050 and it had been abandoned by 1100.


# THE SAGA OF THE PEOPLE OF EYRI

1.  *Ketil Flat-nose*: Father or father-in-law of many of the most prominent settlers in Iceland (among them his daughter Aud the Deep-Minded, a Viking queen in Dublin and a settler in Hvamm in the West of Iceland), whose descendants became some of the most powerful families in the tenth and eleventh centuries (among them several Lawspeakers, who presided over the Althing, and the leader of the most ambitious voyage to Vinland, Thorfinn Karlsefni). Ketil is well known from *The Book of Settlements* and *The Saga of the People of Laxardal*.

2.  *Ingolf Arnarson*: The first permanent settler of Iceland, according to all literary sources. Ari the Learned, in his *Book of the Icelanders* from the early 1100s, dates the settlement to 870 but later versions of *The Book of Settlements* give the year as 874. Analyses of annual snow-layers in the glacier in Greenland have now shown that a volcanic ash layer that covers large parts of Iceland and predates the first settlement in most parts of the country can also be traced in the glacier. That ash fell in 871 (±1 year), showing that these ultimately oral sources are fairly accurate about the first settlement.

3.  *Thorolf carried fire around his land-claim*: Carrying fire around an area of land to claim it as a site of settlement is frequently mentioned in Old Icelandic literature. No one was allowed to claim a larger area of land than he could carry fire around in a single day with the crew of his ship. The smoke from a fire that he lit in the morning

had to be visible from where he lit a fire in the evening. Women were allowed to claim the area of land they could lead a heifer around in a single day.

4. *There he had a temple built*: About the authenticity of the temple description that follows, see the Introduction, pp. xlv–xlvi. 'Helgafell' literally means 'holy mountain'. It is not uncommon that mounds and mountains have a religious function as here and the idea of people dying into mountains is widespread. Helgafell retained its religious role after the coming of Christianity. A medieval monastery was established there and local folkbelief still holds the mountain in high esteem.

5. *elf-frighteners*: Literally 'that which frightens elves away', a euphemism for faeces.

6. *Aud and her son Thorstein*: The lives of Aud and her son Thorstein the Red are portrayed in more detail in *The Saga of the People of Laxardal* and *The Book of Settlements*.

7. *Bjorn settled ... in Bjarnarhofn*: The accounts here and in the following chapters about the various settlements are partly told in more detail in *The Saga of the People of Laxardal* and in *The Book of Settlements*, and partly in more detail here. These varying details indicate that those who put the texts together had access to oral informants whom they relied on, no less than written sources.

8. *Ari Thorgilsson the Learned does not count her among his children*: Ari the Learned only refers to two children of Thorstein the Red, Osk and Olaf Feilan, in the one extant work attributed to him, *The Book of Icelanders*. Those references are not a part of a complete list of Thorstein's children and it is possible that the writer of this saga has thought of Ari as the compiler of *The Book of Settlements*, where the children are listed. Hallstein was the son of Thorolf by a former wife.

9. *Thord Bellower*: The leading chieftain in the district, great-grandson of the Viking queen in Dublin, Aud the Deep-Minded. His status was such that it is enough for the author to link characters up with him to elevate their status. He also appears in *The Saga of the People of Laxardal* and *Hen-Thorir's Saga*.

10. *Bork the Stout*: Features in many sagas, most prominently *Gisli Sursson's Saga*.

11. *Thorgrim married Thordis Sursdottir in Dyrafjord*: Here the saga links up with the subject matter of *Gisli Sursson's Saga* (Ch. 4) and gives a plot summary which leaves no doubt as to who killed Vestein (see also Introduction, p. xxii).

12. *Helgi Droplaugarson and Vemund Fringe*: Both well-known

characters, from *The Saga of Droplaug's Sons* and *The Saga of the People of Reykjadal and of Killer-Skuta*, respectively.

13. *they announced the death of Gisli Sursson ... before he fell*: The following account of Thordis's attempted revenge is also told in *Gisli Sursson's Saga* (Ch. 37). See Introduction, p. xxxvii.

14. *Styr had a lot of influence in the area and many followers*: Styr appears as a great killer and troublemaker in *The Saga of the Slayings on the Heath*, where the story of the berserks is also told in Chs. 3–4 (see Chs. 25 and 28 here).

15. *door court*: A 'civil' court, held not at an assembly but at the home of the defendant. Such courts are not mentioned in other sagas, but are referred to in law books.

16. *Eirik the Red discovered Greenland ... for one winter*: The story of Eirik and the later voyages from Greenland to Vinland is told in *Eirik the Red's Saga* and *The Saga of the Greenlanders*.

17. *At that time Earl Hakon Sigurdsson ruled Norway*: Earl Hakon ruled 975–95.

18. *The Swedish King Eirik the Victorious*: Ruled c.950–93.

19. *Earl Sigurd Hlodvesson of the Orkney Islands*: Appears in other Sagas of Icelanders as well as in *The Saga of the Orkney Islanders* (Chs. 11–12), which tells of his raiding in the Hebrides but does not mention the Isle of Man.

20. *At that time Palna-Toki was the leader of the Jomsvikings*: The town of Jomsborg is bathed in a special aura as the source of legends about the Vikings who fought earls Eirik and Hakon at Hjorungavag in Norway in 994 (as told in *The Jomsvikings' Saga* and *Kings' Sagas* collections). Jomsborg is thought to have been on the Oder estuary in Poland, where a town which flourished during King Harald Black-tooth's reign in Denmark in the latter half of the tenth century was destroyed in the mid eleventh century.

21. *turf-game*: This particular sport is not mentioned elsewhere in the sagas.

22. *Steinthor shot a spear over them for good luck, according to ancient custom*: It is believed to have had Odinic associations to mark an army by throwing a spear towards it – Odin was the supreme god of war and wisdom in the Old Norse mythology. A weapon which is thrown or shot in this fashion in the sagas, without the intention to kill a particular person, often kills the most innocent bystander.

23. *when Geir the Godi and Gizur the White attacked Gunnar inside his house at Hlidarendi*: A reference to the best-known scene of that kind in the sagas, in *Njal's Saga*.

24. *Snorri went to Vinland the Good with Karlsefni ... Skraelings*:

Karlsefni was the leader of the most ambitious exploratory voyage to Vinland, according to *The Vinland Sagas*. He was the great-grandson of Thord Bellower. Skraelings is the term used in the sagas to describe the native inhabitants of the North American continent.

25. *who owned the slaves*: Hallstein's slaves are known from other medieval sources as well as nineteenth-century folklore, which remembers that they were once found asleep while they were supposed to be working. As a result they were promptly punished by their owner, who hanged them.

26. *everyone in Iceland was baptized*: The story of the adoption of Christianity as the official religion in Iceland in the year 1000 is told in several sources, in most detail in *The Saga of Christianity* (*Kristni saga*).

27. *have my body carried to Skalholt*: Expresses Thorgunna's prophetic vision, as Skalholt was later to become the seat of the first bishop in Iceland, in 1056.

28. *Bolli Thorleiksson, Gudrun Osvifsdottir's husband*: Two of the main characters in *The Saga of the People of Laxardal* (in which Snorri the Godi also appears).

29. *Grettir the Strong*: See note 28, p. 203.

30. *Ospak, who quarrelled with Odd Ofeigsson of Midfjord*: That story is known from *The Saga of the Confederates*.

31. *from whom the Sturlung clan is descended*: The Sturlungs were the most influential family in politics and literature in the thirteenth century. Members of the family often held the post of lawspeaker and authored many known literary works.

32. *In the last days of St Olaf*: Saint Olaf, King of Norway, was killed in 1030.

# REFERENCE SECTION

# Family Ties in *The Saga of the People of Eyri*

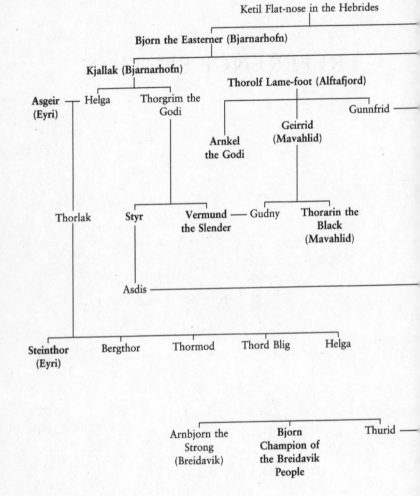

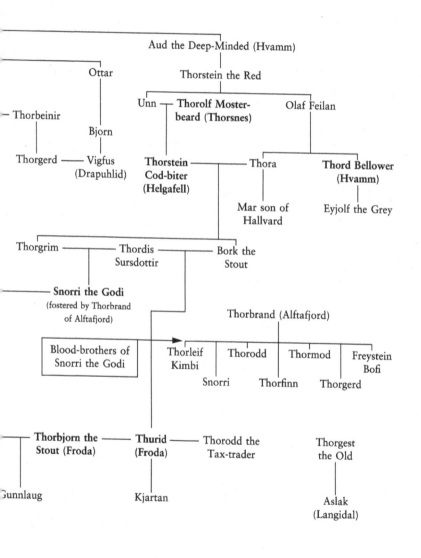

# Structure and Feuds in *The Saga of the People of Eyri*

| AD | Chapters | |
|---|---|---|
| 884–6 | 1–8 | Settlers arrive in Iceland from Norway and the British Isles |
| 932–4 | 9–10 | Feud settled by the sons-in-law of Thord Bellower |
| 980 | 15–22 | Snorri the Godi and other main characters are introduced (Chs. 11–14) |
| | 23 | Eirik the Red is exiled (Ch. 24) |
| 982 | 26–7 | Vermund gets berserks (Ch. 25) |
| 983 | | Styr kills berserks. His daughter marries Snorri (Ch. 28) |
| | 29 | |
| 987–90 | 30–32 | |
| 993 | 35–8 | Thorolf Lame-foot dies and haunts the neighbourhood (Chs. 33–4) |
| 994 | 39 | Clash abroad |
| | 40 | Thurid has a son, Kjartan |
| 997 | 41–6 | Styr fights on both sides and his brother Vermund the Slender settles the feud |
| | | Bjorn of Breidavik goes abroad (Ch. 47), the Thorbrandssons settle in Greenland and go to Vinland (Ch. 48) |
| 1000 | | Christianity is accepted as the official religion in Iceland (Ch. 49) |
| 1000–1001 | | Thorgunna arrives at Froda; the Froda wonders take place (Chs. 50–55) |
| 1008 | | Snorri moves to Tunga and takes part in national politics. Gets rid of Ospak and his band (Chs. 56–62) |
| 1010–12 | 63 | Bjorn the Champion of the Breidavik People has become a chieftain in a faraway country across the ocean to the south-west (Ch. 64) |
| | | Final episode about Snorri and his in-laws' alliances (Ch. 65). Snorri dies in 1031 |

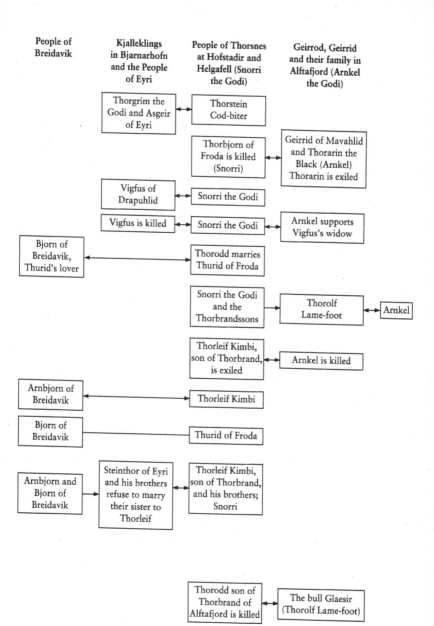

| People of Breidavik | Kjalleklings in Bjarnarhofn and the People of Eyri | People of Thorsnes at Hofstadir and Helgafell (Snorri the Godi) | Geirrod, Geirrid and their family in Alftafjord (Arnkel the Godi) | |
| --- | --- | --- | --- | --- |
| | Thorgrim the Godi and Asgeir of Eyri | Thorstein Cod-biter | | |
| | | Thorbjorn of Froda is killed (Snorri) | Geirrid of Mavahlid and Thorarin the Black (Arnkel) Thorarin is exiled | |
| | Vigfus of Drapuhlid | Snorri the Godi | | |
| | Vigfus is killed | Snorri the Godi | Arnkel supports Vigfus's widow | |
| Bjorn of Breidavik, Thurid's lover | | Thorodd marries Thurid of Froda | | |
| | | Snorri the Godi and the Thorbrandssons | Thorolf Lame-foot | Arnkel |
| | | Thorleif Kimbi, son of Thorbrand, is exiled | Arnkel is killed | |
| Arnbjorn of Breidavik | | Thorleif Kimbi | | |
| Bjorn of Breidavik | | Thurid of Froda | | |
| Arnbjorn and Bjorn of Breidavik | Steinthor of Eyri and his brothers refuse to marry their sister to Thorleif | Thorleif Kimbi, son of Thorbrand, and his brothers; Snorri | | |
| | | Thorodd son of Thorbrand of Alftafjord is killed | The bull Glaesir (Thorolf Lame-foot) | |

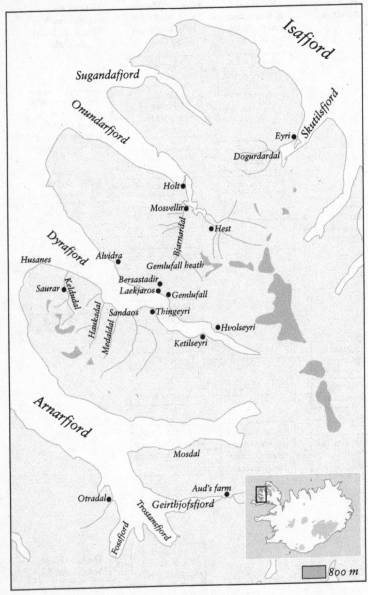

Map 1: The West Fjords

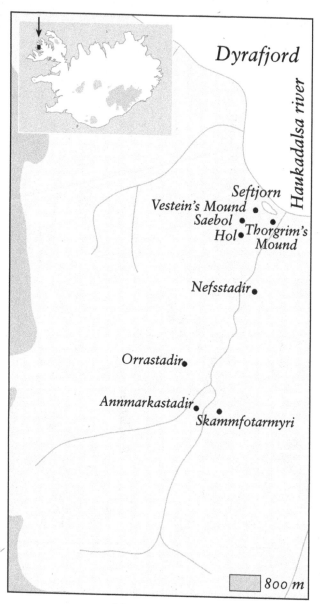

Map 2: Haukadal

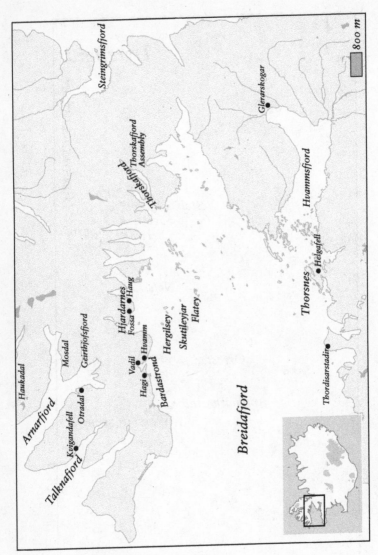

Map 3: Breidafjord

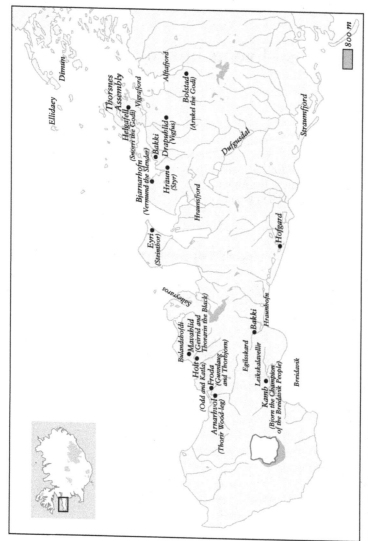

Map 4: Regional feuds backed by Snorri and Arnkel

# Historical Events linked to the Sagas

The settlement of Iceland, mainly from Norway, begins c.870
The establishment of the Althing c.930
Christianity accepted in Iceland 999 or 1000
First trips to Vinland c.1000–1011
Agreement between the Icelanders and Olaf Haraldsson the Saint, King of Norway 1020–30
The *Möðruvallabók* codex of the sagas compiled mid 14th century

## CHRONOLOGY OF GISLI SURSSON'S SAGA

952  Thorbjorn Sur arrives in Iceland (Ch. 4)
960  Attempt at pledging sworn brotherhood between Thorgrim, Gisli, Thorkel and Vestein (Ch. 6)
964  Gisli Sursson exiled (Ch. 21)
977  Gisli Sursson is killed (Ch. 36)

# Social, Political and Legal Structures

The notion of kinship is central to the sense of honour and duty in the sagas, and thereby to their action. Kinship essentially involves a sense of belonging not unlike that underlying the Celtic clan systems. The Icelandic word for kin or clan (*ætt*) is cognate with other words meaning 'to own' and 'direction' – the notion could be described as a 'social compass'.

Establishing kinship is one of the justifications for the long genealogies given in the sagas, which tend to strike non-Icelandic readers as idiosyncratic detours, and also for the preludes in Norway before the main saga action begins. Members of the modern nuclear family or close relatives are only part of the picture, since kinsmen are all those who are linked through a common ancestor – preferably one of high birth and high repute – as far back as five or six generations or even more.

Marriage ties, sworn brotherhood and other bonds could create conflicting loyalties with respect to the duty of revenge, of course, as *The Saga of Gisli Sursson* supremely illustrates, but by the same token they could serve as instruments for resolving such vendettas. A strict order stipulated who was to take revenge within the fairly immediate family, with a 'multiplier effect' if those seeking vengeance were killed in the process. The obligation to take revenge was inherited, just like wealth, property and claims.

Patriarchy was the order of the day, although notable exceptions are found. Likewise, the physical duty of revenge devolved only upon males, but women were often responsible for instigating it, either by urging a husband or brother to action with slurs about their cowardice, or by bringing up their sons with a vengeful sense of purpose and even supplying them with old weapons that had become family heirlooms.

Iceland was unique among European societies in the tenth to thirteenth centuries in two respects in particular: it had no king, nor any executive power to follow through the pronouncements of its highly sophisticated legislative and judicial institutions. The lack of executive power meant that there was no means of preventing men from taking the law into their own hands. This gave rise to many memorable conflicts recorded in the sagas, but it also led to the gradual disintegration of the Commonwealth in the thirteenth century.

The Althing served not only as a general or national assembly (which is what its name means), but also as the main festival and social gathering of the year, where people exchanged stories and news, renewed acquaintances with old friends and relatives, and the like. Originally it was inaugurated (with a pagan ceremony) by the leading godi (*allsherjargoði*), who was a descendant of the first settler, Ingolf Arnarson, in the tenth week of summer. Early in the eleventh century the opening day was changed to the Thursday of the eleventh week of summer (18–24 June). Legislative authority at the Althing was in the hands of the Law Council, while there were two levels of judiciary, the Quarter Courts and the Fifth Court.

The Law Council was originally composed of the thirty-six godis, along with two thingmen for each, and the Lawspeaker, who was the highest authority in the Commonwealth, elected by the Law Council for a term of three years. It was the duty of the Lawspeaker to recite the entire procedures of the assembly and one-third of the laws of the country every year. He presided over the meetings of the Law Council and ruled on points of legal interpretation.

Quarter Courts, established at the Althing around 965, evolved from earlier regional Spring Assemblies, probably panels of nine men, which had dealt with cases involving people from the same quarter. Three new godords were created in the north when the Quarter Courts were set up. The godis appointed thirty-six men to the Quarter Court and their decisions had to be unanimous.

Around 1005, a Fifth Court was established as a kind of court of appeal to hear cases that were unresolved by the Quarter Courts. The godis appointed forty-eight members to the Fifth Court and the two sides in each case were allowed to reject six each. A simple majority among the remaining thirty-six then decided the outcome, and lots were drawn in the event of a tie. With the creation of the Fifth Court, the number of godis was increased correspondingly, and with their two thingmen each and the Lawspeaker, the Law Council was then composed of 145 people in all.

Legal disputes feature prominently in the Sagas of Icelanders, and the prosecution and defence of a case followed clearly defined procedures. Cases were prepared locally some time before the Thing, and could be dismissed there if they were technically flawed. Preparation generally took one of two forms. A panel of 'neighbours' could be called, composed of five or nine people who lived near the scene of the incident or the home of the accused, to testify to what had happened. Alternatively, a party could go to the home of the accused to summons him during the Summons Days, two weeks before the Spring Assembly but three or four weeks before the Althing.

The accused generally did not attend the Thing, but was defended by someone else, who called witnesses and was entitled to disqualify members of the panel. Panels did not testify to the details and facts of the case in the modern sense, but determined whether the incident had taken place. The case was then summed up and a ruling passed on it by the Quarter Court.

Penalties depended upon the seriousness of the case and took the form of either monetary compensation or outlawry. Lesser outlawry lasted for three years, while full outlawry meant that a man must not be 'fed or helped on his way' and was tantamount to a death sentence. A confiscation court would seize the belongings of a person outlawed for three years or life. Cases were often settled without going through the complex court procedure, either by arbitration, a ruling from a third party who was accepted by both sides, or by self-judgement by either of the parties involved in the case. Duelling was another method for settling but was formally banned in Iceland in 1006.

# The Farm

The farm (*bær*) was a basic social and economic unit in Iceland. Although farms varied in size, there was presumably only one building on a farm at the time of the settlement, an all-purpose building known as a hall (*skáli*) or longhouse (*langhús*), constructed on the model of the farmhouses the settlers had inhabited in Norway. Over time, additional rooms and/or wings were often added to the original construction.

The Icelandic farmhouse shown in figures 1–3 is based on information provided by the excavations at Stong (Stöng) in the Thjorsardal valley in the south of Iceland. Stong is regarded as having been an average-sized farm by Icelandic standards. The settlement at Stong was abandoned as a result of the devastating ash-fall from the great eruption of Hekla in 1104.

The plan of the farmstead (figure 1) shows the overall layout of a typical farm. It is based on the measurements carried out by the archaeologist Daniel Bruun, but it should be stressed that the layout of these farms was far from fixed. None the less, the plan indicates the common positioning of the haystack wall/yard (*stakkgarður*) in the often-mentioned hayfield (*tún*). The hayfield wall (*túngarður*) surrounds the farm and its hayfield. Also placed outside the main farm are the animal sheds. With the exception of one cowshed, no barns or other animal sheds came to light during the excavation at Stong, but these must have existed as they did on most farms. Sometimes they were attached to the farmhouse, but more often they were independent constructions some distance away from the building. Sheep sheds, in particular, tended to be built some distance away from the hall, and closer to the meadows used for grazing.

The smithy was also separate (for safety reasons), and the same often appears to have applied to the fire room/fire hall (*eldhús/eldaskáli*). The latter was essentially a form of specialized kitchen. It was not only used for cooking, but was also the site of other daily household activities carried out around the fire. Indeed, sometimes the term *eldhús* seems to

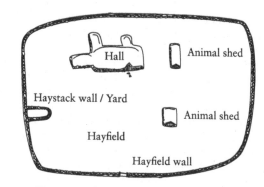

*Figure 1. Plan of an Icelandic farmstead*

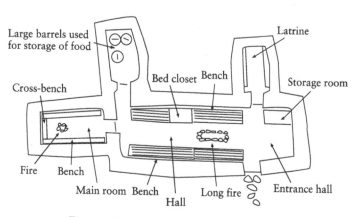

*Figure 2. Cross-section of the hall at Stong*

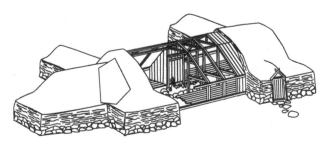

*Figure 3. Layout of the farmhouse at Stong*

refer not to a separate building, but to the farmhouse, used instead of the word *skáli* (hall), stressing the presence of the fire and warmth in the living quarters.

Figure 2 shows a cross-section of the hall at Stong, giving an idea of the way the buildings were constructed. The framework was timber. The main weight of the roof rested on beams which, in turn, were supported by pillars on either side of the hall. The high-seat pillars (*öndvegissúlur*) that some settlers brought with them from Norway might have been related to the pillars placed on either side of the high seat (*hásæti*). The outer walls of most farms in Iceland were constructed of a thick layer of turf and stone, which served to insulate the building. The smoke from the main fire was usually let out through a vent in the roof, but the living quarters would still have been rather smoke-ridden.

Figure 3 depicts the layout of the farm excavated at Stong. The purpose of the area marked 'latrine' is uncertain, but this role makes sense on the basis of the layout of the room. For information about the bed closet, see the Glossary.

See further: Foote, P. G. and Wilson, D. M., *The Viking Achievement*, (London, 1979); Graham-Campbell, James, *The Viking World* (London, 1980).

# Early Icelandic Literature

Enabled by the advent of Christian learning *c*.1000, writing flourished in Iceland from the twelfth century onwards. Native traditions were combined with materials and influences drawn from foreign literature, especially medieval Latin and, later on, French, though the 'native' strand predominates in the most famous branch of the literature, the Sagas of Icelanders. The word *saga* in Icelandic derives from the verb *segja* 'say, tell' and denotes an extended prose narrative that may (to modern perceptions) be located anywhere on the spectrum between seriously historical and wholly fictional, and various groupings of sagas are customarily identified especially on the basis of content and degree of apparent historicity. Some but by no means all of these saga genres were recognized in medieval Iceland. Literacy also enabled poetry to be recorded, some of it oral compositions dating from the Viking Age (approximately ninth to mid eleventh centuries). Some poetry, especially the earlier compositions, and certain prose genres had their genesis in Norway, and for a few texts Norwegian or Icelandic origins are equally possible.

## SAGAS

### Sagas of Icelanders or Family sagas (*Íslendingasögur*)

Composed from the early thirteenth century to *c*.1400 and beyond, based on characters and events from the Icelandic past, especially from the settlement period (*c*.870–*c*.930) to the early eleventh century. Most are concerned with feuding in a pastoral setting, and feature in varying proportions both exceptional individuals and neighbourhoods: hence titles such as *Egil's Saga*, *Njal's Saga* and *The Saga of the Sworn Brothers* on the one hand, and *The Saga of the People of Eyri* and *The Saga of the People of Vatnsdal* on the other. *The Saga of the People of Laxardal* is unusual in featuring a woman, Gudrun Osvifsdottir, as its central figure. Many sagas, including *The Saga of Hrafnkel* and *The Saga of the Confederates*, are concerned with chieftainly power. In *The Saga of Grettir the Strong* and *Gisli Sursson's Saga* the titular heroes spend long periods of outlawry in the Icelandic 'wilderness', and many depict episodes abroad, including *Bard's Saga*, a late work of c.1400, which differs from the 'classic', feud-based sagas in narrating adventures of an often fantastical kind. On the style of the Sagas of Icelanders, see the Introduction, p. xi.

## Contemporary sagas (*Samtíðarsögur*)

*Sturlunga Saga*, 'The Saga of the Sturlungs': a compilation, from c.1300, of sagas based on Icelandic events from the twelfth century to the end of the Icelandic Commonwealth in the 1260s. They were written by various authors. Sturla Thordarson's *Saga of the Icelanders* (*Íslendinga saga*) is the most substantial; shorter items include *The Saga of Thorgils and Haflidi*, which relates the dispute between these two men in the early twelfth century.

## Sagas of Kings (*Konungasögur*)

Mostly about Norwegian kings and earls, but also Danish kings and earls of Orkney (*Orkneyinga saga*). Writing begins, in Latin and the vernacular, in Norway and Iceland, in the mid twelfth century. Some sagas concern individual kings, especially the two missionary Olafs, for instance the sagas of Olaf Tryggvason by Odd Snorrason and Gunnlaug Leifsson, both written originally in Latin, and Snorri Sturluson's *Great Saga of St Olaf*. Others cover a broad sweep of reigns, including the anonymous *Morkinskinna*, *Fagrskinna* and Snorri Sturluson's massive *Heimskringla*, all from the first decades of the thirteenth century. *Flateyjarbók*, a huge manuscript compilation mainly from the late fourteenth century, contains many kings' sagas.

## Short tales (*Thættir*)

Brief narratives, often of encounters between Norwegian kings and low-born but canny Icelanders; these are more or less independent stories, but are incorporated especially in major compilations of the Sagas of Kings such as *Morkinskinna*, *Fagrskinna* and *Hulda-Hrokkinskinna*. Other tales, including some contained in *Flateyjarbók*, are in effect miniature Sagas of Icelanders, or Legendary sagas.

## Sagas / Lives of Saints (*Heilagra manna sögur*)

Mainly translations from Latin; some fragments are preserved from the mid twelfth century, putting these among the earliest type of literature produced in Iceland.

## Legendary sagas / Sagas of Ancient Times (*Fornaldarsögur*)

Usually set in remote times and locations, showing stereotypical heroes in racy though sometimes tragic adventures involving the supernatural – hence giving a generally unrealistic impression. These include *The Saga of the Volsungs* (*Völsunga saga*), c.1260–70, and *Fridthjof's Saga*, c.1400.

## Chivalric sagas (*Riddarasögur*)

Romances: some of these are adaptations of French originals, such as the *Saga of Tristram and Isond* (*Tristan and Isolde*, Norwegian, c.1226); others are original Icelandic compositions in a similar mode. The latter have sometimes been termed 'lying sagas' (*lygisögur*).

## Translated quasi-historical works

These include *The Saga of the Trojans* (*Trójumanna saga*, first half of the thirteenth century), a retelling of the story of the Trojan Wars, mostly based on classical sources, especially the late Latin *De excidio Troiae historia* attributed to 'Dares Phrygius'.

# POETRY

## Skaldic poetry

Usually attached to named poets and specific occasions, skaldic poetry includes praise of princes, travelogue, slander, love poetry and, especially in the earliest surviving poetry (late ninth and tenth century), pagan mythology. Metre, diction and word order tend to be elaborate, though the style of later religious poetry (twelfth to fourteenth centuries) is simpler. Skaldic poetry tends to be preserved as fragmentary citations within prose works, including the sagas of poets. The names of 146 poets, and the rulers they composed for, are preserved in the *List of Poets* (*Skáldatal*), c.1260.

## The Poetic Edda (Eddic poetry)

The poems of this genre are mainly in older, simpler metres, and span the ninth to the twelfth or thirteenth centuries. Topics are drawn largely from pagan mythology or legend. Composed in Norway, Iceland or the wider Nordic-speaking world, the works were preserved mainly (as complete or near-complete poems) in the Icelandic *Codex Regius*, *c*.1270.

# OTHER PROSE WORKS

## Works on Icelandic history

*The Book of the Icelanders* (*Íslendingabók*), by Ari Thorgilsson *c*.1122–33, on the Settlement and the establishment of Christianity.

*Kristni Saga*: a saga history/narrative of the Christianization of Iceland, probably late thirteenth century.

*The Book of Settlements* (*Landnámabók*): the names, also often accompanied by genealogies and anecdotes, of over four hundred settlers, given region by region. There are five main versions, the earliest thirteenth century, but including still older materials.

*Icelandic Annals*: lists of dates and events (Icelandic and foreign), existing in numerous versions, the oldest compiled in the late thirteenth century from older sources.

## Legal writings

*Grágás* ('Grey Goose'): the laws of the Icelandic Commonwealth, as preserved in a range of mainly thirteenth-century manuscripts. These are Christian laws, but to some extent founded on the pre-Christian Norwegian laws brought by early settlers of Iceland.

## Works on poetry, language or grammar

The *Prose Edda* of Snorri Sturluson (*Snorra Edda*, probably composed in the 1220s) comprises a prologue and three parts: on Nordic mythology (*Gylfaginning*, 'The Deceiving of Gylfi' – the most comprehensive medieval account we have); on the diction of skaldic poetry (*Skáldskaparmál*, 'The·Language of Poetry'); and on metre (*Háttatal*, 'List of Metres', 102 illustrative verses with commentary).

*The Third Grammatical Treatise*, by Olaf Thordarson, mid thirteenth century: the fullest of four prose treatises applying classical grammar and rhetoric to Icelandic language and poetry; it is rich in poetic quotations.

# Glossary

The Icelandic terms are printed in italics, with modern spelling.

**Althing** *alþingi*: General assembly. See 'Social, Political and Legal Structures', p. 220.

**arch of raised turf** *jarðarmen*: In order to confirm sworn brotherhood, the participants had to mix their blood and walk under an arch of raised turf: 'A long piece of sod was cut from a grassy field but the ends left uncut. It was raised up into an arch, under which the person carrying out the ordeal had to pass' (*The Saga of the People of Laxardal*, Ch. 18).

**assembly** *þing*: See 'Social, Political and Legal Structures', p. 220.

**ball game** *knattleikur*: A game played with a hard ball and a bat, possibly similar to the Gaelic game known as hurling which is still played in Scotland and Ireland. The exact rules, however, are uncertain.

**bed closet** *hvílugólf*, *lokrekkja*, *lokhvíla*, *lokrekkjugólf*: A private sleeping area used for the heads of better-off households. The closet was usually partitioned off from the rest of the house, and had a door that was secured from the inside.

**berserk** *berserkur*: (Literally 'bear-shirt'). A man who slipped or deliberately worked himself into an animal-like frenzy, which hugely increased his strength and made him apparently immune to the effect of blows from weapons. The berserks are paradoxical figures, prized as warriors and evidently regarded as having supernatural powers (perhaps bestowed on them by Odin, the god of warriors), but in the sagas this mysticism is beginning to wear off. They are often presented as stock figures, generally bullies who are none too bright, and when heroes do away with them there is usually little regret, and a great deal of local relief. Closely related to the original concept of the berserk (implied by its literal meaning) are the *shape-shifters*.

**black** Often used here to translate *blár*, which in modern Icelandic means only 'blue'. The colour was a dark blue-black, often worn by saga characters setting out with murderous intentions.

**bloody wound** *áverki*: Almost always used in a legal sense, that is with regard to a visible, probably bloody wound, which could result in legal actions for compensation, or some more drastic proceedings such as the taking of revenge.

**booth** *búð*: A temporary dwelling used by those who attended the various *assemblies*. Structurally, it seems to have involved permanent walls which were covered by a tent-like roof, probably made of cloth.

**bride-price** *mundur*: In formal terms, this was the amount that the groom's family gave to the bride's. According to Icelandic law it was the personal property of the wife. See also *dowry*.

**compensation** *manngjöld, bætur*: Penalties imposed by the courts were of three main kinds: awards of compensation in cash; sentences of *lesser outlawry*, which could be lessened or dropped by the payment of compensation; and sentences of *full outlawry* with no chance of being moderated. In certain cases, a man's right to immediate vengeance was recognized, but for many offences compensation was the fixed legal penalty and the injured party had little choice but to accept the settlement offered by the court, an arbitrator or a man who had been given the right to *self-judgement* (*sjálfdæmi*). It was certainly legal to put pressure on the guilty party to pay. Neither court verdicts nor legislation, nor even the constitutional arrangements, had any coercive power behind them other than the free initiative of individual chieftains with their armed following.

**confiscation court** *féránsdómur*: See 'Social, Political and Legal Structures', p. 221.

**cross-bench** *pallur, þverpallur*: A raised platform or bench at the inner end of the *main room*, where women were usually seated.

**directions** *austur/vestur/norður/suður* (east/west/north/south): These directional terms are used in a very wide sense in the sagas; they are largely dependent on context, and they cannot always be trusted to reflect compass directions. Internationally, 'the east' generally refers to the countries to the east and south-east of Iceland, and although 'easterner' usually refers to a Norwegian, it can also apply to a Swede (especially since the concept of nationality was still not entirely clear when the sagas were being written), and might even be used for a person who has picked up Russian habits. 'The west', or to 'go west', tends to refer to Ireland and what are now the British Isles, but might even refer to lands still farther afield; the point of orientation is west of Norway. When confined to Iceland, directional terms sometimes refer to the *quarter* to which a person is travelling, for example a man going to the *Althing* from the east of the country might be said to be going 'south' rather than 'west', and a person going home to the West Fjords from the Althing is said to be going 'west' rather than 'north'.

**dowry** *heimanfylgja*: Literally 'that which accompanies the bride from her home'. This was the amount of money (or land) that a bride's father contributed at her wedding. Like the *bride-price*, it remained legally her property. However, the husband controlled their financial affairs and was responsible for the use to which both these assets were put.

**drapa** *drápa*: A heroic, laudatory poem, usually in the complicated metre preferred by the Icelandic poets. Such poems were in fashion between the tenth and thirteenth centuries. They were usually composed in honour of kings, *earls* and other prominent men, living or dead. Occasionally they were addressed to a loved one or made in praise of pagan or Christian religious figures. A drapa usually consisted of three parts: an introduction, a middle section including one or more refrains, and a conclusion. It was usually clearly distinguished from the *flokk*, which tended to be shorter, less laudatory and without refrains.

**duel** *hólmganga*: A formally organized duel, literally meaning 'going to the island'. This is probably because the area prescribed for the fight formed a small 'island' with clearly defined boundaries, which separated the action from the outside world; it might also refer to the fact that small islands were originally favoured sites for duels. The rules included that the two duellists slashed at each other alternately, the seconds protecting the principal fighters with shields. Shields hacked to pieces could be replaced by up to three shields on each side. If blood was shed, the fight could be ended and the wounded man could buy himself off with a ransom of three *marks* of silver, either on the spot or later. The rules are stated in detail in *Kormak's Saga*:

The duelling laws had it that the cloak was to be five ells square, with loops at the corners, and pegs had to be put in of the kind that had a head at one end. They were called tarses, and he who made the preparations was to approach the tarses in such a way that he could see the sky between his legs while grasping his ear lobes and uttering the invocation that has since been used again in the sacrifice known as the tarse sacrifice. There were to be three spaces marked out round the cloak, each a foot in breadth, and outside the marked spaces there should be four strings, named hazel poles; when that was done, what you had was a hazel-poled stretch of ground. You were supposed to have three shields, but when they were used up, you were to go on to the cloak, even if you had withdrawn from it before, and from then on you were supposed to protect yourself with weapons. He who was challenged had to strike. If one of the two was wounded in such a way that blood fell on to the cloak, there was no obligation to continue fighting. If someone put just one foot outside the hazel poles, he was said to be retreating, or to be running if he did so with both. There would be a man to hold the shield for each one of the two fighting. He who was the more wounded of the two was to release himself by paying duel ransom, to the tune of three marks of silver. (Ch. 10)

The duel was formally banned by law in Iceland in 1006, six years after the Icelanders had accepted Christianity.

**earl** *jarl*: A title generally restricted to men of high rank in northern countries (though not in Iceland), who could be independent rulers or subordinate to a king. The title could be inherited, or it could be conferred by a king on a prominent supporter or leader of military forces. The earls of Lade, who appear in a number of sagas and tales, ruled large sections of northern Norway (and often many southerly areas as well) for several centuries. Another prominent, almost independent, earldom was that of Orkney and Shetland.

**east** *austur*: See *directions*.

**fire room** *eldaskáli*: In literal terms, the fire room was a room or special building (as perhaps at Jarlshof in Shetland) containing a fire, and its primary function was that of a kitchen. Such a definition, however, would be too limited, since the fire room was also used for eating, working and sleeping. Indeed, in many cases the word *eldaskáli* seems to have been synonymous with the word *skáli* meaning the *hall* of a farm. See 'The Farm', p. 222.

**follower** *hirðmaður*: A member of the inner circle that surrounded the Scandinavian kings, a sworn king's man.

**foster-** *fóstur-, fóstri, fóstra*: Children during the saga period were often brought up by foster-parents, who received either payment or support in return from the real parents. Being fostered was therefore somewhat different from being adopted: it was essentially a legal agreement and, more importantly, a form of alliance. None the less, emotionally, and in some cases legally, fostered children were seen as being part of the family circle. Relationships and loyalties between foster-kindred could become very strong. It should be noted that the expressions *fóstri/fóstra* were also used for people who had the function of looking after, bringing up and teaching the children on the farm.

**freed slave** *lausingi, leysingi*: A *slave* could be set or bought free, and thus acquired the general status of a free man, although this status was low, since if he/she died with no heir, his/her inheritance would return to the original owner. The children of freed slaves, however, were completely free.

**full outlawry** *skóggangur*: Outlawry for life. One of the terms applied to a man sentenced to full outlawry was *skógarmaður*, which literally means 'forest man', even though in Iceland there was scant possibility of his taking refuge in a forest. Full outlawry simply meant banishment from civilized society, whether the local district, the province or the whole country. It also meant the confiscation of the outlaw's property to pay the prosecutor, cover debts and sometimes provide an allowance for the dependants he had left behind. A full outlaw was to be neither fed nor offered shelter. According to one legal codex from Norway, it was 'as if he were dead'. He had lost all goods, and all rights. Wherever he went he could be killed without any legal redress. His children became illegitimate and his body was to be buried in unconsecrated ground.

**games** *leikar*: *Leikur* (sing.) in Icelandic contained the same breadth of meaning as 'game' in English. The games meetings described in the sagas would probably have included a whole range of 'play' activities. Essentially, they involved men's sports, such as wrestling, *ball games*, 'skin-throwing games', 'scraper games' and horse-fights. Games of this kind took place whenever people came together, and seem to have formed a regular feature of *assemblies* and other gatherings (including the *Althing*) and religious festivals such as the *Winter Nights*. Sometimes prominent men invited people together specifically to take part in games.

**ghosts/spirits** *draugar*, *afturgöngur*, *haugbúar*: Ghosts in medieval Scandinavia were seen as being corporeal, and thus capable of wrestling or fighting in other ways with opponents. This idea is naturally associated with the ancient pagan belief in Scandinavia and elsewhere that the dead should be buried with the possessions that they were going to need in the next life, such as ships, horses and weapons. The suggestion was that somehow the body was going to live again and need these items. There are many examples in the sagas of people encountering or seeing 'living ghosts' inside grave mounds. These spirits were called *haugbúar* (lit. 'mound-dwellers'). Because of the fear of spirits walking again and disturbing the living, there were various measures that could be taken to ensure some degree of peace and quiet for the living. See, for example, *Gisli Sursson's Saga*, Chs. 14 and 17, and *The Saga of the People of Eyri*, Chs. 33–4 and 63.

**godi** *goði*: This word was little known outside Iceland in early Christian times, and seems to refer to a particularly Icelandic concept. A godi was a local chieftain who had legal and administrative responsibilities in Iceland. The name seems to have originally meant 'priest', or at least a person having a special relationship with gods or supernatural powers, and thus shows an early connection between religious and secular power. As time went on, however, the chief function of a godi came to be secular. The first godis were chosen from the leading families who settled Iceland in c.870–930. See 'Social, Political and Legal Structures', p. 220.

**godord** *goðorð*: The authority and rank of a *godi*, including his social and legal responsibilities towards his *thingmen*.

**halberd** *atgeir*: *Atgeir* is translated as 'halberd', which it seems to have resembled even though no specimens of this combination of spear and axe have been found in archaeological excavations in Iceland.

**hall** *skáli*: This word was used both for large halls such as those used by kings, and for the main farmhouse on the typical Icelandic farm. See fig. 3 in 'The Farm', p. 222.

**hayfield** *tún*: An enclosed field for hay cultivation close to or surrounding a farmhouse. This was the only 'cultivated' part of a farm and produced the best hay. Other hay, generally of lesser quality, came from the meadows, which could be a good distance from the farm itself. See fig. 1 in 'The Farm', p. 223.

**hayfield wall** *túngarður*: A wall of stones surrounding the *hayfield* in order to protect it from grazing livestock. See 'The Farm', p. 222.

**hersir** *hersir*: A local leader in western and northern Norway, whose rank was hereditary. Originally the hersirs were probably those who took command when the men of the district were called to arms.

**high seat** *öndvegi*: The central section of one bench in the *hall* (at the inner end, or in the middle of the 'senior' side, to the right as one entered) was the rightful high seat of the owner of the farm. Even though it is usually referred to in English as the 'high seat', this position was not necessarily higher in elevation, only in honour. Opposite the owner sat the guest of honour.

**high-seat pillars** *öndvegissúlur*: The *high seat* was often adorned with decorated high-seat pillars, which had a religious significance. There are several accounts of how those emigrating from Norway to Iceland took their high-seat pillars with them. As they approached land they threw the carved wood posts overboard. It was believed that the pillars would be guided by divine forces to the place where the travellers were destined to live.

**homespun (cloth)** *vaðmál*: For centuries wool and woollen products were Iceland's chief exports, especially in the form of strong and durable homespun cloth. It could be bought and sold in bolts or made up into items such as homespun cloaks. There were strict regulations on homespun, as it was used as a standard exchange product and often referred to in *ounces*, meaning its equivalent value expressed as a weight in silver. One ounce could equal three to six ells of homespun, one ell being roughly 50 cm.

**hundred** *hundrað*: A 'long hundred' or one hundred and twenty. The expression, however, rarely refers to an accurate number, rather a generalized 'round' figure.

**judgement circle** *dómhringur*: The courts of heathen times appear to have been surrounded by a judgement circle, marked out with hazel poles and ropes, where judgements were made or announced. The circle was sacrosanct, and weapons were not allowed inside it – nor was violence.

**knorr** *knörr*: An ocean-going cargo vessel.

**lesser outlawry** *fjörbaugsgarður*: Differed from *full* or *greater outlawry* in that the lesser outlaw was banished from society for only three years. Furthermore, his land was not confiscated, and money was put aside to support his family. This made it possible for him to return later and continue a normal life. *Fjörbaugsgarður* means literally 'life-ring enclosure'. 'Life-ring' refers to the silver ring that the outlaw originally had to pay the *godi* in order to spare his life. (This was later fixed at a value of one *mark*.) 'Enclosure' refers to three sacrosanct homes no more than one day's journey from each other where the outlaw was permitted to stay while he arranged passage out of Iceland. He was allowed limited movement along the tracks directly joining these farms, and en route to the ship that would take him abroad. Anywhere else the outlaw was fair game and could be killed without redress. He had to leave the country and begin his sentence within the space of three summers after the verdict, but once abroad regained normal rights.

**longship** *langskip*: The largest warship.

**magic rite** *seiður*: The exact nature of magic ritual, or *seiður*, is somewhat obscure. It appears that it was originally a ceremony that was only practised by women. Even though there are several accounts of males who performed this (including the god Odin), they are almost always looked down on as having engaged in an 'effeminate' activity. The magic rite seems to have had two main purposes: a spell to influence people or the elements (as in *Gisli Sursson's Saga*, Ch. 18), and a means of finding out about the future. There are evidently parallels between *seiður* and shamanistic rituals such as those carried out by the Lapps and Native Americans.

**main room** *stofa*: A room off the *hall* of a farmhouse. See also 'The Farm', p. 222.

**mark** *mörk*: A measurement of weight, eight *ounces*, approximately 214 grams.

**Moving Days** *fardagar*: Four successive days in the seventh week of 'summer' (in May) on which householders in Iceland could change their abode.

**north** *norður*: See *directions*.

**ounce, ounces** *eyrir*, pl. *aurar*: A unit of weight, varying slightly through time, but roughly 27 grams. Eight ounces were equal to one *mark*.

**outlawry** *útlegð, skóggangur, fjörbaugsgarður*: Two of the Icelandic words, *útlegð*, literally meaning 'lying, or sleeping, outside', and *skóggangur*, 'forest-walking', stress the idea of the outlaw having been ejected from the safe boundaries of civilized society and being forced to live in the wild, alongside the animals and nature spirits, little better than an animal himself. The word *útlagi* ('outlaw') is closely related to *útlegð*, but has also taken on the additional meaning of 'outside the law', which for early Scandinavians was synonymous with 'lying outside society'. Law was what made society. See also *full outlawry* and *lesser outlawry*.

**quarter** *fjórðungur*: Administratively, Iceland was divided into four quarters based on the four cardinal directions. See 'Social, Political and Legal Structures', p. 220.

**sacrifice, sacrificial feast** *blót*: There is great uncertainty about the nature of pagan worship and cult-activities in Scandinavia, and just as the theology and mythology of the Nordic peoples seem to have varied according to area, it is highly questionable whether any standardized rules of ritual practice ever existed there. It should also be remembered that the population of Iceland came from all over Scandinavia, as well as from Ireland and the islands off Scotland. Religion was very much an individual matter, and practices varied. The few references to sacrifices in the sagas are somewhat vague, but these sometimes seem to have involved the ritual slaughter of animals.

**scorn** *níð*: In the sagas *níð* refers to two forms of slander that need to be distinguished. The physical form of scorn generally refers to figures made of wood that were understood by all to represent one or more persons in local society. These figures were sometimes depicted in some compromising sexual position. Such a public insult attracted attention and seriously damaged the honour of the person or persons in question. The figures were strictly illegal, and a common reason for killings and/or local feuds. See, for example, *Gisli Sursson's Saga*, Ch. 2. *Níð* could also take a verbal form, a slanderous lampoon.

**shape-shifter** *hamrammur*, adj.: Closely associated with the *berserks*, those who were *hamrammir* (pl.) were believed to change their shape at night or in times of stress, or leave their bodies (which appeared asleep) and take the physical form of animals such as bears or wolves. There are again faint associations with shamanistic activities and figures known in folklore throughout the world, such as the werewolf. The transformation was not necessarily intentional.

**slave** *þræll*: Slavery was quite an important aspect of Viking Age trade. A large number of slaves were taken from the Baltic nations and the western European countries that were raided and invaded by Scandinavians between the eighth and eleventh centuries. In addition, the Scandinavians had few scruples against taking slaves from the other Nordic countries. Judging from their names and appearance, a large number of the slaves mentioned in the sagas seem to have come from Ireland and Scotland. Stereotypically they are presented as being stupid and lazy. By law, slaves had hardly any rights at all, and they and their families could only gain freedom if their owners chose to free them, or somebody else bought their freedom: see *freed slave*. In the Icelandic commonwealth, a slave who was wounded was entitled to one-third of the compensation money; the rest went to his owner.

**south** *suður*: See *directions*.

**Spring Assembly** *vorþing*: The local assembly, held each spring. These were the first regular assemblies to be held in Iceland. Held at thirteen sites and lasting four to seven days between 7 and 27 May, they were jointly supervised by three *godis*. The Spring Assembly had a dual legal and economic function. It consisted of a court of thirty-six men, twelve appointed by each of the godis, where local legal actions were heard, while major cases and those which could not be resolved locally were sent on to the *Althing*. In its other function it was a forum for settling debts, deciding prices and the like. Godis probably used the Spring Assembly to urge their followers to ride to the Althing; those who remained behind paid the costs of those who went. See 'Social, Political and Legal Structures', p. 219.

**sprinkled with water** *vatni ausinn*: Even before the arrival of Christianity, the Scandinavians practised a naming ceremony clearly similar to that involved in the modern-day 'christening'. The action of sprinkling a child with water and naming it meant that the child was initiated into society. After this ceremony, a child could not be taken out to die of exposure (a common practice in pagan times).

**Summons Days** *stefnudagar*: The days during which someone could be summonsed to appear at a given *Spring Assembly* or *Althing* for a legal case.

**sworn brotherhood** *fóstbræðralag*: This was seen as another form of foster-brotherhood, but instead of being arranged by the parents (see *foster-*), it was a relationship decided by the individuals themselves. Sworn brothers literally were 'blood-brothers': they swore unending loyalty to each other, sealing this pact by going though a religious ceremony involving a form of symbolic rebirth, in which they joined blood and passed beneath an *arch of raised turf*. See *Gisli Sursson's Saga*, Ch. 6.

**temple** *hof*: In spite of the elaborate description of the 'temple' at Hofstadir (lit. 'Temple Place') in *The Saga of the People of Eyri*, Ch. 4, and other temples mentioned in the sagas, there is no certainty that buildings erected for the sole purpose of pagan worship ever existed in Iceland or the other Scandinavian countries. To date, no such building has been found in archaeological excavations. In all likelihood, pagan rituals and *sacrifices* took place outdoors, or in a specified area in certain large farmhouses belonging to priests, where the idols of the gods would also have been kept.

**Thing** *alþingi*: See *Althing*.

**thingman/men** *þingmaður/þingmenn*: Every free man and landowner was required to serve as a thingman ('assembly man') by aligning himself with a *godi*. He would either accompany the godi to *assemblies* and other functions or pay a tax supposed to cover the godi's costs of attending them. See 'Social, Political and Legal Structures', p. 219.

**troll** *tröll*: Trolls in the minds of the Icelanders were not the huge, stupid figures that we read about in later Scandinavian wonder-tales and legends. At the time of the sagas, they were essentially evil nature spirits, a little like large dark elves. It is only in later times that they come to blend with the image of the Scandinavian giants.

**Viking** *víkingur*: Normally has an unfavourable sense in the Sagas of Icelanders, referring to violent seafaring raiders, especially of the pagan period. It can also denote general bullies and villains.

**weight** *vætt*: The equivalent of 160 *marks*, or about 40 kilos.

**west** *vestur*: see *directions*.

**Winter Nights** *veturnætur*: The period of two days when the winter began, around the middle of October. In the pagan era, this was a particularly holy time of the year, when *sacrifices* were made to the female guardian spirits, and social activities such as *games* meetings and weddings often took place. It was also the time when animals were slaughtered so that their meat could be stored over the winter.

# Index of Characters

# Njal's Saga

Full of dreams, strange prophecies, sexual slander, violent power struggles and fragile peace settlements, *Njal's Saga* is a compelling chronicle of a fifty-year blood feud.

Written in the late thirteenth century, it is the most powerful and popular of the great Icelandic Family Sagas and teems with memorable and complex characters such as Gunnar of Hlidarendi, a powerful warrior with an aversion to killing, and the not-wholly-villainous Mord Valgardsson. Alongside the heroism and prowess there is also blood spilt in acts of cowardice and cruelty. Despite its distance from us in time and place, *Njal's Saga* explores perennial human problems: from failed marriages to divided loyalties, from the law's inability to curb human passions to the terrible consequences when decent men and women are swept up in a tide of violence quite beyond their control.

The text for this new translation has been taken from *The Complete Sagas of Icelanders*, published by Leifur Eiríksson, of which *The Times Literary Supplement* said, 'The translations are generally excellent; accurate and readable, they are sure to become the standard versions.'

*Translated and edited by* ROBERT COOK

# Sagas of Warrior-Poets

A famous poet and fighter spends an illicit night with a woman he failed to marry long ago. Her husband has no choice but to seek redress . . .

All the Icelandic sagas portray a world well aware of the power of words: to praise, to blame, to curse and to taunt. Yet these five stories are unusual in putting a skald, or poet, centre stage and building the plot around his travels to seek fame, his doomed love for a married woman and his hostilities against her menfolk.

Although the mainly thirteenth-century authors drew on semi-historical traditions about people and events over two centuries before, they portrayed vivid and enduring scenes of everyday life in the farmsteads of windswept Iceland – making hay, hunting seals, rounding up sheep and struggling through blizzards. Most of the poet-heroes are notably difficult characters, whose restless energy threatens the peace of their communities, and whose own faults, as much as fate, bar them from happiness. Full of fights, invective and voyaging, these sagas also deploy their terse prose and intricate verse to explore human motive and behaviour in non-aristocratic society, and as such they are almost unique in the medieval literature of Europe.

*Edited with an introduction by* DIANA WHALEY

HOMER

# The Odyssey

*'I long to reach my home and see the day of my return. It is my never-failing wish'*

The epic tale of Odysseus and his ten-year journey home after the Trojan War forms one of the earliest and greatest works of Western literature. Confronted by natural and supernatural threats – shipwrecks, battles, monsters and the implacable enmity of the sea-god Poseidon – Odysseus must test his bravery and native cunning to the full if he is to reach his homeland safely and overcome the obstacles that, even there, await him.

E. V. Rieu's translation of *The Odyssey* was the very first Penguin Classic to be published, and has itself achieved classic status. For this edition, Rieu's text has been sensitively revised and a new introduction added to complement his original introduction.

'One of the world's most vital tales ... *The Odyssey* remains central to literature' MALCOLM BRADBURY

*Translated by* E. V. RIEU
*Revised translation by* D. C. H. RIEU
*With an introduction by* PETER JONES

# Beowulf
## A Verse Translation

*'With bare hands shall I grapple with the
fiend, fight to the death here, hater and hated!
He who is chosen shall deliver himself to
the Lord's judgement'*

*Beowulf* is the greatest surviving work of literature in Old
English, unparalleled in its epic grandeur and scope. It tells
the story of the heroic Beowulf and of his battles, first with the
monster Grendel, who has laid waste to the great hall of the
Danish king Hrothgar, then with Grendel's avenging mother
and finally with a dragon that threatens to devastate his homeland. Through its blend of myth and history, *Beowulf* vividly
evokes a twilight world in which men and supernatural forces
live side by side, and celebrates the endurance of the human
spirit in a transient world.

Michael Alexander's landmark modern English verse translation has been revised to take account of new readings and
interpretations. His introduction discusses central themes of
*Beowulf* and its place among epic poems, the history of its
publication and reception, and issues of translation.

**'A foundation stone of poetry in English' ANDREW MOTION**

*Revised edition*
*Translated with an introduction and notes by*
MICHAEL ALEXANDER